THE HIT

DENISE RYAN

First published in Great Britain in 1999 by
Judy Piatkus (Publishers) Ltd of
5 Windmill Street, London W1P 1HF

This edition published 1999

A catalogue record for this book
is available from the British Library

ISBN 0 7499 3140 X

Set in Bembo by
Phoenix Photosetting, Chatham, Kent

Printed and bound in Great Britain by
Mackays of Chatham PLC, Chatham, Kent

I dedicate this book first
and foremost to Peter,
my husband

Also to my family: Michael Joseph Ryan, my late brother;
Dorothy Ryan, my mother; Michael, my brother;
Elizabeth, my sister; neices and nephews, especially
the newest member of the gang, Baby Fergal

My godmother, Dorothy Rhodes

and to these friends: Sigrid, Corina, José, Famke, Margaret

I would like to thank Kerith Biggs of the Darley Anderson Literary, TV & Film Agency for her invaluable advice, guidance and enthusiasm, and all her efforts on my behalf.

Also the man himself: Darley Anderson

Part One

Chapter One

'She never wanted sex. She never cooked. She expected me to look after the children as well as be a full-time accountant.' The young man in the dock, florid-faced, red-haired and neat in his pinstripe suit, glared at Shannon Flinder, the prosecuting solicitor. Bloody bitch, he thought. She was out to get him. They were all the same.

'Well, you are their father, Mr Hankin,' Shannon said icily. Some things never changed.

'She's a bad mother and a useless wife!' he shouted. 'She's had affairs. I couldn't take anymore.' He banged his fist on the dock and winced. The magistrate, Mrs Theodora Cooke, tutted and frowned at him over her magnifying-glass spectacles. A long sigh from Philip Manning, the defendant's solicitor, was audible. The bad-tempered bastard was going to hang himself with his own rope. 'Yes, of course I'll stay calm.' Fat chance! Manning's job would be as easy as his GP wife's if he too could prescribe sackfuls of Valium. Shannon Flinder was going to wipe the floor with him. Again.

'Mr Hankin, I'm afraid the demands of childcare and the *alleged*,' she emphasized the word loudly, 'infidelities, don't give you the right to rape your wife, stab her with a kitchen knife and fracture her skull with a spanner.' People looked at one another and gasped. 'A week in intensive care, and that's just for starters. Not surprisingly, she's lost the baby.'

There were more gasps and murmurs. She looked round and noticed the red-haired, middle-aged woman in the fur coat who was still staring at her with hatred, barely able to contain her rage. Who was she?

'I didn't rape the b— her,' Hankin burst out, purple in the face. 'She wanted it – asked for it!'

'I thought you said she never wanted sex? You also threatened, in the presence of witnesses, to 'finish the job' if she pressed charges. Which she has in fact been courageous enough to do.' Now you lot do your job, she thought, as she turned to face the bench.

Shannon was five foot five and slim, with a small waist and full bust. She wore a tight black suit and red silk shirt. Her thick blonde wavy hair fell around her shoulders and Philip Manning could smell her perfume, Obsession. She had a heart-shaped face, curved mouth and soft fair skin, faintly flushed across the wide cheekbones. Her violet blue eyes glared back at the defendant for a second.

'I therefore submit that there is a case to answer, madam,' she said firmly to Theodora Cooke. 'The bail application is opposed, of course. The defendant has, as I mentioned earlier, made repeated threats against my client, and would be a continual danger to her if he were allowed to remain at large.'

Jenny Fong, the legal executive, glanced at her notes. This was a man with a bad temper, as the list of previous convictions for assault and drink driving showed. Theodora Cooke bent her grey head and conferred with her two male colleagues for a moment.

'I agree,' she said finally, glancing at Shannon. She took off her glasses and looked sternly at Hankin. 'Defendant will be remanded in custody until he is brought to trial at the Crown Court, for which a date will be set.'

'And may God have mercy on your soul!' Jenny murmured, grinning to herself. Philip Manning gathered his papers, stood up and marched out. The red-haired woman in the fur coat began to push her way towards him. Hankin was led away by two policemen.

'Well done!' Jenny stood up and patted Shannon's shoulder.

'Didn't take much. What a creep!' she sighed. 'Why can't he just stick to doing what his name rhymes with and give us all a bit of peace? I'll call Joanne in a minute, give her the good news. At least she'll have the comfort of knowing she'll be safe for a while.'

'How's she doing?' Jenny asked as they left the courtroom.

'Not great. I went to see her yesterday. She's terribly upset about losing the baby, not to mention the other injuries. Her face is a right mess. She lost so much blood she had to be transfused.'

'My God!' Jenny looked at her in horror. 'I wouldn't fancy a transfusion nowadays.'

'That's the least of her worries, Jenny. The risk of HIV from a transfusion is incredibly remote.'

'But it exists.'

'Three kids, violent husband, miscarriage, fractured skull ... how does she get through tomorrow, never mind the rest of her life? As I said, she's got enough to worry about.' She shook her head. 'Poor girl.'

They walked down the busy corridor filled with barristers, solicitors and their nervous or cocky clients. A few policemen stood around talking and there was a smell of instant coffee and forbidden cigarette smoke.

'I fancy a double espresso.' Shannon glanced at her watch. 'Hey, it's nearly lunchtime,' she exclaimed. 'I thought I was starving. I could murder a cow pie.'

'It might murder you.' Jenny grinned. 'I don't know how you stay so slim, the way you eat. Still, I only see you in black clothes, don't I?'

'Bitch! I'll scratch your eyes out. Want to join me?' she asked. 'My treat. Seeing as you're the poor but loyal legal executive, that dying breed.'

'No, thanks. I'll stroll back to the office and my tub of cottage cheese.'

'Bloody hell!' Shannon pulled a disgusted face. 'I won't tell you what that stuff reminds me of – not when I'm sober anyway. I never heard of a Chinese girl who ate cottage cheese,' she laughed.

'That's because you have racist preconceptions about Chinese girls,' Jenny said loftily. 'I suppose you think I learned Kung-fu and spent my early life helping in a takeaway? And now I hand over all my earnings to my father, or our local Triad gang, who will inflict the death of a thousand cuts if I don't pay up?'

'Yeah, right.'

They walked out of the Magistrates Court into autumn sunshine. The chill air smelled of wood smoke and the usual stink of molasses drifted up from the docks.

'I love this weather.' Shannon smiled and looked up at the pale blue sky. 'Autumn's my favourite season. I don't care about summer.'

'Shannon!' Jenny screamed. 'Look out!'

'What . . .' she gasped and staggered forward as a blow to the small of her back sent her reeling. The briefcase fell and burst open, spilling yellow and white papers over the sandstone flags. The red-haired woman in the fur coat kicked the briefcase and pushed Jenny away as she tried to go to Shannon's aid.

'How dare you do this?' she screamed. 'How dare you send my son to jail? You and his bitch of a wife conspired against him from the start. He should never have married that woman.' She grabbed Shannon's hair, punched her in the stomach and kicked her to the ground. Passers-by stopped and stared.

Shannon curled up foetus-like, a blur of fur and clumpy black shoes before her eyes. She hoped someone would call the police before the mad mother kicked her head in.

'My son can't go to jail!' the woman screamed. 'He can't! His life will be ruined. How dare you do this to my family? I'll kill you!' She kicked Shannon hard in the hip and stomach.

She coughed and retched and rolled on the ground, swallowing saliva. They didn't warn me about this at the College of Law, she thought, and managed to grab the lunging foot and bring the woman thudding down on her fat bottom.

'Your son should have thought of that before he beat up his wife and caused her to have a miscarriage,' gasped Shannon. She jumped astride the spitting, snarling woman and twisted her arms up behind her back, recoiling as if from an adder. 'He's lucky he's not up for murder. You should see her in the hospital – she's not a pretty sight.'

'Hey, come on. Break it up, girls.' Two policemen ran up and hauled them apart, pulling them to their feet. 'Fighting's not very ladylike, is it?'

'That evil bitch sent my son to jail!' the woman shouted,

pointing at Shannon. Her son had inherited her temper, Shannon thought. 'His life will be ruined. He's innocent – it's a conspiracy.'

''Course it is, love.' The older policeman laughed. 'Now you get off home and don't be causing trouble.'

'How dare you speak to me like that?' She turned on him, narrow hazel eyes blazing. 'I'll make sure you lose your job. I'm not just anybody, you know. My husband's a personal friend of the Chief Constable.'

'Isn't that nice?' His smile disappeared. 'Now get off home or we'll have to lock you up as well. Go on, I mean it.'

She picked up her unfashionably big brown handbag and backed away like a hyena frightened by lions. A minute later she turned and hurried away from the court building and past the statue of Queen Victoria on her stone throne, walking in the direction of the Pier Head.

'You all right, love?' The younger policeman looked at Shannon with interest as she got to her feet and brushed sandstone dust and papery autumn leaves from her suit. Her hip, back and stomach ached and she felt sick. Jenny ran around picking up papers.

'I think so.' She straightened up, rubbed her sore back and looked at her friend. 'I'm disappointed in you,' she said. 'I thought you'd do an Eric Cantona on her.'

'Don't I know you, love?' The policeman stared harder at her and laughed. 'Yeah! You're Rob Flinder's wife. I saw you in some club with him in the summer. A solicitor and a detective constable!' He laughed. 'How the hell did you two get together? Must be a marriage from hell, that.'

'My marriage has got asterisk all to do with you,' she said briskly. '*Love*.'

'Sensitive subject, is it?'

'Get stuffed. Fancy you shouting "break it up" like that,' she said sweetly. 'Just like the telly. Thanks for rescuing one of the undead from a kicking.'

'All part of the service.'

They walked off, laughing, and she brushed more dust off her suit. What idiot said black clothes didn't show the dirt?

'Here's your briefcase,' Jenny said. 'Oh, God, Shannon, are you all right?'

'I think so.' She blinked back tears. 'Why do I do this stupid job?'

'Because when you were at school your silly old bitch of a domestic science teacher, who did careers in her spare time, told you to be a typist. Great motivation. We should all be that lucky.'

'It's just the shock,' she said as Jenny put one arm around her. 'I'm all right, really. At least Hankin's banged up for now. That's all that matters.'

'Let's get back to the office,' Jenny said. 'We'll order a sandwich or something. Wait here while I find us a taxi.' She looked up and down the road for one of the shiny black cabs that cruised between Pier Head and the city centre.

'Shannon!' a man's voice called. 'What's going on?'

'Oh, Nick! Hello.' Her accountant friend, Nick Forth, strode up looking anxious, followed by another man.

'Enraged mother took offence at seeing wife-beater son remanded in custody until his trial at the Crown Court. I managed to see her off,' Shannon said with a shaky laugh.

'For God's sake!' Nick took her arm. 'Are you all right?'

'Yep. Nothing broken or dislodged.' As she rubbed her sore hip and back she became uncomfortably aware of Nick's companion or client, a tall thin broad-shouldered man in his early thirties with a close-trimmed beard and shortish wavy black hair. I must look a right scruffball, she thought, taking in his grey Armani suit and white collarless shirt. He had a narrow face, pale skin and startlingly green eyes, which barely flickered as he gazed down at her. She looked into them and her mouth went dry. She found she couldn't move.

'Am I wearing something of yours?' Shannon asked coldly, to hide her shyness, amazed she could still feel shy after just being punched and kicked to the ground. He didn't answer, only smiled slightly. She felt stupid.

'Shannon.' Nick glanced from one to the other. 'This is Finbar – Finbar Linnell. He's a client and friend of mine. Finbar, this is Shannon Flinder. We were at university together, she's a solicitor now. Criminal law.'

'That's interesting.' Finbar held out his hand. 'I'm pleased to meet you, Miss Flinder.'

His self-possession, the look in his green eyes and that soft Galway accent combined to make her shiver. Get a grip on yourself, she thought irritably. You're a twenty-six-year-old married lawyer, not a bloody sixth former. He took her hand and slid one warm finger across her pulse, pressing lightly. She blushed and pulled away as an electric shock of desire ran through her. She'd never believed in lust at first sight. Until now.

'It's Mrs,' she said. 'Actually.' Why had she said that? She usually called herself Ms, telling anyone who cared to listen that she refused to be defined by her relationship to a man.

'Sorry. Mrs Flinder. Did the demented woman with the poor dead animal on her back think you were something to do with the strange goings-on up at Castle Dracula?'

'Unfortunately I *am* something to do with the goings-on at Castle Dracula,' she said wryly. 'Are you a lawyer, Mr Linnell?'

'Ah, no. No, indeed.' The green eyes sparkled with sudden mirth. 'But I sometimes make use of their services.'

They couldn't take their eyes off one another, Nick thought uneasily. Jenny giggled nervously. A car horn hooted behind them and they looked round to see a black BMW parked on yellow lines, tinted windows glinting in the sunshine. The male driver waved.

'I hate to do this.' Finbar glanced at his watch. 'But I'm afraid I'll have to love you and leave you.' He smiled at Shannon. 'I'll see you, Nick,' he said quietly. 'Don't let me down now, will you? I need that report by Thursday.'

'Of course.' Nick looked at the ground and shuffled his feet like an embarrassed schoolboy.

'Goodbye, *Mrs* Flinder.' Finbar's green eyes bored into her blue ones. 'I hope we meet again very soon. Bye now!' He ran to the BMW and got in. The car drove away, slowing as it joined a queue of traffic further down the crowded street.

'How about lunch, Shannon?' Nick smiled at her. 'I'll take you to Hale's Bistro. Steak and kidney pie and a couple of glasses of South Aussie Cabernet Sauvignon should make you feel the business again. You can even have one of those bloody awful whipped cream, ice cream, meringue and fruit things that make me feel sick just to look at them.'

'Thanks, Nick.' She smiled up at him. 'Seeing as I don't feel sick anymore, that would be lovely.'

'Well, see you later, Shannon.' Jenny walked off, cross at being ignored by the gorgeous green-eyed Irishman and by handsome Nick, on whom she nursed a secret painful crush. It was obvious they both fancied Shannon. Everyone fancied Shannon. 'If she wasn't so nice I'd hate her. Sod the cottage cheese,' she said to herself. 'I'll have a chicken tikka and salad baguette. *And* a strawberry tart.'

Shannon stared after the BMW and took a deep breath to calm her racing heart. 'What does Mr Finn MacCool do?' she asked sarcastically. 'He didn't say.'

'He's a businessman.' They began to walk along the street of Victorian office buildings, heading for Exchange Flags and the side street where the bistro was. 'He owns a club in town – someone manages it for him – and he runs an air cargo business out of Speke. He's got offices in India Buildings, pretty near you. He lives by himself in one of those Albert Dock apartments.'

'God, how Eighties!' she laughed. 'Those places cost a fortune. He's not married then?' she asked shyly.

Nick laughed. 'He's not married. He's been in Liverpool about four years, he used to live in Dublin. I think he had someone there, but he doesn't talk much about his personal life. I don't want to pry. You fancy him, don't you?'

'Don't be ridiculous!' she lied, blushing. 'Anyone would say he was gorgeous. Those green eyes, that southern Irish accent. I could tell there was a party going on in Jenny's pants.' Never mind her own.

'He's also got business interests abroad.'

'I'll bet he does. How did you get involved with him?' she asked curiously.

'I shouldn't really tell you, it's confidential. He's got an Isle of Man bank account, I look after that for him.'

'Oh, my God!' She laughed. 'Luxembourg, Gibraltar and the Cayman Islands too, I suppose? Does he know he can get diplomatic status in the Seychelles for only ten million dollars US? You have a duty of care to check that your clients' money isn't dodgy these days, Nicholas dear, you do realise that?' she teased. 'Otherwise you too could be up shit creek with the old chicken wire paddle.'

'Shannon – offshore companies, trusts and bank accounts are used every day by people pursuing perfectly legitimate business,' Nick said irritably.

'Of course they are!' She grinned. 'What is he then, an arms dealer? Drugs trafficker? Importer of illegal aliens? All three? You launder his dirty money. Hey!' She nudged him, seeing his annoyed expression. 'I'm just having a laugh. I need it after being attacked by the mad lady from the manor.'

'I don't know much about Finbar, but my investigations haven't turned up anything dodgy,' said her friend stiffly. 'I can assure you of that.'

Touchy, she thought. 'How's the Australian gold mine?'

'Oh, that.' He looked relieved. 'They're not giving any free samples.'

'And how's gorgeous baby girlie?'

'Helen's fine. You and Rob still on for dinner tonight?'

'Of course.'

'I told Caroline you both want to start trying for a baby, but she says don't have kids unless you're prepared to go without sleep indefinitely.'

'Oh, really? I thought she'd encourage me and tell me she's glad we've decided to go ahead and that we don't know what delights we're missing.'

'That's not the word that springs to your jaded brain at three a.m. when you get woken by the strongest pair of lungs in the Western Hemisphere. How anything so little can make so much noise!'

'Hey, gerl! Penny for the guy!'

A gang of boys on the street corner were grouped around a hideous slumped guy with a red slash for a mouth and ripped tartan scarf for its clothing.

'Twenty quid, more like,' Nick said crossly. He glared at them. 'The little bastards are never in school.'

'Hitler said most people should have just enough education to read road signs.'

'I bet they can't even do that. They're all brain dead these days. Must be all that junk food and the lead in petrol. And the education system.'

'You're getting old, Nick. Old Nick!' Shannon laughed. His company and the crisp weather made her feel better. She pushed Finbar Linnell out of her mind, dismissing her reaction to him. She had Rob, they were happily married. She wanted a baby. Two babies. On impulse she ran up to the boys and thrust a ten pound note into the hand of their leader, a tall boy with smooth milk chocolate-coloured skin and a pineapple haircut.

'Wow, a tenner! Thanks, gerl. Look, you lot.' He flourished the note, grinning with pleasure.

'You're mad, Shannon,' Nick said disapprovingly when she ran back to him. 'They'll only spend it on drink or drugs or cigarettes.'

'Oh, Nick! They wouldn't get much change out of a tenner. They might even spend it on sweets, you know. There are still a few normal children left. Don't believe everything you hear from social workers who want to justify their existence and control everyone.'

The BMW was still stuck at traffic lights. Finbar twisted around in his seat for a last look at Shannon. He felt devastated, physically shattered by the intensity of the feeling that had gripped him when he saw her. He knew immediately that he loved her, wanted her for the rest of his life. Even with Majella he had not experienced that incredible instant recognition. The overwhelming desire. But Shannon was married. Happily married. He didn't think she'd liked him much. He had made her uneasy. His expression was brooding as he watched her with the laughing boys, the midday sun turning her blonde hair to a halo around her heart-shaped face. She rejoined Nick and fished out a mobile phone.

'Come on,' Finbar murmured to the driver. 'I'll never make that Amsterdam flight.'

'Bad news?' Nick asked as Shannon swore, switched off her phone and threw it in her briefcase.

'The beaten wife calling from her hospital bed,' she said disconsolately. 'She wants to drop the charges.'

* * *

'But how could the stupid bitch drop the charges?' Caroline Forth looked indignantly at Shannon over her glass of white Burgundy. She tossed back long lank brown hair. 'After all you did for her? *Way* beyond your job description. Some women are their own worst enemies, they really are.'

'It's not that simple, Caroline,' Rob Flinder broke in, glancing worriedly at Shannon. She looked exhausted, he thought. They shouldn't have come out tonight. 'When someone's slapping you up all the time and telling you how useless and hopeless you are, eventually you start to believe them. Women treated that way have such a low sense of self-worth, you can't imagine.' Just as some people's was too high. 'I see it all the time,' he went on, picking up his glass of wine. 'I'm surprised she got as far as pressing charges in the first place.'

'But this means the bastard's just going to get *away* with it!'

'Tell me something I don't know,' Shannon said wearily.

'He'll probably kill her next time. Blacken her character enough to plead manslaughter and walk out laughing within three years. Who said provocation is no defence anymore!'

'It's incredibly frustrating,' Shannon agreed. She looked at the empty lobster shell on her plate and stifled another yawn. Her back and hip still hurt, probably more from tiredness than the kicking. A hot shower would help. Thank goodness tomorrow was Saturday and she could sleep late. Rob was looking at her and she laid one hand gently on his, stroking the warm skin lightly scattered with fine dark hairs. She felt a surge of desire, despite her tiredness. They smiled at each other and she knew he was as bored with Caroline as she was. She loved the look of warmth and humour in his deep brown eyes, his narrow face and thoughtful expression, his broad shoulders. He had fine lines around his eyes but had otherwise barely changed since he was a teenager.

Nick watched them enviously. They still fancied each other after nearly two years of marriage. He wished Caroline would shut up. She always wanted a heated debate after a few glasses of wine.

'Anyone for dessert?' He tried to catch the waiter's eye.

'Not for . . .' Shannon began.

'Yes, *please*!' Caroline emptied her wine glass and poured more, ignoring Nick's critical look. 'Something chocolatey and creamy.'

'You'll get the baby pissed if you drink anymore of that wine,' he remarked.

'Might make her sleep through the night for once, little madam! But if not, it won't be you who gets up, will it?'

'I haven't got tits full of milk,' he protested. 'You're the one she needs most. If you fed her more often, instead of yourself, she wouldn't cry so much.'

Caroline looked at Shannon. 'I can't stand these bloody born-again fathers, can you?' she said loudly. 'They're full of patronizing, half-baked advice and always ready to wank on about the joys of fatherhood, but when it comes to practical help, forget it. I bet Doctor bloody Spock sat locked in his study writing all that bullshit while his wife dealt with the kids.'

'Let's forget dessert.' Rob smiled at them. 'I think we'll get home. Shannon's had a hell of a day.'

'She *thinks* she's had a hell of a day! Wait until you've got a screaming baby clamped to your tits. No adult company except the milkman and the bloody interfering health visitor. The *occasional* appearance of a disinterested husband . . .'

They left Nick and Caroline to their bickering and took a cab home to West Derby. The big detached house was warm and quiet and welcoming, a refuge from the noisy restaurant and cold misty night. Shannon ran upstairs, pulled off her clothes and stood under a hot shower, lifting her face to the hard hot stream of water. She gasped with relief and pleasure as her sore body relaxed. What a day! she thought. What a bloody day! She thought of poor battered Joanne Hankin in her hospital bed, her mad mother-in-law who would defend – as if he needed it! – her violent son against anyone who tried to stop him. She couldn't feel angry with Joanne for dropping the charges, only disappointed and frustrated. What would her husband do now? Not attack her at the hospital, he wasn't stupid enough for that. Could she make it to a refuge in time?

She stepped out of the shower, wrapped herself in a thick, apricot-coloured towel and snapped the bathroom light off.

'I think I'll visit Joanne tomorrow,' she said as she strolled into the bedroom, drying herself. 'See how she's doing.'

'Again?' Rob was sitting up in bed, lamplight falling on his bare shoulders. 'I don't see that you can help her any further, Shannon.' He frowned slightly. 'If she won't press charges, that's it.'

'I could maybe help her and the kids get a place in a refuge. I mean – if that's what she wants, of course.'

He yawned and stretched his arms above his head. 'I'll come with you,' he said. 'God knows what could happen with that husband on the loose. Not to mention his bloody mother.'

'Thanks.' She smiled at him. 'Just a quick visit. Then we've got the rest of the weekend to have fun.'

'Yes,' he said, watching as she dropped the towel and studied her naked body in the wardrobe mirror, turning and twisting to view her hip and back.

'No bruises,' she murmured. 'I couldn't *believe* that woman. Mad bitch!'

'Could have been a mad bitch with a knife or gun.'

'But it wasn't. Don't worry, I'm all right. Really.' She crossed to the dressing table and sprayed spicy perfume between her breasts and thighs, aware of his gaze.

'You're bloody lovely,' he murmured as she got on the bed and he took her in his arms, kissing her and stroking her breasts. He laughed suddenly. 'D'you think we'll get like Nick and Caroline once we've got a baby?'

'We'll *never* get like Nick and Caroline. I was really fed up with her tonight. She's not interested in anyone but herself. Anyway, they were like that before they had Helen. Always bitching at one another.'

'Your skin is so soft.' He slid a hand between her legs and stroked, softly at first. She gasped and put her arms around him.

'You still fancy me after eighteen months of marriage then?'

'You and your insecurity,' he murmured, half exasperated. 'Of course I still fancy you. I love you, you're my life.'

'You won't get sick of me?' she teased.

'For Christ's sake!' He stopped stroking, pushed her thighs further apart and surged inside her, making her cry out with pleasure. He looked into her eyes.

'*No* chance!'

Chapter Two

'That was a great night, Finbar!' The bald stocky man in the filthy sheepskin jacket lurched out of the Carmen Club and stumbled down the steps. 'Jesus, Mary and Joseph!' He tripped and grabbed at the railings. 'Had a bit too much of the old water of life. Hey!' Two young girls across the street giggled uncontrollably as they held on to one another. 'You're pissed!' he yelled at them. 'Bloody lesbians!'

'Come on now, Conal. Mind how you go.' A tall thin broad-shouldered man with a pointed beard and black hair stood at the top of the steps flanked by two bouncers, hands clenched in his trouser pockets. He wore a dark suit and a white collarless shirt. A pale blue November dawn shed cold light over the River Mersey and the Liver Buildings. He could smell the river, molasses from the docks.

'You're a great man, Finbar!' Conal McCartan slurred, clinging to the railings. 'A generous man. I'm glad we got the misunderstanding sorted out. A second chance. Not every man gets a sec–'

'Jesus Christ!' Phil, one of the bouncers, looked away in disgust as Conal bent and retched, bringing up the mixture of cottage pie, chips and the litre of Bushmill's malt swilling around his stomach. The vomit splashed on to the pavement. Finbar waited patiently while Conal retched, coughed, spat and unzipped his trousers. A stream of hot urine poured on to the steaming vomit.

'Billy Connolly says it's always got carrots in it.' He laughed and lurched round to face them. 'Sorry about that, Finbar,' he mumbled as he zipped up his baggy jeans.

'You're a real pig, Conal.' Finbar spoke in a low voice, almost a murmur. He glanced at his Rolex and looked up and down the street of terraced Georgian houses, now renovated and split into apartments and lawyers' offices. 'I don't know how your wife puts up with you.'

'That bitch!' Conal spat. 'That Medusa! If it wasn't for the wee girl . . .'

'Go home and get to bed, Conal.'

'I will, Finbar. I'll do that.' He rooted in his pockets, dragged out a bunch of keys and dropped them in the vomit. 'Holy fuck!' He laughed and stood swaying in the dawn light. Finbar came down the steps.

'Never mind the keys,' he said. 'You can't drive in that state. You'll never make it home.'

'I drive better after a few drinks!' Conal protested loudly. 'And I've brought it all up. Best feeling in the world, a good puke!'

'I'll get someone to drop you off home.' Finbar recoiled from the stink of vomit, whisky, stale sweat and fresh urine. 'Eddie?'

'Yes, Finbar?' The bouncer with the shaved head came running down the steps.

'Make sure this tosser gets home safely. Use your car.'

'Yes, Finbar.' Eddie nodded reluctantly. If that drunken bastard chucked up in his Pontiac Firebird, he'd be sorry.

'Thanks, Finbar.' Conal's sunken bloodshot eyes filled with tears. 'You're the best. I love you, man!' He stretched out his arms and Finbar stepped back. 'Four years I've known you since you came to this town, and I love you,' he cried. 'I'll never let you down again.'

'I know you won't.' Finbar smiled slightly, his green eyes calm. His narrow face was pale and tired-looking. 'Go on home now,' he repeated.

'Goodnight, Finbar. Goodnight now.' Eddie's car pulled up and Conal collapsed into the passenger seat and slumped back in it, his mouth falling open as he passed out. The car sped down the quiet road, Finbar staring after it. One thousand Es nicked from the latest consignment and flogged in clubs all over the city. No,

Conal wouldn't let him down again. One rip deal was one too many.

He shivered, turned and ran back up the steps into the club. A group of men sat talking quietly in a corner and the video screen was blank. The music was off. Finbar sat on a bar stool and leaned his elbows on the polished bar. Exhaustion swept over him. In a few minutes he would drive back to his Albert Dock apartment, make a cup of coffee and get some sleep. He loved coffee and it never stopped him sleeping. It was other things that did that. The pain, the anguish that would stay with him for the rest of his life.

'Mineral water,' he said to the young barman.

'Feenbar! I miss you all night.' The young blonde girl in the black silk mini dress with spaghetti straps pouted up at him and pushed her big breasts against his chest. 'You don't talk with me. You never talk with me!'

'What's to talk with you about?' he asked mildly. 'The state of the economy? Tony Blair's chances of re-election? The pros and cons of a single currency?' He sipped his mineral water and turned away.

'Feenbar, you take me back to your beautiful apartment by the river?' she pleaded. Her hardened nipples were visible beneath the black silk.

'How do you know it's beautiful? You've never seen it. You'll never see it.'

She slid on to a bar stool beside him. 'I give best blow job in Liverpool – in whole of Europe.' She ran her tongue slowly over her shiny pink lips. 'And for you, without the condom.'

'I wouldn't shag you, with or without a condom,' he said coldly. 'Go away. I'm busy.'

'Please, Feenbar!' She pulled the straps down and exposed her breasts, attracting whoops and whistles from the group of men in the corner. 'I am wet for you,' she said. She grabbed his hand and pressed it to her crotch. 'Feel!'

'You peasant slapper!' He pulled his hand away as if stung. 'Put those tits away, they're an act of aggression.'

'You know you want me.' She got off the bar stool and twined her arms around his neck. 'Take me home with you. Now.'

'I said, go away!' He pushed her in the face and she staggered back and crashed down on a table full of empty pint glasses, screaming in pain and fright as glass cut into her naked back. 'I don't want you.' He looked down at her coldly. 'I never have and never will. Don't bother me again.'

Majella's smiling, heart-shaped face, blue eyes and silky blonde hair flashed into his brain, and he heard Roiseann's gurgling baby laughter. How could this bitch be alive when they were dead, torn from him forever? Four years now, and it still felt like yesterday. He looked at his watch again and turned back to the bar. His hand tightened around the glass.

'Wake up, you drunken bastard Mick!' Eddie shook Conal roughly, and he groaned and mumbled. 'Get the hell out of my car, stinking it up with your puke!'

'All right, all right.' Conal stirred and opened his eyes. Eddie leaned across and pushed the door open. 'I'm out of here, I'm out. Christ, it's bloody freezing!'

He stood on the pavement, pulling his sheepskin jacket tightly around him as the Pontiac drove off. His stomach ached and a million sledgehammers were trying to bang their way out through his skull. It's the dehydration, he thought. I'll drink a pint of water before I go to sleep. That bitch Dervla would be up, but there was no more chance of her making him a cup of tea than there was of Boris Yeltsin running the London Marathon.

He stood there groaning, holding his head, scratching his stubbled jowls. The narrow street of small terraced houses was silent in the chill dawn. There weren't many who had work to get up for in this town anymore. He turned and staggered towards his house, feeling in his pockets for the keys. Good job they weren't kept on the same ring as his car keys! 'Jesus, Mary and Joseph!' he chuckled.

He stopped and stared open-mouthed at the stiff pink carrier bag that hung from the front door knob, 'Sweetheart' printed across it in curvy yellow letters. Bunches of thin shiny pink ribbons were knotted around both handles.

'Oh, Jesus!' he gasped. 'It's the wee girl's birthday. Nine today. God, the time flies.'

'Sweetheart' was the name of the big posh new sweetshop in

town where his daughter Rosie always begged to be let loose. It must be a present for her. He'd have to sneak out later and buy her something. One of her little friend's mothers must have left the bag there on her way to or from a shift. He shook his head drunkenly. There were more women than men in work these days. It wasn't right. Conal grabbed the bag and stuck his key in the lock.

The explosion destroyed his house and the houses to either side and set car alarms wailing the length of the street. People awoke terrified and confused.

'What the *hell* was that?' The young couple opposite cowered in their bed, staring at the glass blown from their windows that covered the flowered quilt.

'We don't live under a flight path. Must be a gas explosion.' They couldn't get out of bed, the floor was covered in glass. 'Oh, my God!' the woman gasped, sitting up and looking out. 'Look at the McCartan house – it's *gone.*'

The three-metre long and two-metre wide crater in the road seemed to confirm a gas explosion. A raw bloody severed hand, two fingers missing, and one of Conal's feet in a bloodied emerald sock and scuffed brown brogue flew through the air and landed at the end of the street where two men sat in a stolen blue Ford Mustang.

'For Christ's sake!' The man in the passenger seat laughed. 'Dean, man, the boss said to blow up Conal. Not the whole frigging street.'

'Wonder what the blast geometry of that one was?' the driver murmured. He had thick grey hair and black eyebrows that met in the middle. 'Let's see, equal parts of trinitrotoluene –'

'You *what*?'

'TNT to peasants. Penthrite plastic, T4 plastic ... Ugh!' He grimaced at the bloody foot on the road. 'Let's get out of here before I get put off me bacon and sausages and fried bread.'

The man in the passenger seat pulled out a mobile phone and punched in a number as the Ford Mustang reversed out of the street and sped off, heading for the city centre.

'Okay. Good.' Finbar put down the phone and got off the bar stool. 'Guy!' he called. 'I'm off now.'

'Right, Finbar. Goodnight.' A balding heavily built man in his late thirties, wearing an evening suit, waved to him from across the room. The injured girl sat crying in his office; he would take her to Casualty in a minute. Leave the boss alone, he'd warned her earlier. He doesn't want to know. The silly cow had ignored him and this was the result.

Finbar decided to leave the Maserati in its parking space down the road and walk the short distance to the Albert Dock. He needed to breathe the fresh cold air. It was daylight now. He walked down James Street, past the graceful old building on the corner that had once housed the offices of the White Star Line, and paused to watch a pale gold autumn sun rise over the Mersey. The pilot boat was out, rocking up and down with the gentle swell of the river.

'"Big confusion under the sky",' he murmured, quoting the immortal words of Mao Tse Tung, '"then the situation is excellent."'

Chapter Three

'Thanks for the lift, Mr Flinder.' The girl glanced shyly up at Bernard and blushed as his gaze left her face and dropped to her smooth bare brown thighs under the navy blue pleated school skirt.

'You're welcome, Patricia.' He smiled.

'Pattie.' She hated being called Patricia. Patricia was a clueless bitch who didn't know which way was up. She opened the Volvo door and reached down to grab her bag, pressing her knees together.

'Pattie. Er – just a minute!' said Bernard Flinder urgently. His smile faded, not that old Fish Eyes Flinder ever really smiled. He laughed a lot, a creepy laugh, at things you didn't realize were funny. He'd got Jed Markie and that gang of bitches off her back, though, she was grateful for that. He was a big fat bastard, with a bush of wiry black hair going grey, hairy ears, a pouchy putty-coloured face, thin lips under the out-of-control moustache and little black eyes that looked at you as though you were a dissected rat from the science lab. Sharp white teeth. He wore dark grey trousers, a red-and-black striped tie and one of his double sad tweed jackets with leather elbow patches. He always sounded like he had a cold.

'Yes, Mr Flinder?' Was he going to wank on about her missing the bus or wearing her skirt too short? The waistband was rolled over and pulled up around her chest, the way the other girls had shown her at lunchtime in the toilets. Jacintha Fenn had said she had good legs. The car door swung shut. The leather seat was hot and sticky under her bare thighs and she could smell his disgusting pine aftershave.

'Going to watch a bonfire and firework display tonight?' He laughed his creepy laugh.

'Yes.' She nodded, relieved to be let off a lecture. 'Some boys have built a bonfire on the field around the corner.'

'Good. Great. And how are you liking your first term at St Fidelma's?' He longed to stroke her soft neck and thick corn blonde plait; to knead a handful of satin thigh. Would she object? They looked so innocent in their navy blue school uniforms. But they weren't innocent. Not nowadays.

'Oh, it's fine,' lied Pattie. She hated the place, like everyone else. 'I like it very much. Lots of friends from primary school are there.'

'Made any new ones?'

'A few.' She glanced at her house. The television flickered through the living room curtains. Her brother would be home, hogging the screen, stuffing himself with crisps and chocolate cake. Or doughnuts. She swung the door wide and edged away.

'If you have any more problems, you come to me,' said Bernard. 'All right?' He stared at her, sweaty hands slithering on the wheel. 'I'm the headmaster, I can help you. Any bullying in my school I take as a personal affront. I won't tolerate it. If I hadn't caught those girls hitting you, you wouldn't have said anything, would you?' She was silent. 'Don't forget, my door's always open.' He started. 'Is that your mother?' A plump blonde middle-aged woman in a pink shell suit had come out of the house and was looking crossly up and down the tree-lined road.

'Yes.' Pattie flinched with embarrassment. 'That's her.'

'It's nice she's home when you get back from school. A lot of mums have jobs nowadays. Different priorities.'

'Yes,' Pattie said politely. What the hell was he on about? She wished the narky bitch would go straight from the margarine factory to the pub every night and stay until chucking-out time. She cringed as her mother spotted the Volvo, waved excitedly and ran forward.

'Good afternoon, Mr Flinder!' She put on her gruesome, high-pitched posh voice. 'How lovely to see you again!'

'Good afternoon, Mrs O'Neill.' He coughed and cleared his throat. Ugly bitch, he thought. 'I'm just delivering Patricia to you. She missed the bus.'

'Did she? Silly girl. Thanks very much for bringing her home, Mr Flinder,' she said gaily. 'It's very kind of you.'

'Not at all. I wouldn't want my daughter hanging around waiting for a bus that didn't come.' He turned the key in the ignition. 'Well, I must be off. Have a good Bonfire Night!'

'Same to you, Mr Flinder.'

Pattie got out and slammed the door. Ginette O'Neill waved exaggeratedly as the Volvo pulled away down the road and turned left. Then the flirtatious smile disappeared as she turned and slapped Pattie's face.

'How many times have I told you not to go frigging around after school?' she shouted hoarsely. She pushed Pattie, making her stumble against the low garden wall. 'If you miss that sodding bus again, I'll belt you so hard you won't sit for a week. I've told you about them perverts who hang around waiting for silly little bitches like you to come waltzing along. Good job Mr Flinder gave you a lift. And what have you done to your skirt?' she yelled. 'Get in there and change out of that frigging uniform before it's ruined. Cost me a sodding fortune.'

'No, it didn't.' Pattie rubbed her stinging cheek. 'You got it secondhand. People make fun of me because of that.' Not anymore, she hoped, now that Jed Markie was threatened with expulsion.

'Shut it! Don't you frigging well answer me back! Christ, who'd have kids? Bloody waste of space and money.' She shoved her daughter into the porch. 'Get in that bloody house, I'm freezing my tits off out here.'

Pattie's brother Martin came into the hall, mouth full of jam doughnut.

'Old Flinder fancies you.' He sniggered. 'I saw him perving at your legs. Mum – Fish Eyes Flinder fancies our Pattie. He's always talking to her in school and staring at her. He's waiting for her to grow tits.' He dodged as Pattie swung her heavy bag at his crotch.

'At least he takes a bit more trouble than the other teachers at that bloody school,' Ginette said crossly. 'Good job they've got him as headmaster. He was really lovely to me at the parents' evening. You wash your mouth out with soap, Martin, or I'll phone your dad and tell him not to take you to the football tomorrow night.'

Martin looked downcast. 'If he remembers he's taking me.'

'Don't look at me like that, it's not my fault he's useless.'

Pattie ran upstairs, threw the bag on her bed and stared at herself in the round dressing table mirror. The smell of frying chips drifted in. She dragged off her school blazer and pulled down her skirt until it covered her knees. That's that, she thought. I won't eat tonight. I don't want to have a Rottweiler face and grow tits like hers. Not me – ever.

Bernard was restless and full of energy, even after striding the school corridors all day and chairing a long futile meeting about changes to the autumn term timetable. The usual squabbles, with no one willing to concede. He had ended up pulling rank.

He parked the car near a row of shops and smoked a cigarette, something he never did at school for fear of setting a bad example. He wanted a big Scotch, but that would have to wait until he got home. Margaret could wait too, useless bitch! Which carton or packet would be pulled out of the freezer and stuck in the microwave for tonight's gourmet dinner? She'd have spent the day daubing her pathetic watercolours in the attic, drinking gin or white wine and dreaming about being an artist. Her part-time job in a florist's was the nearest she would get to that. Shannon, his daughter-in-law, was an excellent cook, but she hated him and Margaret, and had stopped Rob from inviting them round. She had her law career, made more money than he and Rob put together. A different set of priorities.

Dusk was falling and the cold crisp air smelled of woodsmoke and cordite. The evening star glittered over houses, shops and office blocks. Every minute there was the crack and bang of an exploding firework. Liverpool would look and sound like the West Bank before the night was out. He started the car again and drove through the city centre, past crowds of commuters hurrying into Central Station. Some of the lighted department store windows already had Christmas displays. He followed signs for Woolton and Childwall.

Darkness came suddenly. He left the city behind, circled a roundabout and cruised down a quiet tree-lined road of Thirties' detached houses, the orange streetlights obscured by the heavy branches of the double file of trees. He caught his breath and stopped the car as a small girl in shiny boots and woolly hat and scarf ran out of a driveway and down the road, the colours of her clothes washed out by orange light. He accelerated past the little running figure, stopped the car again and got out, leaving the engine running. So innocent. He stood in her path and smiled at her as she ran up to him.

'What are you doing out here, love?' He kept his voice low.

She stopped and stared up at him uncertainly, pushing back the dark curly mass of hair that fell over her shoulders. He liked her pale earnest little cat face and big dark eyes. She clutched a half-naked Barbie doll dressed in a pair of cotton jeans, the top button missing. She looked about four years old.

'I'm hiding.' She gave a little gasp, half a sob, of excitement. 'I'm hiding from my Mummy and Daddy. I was in the back garden. I ran out. Daddy's just going to light the bonfire. I ran out,' she repeated.

'Hiding from your Mummy and Daddy?' Bernard stepped closer and glanced up and down the deserted road. 'Why's that, love?'

'I'm cross with them,' she said breathlessly. She clutched the Barbie doll and stared up at him. 'We're going to have a bonfire in our back garden.' Her baby teeth chattered with cold. 'Mummy and Daddy won't let me throw my old coat on the fire. I want to burn it. They won't let me.'

'That's a bit mean.' He laughed and glanced up the road again. 'Especially on Bonfire Night.'

'Yes.' She nodded solemnly. 'It's mean. I want someone else to look after me.'

'Let's get in my nice warm car and drive around the block,' he suggested. 'Just for a minute. I've got some lovely sweeties for you. Jelly babies.'

'They're for babies!' she shouted. And stamped her little feet in their shiny boots.

'Shhh!' he said nervously. 'Dolly Mixtures. D'you like those?' He stooped and grabbed her hand. 'Come on, I'll give you some Dolly Mixtures.'

'No! Don't want any.' She stumbled and he swung her up and carried her to the car. 'I want to go back!' she shouted, struggling in his arms. He felt her baby breath on his cheek. Margaret had a plant called Baby's Breath. 'I want to go back to my Mummy!'

'Shut up.' He bundled her into the back seat and slammed the door. She began to wail.

'I want to go back to my Mummy.' She drummed her feet on the floor and screamed as he drove away, climbing on to the seat and hitting the window with her little fists.

'I said, shut up!' He glanced at her terrified face in the driving mirror. Huge frantic dark eyes stared back at him. She looked like his daughter Melanie had at that age. 'If you don't stop that noise I'm going to get very cross.' Same words. 'You can go back to Mummy in a minute, I promise. Here.' He fumbled in the glove compartment and tossed the packet of Dolly Mixtures on to the back seat.

'I want my Mummy, I want my Mummy!' she gulped and hiccoughed and went on sobbing. 'I want my Mummy.'

'I told you, you can go back to your Mummy in a minute,' Bernard said soothingly. 'I just want to talk to you for a while. You're a lovely little girl.'

He screeched to a halt at some crossroads and swerved left, heading for Calderstones Park. Near the park he slowed, startled by shouts from a group of excited children. Bonfire Night. There was a bonfire in the park. And a firework display. There was a crack as a shower of red and green jewelled stars shot into the sky and exploded over the tree tops. He reversed into a side street and drove off again, glancing in the mirror. She was quiet now.

'Just another minute and you can go home,' he promised. He circled the park railings, past crowds of children and adults, swathed in scarves, coats, hats, quilted jackets, all heading for the bonfire site and firework display. He found a dark narrow tree-lined track, bumped the car down it and parked in a small space among the trees. It looked like a kind of lovers' lane, but it was too early for lovers. They would be along later, after they had had their fill of beer and wine and baked potatoes and burnt sausages. More fireworks cracked like gunshots and whooshed into the sky. A full moon had risen.

He switched off the engine and headlights, pulled on a pair of latex gloves and got into the back seat beside her. Barbie lay on the floor, her bare nippleless breasts thrusting upwards, tarantula-lashed doll's eyes blank and accepting.

The engine dead, there was silence among the trees. The car smelled of stale cigarette smoke and the child's fear. She had wet herself.

'What's your name, love?' He shifted closer.

'Bianca.' She shrank back, big dark eyes staring up at him. Her round smooth cheeks were pale in the moonlight and wet with tears.

'Bianca.' Bernard shifted again, feeling himself harden. He pulled at the hem of the little tartan kilt she wore. 'That's a pretty name.' Even if it did sound like an Italian aperitif. 'You're a very pretty little girl.'

'Are you a bad person who hurts children?' she gulped and her voice trembled.

'I don't hurt children,' he said softly. 'I love children. Especially little girls.'

Excitement surged in him. He felt no pity for her terror and vulnerability, just overwhelming excitement. People would say he was sick. Evil and sick. Or just evil. Evil was in, sick was out. People were tired of psychiatrists and social workers wanking on about impoverished backgrounds, physical abuse, emotional neglect. An evil pervert. Someone for whom hanging should be brought back. Or chemical castration introduced. He tugged at the kilt and stared at Bianca, his breath quickening.

'I want you to do something really nice for me.' He unzipped his trousers. 'Then you can go home.'

'If you're a bad person . . .' more tears glittered in her eyes and rolled down her cheeks . . . 'can I say my prayers first?'

Chapter Four

'You'll be there a couple of hours? What's going on?' Shannon sipped her champagne. 'I might have known this would happen,' she said crossly. 'I thought we were going to watch the bonfire and firework display in Croxteth Park, and then order pizza? I'm starving!'

'We are,' Rob said. 'We will. But Melanie's in a state again.' His voice sounded strained. 'She's confused.'

'You've got that right.' Shannon sipped more champagne, fingertips cold on the chilled frosted glass. 'Your sweet little sister might be less confused if she stopped swilling vodka for five minutes at a stretch,' she went on, angry at the prospect of a wrecked Bonfire Night. 'Student loans are supposed to be spent on books. Still, what's the point when she's too *confused* to drag herself out of bed and go to college?'

Rob chuckled. 'You're a wicked lady.'

'A wicked lady drinking champagne alone. I wanted to celebrate with you.'

'Celebrate what?'

'Rob.' She hesitated. 'I've been offered a partnership. Gavin told me this morning. To take effect from next month.'

'Shannon, that's fantastic!' His voice rose. 'You're bloody brilliant, I'm so proud of you! Congratulations! You deserve it.'

'Thanks.' She grinned. 'I wish you were here. You should be congratulating your beloved wife instead of consoling your bewildered sister. Especially after me nearly getting my head kicked in the other day.'

'I know. I'm really sorry.' He sighed. 'She phoned me at work. She's a mess, Shannon. That bastard Paul thumped her again.'

'For God's sake!' Shannon stretched out on the burgundy leather Chesterfield in the lamplit sitting room. The television was on, sound turned down. A vase of red roses stood on the pine coffee table. I shouldn't have to buy my own champagne and roses, she thought. And celebrate alone. She could call a friend. But she wanted Rob. 'Is he there now?'

'No,' her husband said grimly. 'Luckily for him. Melanie just nipped out to buy more cigarettes. I thought I'd give you a quick call.'

'*Cigarettes!*' She pulled a face. 'Make sure you don't breathe her smoke and damage your sperm. They're always telling wannabe mothers not to drink, smoke, fly or eat hamburgers and gorgeous soft cheeses, but no one nags wannabe fathers to protect their sperm.'

'You can rely on me, *Mrs* Flinder.' A door slammed in the background and feet pounded upstairs. 'That's her now.' He lowered his voice. 'I'll see you later, okay? I'll be home around nine. You order your pizza if you're starving. I'll be as quick as I can, but I just have to make sure she's okay. I'm really worried about her, Shannon.'

'All right,' she said sadly. 'But it's seven o clock now, the bonfire will be ashes by nine. I might go out and look at it after I've eaten.'

'Well, watch out for illegal fireworks wielded by irresponsible idiots.'

'Don't worry.'

'I'll see you later,' he said. 'I love you.'

Rob Flinder put down the phone and turned as his sister Melanie walked into the cold cavernous living room of her flat on the top floor of a Victorian house overlooking Sefton Park. A lamp on the high mantelpiece shed a weak pool of light. The dismal room was furnished only with a tattered cigarette-burnt beige sofa and two matching armchairs. Ancient filthy lace curtains hung at the four sash windows, and the black ceiling and purple walls were obviously the work of some stoned tenant from the late Seventies. The television was off because it was damaged; Melanie had spilt vodka down the back.

'Been phoning wifey to tell her you'll be late for your Thai prawn curry with kaffir leaves?' She laughed contemptuously. 'She'll nail your dick to the cooker!' Melanie pulled two packs of cigarettes from the pocket of her heavy fringed leather jacket and dropped them on the orange box that was her coffee table.

He winced. 'My wife's got a name, you know.'

'Yeah. D'you want me to say it?'

Rob moved to the windows and looked out over the dark mass of Sefton Park. Through the bare trees flames flickered and flared. They were lighting the bonfire. Within minutes it was burning fiercely, gorging on the old clothes, broken furniture, branches, sticks and chewed carpet that had been piled on it for the past week. He stared uneasily at the pagan scene of dark figures dancing around a fire, exulting in and worshipping the flames. A pall of smoke already hung over the park, and the smell of cordite was everywhere. He longed to be with Shannon; he'd leave as soon as possible.

'She works hard at being perfect.' Melanie joined him at the window, watching with him as red, green, yellow, orange and white trails shot through the sky and showered down, causing distant whoops and screams of excitement. The soft coloured lights flickered over the dark bruise around her left eye and cheekbone. 'Perfect wife, perfect criminal lawyer, perfect mother when she decides the time's right. I can see it now.' She dragged on her cigarette and laughed huskily. 'Dinner parties, champagne, baby laughter, sex three times a week. All in the desirable detached des-res in West Derby, far from the madding scumbags. Beautiful blonde, blue-eyed, angelic Shannon presiding over it all.' Melanie glanced down and a curtain of shining hennaed hair fell across her battered face. 'Worse than a bloody soap!' She gasped and sucked in more smoke. 'If someone wrote a script about her they'd say it wasn't realistic.'

'You'd think that cigarette was a life support machine,' he said angrily.

'It is.' She sucked again.

'You've always been jealous of Shannon, haven't you?' he said, pained. 'It wouldn't do you any harm to try a bit harder, you know.' He looked down at her. 'Instead of slagging off Shannon all the time, why don't you try to get on with her for a change? She tries hard enough with you. And look at your own life. You risk HIV and God knows what by shagging one creep after another, you chain smoke, you drink too much–'

'Thanks for reminding me.' Melanie crossed to the mantelpiece and picked up a full bottle of vodka. A small old-fashioned gas fire hissed in the grate.

'You could get a great job with a computer studies degree but you never go into college anymore,' he said worriedly. 'And now you've let this bastard move in. Where is he, by the way?' he demanded. 'Not in the university library, I'll bet.'

'Out,' his sister said sullenly. 'Don't know where.' She dared not tell him that Paul was a drugs dealer. She poured vodka into a squat glass and added a splash of tonic. 'No ice, no slice. Just the way I like it.' She giggled and took a gulp. 'Fancy a drink?'

'No.' Rob moved away from the window and stood by the gas fire. 'It's bloody freezing in here,' he complained, pulling his grey padded jacket around him. 'I don't know how you stand it.'

'This house was built in the days when they had great roaring fires and millions of housemaids to keep them going round the clock.' Melanie swigged more vodka. 'After the First World War and the consequent shortage of domestic staff they installed gas fires and converted the houses to flats. Look.' She pointed her glowing cigarette at the horrible purple wall above the mantelpiece. 'You can still see the old gas bracket. And the bell they rang when the mistress wanted her afternoon gin or the master his blow job from the poor but beautiful servant girl who would wreak bloody revenge and go on to build her own empire. I expect she looked a lot like Shannon. There's a row of cute little bells above the kitchen door. They don't work now. Or I can't find the wire or whatever.'

'The place is a bloody museum,' said her brother disapprovingly. 'Are you going to get that bruise looked at?'

'No. It'll fade in a day or two.' Melanie poured more vodka, pulled off the leather jacket and sat down on the sofa, crossing one thin blue-jeaned leg over the other. She stubbed out the cigarette and lit another, leaving it smouldering in the diamond-shaped glass ashtray while she pulled the long sleeves of her green sweater down over her bitten fingernails.

A pang shot through him. She looked so vulnerable like that, the shining hennaed hair falling around her poor battered face. She looked and acted tough, but she wasn't. Shannon looked like an angel, but Rob had watched her tear apart witnesses in court and square up to his domineering father – on the rare occasions she agreed to see his parents. His father's charm, when he chose to exercise it, definitely didn't work on her.

'The bruise might fade, but broken bones or brain damage won't,' he warned. 'For Christ's sake, Mel! Throw him out. If you don't, I will. The worst injuries, the worst murders we see, are domestics. You wouldn't believe what men do to their wives and girlfriends. Even their daughters.' He slumped down in the armchair.

'I would,' she said slowly. 'Oh yes, I would.' She finished her drink. 'Rob – are you and Shannon planning to have a baby soon?' Her fingers trembled around the cigarette.

'We're using condoms until Shannon's been off the Pill for a year. There's another month to go before we start shagging like rabbits. Nothing wrong with wanting a baby, is there?' he asked defensively. 'I mean, it's not abnormal. Mel, what's the matter? What's wrong?'

Tears poured down her face and she brushed them away, smudging the awful black eyeliner. He got up, took the half smoked cigarette from her shaking fingers and sat beside her. She leaned forward and buried her head in her arms, shoulders heaving.

'Mel, what is it?' he asked softly. 'Talk to me, please. You're my little sister, I love you. I want to help.'

'Get me another drink,' she said, voice muffled.

'Okay,' sighed Rob. He got up and poured more vodka and tonic, adding as much tonic as he dared.

'I can't take anymore,' she moaned, and gulped the drink he handed her. 'I can't go on like this. It's doing my head in.'

'Of course it is.' He put his arm around her, holding her close. 'You've got to get away from that bastard. Men who hit women never change. The more they get away with it, the more violent they become. Pack some of your stuff,' he urged. 'I'll sort him out. Come home with me now.'

'Shannon would love that, wouldn't she?' Melanie laughed huskily. 'Cigarette ash all over the parquet, the sink full of empties.'

He hesitated. 'I know you – we – don't get on great with Mum and Dad. We never did. But would you consider moving back to Woolton for a while?' he asked. 'I'm sure they wouldn't mind. You'd get away from Paul, take time to sort yourself out, get help–'

'No!' Her shoulders went rigid and she jumped in fright as another firework cracked and whooshed in the sky outside. 'Are you crazy?' She pulled away from him. 'You're so fucking naive!' she shouted. 'I can't believe how naive you are.' She tossed back the rest of her drink. 'Go back to Mum and Dad!' she sneered. 'You just don't have a bloody clue, do you? After all these years, you still don't have a bloody clue.'

'What are you talking about?'

She stood up, went to the mantelpiece and unscrewed the vodka bottle. 'Should have got another of these while I was out,' she said thoughtfully. The bottle clinked against the rim of the glass as she poured. 'It's Dad.' She faced him, panda eyes accusing. 'The main theme from which all my sub-plots run. I don't see why I should keep it secret any longer. Protect everyone except me.'

'Dad?' Rob looked puzzled. 'Keep what secret? Look,' he said uneasily, 'I know he's been a bastard to us at times, always putting us down. Especially you. He's very negative about women. In private, of course.'

'Exactly.' The lighter snapped again and Melanie blew out smoke. 'So why did he always say little girls were better than little boys? That he wished you'd been born a girl?'

'I don't know.' Her brother shrugged. 'I often wondered about that. I put it down to his weird sense of humour. Always laughing at nothing. It made me mad the way he was so nice to everyone except you and me and Mum,' he said moodily. 'The people at St Fidelma's, the social club, the Catholic macho – they wish! –

Knights of St Columba, all think the sun shines out of his arse. Even that silly old cow Irene, his secretary. They'd never believe what a bastard he can be! Laughing and joking, telling people what their brain dead kids are capable of achieving. All he ever did with us was tell us how thick we were – how I'd work in a chippie and you'd end up selling knickers in Woolworth's.'

'There are worse things,' she murmured.

'Come off it, Mel! Remember when you got three As and a B in your "A" levels last summer? He mentioned some drinking crony's retarded brat who'd got a certificate in basket weaving.'

'I remember.' Melanie laughed and dragged on her cigarette. 'But you still don't get it, do you? Detective bloody Constable.'

'Look, what is this?' he asked angrily. 'Just tell me, for Christ's sake! What about Dad? Melanie?' He did not dare glance at his watch or tell her he had promised to go with Shannon to the bonfire in Croxteth Park.

'Okay.' She clenched the glass so tightly he half rose, afraid it would shatter in her hand. 'I wasn't born with a silver spoon or a teat in my mouth,' she said dully. 'Only his dick.'

'*What?* What did you say?'

It was like one of the nightmares in which he fell off a cliff or dreamed Shannon had been killed in a car crash. Or the time an escaping car thief had slammed a baseball bat into his solar plexus. 'Are you saying he . . .?' Rob's chest felt constricted. He could not breathe. 'That he . . .?'

'First his finger.' She took a swallow of vodka. 'Then his dick. Every which way. It started when I was three.'

'Three!' He stared at her in shock.

'He used to come in my bedroom at night. Mum was out of her head on Valium or Mogadon or whatever. He said I had to keep quiet because what we were doing – *we*! – was very secret and if anyone found out I'd be taken away from you and Mum and sent to a place where people would hit me and not give me enough to eat and lock me in a cold dark room where there'd be rats and big spiders. I had nightmares, I'd wake up screaming. Remember?'

A memory came to him of his father standing in Melanie's bedroom, her nightlight shining on the teddy bear wallpaper. He wore only a striped pyjama top, his long bare legs covered with black hairs. Melanie sat up in bed, her mouth open and big dark eyes dilated with terror. 'Get back to your room,' his father had said roughly to the sleepy boy rubbing his eyes. 'Your sister's had another nightmare, I'm comforting her.'

'No, Daddy! Go 'way, go 'way!'

Rob could hear the cries now. Where was his mother? He could not remember her being there.

'Sometimes he did it to me in the bath,' Melanie went on remorselessly, her brown eyes stony. 'He loved that. Loved my skin wet and slippery. He'd tell me to bend over. He brought me sanitary towels for the blood and gave me Junior Disprin when the pain was bad.' She glanced out of the windows as more fireworks exploded over the trees. 'Miss Jackson, our PE teacher, saw the sanitary towel once during a swimming lesson. I told her I was imitating the big girls who had periods and that the blood came from a cut on my knee.' She giggled. 'Luckily I had one! She said I'd have more than enough of wearing those things later on, and not to be so stupid. She thought I was mental.'

She looked at her brother who sat staring at her in shock, hands clenched like an old man with rheumatism. Suddenly she wanted to hug him tight and run her hands through his thick brown hair, the way she had when she was little. His oval face was pale, the usual carefree humorous glint in his brown eyes gone, replaced by shock and stunned disbelief. Suddenly she felt frightened, steeped in guilt. In a split second Rob had changed. He would never be the same person again because of what she had told him. He looked older, weighed down, tainted by the hideous knowledge.

'Well?' she asked harshly. 'Haven't you got anything to say? Don't look so bloody dumb!' She drank the vodka and crashed the glass down on the marble mantelpiece. 'Bloody well say something!'

'I don't know what to say.' He felt as if he had to concentrate on breathing and speaking, that they were suddenly difficult things to do. He had a crazy urge to feel himself all over, like someone checking themselves for damage after a fall, to make sure his body was still in one piece. His whole life was an illusion; nothing was as it had seemed.

'How long did he – how long did it go on?' He felt dazed, dizzy.

'Until I left home last year.' She pulled another cigarette from the pack and stuck it between her lips. 'He was furious when thick little Melly-Mel got four good "A" levels. Didn't want me to leave home and go to college. He said I was a slag and I'd get out of control. *Control*!' she spat, and threw the lighter on the orange box.

'He did it until *last year*? I thought people like that . . .' Rob swallowed. 'I thought he wouldn't want to do it once you reached puberty?'

'I wish! For a copper you've got a very stereotyped view of perverts. It wasn't just sex, it was *power*. His way of exerting power over me.'

'I know this is a stupid question, but why didn't you tell anybody?'

'He frightened me. Blackmailed me, like I told you. And I –' She hesitated. 'When I got older I sort of – used him.'

'*You* used *him*?'

'To get things. If I wanted money or new clothes or to stay at a party all night I'd give him a blow job or let him fuck me. Pretend to enjoy it. You know what he said?' She laughed, bending over and clutching her stomach. 'He said he was disappointed because I'd lost my innocence.' She gasped and straightened up. There were tears in her eyes now. 'I told him I'd never had any innocence to lose. He went mental and thumped me. Mum came in then. He told her he was angry because I'd cheated in a Maths exam.'

'I never knew – I never thought,' Rob faltered. 'I knew he was a bastard, but I never imagined . . .' He shrugged helplessly. 'It's amazing what you don't see when you're not looking for it.'

'You're thirty, Rob. I'm nineteen. That's a big age gap. How could you know? Like you say, it's not the sort of thing you think about. You were playing football, cricket, studying, staying over at friends' houses.' She laughed. 'Discovering sex.'

'I should have been there,' he said dully. 'I should have protected you. This is what's wrong, isn't it? This is why you're such a mess.'

'Right.' She bent and stubbed out the cigarette. 'Promiscuous behaviour, dependence on Class A substances, inability to form normal *healthy* relationships. Non-existent sense of self-worth. I've got the symptoms, I know all that shit. I just don't have a clue what to do about it.' She laughed again. 'Remember that weekend I went camping in the Lake District?' she asked. 'When I was thirteen?'

He nodded, not trusting himself to speak.

'I wasn't camping,' she said, watching him closely. She reached for another cigarette. 'I was having an abortion.'

He stumbled to the sordid freezing bathroom and threw up. Rinsing his mouth at the ancient cracked sink, he noticed the used syringes on the floor by the lion's paw bath foot. He wiped his mouth and watering eyes, straightened his tie and stared at his own white face in the dirty spotted mirror. He felt ten, twenty years older. Melanie was sitting in an armchair when he got back, smoking and twisting the greasy glass in her hands. He flopped on the sofa and leaned his head back, exhausted.

'Are you okay?' she asked anxiously.

'I'll have some of that vodka and tonic if you can spare it,' he said. She got up, went downstairs to the kitchen for another glass and poured him a drink.

It was too strong, the way she liked it, but he gulped it down, enjoying its healing warmth.

'Mr Catholic headmaster, Knight of St Columba, made me have an abortion,' Melanie went on, sitting down again. 'He told the doctor I'd been date-raped by a boy at school and that he wanted it hushed up because I was very young and otherwise I'd suffer more trauma. The doctor understood. Said I should go on the Pill afterwards. Dad thought that was a great idea.'

Rob slumped back again and wiped his sweaty forehead on his bulky grey sleeve. The vodka warmed his stomach and thighs and he wondered why he did not drink more often.

'Are you okay, Rob?' his sister asked again. 'I wish I hadn't told you. Only I was upset after Paul hit me again and –'

'Oh, I'm great,' he said tiredly. 'I'm cool.' He held out the glass. 'Get me another one, will you? Bit more tonic this time.'

'You hardly ever drink.' She got up and replenished their

glasses. 'Shannon drinks more than you. Good job she's a lawyer, she can afford her champagne.'

A twinge of guilt stabbed him. 'Well, I'm drinking now,' he said coldly. 'Are you happy?' He took the glass and sat back. 'Sorry,' he muttered. 'I'm sorry. I just can't take this in, I feel numb.' A thought struck him. 'Where was Mum in all this?'

'Oh, you know her!' Melanie grinned. 'Drinking, fantasizing about being an artist. Her *little job* at the florist. The Meals-on-Wheels, being Mrs Headmaster. She only had kids because she was Catholic and it was the thing to do. She hasn't a maternal bone in her whole fat body. Those big saggy tits . . . what a waste! I don't think she ever liked sex. Well, who would with him? Not that he ever bothered her.'

'Did she know about–'

'No, I'm sure she didn't. She didn't *want* to know anything about us, and wouldn't have believed me if I'd told her. She gave us meals and clean clothes. That was her idea of motherhood. When I got my first period she told me I should watch out because now I was capable of having a baby. Dad had already provided the rest of my sex education.'

Rob drank and closed his eyes. 'Why are you telling me this now?'

'I've wanted to tell you for years, but I was too scared.' She puffed on the cigarette. 'Guilty and ashamed. But now that you're planning to have a kid – don't let him anywhere near it!' she warned fiercely. 'Don't, Rob. Even if it's a boy. It does my head in, seeing him go on living his life, being liked and respected by people who don't know what he is. And me . . . sometimes I want to die.' She bent her head and burst into tears again. 'I think he's done it to other girls. Not just me.'

He jerked upright as the feeling of shock slammed into his solar plexus again. 'What makes you say that?'

'He was always out, remember?' Melanie wiped her eyes on her sleeve. 'Always going off by himself, no one knew where. I saw a programme about men like him. They never do it just – *just!* – once, or to one person. Most paedophiles molest an average of one hundred children in their lifetime. Lots of them are married with kids, hold down good jobs. Pillars of the community. Like him. Most of them never get caught.'

'I know,' he said wearily. 'I haven't spent the past ten years sitting in police cars eating hamburgers.' He finished his drink and looked at his watch. 'Come home with me now,' he urged again. 'You need to get away from here. And we need to talk.'

'No.' She shrank back in the armchair. 'Paul might come home soon. I'm staying here. He didn't mean to thump me, he was just in a bad mood. He'll be sorry when he gets back. He'll buy me another bottle of vodka.'

Pointless to mention the used needles in the bathroom. Rob could not be bothered now. His limbs felt heavy, his brain numb. This is derealisation, he thought, my self-protection mechanism taking over until I can cope with this horror.

'I'm sorry, Mel,' he said. 'I have to go home.' He got up slowly, stooping like an old man. His body felt unbelievably heavy. 'Think about what you've told me. I can't take it in just now. I have to think what to do. I'll talk to you again soon. Maybe you should get some counselling?' he suggested. 'That might help.'

She stuck two fingers in the air. 'I won't listen to a load of psychobabble from some stupid social worker. I can't stand those wankers.'

He smiled. 'Shannon hates social workers too. She thinks they cause more trouble than criminals.'

'Then we've got something in common after all.' She stared at her brother's pale drawn face. 'You didn't look thirty before,' she remarked. 'You do now. You look like your light's gone out.'

'Thanks, Mel!' The vodka and her revelations made his head spin. He hoped he could drive home without killing himself. Or someone else. He zipped up his jacket.

'Rob?' she said hesitantly. 'Could you spare me a few quid? I need to go shopping.'

'For food, I hope.' He unzipped his jacket again and took out his wallet. 'Make sure you spend it on yourself – get some fresh food, eat properly. And throw that bastard out.' He knew she wouldn't.

'What are you going to do?' she asked. 'About Dad, I mean.'

'I don't know,' he said tiredly. 'I told you, I can't handle this right now. I have to think things through. I need time to think.' He handed her five crackly twenty-pound notes and she sniffed them before stuffing them into the back pocket of her jeans. She loved the smell of new money.

'I'll see you, Mel.' He walked to the door. 'I'll phone or come round tomorrow or the day after. Take care.'

She nodded, still staring at him. He went out of the room and down the dark stairs. The damp building stank of cigarettes and fry-ups and stale clothes. Downstairs in the hall the light was not working. He sneezed, trying not to breathe too deeply the musty air tainted with years of cigarettes. He slammed the front door and ran down the stone steps. The fireworks had stopped.

'Good evening, Detective Constable!' Paul Ashton's quiet voice came out of the darkness, his feet crunching on the gravel drive. He was twenty-two, small and thin, and wearing a long black coat, jeans and trainers. His straggly blond hair was tied back in a ponytail and he held a carrier bag in one hand. 'How are you this evening?' Hopefully big brother had slipped Melanie a few quid. She wouldn't deny it after a slap or two. Paul took out his house keys.

'Give me those.' Rob blocked his path, towering over him. 'You don't live here anymore. As from now.'

'What?' Paul stared up at him, his unshaven rabbit jaw set. 'Why?' he asked, trying to sound confident. 'What's wrong?' He shivered in the cold darkness. Shouts and laughter came from the park across wide potholed Swanmere Drive.

'You know what's wrong. Melanie doesn't know which way's up,' Rob said harshly. 'The last thing she needs is a sad bastard like you knocking her about.' He held out his hand. 'Keys!'

'I didn't knock her about.' Paul stepped back. 'She must have fallen or something. You know she drinks too much.' He swallowed and blinked nervously. He'd told Melanie to keep her mouth shut. 'I didn't touch her, I swear!'

'Don't lie to me, you little shit!' Rob grabbed him by his permed hair and slammed his face against the brick wall, smashing his nose and fracturing his right cheekbone. The keys fell on the gravel and gleamed dully in the pale blue light from the Edwardian streetlamp. Dark shiny blood streamed from Paul's nostrils and the corners of his mouth.

'Who do you think you are?' he gasped in agony. 'Clint Eastwood?'

Rob shoved him back against the wall and began punching him in the face and stomach and around the head until he slid to the ground in a whimpering heap. Rob took out a handkerchief and wiped blood off his knuckles, picked up the keys and put them in his own pocket.

'Listen.' He squatted beside the heap of overcoat and tangled matted blond hair. 'I want you to regard this as a friendly warning. If you go near Melanie again or lay one finger on her you'll have as much chance of survival as you will of getting a job with a Philosophy degree.' He stood up and kicked the crumpled body twice. Paul groaned and swore. 'Get the hell out of here!' said Rob. 'Freeze to death in the park for all I care. But leave my sister alone!'

He coughed, his nose and throat dry and itchy with cordite fumes. His knuckles hurt. He'd never hit anyone in his life. He got into his Vauxhall Astra, reversed between the stone gateposts of the drive and sped off into the night. Suddenly he didn't feel like going home, couldn't face Shannon or telling her what had happened. Not yet anyway. He'd find a pub instead, have a quiet drink.

The smoky sky was lit by the red glow from bonfires that burned all over Liverpool. Old people peering out of their curtained windows were reminded of the May Blitz of 1941.

Chapter Five

'I told him to blow up Conal,' Finbar said moodily. He tapped his sharpened pencil on the polished mahogany desk. 'Not the whole bloody street!'

'That's what I said.' Guy nodded eagerly. 'But once he gets going with his Penthrite plastic and . . .'

'It only takes two hundred grams of Semtex to blow up a Boeing 747-400. What was he playing at? You told me he was an expert.'

'He is. Dean's the best.' Guy took out a pack of cigarettes then stuck them back in his pocket as he caught Finbar's glare. 'But he likes to practise. And he's a bit of a psycho. Gets carried away.' He shrugged. 'Does it matter?'

'Does it matter?' Finbar echoed icily. 'Conal's wife was killed too. The girl only survived because she was asleep in a back bedroom. It's not her fault she had a tosser for a father, and she didn't deserve to lose her mother like that.' He hurled the pencil across the room and leaned back, gripping the chair's leather armrests.

Guy dropped his gaze to the woodblock floor, stubby fingers closing around the cigarette pack in the pocket of his black leather jacket. He dared not argue. But what did the bastard expect? Ordering Conal McCartan to be blown to kingdom come for ripping off a few Es then getting all upset about poor little orphan Rosie. 'These things happen,' he wanted to say. But the sentimental ones were more dangerous than the psychos. Guy still couldn't quite decide which category Finbar belonged in. But he would keep his opinions to himself.

He raised his head and glanced at the panelled walls, the long sash windows and the ceiling with its plaster pattern of vine leaves and grape-guzzling cherubs. Two bottle green leather sofas with a glass coffee table in between stood at the other end of the big bare room. What a dump, he thought. No cigars, pictures, plants, eighteen-year-old blonde secretary with Lycra micro round her ears. India Buildings looked classy from the outside; he had strolled along its ground-floor arcade of old-fashioned expensive little shops before coming up here.

Say something, you moody bastard, he thought, listening to the hum of traffic far below as the miserable grey November afternoon faded into twilight.

'Worst of all,' Finbar resumed, 'the police might think this is more than a hit. They'll comb Liverpool for arms and explosives now, check the airports. And why did Dean have to do it that way?' he fumed. 'A bloody carrier bag hanging on the door? What's wrong with an ex-INLA on a motorbike?'

'Well, that's more your patch than mine, Finbar.' Guy laughed nervously and was met by another chilly stare. 'I told you,' he repeated. 'Dean's a psycho and he likes showing off.' He rubbed his stubbly chin and sniffed his nicotine-stained fingers. 'I wouldn't worry about the police. They'll be too busy looking for the pervert who murdered that little girl on Bonfire Night.' He shook his head. 'Terrible, that.'

'Finbar.' His secretary, a woman in her late twenties with long lank black hair and fierce pale grey eyes, stuck her head round the door. A tight black top and purple leggings hugged her thin figure. 'There's someone to see you. Hey, you, wait a minute!' she said indignantly as a fat middle-aged man in a black suit pushed past her, breathing heavily.

'You can go.' Finbar nodded coldly at Guy. 'Tell your friend to be more careful next time.' He reached into a drawer, took out a padded brown envelope and tossed it across the desk.

'Next time?' Guy echoed, and smiled ingratiatingly as he picked up the envelope. 'When's next time?'

'Slip of the tongue. Figure of speech. None of your business. Get out.'

'Will you be at the club later?'

'I might look in. Then again, I might not. So you'd better have everything in order. Stay away from the women and the single malt. You're there to manage the club. Don't forget that.'

Guy turned and left, stuffing the envelope into his pocket. He followed the secretary to her desk in the outer office and grabbed her by the waist, thrusting himself against her flat purple bottom.

'When are you and me going to make a night of it, sweetheart?' he murmured, lifting a strand of hair to kiss her neck.

'Get off me, you bastard!' She pushed him away and whirled round, pale eyes blazing. 'Never!'

'Why not?' he grinned. 'Why don't you like me?'

'You want a list?' she asked contemptuously. 'Okay. You grow thirty centimetres taller, you lose fifteen kilos, you grow hair on your head, you turn the clock back ten years . . .'

'And call myself Finbar Linnell? You rotten bitch,' he said good-naturedly, seeing her flush. 'Ta-ra!' He opened the glass door and lit the longed-for cigarette while he waited in the corridor for the ancient lift to wheeze its way up six floors.

'There are two bags of rubbish in my car,' the fat man said tersely to Finbar. He dropped some keys on to the desk. 'Take them. And this.' He thrust a slip of paper at him. An account number in an American bank was scribbled on it. 'Goodbye.' He hurried out, slamming the door behind him.

'Mariska!' Finbar called. The woman came back and lounged in the doorway. It struck him that with her pale eyes and sharp chiselled cheekbones she looked like a wolverine.

'That bastard Guy!' she spat. 'He puts his dirty hands all over me.'

'Take these keys and go and get the bags from Mr Koper's car.' He handed her the slip of paper. 'This is the dollar account number. I'd like you to go to Zurich this weekend.'

'Okay. Are you coming?'

'Not this time.'

'Pity.' She crossed to the window and leaned on the broad stone sill, looking down into the street. The lights were on and rush hour traffic was gridlocked. She straightened up and turned round. 'It's nearly six. Shall we go for a drink at the club?'

'No.'

'Don't you ever want anyone?' she asked curiously, coming forward. 'You're not gay, but you never seem to fancy any women.'

Her included. She gazed longingly at his beautiful green eyes and broad shoulders and chest, that long elegant body. She'd never seen such a sexy man. There was something about him . . . she couldn't tell what it was. She only knew she longed to spend a night with him. Many nights. Finbar leaned forward, fingertips touching in an attitude of prayer.

'That's none of your business, Mariska.' He thought for a moment. 'Did that industrial helicopter parts consignment arrive?'

'This morning,' she said petulantly. 'I told you.'

'That's right, you did.' He stood up. 'I'm finished here. You can go when you've brought the bags up.'

She tried again. 'Sure you don't want to come for a drink with a sexy Dutch girl?' she asked, smiling.

He didn't smile back. 'I've never seen any sexy Dutch girls,' he remarked. 'They either look like milkmaids or overblown tulips.'

'You would be a good priest,' she said stonily. 'A Jesuit.'

'Thank you, Mariska.'

'Although, I don't know.' She walked to the door, trying to swing her thin hips. 'Priests screw anything and everything these days. Like in the Middle Ages.' She laughed. 'Will you do it with me if I promise to say a Hail Mary afterwards? *Penance*, – how sexy!'

'The bags, Mariska.' He tossed her the car keys. 'Then goodnight.'

She flounced out and he sat down and leaned back again, thinking of Shannon Flinder's violet blue eyes and the cloud of gossamer blonde hair that framed her heart-shaped face. She looked sensitive, intelligent, humorous when she wanted to be. He thought there was a side to her she didn't often reveal. What was she doing now? Would she rush home to be with the lucky bastard who was her husband? Drink wine, eat, talk? Make love? He couldn't bear to think about that. What would it be like to make love with her? She had a beautiful body, a bust that was full but not too full, a slim curved waist that he longed to put his hands around. He remembered the faint smell of her perfume. Imagined her dark blue eyes staring up at him, filled with pleasure and passion and longing – longing for him. Kissing her beautiful mouth.

He jumped as Mariska slammed the outer door. Her horrible musky perfume lingered on the chill air. Where did Shannon live? Work? Devastation swept over him again. She was the first woman since Majella to disturb his monk-like existence. *Disturb* was a massive understatement.

Majella! He took the bottle of Kilbeggan from the bottom drawer of his desk and poured himself a measure, swilling it around the thick-bottomed glass before he drank. He coughed as the pale golden liquid burned his throat. Beautiful Majella, murdered by a trigger-happy Brit squaddie at a border checkpoint after her first and last visit to the cousin in the North she had always wanted to meet. She had taken Roiseann, their nine-month-old baby daughter. Both of them were shot dead, Majella lying on the narrow country road, Roiseann still strapped in her baby seat. The official enquiry had exonerated the squaddie, said mother and daughter had been caught in crossfire, but of course no one believed that.

He had left Dublin after the funeral, for good. Shock and disbelief faded in the months that followed and were replaced by pain: the agonizing, the intolerable pain of loss. And anger. His PIRA contacts suggested he move to London, but Finbar preferred Liverpool. There was less of a security presence there. The Isle of Man was nearby. He liked the city, felt at home there.

And now he was rich. The industrial helicopter parts consignment were actually military helicopter parts, on their way from Belgium to Iran via Malta, one of the best transit areas to dodgy countries. His legitimate air cargo business was thriving now; he'd decided recently he would stop the drugs and weapons, sever his contacts with PIRA. He had paid them back many times over. After this last big 'next time' he would finish with them. More trouble could break out anytime soon. They were seriously bored with the latest ceasefire, that was for sure.

He sipped his whisky, thinking of that triple-chinned, loud-mouthed, balding bastard, Rupert Eastbrook, Defence Secretary, with his hideous striped suits and stunningly banal pronouncements. Who in the name of God christened a child *Rupert*? Like most politicians, he spoke to press and public as though they were retarded children who did not know what was good for them. Finbar would have hit him for the suits alone. He was in power, had been in power, when Majella and Roiseann were murdered. He and his government were responsible for their deaths. And he would pay.

Eastbrook was due to visit the military aircraft division at Salmesbury the following March and for some incomprehensible reason, probably a desperate vote-grabbing exercise, would visit Liverpool afterwards, to honour the Merseyside Maritime Museum with his arrogant presence. The visit would be made public a day or so beforehand. Time enough to dig out the bags of flour and rotten eggs. And Czechoslovakia's biggest export success. Maybe this hit would stop the wormwood eating away at Finbar's heart. Or not. He put down the glass, picked up the phone and punched a number.

'Nick? Finbar. There's a little favour I want to ask you.'

'Oh yes? What is it?'

He smiled at the nervousness in Nick's voice. He was well paid for managing the offshore trusts and there was hardly any risk in it for him, but he wasn't happy about it. Finbar liked shy nervous people. They worked hard, kept their mouths shut and did not screw up.

'Just a phone number,' he said. 'I'd like the phone number of your beautiful brainy lawyer friend from university days – Mrs Flinder.'

'Shannon has an unlisted phone number, Finbar.' Nick swallowed. 'I couldn't give it to you without her permission.'

'I'm sure she wouldn't mind,' he said patiently. 'I've got some business I'd like to discuss with her.'

I bet you have, Nick thought. He hesitated. 'I really don't think I should.'

'The number, Nick. If you please.'

'All right,' he said reluctantly. 'Just a second.' Pages rustled. 'It's a West Derby number.' He read it out slowly.

'Thanks very much, Nick.' Finbar scribbled it on a yellow

post-it pad. 'Have a good evening now. Say hello to Caroline and Helen for me, won't you?'

'Finbar – Shannon's very happily married. She really loves Rob and he's crazy about her too. She'd never have an affair with anyone.'

'I'm very glad to hear it,' he said coldly. 'Bye, Nick.'

He wanted a lot more than a sordid soulless affair. He hung up and dialled Shannon's number, hoping she would answer.

'Hello?' she said breathlessly. 'Shannon–'

'Mrs Flinder? Good evening! This is Finbar Linnell, we met last week.' He paused. 'D'you remember me?'

Remember him! Her scalp prickled and her heart raced at the sound of his unnervingly soft voice. He'd been on her mind for days, she couldn't shake his image and was furious with herself. He was almost a guilty secret, when in fact she had nothing to feel guilty or secretive about. 'Yes, I do. How . . .?'

'Nick gave me your number,' he said, anticipating her question.

'He shouldn't have done that without asking me,' she said, voice hardening. 'What do you want?' she asked rudely.

He was disappointed by her tone. Maybe she really couldn't stand him. It was possible. Wishful thinking could be very dangerous.

'I'd like to invite you to have dinner with me one evening,' he said. 'I've got a number of business deals going and I–.'

'Mr Linnell, I'm a criminal lawyer,' she interrupted. 'I do criminal work, not commercial. You don't want a criminal lawyer. Unless you end up in court on a murder charge or something,' she added lightly. Then she remembered his green eyes glinting down at her outside the court, and shivered. She glanced across the steamy kitchen. Rob stood at the cooker, mechanically stirring a panful of bubbling spaghetti. He did not look round or mouth 'Who is it?' the way he usually did.

'Sorry. Of course you are.' Finbar kicked himself for his stupidity. There was a pause. 'Have you recovered from your unpleasant experience of a week ago?' he asked, closing his eyes.

'Oh, the demented woman in the fur coat?' Shannon smiled. 'Yes, thanks.' Suddenly she felt sure he would have blown the woman away without a thought. 'It comes with the territory,' she said.

'You mean, that kind of thing happens to you on a regular basis?' he asked, horrified.

'Oh, no! No,' she said hastily, startled by the concern in his voice. 'I just mean – you can't please everyone, that's all. The legal system's not great, but it's the best we've got. I keep repeating that like a mantra lately,' she said, embarrassed.

'I'm glad you're all right,' he said. 'I was worried about you.'

It was crazy, but she wanted to go on talking to him, hearing his voice. She suddenly felt intensely close to him, knew what he was thinking. He wanted her. It was that simple. That terrible. She looked at Rob, who was stirring the spaghetti as if mesmerized, and crashed back to earth. This was insane. What was she doing talking to this man? She had enough to worry about lately.

'Will you have dinner with me anyway?' he persisted. 'I'd like to spend an evening with you. Just to talk. I think we have a lot in common. We already have Nick as our mutual friend.'

'I'm afraid that's impossible,' she stammered. 'I'm very busy during the day and I don't go out much in the evening. When I do it's usually with my husband.'

'I see.' Another silence. 'Well, if you ever need me, you can get in touch with me through Nick,' he said quietly. 'Thanks for your time. Goodnight, Mrs Flinder. Take care of yourself.'

'Why would I need you?' Shannon asked the dead phone. She listened to the dial tone for a few seconds, hung up and glanced, blushing, at Rob. He ignored her.

'Rob, the spaghetti!' She dashed to the cooker and snatched the wooden spoon from him. 'What are you doing, trying to turn it into polenta? It'll be inedible.' She seized the stainless steel colander, dumped it in the sink and emptied spaghetti into it. Clouds of steam rose. 'What's the *matter* with you?'

He stood back, rolled down the sleeves of his denim shirt and stuck his hands in the pockets of his jeans, blank brown eyes avoiding her worried gaze. He wanted to cry, shout, throw something, anything to relieve the terrible oppression of the chaos whirling inside him. Fact: his father had abused his sister since childhood. He couldn't think straight, couldn't take it in. Maybe he was like his father. He didn't know anything. His life was – always had been – an illusion. He couldn't stand it. It took all his control not to explode in panic. Or rage.

'Rob, what's wrong?' pleaded his wife. 'Why won't you talk to me?'

He didn't answer. Stood staring into the dark back garden as she carried the spaghetti and and a pot of fragrant herby bolognese sauce to the table. She'd rushed home from work, picking up a load of groceries on the way, hadn't even had time to get changed. She ladled spaghetti and sauce into two big willow pattern soup plates and sprinkled freshly grated Parmesan on top. 'I wish you'd tell me what's the matter with you lately,' she said sadly. 'You're like a bloody zombie. It's driving me crazy.'

'Nothing's the matter,' he said at last. He emptied his glass of red wine and poured another, the fourth in half an hour. She was on her first.

'What *is* it?' she asked again. 'I don't want to nag you but–.'

'Then don't.'

She sat down and looked at her plate, smelled the rich meaty oregano-flavoured sauce. She wasn't hungry. 'You've been terrible these past few days,' she said miserably. 'I feel as if I don't know you anymore. You ignore me, you don't talk. It's like you're on another planet. Is it something at work?'

'I've told you, it's nothing to do with work. Just leave me alone.' He clenched his hands. 'I'll be fine. I *am* fine.' I can't go on any more, he thought. I can't take this.

'You're not fine. Please, Rob, can't we have dinner and talk about whatever's bothering you?' He hardly spoke her name any more. She watched as he gulped more wine. 'You're drinking like Melanie,' she said nervously. 'I can't believe it! It's so unlike you.'

'Leave her out of this!' he shouted, and hurled his glass across the kitchen. It smashed against the white wall, dribbling Australian Shiraz Cabernet on to the tiny red brick Thirties floor tiles. Shannon jumped up and gasped with shock.

'Leave Melanie alone!' he shouted again. 'You hated her from the start, you never gave her a chance. You're so bloody superior to everyone, aren't you?'

'Rob, for Christ's sake!' Shannon's knees felt weak. 'You know that's not true. Why are you yelling at me like this? You never yell.'

He took no notice. 'You don't know anything about her.' He turned away, face contorted. 'You know nothing about her life. What she's been through. How she's suffered.' He stopped, his fists clenched.

'Okay, I don't know much about Melanie.' Her voice shook. 'But no one told her she had to be out of her head on vodka and Class A drugs all the time and have sex with the kind of men who think a black eye or a punch in the mouth is foreplay. I've really tried to get on with her but . . .'

'Shut up!' he blazed. Shannon stepped back and stared at him, horrified, one hand to her mouth. 'What the hell do you know? You haven't a clue.' The defensive gesture infuriated him. 'You, with your lowlife clients that you keep out of jail so they can go on screwing up more people's lives. And your precious friends. *Nick! Gavin!*'

'Gavin's not my friend.'

'And your bloody partnership and salary raise!'

'I can't believe that's what this is about.'

'*Shut up!* When did you ever suffer?' He took a step towards her. 'I suppose missing a party or ballet lesson or not being able to screw someone you fancied was your definition of torture?'

'Rob, why are you talking like this?' She was crying, licking warm salt tears from her trembling lips. 'I've never seen you like this before *Please* tell me–.'

'Okay.' He took a deep breath as they faced each other. 'I don't want us to be married anymore.' The numb feeling returned.

'*What?*' She couldn't believe she'd heard right.

'I want us to split up.' He looked her in the eye for the first time. 'I've got to get away, I can't go on like this.'

'Go on like *what*?' she whispered. Her body felt weak. 'What the hell do you mean?'

'I've got to be by myself, be alone,' he said dully. 'I want this to happen as soon as possible. I'll find another place, give you a chance to get used to the idea. Sort things out. Say, in about a month.'

'I don't believe this!' Tears rained down her white face. 'You want us to split up? Within a month? Get–.' Her voice broke – '*divorced*. But we're happy, we love each other. I don't understand.'

'It's not possible anymore,' he said. And was surprised not to feel sorry at her distress.

'*Why?* What's happened?'

'I don't want to talk about it.'

'You've got to bloody well talk about it!' she cried. 'You can't just tell me you don't want to be married anymore and *not talk about* it. What d'you expect me to say? Oh, all right, fine?' She wiped her streaming eyes on her jacket sleeve. 'You can't do that, Rob. You can't! We love each other, we're happy, we want to have a baby . . .'

'Don't say that,' he said stonily. 'Shut up.'

'Don't tell me to shut up! What the hell is going on? You don't drop a bombshell like this and then tell me to shut up! You've got to talk to me,' sobbed Shannon. Woman's world falls apart over dinner, she thought. How original!

'I said, shut up!' He moved away from her. He had to get out.

'Where are you going?' Shannon clung to him as he tried to walk out of the kitchen. 'Have you got someone else?' she demanded. 'Is that it?'

'No.' If only it was that simple! 'I don't want anyone.' He smelled her hair, her perfume, looked into the blue eyes glittering with tears. Felt nothing. 'I don't want you,' he said. 'Don't question me.'

'You're not going out, we have to talk.' She pulled at his denim shirt. 'Stay here, Rob, please.'

'Leave me alone.' He grabbed her arms and shoved her viciously, sending her stumbling against the wall. She tripped over the chair leg and fell, knees hitting the cold tiled floor, outstretched hands sweeping the plates of spaghetti off the table as she tried to save herself.

'Sorry,' he said. 'I didn't mean to do that.' He looked down at her. 'If you give me a hard time about this, I'll leave sooner. And don't tell anyone what's happened. I don't want any hassle.'

Curled spaghetti strands, fractured bits of willow pattern and bolognese sauce mingled with the pool of red wine Shannon knelt in. He grabbed his jacket from the chair and strode into the hall.

The front door slammed and a car engine roared in the drive.

She stayed on her hands and knees for what seemed like ages, staring at the mess through her tears, trying to make sense of the crazy scene. She felt as though she had been dumped in the middle of nowhere without map or compass. The house was silent except for her sobs and the hum of the central heating. She got to her feet. Her black tights were ripped and her hands and knees and the red skirt of her suit stained dark with sauce and wine.

Rob had changed, literally overnight. She could not believe it, could not believe this aggressive stranger who drank non-stop, ignored her except to yell, and now said he didn't want to be married to her anymore. She felt dazed. Bonfire Night, a week ago, it had started then. He hadn't talked to her or touched her since. He flinched away from kisses and hugs as though she were a bag lady to whom dentists, showers and clean clothes were a distant memory. In bed he pushed her away and rolled on to his side, muttering impatiently about being 'knackered'. I don't know him anymore, she thought. I don't know what to do. How can he want us to split up? I don't believe it! Something's upset him. But *what*?

She cleaned up the spaghetti and wine mess, threw away the smashed plates and stood in the silent kitchen trying to think. She would need all her strength to deal with this calamity. He didn't mean it, he *couldn't*. Was it her fault? she wondered. Something she'd done – or not done? It couldn't be the partnership, Rob wasn't the type of idiot who'd get jealous or feel threatened by his wife's career. There was nothing she could think of.

'It's not my fault,' she said out loud. Her voice sounded small and shaky in the empty house. Empty without Rob. She opened a bottle of Riesling, poured herself a glass, gulped it down. 'Go on, take to drink,' she said. 'More highly original behaviour! God, you're pathetic! You've got to deal with this.' She trembled with shock and upset.

Was Rob having second thoughts about starting a family? she wondered suddenly. No! He wanted children as much if not more than she did. He loved children and they loved him. He adored Helen, Nick and Caroline's baby daughter. That didn't explain anything either. What the *hell* was going on? Whatever it was, she had to cope with it. Not cry and fall apart. First she had to clean herself up, get changed.

She went upstairs and was lying in a hot bath perfumed with citrus oil when she suddenly sat upright, oiled water droplets clinging to her satin skin. Melanie! She might know something. Why had Rob exploded the second her name was mentioned? He paid her final warning phone, gas and electricity bills, gave her money for food - no doubt spent on drink, drugs and abusive boyfriends instead. He sat for hours in the sordid living room of that Victorian mausoleum, listening to her moan about her problems. Problems, it had to be said, that were entirely of her own making.

'It's time you got a life, Melanie!' Shannon said aloud, welcoming the surge of positive anger. Rob loved his younger sister very much, but her problems and warped personality couldn't be allowed to wreck their marriage. Maybe she'd told him some terrible lie. That would be typical. 'You always hated me, didn't you?' Shannon murmured. Well, this had to be sorted. Tonight.

She climbed out of the bath and dried herself. She couldn't stop crying. She stared at her slender curved naked body and flushed face in the steamy mirror, remembering that bright summer day eighteen months before. Her parents, bored and indifferent, longing to get back to Little Crosby and their garden and Mozart piano concertos. Rob's father, turning his charm on for the guests but glowering with disapproval at her because she and Rob were not getting married in church. She'd worn a simple, straight, ankle-length ivory silk dress instead of the filmy veil and meringue and whipped cream confection he considered suitable for a bride. Rob's mother Margaret, hiding beneath her yellow silk hat brim, not saying anything much. Their friends, happy for them, shouting and laughing. A few of Rob's less obnoxious police colleagues smirking in the background, not mixing. Melanie had missed the service and turned up drunk at the reception, her hennaed hair wild, wearing ghoulish make-up and a black silky mini dress that looked like underwear. No one dared ask why her left arm was badly bruised. Afterwards Shannon and Rob had spent a fantastic honeymoon at a luxurious Caribbean resort where children were forbidden, joking that it was their first and last time at such a place.

She pulled on black Calvin Klein jeans, purple velvety sweater and black leather jacket, took her car keys and left the warm comfortable house which didn't feel like a haven anymore. The frosty air smelled of woodsmoke. She wiped her eyes again and glanced at her watch. Nine-thirty. Rob had taken the Astra and driven off God knew where, with a bottle of fourteen percent proof Australian red wine inside him. He was probably at Melanie's Sefton Park slum. Well, that was fine. They could all have an honest discussion. Shannon had to save her marriage.

She backed the baby blue Nissan Nomad out of the garage and down the drive and sped off along curving, tree-lined Eaton Road.

Chapter Six

'I don't want to talk about that!' Melanie said tiredly. 'I'm not having a good evening.' She upended the empty vodka bottle and thumped it down on the orange box coffee table. 'Anyway, do I look stupid or what?' she asked crossly. 'I'm not doing it, I'd be terrified. And with my luck, I'd be bound to get caught.' She lit a pink Sobranie given to her by Paul's mate, Guy Menand, manager of the Carmen Club in town. 'These are nice,' she said appreciatively. 'I've never had them before. I love the pretty colours.'

Paul Ashton and Guy, sitting on the dirty beige sofa, exchanged bored glances. Paul had spent the day in bed and wore Melanie's red-and-black striped bathrobe. Purple bruises showed around the edges of the fluffy white dressing that covered his nose and fractured cheekbone and he was on painkillers, chalky white torpedo-shaped things that he swallowed every four hours with whatever drink was to hand. The packet had advised against alcohol, but that meant nothing. They said it for their own protection. He had taken Melanie's keys and had copies cut and she was under strict instructions to provide advance warning of her brother's visits.

'Freeze to death in the park!' He winced as another shaft of pain shot through his nose and across his cheekbone, bringing tears to his eyes. A fracture was more painful and harder to treat than a break, the abrupt young doctor in Casualty had said. His head throbbed.

'You won't get caught, Melanie,' Guy said calmly. He took a bottle of Smirnoff Blue from the carrier bag at his feet, unscrewed it and refilled her glass. Paul grunted and held out his. 'You'll just be a young lady on holiday, no one will have any reason to suspect you.'

'Being a woman alone on holiday *is* suspicious, or haven't you heard?'

'Thousands of people make the same trip every day,' he went on, as though she had not interrupted. 'You only get caught if someone grasses you up, and no one's going to do that to you. They can't check every passenger, it's impossible. There's nothing to worry about.' He chuckled. 'Except the airline food.'

'I'm not thick, you know!' she said aggressively, blowing smoke at him. She stared at his jowly tanned face and shiny balding head, the sparse black hair that was left slicked down with gel. He looked a lot older than Paul, in his late thirties or early forties. He wore designer jeans, an expensive tweed jacket and a hideous Ralph Lauren sweatshirt. The thick gold signet ring on his fat little finger looked more like a weapon than a piece of jewellery. There was a sinister-looking Celtic design engraved on it. He stank of some crass aftershave or men's cologne.

'Listen, Melanie–.' Paul lifted his glass and drank. 'Guy didn't have to give you this chance, you know. He could have picked anybody. Someone with experience. But he wants someone he knows he can trust.'

The bitch was not cooperating, making him look stupid. He'd told Guy she'd be up for it. Guy glanced at him again and Paul shrugged apologetically.

'It's dangerous,' Melanie whined, twisting a strand of hennaed hair around her little finger. She sucked on the Sobranie and dropped her eyes, voice low. 'If I'm caught, I could get twenty-five years. Or the death penalty.' She shuddered. 'I've seen *Bangkok Hilton*.'

That made Guy laugh, a low wheezy sound. 'This is Singapore, Melanie. Not Thailand.'

'Same bloody difference. They have the death penalty there.' She stubbed out the cigarette and took a swig of neat vodka. 'They hang drug traffickers every Friday morning in Changi prison. They weigh you beforehand, calculate the drop so you don't get decapitated or slowly choked. But it must go wrong sometimes,' she said thoughtfully. 'People are always fucking up.'

'You know a lot, don't you?' Paul said threateningly.

'Melanie.' Guy sat forward, his banana hands clasped. The signet ring gleamed. 'I can understand you're nervous about this but, believe me, you've got as much chance of being caught as you have of winning squillions in the Lottery. Or being killed in a plane crash.' He laughed his throaty growl and Paul joined in with his hyena giggle. What a pair of sad bastards, she thought. 'And we're not talking Monopoly money here,' he went on. 'You can expect more than the usual few grand. The stuff you'll be shifting there and back is worth two million. Your cut is five percent. That's one hundred thousand pounds, Melanie.'

It was a lie of course. Mules were never paid anything like that. She would be lucky to get ten grand. She could hardly go running to the police – if she made it back to the UK. Say yes, you stupid cow, he urged her silently, his round face impassive. Finbar wanted the job done quickly by an unknown, someone with no contacts or police record. Paul had suggested his nailbiting, alcoholic, hennaed slapper of a girlfriend. Even at his age he could do better than her, he thought, looking at her bruised face, smudged eyeliner, tatty bottle-green sweater. Look at the state of that.

'One hundred thousand *pounds?*' Melanie breathed. Her dark brown eyes shone. 'I never imagined it would be that much.'

'Oh, yes. In this case.' Guy nodded solemnly, trying not to smirk. He felt Paul shake with silent laughter and glanced contemptuously around the cavernous living room, at the huge television and the two red candles dripping wax on to the orange box. 'You'll be set up for life,' he said. 'You can move out of this dump, give up that computer course you hate.'

'It's not exactly a computer *course*.'

'Whatever.' The lamp on the mantelpiece was scorched at the top. 'Do what you like. You'll be somebody.' He smiled encouragingly. 'People with that sort of money don't get messed around.'

'No. That's true.' Melanie was silent for a moment, drinking and smoking and staring at the blank television screen. 'Can I think about it some more?' she asked finally.

'For Christ's sake!' Paul sighed and lit another cigarette.

'We can't fool around, Melanie,' Guy said patiently. 'This is important. It's Thursday, I need your answer by Saturday. Ten o' clock at the Carmen. I want your answer then.'

'Which will be *yes*.' Paul stared at her. 'If you want your precious brother to stay in one piece.'

'What? What do you mean?' She crushed out the cigarette, shocked and frightened. 'What about Rob?' she asked wildly.

'What about *Rob*?' Paul hauled himself slowly and painfully up from the sofa and stood over her. She glanced up fearfully and shrank back in the armchair, empty glass clutched to her stomach. It wouldn't be the first time he'd hit her in front of one of his mates. They probably did the same to their wives and girlfriends, socially acceptable acts of male solidarity.

'He did this to me, remember?' He pointed to his face, voice thick and nasal because of the swelling. 'Told me to freeze to death in the park. Thinks he's Clint Eastwood. You don't think I'm going to let him get away with it, do you?' He jabbed a warning finger at her. 'I know people who'll do whatever I want to him.'

'Don't hurt Rob!' Melanie's eyes filled with tears. 'Please don't hurt Rob,' she began to wail in panic.

'Shut up, Melanie!' He grabbed a handful of slippery hennaed hair, jerked her head up and slapped her across the face, groaning and breathing hard at the pain from his bruised ribs. Her glass fell on the floor and rolled away.

'All right, Paul,' Guy warned him. 'Let's keep it polite.' He let go of her hair and she cowered sobbing in the armchair, hands over her face. Warm blood flowed from one nostril.

'I haven't decided if it'll be intensive care or a body bag.' Paul smiled, eyes full of contempt as he looked down at her. He took a deep breath against the pain. 'The only way the Detective Constable stays in one piece is if you get on a plane to Singapore when we tell you. You should do it just for him, you're lucky to get paid anything.' He wanted to hit her again but the pain was too much. 'You're useless,' he said. 'People are always on the lookout for this sort of job. Anyone else would be up for it right away.'

He made a possible death sentence sound like some fantastic

career opportunity. Any other time it would have made her laugh. The sharp ringing of the doorbell shocked them into silence. Melanie jumped up and ran crying to the door.

'It's Rob,' she wailed. 'Don't hurt him – please don't hurt him!'

'That depends on you, doesn't it?' Paul hissed.

'No one's going to hurt him.' Guy was on his feet, grabbing her arm. She smelled his horrible aftershave, sickly sweet, like something decayed. 'It's all right,' he said calmly. 'All right, Melanie. Let him in, have a nice brother and sister chat. We'll wait in your bedroom until he's gone.'

'Keep your mouth shut about the job,' Paul threatened. 'We'll be listening.'

They went out of the living room and crossed the landing to Melanie's sparsely furnished bedroom. She ran downstairs, wiping her face, tears, blood and black liquid eyeliner smearing the back of her hand. She imagined Rob being beaten with baseball bats, herself choking on the end of a thick rope, hands and legs tied. Or did Changi prison use thin rope?

'What the hell do you want?' she asked, astonished to see Shannon standing at the flat door. Her face was pale and her eyes reddened.

'Hello, Melanie,' she said quietly. 'I'm sorry to bother you. Can I come in? I won't keep you long.' Melanie stood back to let her in. 'Is Rob here?'

She ran lightly up the stairs, walked into the huge living room and looked disgustedly at the vodka bottle and overflowing ashtrays on the orange box, the takeaway cartons on the floor by the sofa. Cigarette smoke crept into her mouth and up her nostrils and clung to her clothes and hair. She would need another bath or shower when she got home. Melanie's flat made her itch all over.

'No, he's not.' Melanie followed her into the room and collapsed, trembling, into an armchair. Blood trickled from her nostril and her lip was cut. She sniffed hard. 'Have you got a tissue?'

Of course Melanie wouldn't waste money on tissues. Shannon pulled a pack from her bag and handed them to her. She watched as her sister-in-law lit another cigarette, retrieved her glass and poured herself more vodka, dabbing at her bruised, tear and eyeliner-stained face. She blew her nose, spraying blood on to the white tissue.

'Want a drink?' she asked, voice muffled.

'No, thanks.'

'No, you only like champagne, don't you? Snotty bitch! He's not here,' she repeated. 'I thought you were him.' She looked up at her slim, blonde sister-in-law, at her set mouth and the anxiety in the normally cool, confident dark blue eyes. 'Don't you know where he is?' Melanie asked incredulously. She started to laugh. 'I thought you had him electronically tagged on your wedding day.'

'What would you know about my wedding day?' Shannon asked. 'You were so drunk, I bet you don't even remember giving Rob's friend Martin a blow job in the little girls' room. It certainly ruined the front of that tasteful black dress you chose with such obvious care and attention.'

Melanie gaped at her. 'I never gave anyone a blow–.'

'You see, you don't remember.' Shannon trod on an empty cigarette pack and kicked it away. 'What's happened to Rob, Melanie?' she asked. 'He's suddenly so different. Please tell me. I'm worried sick about him lately.'

'Happened?' she echoed. 'Nothing's *happened*. I don't know what you're on about.' She swigged vodka, her hand shaking. 'Don't you barge in here interrogating me, you hardfaced bitch!' she said sullenly.

'I didn't.'

'You're not in court now. People like you think they can control everybody.'

And losers like you think everyone owes them an existence, Shannon felt like replying. Why was Melanie always so aggressive towards her?

'Please,' she begged. 'Something's happened to him, you must know what I mean. He's not himself. He's changed, literally overnight. He's really freaked out about something. I can't believe what's happened – I don't recognize him anymore.'

'Freaked out?' Melanie looked nervous.

'He's so different! Like I said, he won't talk to me. I don't know what to do. He–.' She stopped, blinking back tears. She didn't want to break down. Melanie stared at her and Shannon looked away, embarrassed.

'You've been crying, haven't you?' Melanie asked, twisting round in the armchair to get a better look. 'Did he hit you? I bet he did!' She burst out laughing. 'He hit you. Rob decked you one. Good on him!'

'He didn't hit me.' She tried to control her anger. 'Melanie, *please* tell me!' she begged again. 'I know it's something to do with you. What have you said – or done?'

'I haven't *done* anything,' Melanie shouted. She stopped laughing and swigged more vodka. 'Now, get lost!' she ordered. 'This is my home and I decide who visits.'

Was that what she called this hole? Shannon moved to the sofa but did not sit down.

'I just care about Rob,' she said, voice shaking. 'I love him, I want to help him. I want him to be happy.'

'You mean, you want *you* to be happy. Everything's got to be perfect in Shannon's world, hasn't it?'

'I want to help him,' she repeated desperately. 'To do that I need to know what's happened. I'm his wife, for God's sake.'

'No one with that sort of money gets pushed around.' Melanie laughed softly.

'What are you talking about?' Shannon looked at her, astonished. Melanie hated her, for whatever reason – no reason! – and she was obviously drunk. It was no use trying to talk to her. She felt helpless. Suddenly, unwillingly, she thought of Finbar Linnell. He would never let Melanie stand in his way.

'None of your business,' the girl said slyly. She was loving it, loved seeing Shannon upset like this. But she felt guilty about Rob.

'I wish you wouldn't bother him so much, Melanie.' Shannon wiped her eyes. 'He's got enough problems.'

'Being married to you, you mean?'

'Please don't be so demanding.'

'Or you'll what?' Melanie laughed drunkenly and pushed back her curtain of hair. 'Princess Shannon's warning me!' she jeered. 'What will you do? Have me kneecapped if I set foot in Toy Town? Refuse me a visa for Fairyland?' Would she need a visa for

Singapore? she wondered. 'I'm shaking in my Reeboks.' She sniggered again. 'Listen, you bloody stuck-up bitch of a lawyer!' She shook her glass at Shannon. 'Don't take it out on me because your precious husband finally decked you one and escaped for the night. What did he do, come up for air? Oh!' She laughed. 'That's really funny!'

'Tell me what's happened!' Shannon shouted despairingly. 'Just bloody well *tell* me. I know you hate me, but surely you care about Rob? You've got to tell me so I can help him. He's falling apart, Melanie. It's like he's having some sort of breakdown. I *know* it's because of you! You've told him some terrible lie - he says he wants us to split up! He doesn't want to be married to me anymore!' she cried. '*What* did you say to him?'

'Nothing! I'm sick of being treated like dirt!' Melanie burst out suddenly. She wrapped her arms around herself and started crying noisily.

'What *is* it?' Shannon repeated, exhausted and desperate. 'What did you tell him? Why is he so upset?'

'Everybody thinks they can push me around,' Melanie wailed. 'Well, I won't let it happen anymore. I'm going to be somebody.' She sat up and looked defiantly at Shannon, tears running down her cheeks. 'Rob's *upset* because I told him that my father's been screwing my brains out since I was three years old,' she spat. 'And it's not a lie.'

'You *what*?' Shannon stared at her, rigid with horror again.

'You heard. He got me pregnant when I was thirteen and made me have an abortion. Rob feels guilty,' she said miserably. 'Thinks it's his fault for not protecting me. He might think he's like Dad too. God knows what he thinks. I wish I hadn't told him now. I don't know why he wants to split up with you, though.' She shrugged. 'He's probably just upset. He'll get over it. Unlike me.'

There was silence as Shannon continued to stare at her, stunned with shock. It isn't true, she thought. It can't be true. She felt cold, could not move. Melanie got to her feet and brushed cigarette ash from her jeans and horrible greasy stained sweater.

'You're lying,' Shannon said harshly. 'Don't tell me that's the best you can come up with to freak me out, because it won't work. I thought you cared more about Rob than to damage him like this with such a terrible sick lie! You're evil, Melanie.'

'I do care about Rob! And it's true! Don't you dare call me evil and a liar, you bitch!' Melanie screamed at her as she backed away, dark eyes furious.

Shannon turned to leave. She felt sick and her legs were weak. She dropped the car keys and picked them up. Don't listen, she told herself. It's a lie. She's mental as well as drunk.

'It's true!' Melanie screamed again. She stumbled over an empty coffee mug and stepped back. Her feet crunched on bits of broken glass. 'Why do you think he's in such a state? Why? There's no other reason.' She began to cry again. 'I'm sorry I told him,' she moaned. 'I wish I hadn't. He was so happy, so wrapped up in you – so bloody unaware! And I was so freaked – I couldn't stand it any more, keeping secrets so that everyone except me could be happy. I've never told anyone except Paul,' she went on. 'He asks me about Dad before he screws me. It turns him on.'

Shannon shivered with revulsion. The car keys dug into her clammy palm, hurting her. A long wardrobe mirror propped against the purple wall showed her own white face and staring reddened eyes. She turned back to Melanie.

'None of this – if it's true – is Rob's fault,' she gasped. '*It's not his fault.* I'll help him . . . he has to let me help him. You leave him alone from now on. Leave *us* alone. You've done enough damage. How *dare* you hurt him like this?' she said fiercely. She wanted to hit Melanie. 'Why don't you swallow your filthy revelations along with your vodka and party pills!'

She ran out of the room, slammed the door and stumbled down the dark stairs. Her breath came in little gasps. Don't let it be true, she thought, tears stinging her eyes. Don't let this destroy us. She thought of Rob in the kitchen earlier – shouting, shoving her. His eyes had changed. The warmth and humour and openness and laughter were gone, replaced by rage and despair. How can I deal with this? she thought. Get through it? I have to help him. We'll be all right, we have to be all right.

Melanie ran after Shannon and hung over the carved wooden banister, auburn hair falling over her face.

'Don't tell me what to do!' she screamed. 'I'm going to be somebody!'

The downstairs front door slammed. Paul and Guy came grinning out of her bedroom and she whirled round to face them.

'Now there's a lady I'd like to get to know.' Guy laughed. 'She could work for me.'

'In your dreams!' Melanie said scornfully. Paul stepped forward, glaring at her and she cowered against the wall.

'I'll do it,' she gulped, brushing away tears. 'I'll do it. But you musn't hurt Rob.'

'Good girl.' Guy smiled and nodded encouragingly. 'Don't worry about anything. You'll be fine. You'll do a great job. No one's going to hurt your brother.'

'I want Singapore Airlines Raffles Class,' she said boldly. 'Not riff-raff.'

'Pity I can't come with you. I don't half fancy those Asian birds.' Paul grinned as he lit another cigarette. 'They're trained from birth to please men – think they're gods.' He laughed and caught his breath as another pain stabbed his ribs and cheekbone. 'Bloody hell!' he gasped. 'Get me another vodka, will you, Mel?'

Chapter Seven

'He's a good-lookin fella, that Saddam.' Josie Duffy paused in the act of wiping the double sink and stared at the television on the kitchen counter, wet dishcloth dripping in her raw hands. 'The spit of your Bernie,' she added nastily, her nasal voice and laughter made harsher by a cold. And the sixty-a-day cigarette habit. Water gurgled down the plugholes.

Margaret Flinder choked on her mouthful of smoked salmon and cream cheese bagel and glared at her cleaning lady.

'It's *Mr Flinder*, if you don't mind!' she said icily. The insufferable woman was not even a good cleaner, she couldn't think why Bernard insisted she be kept on. 'And you're not being paid eight pounds fifty an hour for your opinions,' she added.

'I beg your pardon, I'm sure!' Josie wrenched at both taps. Margaret studied her long red nails and patted her blown-out mass of dry dark hair, the grey covered by a fresh application of chestnut brown tint. She was a tall, heavily built woman with a big bust, truculent dark brown eyes and a square jaw.

'Have you finished the upstairs, Mrs Duffy?' she enquired, picking up her glass of white wine. 'You needn't bother with my studio or *Mr Flinder's* study today.' She sipped the wine.

Study. Studio. Snotty cow! Josie laughed again and squeezed the dishcloth viciously, turning back to the sink as newsreel pictures of Saddam Hussein in beret and green army uniform were replaced by shots of the latest MP caught with his pants down and fingers in the till, fresh from taking part in a television debate about how society's shredded moral fabric could be repaired.

'Bastard won't resign,' she muttered. 'They never do. Bloody politicians. Want drowning, the lot of them!' She stared out of the kitchen window at the over-the-top ornamental back garden, with its gnomes and plastic Greek urns and the little marble slapper with her kit off, nothing but a wreath of marble roses between her and decency. She dropped the dishcloth and coughed productively, groping in her yellow overall pockets for the crumpled piece of toilet roll. Margaret winced.

'The upstairs?'

'I'm goin', Margie, luv. Keep your G-string on.' Josie crashed out of the kitchen, sniggering at her employer's stony glance. She longed to light a cig and blow smoke into the bitch's ugly gob. But that would be pushing it.

She paused in the hall, studying her hollow staring eyes and coarse dyed red hair in the mirror. Plucked pencilled eyebrows gave her a permanently amazed expression. She dragged the vacuum cleaner up the thickly carpeted stairs. Don't go in the study, Mrs Duffy. Mr Flinder doesn't want you to clean the study. We knew why, didn't we? Bernie didn't want anyone seeing his pictures of naked little girls, legs spread to show hairless crotches, posed in positions you wouldn't think existed. Smiling at the camera while unbelievable things were done to them. Bloody pervert! There was a stack of unlabelled videos on the desk by the television and she bet the computer wasn't just for letters and school timetables.

Josie laughed, remembering the summer morning when he'd come rushing home in a sweat after leaving the study door unlocked. Too late; she'd had a good root round. He'd given her a hundred quid when she'd smirked and remarked on how much kids' school things cost. 'Terrible, isn't it, Mr Flinder? You must know, being a headmaster.' Josie hated him and his snotty bitch of a wife, but she needed the wage and his handouts – who could afford morals these days? That was months ago now. Maybe it was time the price of her silence went up! She grinned as she manoeuvred the vacuum cleaner into Melanie's old bedroom with its flowered curtains, blue walls, blue carpet and unmade single bed. She switched it on, opened the casement window and leaned out into the raw November afternoon, feeling in her overall pocket for cigarettes and red plastic lighter.

'Margaret? It's Angie.' Her friend's mannish voice boomed down the line. 'How are you? I'm not interrupting your lunch, I hope?'

'No.' *Yes.* 'Just a minute, Angie,' She swallowed the last mouthful of chewy bagel and turned the television down. 'I'm fine,' she said brightly. 'Fine, thanks.' Fancy calling yourself Angie when you were a haggard fifty-four and badly in need of HRT! 'How did the Meals-on-Wheels go this morning?' she asked, trying to sound interested. Angie had an uncanny habit of phoning the minute she was about to go up to her studio.

'Oh – that bloody Mr Fisher complained the vegetables were overcooked. Although, with a mouth full of brown stumps and NHS dentures, I don't know how he imagines he could handle anything more *al dente.*' She burst into a raucous laugh and Margaret shuddered and closed her eyes. 'I'm fed up with the miserable old bastards,' shouted Angie. 'I have to have enormous gin-and-tonics the minute I get home. I don't know why I bother. They should be sweet and grateful and uncomplaining, but all they do is go on about how they haven't fought Hitler and paid National Insurance to be offered overcooked vegetables and grisly lamb in their twilight years. One of them even called me a bitch – an *old* bitch, if you please! Anyway, never mind the undeserving poor,' she said briskly, 'what I really phoned about is to ask if you and Bernard are free for dinner next Friday?'

'Well, I–'

'That pompous young sod Father Sean has invited himself, but there'll be a few interesting people too. Jennifer Rothwell's coming, the local artist the *Echo* did a feature on. Remember? She might give you a few tips.'

'Jennifer Rothwell?' Margaret felt a thrill of excitement. 'I didn't know you were friendly with her. How wonderful! Yes, I'd love to meet her.' She hesitated. 'We – I'd – love to come, Angie. Thank you. I'd say yes right away only–.'

'Only you don't dare because you have to ask Bernard's

permission first.' Angie laughed. 'You submissive wife, you!' Silly bitch, she thought contemptuously.

'I just have to check he hasn't got a staff meeting or fund raiser or something. He never tells me anything until the last minute. Can I ring you back?'

'Of course,' Angie boomed. 'But don't leave it too long. I'm going to do one of my Chinese banquets,' she said proudly. 'Father Sean will hate that, he only likes English food. I need to buy the beef and lamb and marinate it a day in advance. Not to mention getting up at dawn to go to the bloody fish market.'

'You know you love it,' Margaret laughed.

'I've got it all worked out,' Angie said excitedly. 'Your Bernard and Father Sean can get into a boring after-dinner discussion about the moral degeneration spread by single mothers and childless career women, and leave the rest of us to party. What do you think?'

'Sounds perfect. Thanks, Angie. I'll call you back.'

Margaret replaced the receiver, hoping Josie had not been eavesdropping on the bedroom extension, and sat at the kitchen table to finish her wine. This would need careful handling. Bernard hated Angie, as he hated most of her friends, and considered her rich building contractor husband Dennis a jumped-up toerag. Although they liked him; Bernard was always charming when they met. He hated anything or anyone 'arty', so that was Jennifer Rothwell off the list too. Bernard was not one to retreat to the corner of the sofa for a quiet chat, he liked to dominate the conversation. But he would listen too, just enough not to irritate people. They'd never believe how rude and indifferent he was to his wife in private.

Margaret felt a frisson of anger. He was a good husband in the sense that he didn't drink too much, gamble, chase other women – or men! – any of the nightmare marriage scenarios one read and heard about. She thought of Angie. Dennis had had an affair with his twenty-three-year-old 'personal assistant' last year, and Angie considered herself lucky when he crawled back waving his Gold Card as a white flag after the girl ditched him for someone her own age. It was fine to talk about women's rights, fulfilment, etc, but any woman over thirty without husband and children – or husband at least – was still regarded as a joke or an aberration by most people. And a woman over forty or fifty . . .! At fifty-one Margaret had her reward. Comfortably off, respected as headmaster's wife and local do-gooder, time to pursue her 'little hobby', as Bernard referred to her painting. He hadn't touched her for years and she was grateful, but at the same time felt sad because she knew she'd missed out on sex, good sex with a loving caring partner. It was too late for that now. But whose life was perfect? Things could be a lot worse. She poured herself another glass of wine.

'I'm happy,' she whispered. 'I am happy.'

Should she phone Bernard about Angie's dinner party now, or wait until this evening? No, he was always in a terrible hurry to get to his study, twitching like a nervous horse. He spent hours locked in there; it was staggering, the amount of administrative work headteachers had nowadays. And there was the matter of bold, platinum blonde Miss Siobhann O'Kane, the PE teacher at St Fidelma's who was going to marry a divorced man. Bernard was furious about that, storming home in a rage, swearing to have her dismissed. Better phone now. He would be finishing lunch.

'–and a line of police officers carefully comb through Calderstones Park where the strangled battered body of little Bianca Mitchell was found, searching for clues that might have been missed first time around. Despite appeals by Bianca's parents, no one has come forward with information. Bianca had her favourite Barbie doll with her. The doll, dressed in a pair of pink cotton jeans with a button missing–.'

Margaret got up, snapped off the television and frowned as the doorbell pealed. She wanted to take her glass of wine and shut herself in the attic until six, Josie Duffy interruptions permitting. She thought of the painting she was doing: a Lake District scene of a cottage by a stone bridge, rainclouds low over the fells. It should be ready for another wash of yellow ochre.

She went into the hall, smoothing her red sweater and tartan kilt. Josie had sprayed too much lemon air freshener again. Margaret stopped and frowned. The place smelled like a lavatory.

'Robert!' she exclaimed, astonished to see her tall, brown-haired son standing in the plant-filled porch, hands clenched in the pockets of his grey padded jacket. He wore jeans and scuffed trainers. It was usually a suit. She smiled, ignoring his grim staring expression and the two or three days' growth of beard. He was pale and his narrow face looked thinner, the brown eyes hollow. His straight dark eyebrows were drawn together in a frown. He smelled musty, as though he hadn't changed clothes or taken a shower in days.

'What a state you're in!' Margaret laughed nervously. 'What are you doing here in the middle of the day? Have they got you involved in some kind of undercover work?' Did his breath smell of alcohol? Impossible! 'Or have you come from a tussle with some of the drugged unwashed who roam the streets of Liverpool and hurl abuse when I tell them I'm not a human cash dispenser?' she asked gaily. 'Has your washing machine broken down?' she rattled on. 'I don't suppose Shannon has time or inclination to launder her husband's shirts. If she spent more time in her kitchen than she does in that courtroom . . .' A thought struck and she turned eagerly as he brushed past her and strode down the hall. 'I don't suppose you've come to tell me I'm going to be a grandmother at last?'

'A grandmother?' He barked a laugh, the first time he'd laughed since Bonfire Night. She followed him to the kitchen and watched in amazement as he helped himself to a glass of her wine and gulped it down.

'Think you'd make a good grandmother, do you?' He sloshed more wine into the glass. 'No, you're not going to be a grandmother,' he said dully. 'You never will be. Not now.' Children, marriage, a 'normal' happy existence, those things were denied him forever. He felt guilty and embarrassed even talking to people. They didn't know him for what he was: the flawed son of a monster. There was no going back on that now. He was a fraud, an outcast.

'What do you mean? Robert, what is going on?' She cocked her head, listening for the roar of the vacuum cleaner overhead. She closed the kitchen door and faced him. 'Are you ill?' she asked. 'You don't look well – very pale. I don't suppose Shannon's noticed. Always thinking of herself and her career.'

'Never mind Shannon,' he said tiredly. 'It's Melanie I'm here to talk about.'

'Melanie?' Margaret rolled her eyes in exasperation. 'What's she done now? That girl's a disgrace to this family. After all we've done for her.'

'I went to see her the other night and she told me – she *told* me!' He stopped and held up the empty wine glass. 'Haven't you got anything stronger than this?'

'Told you what?' His mother's thin lips tightened into the familiar line of disapproval. 'I wouldn't listen to anything Melanie told you,' she said aggressively, then added, 'Do you think you ought to be drinking in the middle of the day when you've got an afternoon's work ahead of you?'

He went out of the kitchen and fetched himself a Scotch from a decanter on the dining room sideboard. Shannon hated decanters, he thought, looking at the row of heavy ponderous cut glass things. He forced her beautiful image out of his mind – he couldn't think about his wife anymore. She belonged to another world. A world from which he was now excluded.

He strode back to the kitchen. His mother still stood there, looking puzzled and angry. She straightened her Channel swimmer shoulders at the sight of him, patted the permed mass of dark hair, the way she did when dropping false brightness for chilly distance. He hated the cold brown eyes ringed with black eyeliner and blue shadow, the thin obstinate mouth and truculent set of her jaw. Her powdery complexion looked parched, her nose and heavy cheeks covered with thread veins.

'What has Melanie told you?' she asked icily. 'I know her lifestyle leaves a lot to be desired, but she's nineteen now and I can't–.'

'I'm not talking about her *lifestyle*!' Rob interrupted. He felt as if he was wading through sand. 'I'm talking about what he – what Dad did to her. I want to know how you could let that happen and do nothing about it? Where *were* you?' he asked. 'What the hell were you doing?' He took a gulp of Scotch and set the glass down on the counter, his hand shaking.

'Let what happen? What do you mean?' Margaret stared at him.

'I don't like your tone, Robert. How dare you come here and speak to me like this!'

'He's been abusing her – *fucking* her! – since she was three years old!' he shouted suddenly. 'How could he do that? How could you let him?'

Margaret groped for a chair and sat down, legs weak. 'Don't you dare make such a terrible accusation!' she whispered. 'What a ghastly lie!'

'You're not getting away with it,' he said, circling the table. 'Putting on your superior headmaster's wife airs. I want answers. That bastard's ruined my sister's life. Ruined *my* life. I feel like a bloody idiot. Not to mention what Melanie must feel.'

'It's not true!' Margaret gasped. 'It's just not true. I won't listen to this.'

Neither of them noticed that the vacuum cleaner continued to roar on the same spot above their heads. Josie had seen Rob's car and was creeping downstairs to eavesdrop.

'It's not true,' Margaret whispered again, long red nails digging into her palms. 'It's a disgusting, filthy, horrible lie. Melanie's wicked – she always hated your father.'

'Don't say "*your father*" like that.' Rob stood over her, glaring down. 'He's our father only in the biological sense. Why else do you think she's always hated him?' he shouted in her ear, making her jump.

'She's lying,' Margaret repeated. 'I told you, I won't listen to this,' she said, trying to sound bold. She raised her shaky voice. 'It's ridiculous, outrageous what she says. Melanie's wild, always has been difficult to control. He had to be strict with her. Look at her now. She's confused, disturbed. She's upset you with these terrible lies.'

'You'd be confused and disturbed if your father had been screwing your brains out since you were three years old.' Rob felt helpless in the face of her stubbornness, her absolute refusal to accept the truth. 'I should have known.' His voice broke and he buried his face in his hands, rubbing at the rough stubbly skin. 'It's my fault,' he moaned. 'I'm useless. I should have protected her.'

'Robert, all this is nonsense.' Margaret got up and faced him, pushing her chair back. 'One thing it does illustrate is how confused Melanie is. She's obviously very disturbed. I really think she needs professional help.' She grabbed her glass, took a swift gulp of wine. 'Perhaps you could talk to her, make her see that? Spreading terrible lies about her father won't achieve anything.'

'You know,' he stared at her, 'you were nearly a grandmother when Melanie was thirteen. Although not quite in the way you'd have wanted.'

Another horrible wave of shock jolted her heavy body. 'What are you talking about now?' Margaret asked aggressively. How dare he come here and upset her like this! She needed a Valium but the bottle was on her bedside table.

'He got her pregnant and made her have an abortion,' cried Rob. He wiped his face on his jacket sleeve. 'She wasn't camping in the Lake District, she was in hospital having his foetus sucked out of her. How does that grab you?' he shouted, clenching the chair's back. 'Remember you went mental when you found those Pill packets in her drawer? He put her on it so she wouldn't get pregnant again.'

'You're lying! You're lying! *She's* lying. How dare you?' Margaret gasped with horror and put her hands over her ears. She groped for the chair and sat down again. She thought she might faint.

'You're lying to yourself,' Rob said. He felt exhausted, totally helpless. He didn't know why he'd come here. 'My life – your life – they're just an illusion, a sick joke. You don't want to see the truth. And me!' He banged his chest. 'What about me? I'm the son of a paedophile. I could be a monster! Why didn't you tell me? I had a right to know. I got married. I wanted kids!'

'Get out of here,' she gasped, her head whirling. 'Leave me alone. Don't talk to me about your *rights*. I won't listen to these lies.' She raised her head and looked at her son, his mouth twisted, brown eyes full of pain and bewilderment. 'You're not welcome in this house anymore,' she said shakily. 'And neither is Melanie. Not that you ever come here! But you're not welcome anymore. Until you both apologize.'

'I don't believe it! You're putting me – us – in the wrong.' He was silent for a few seconds. 'Mum,' he begged, 'talk to me. Please! You must have known what was going on? Or maybe you really didn't. What happened? Were you scared of him? Tell me. I want to understand. Please talk to me – tell me so I'll understand. This is doing my head in!'

He felt like a small boy again, trying to tell her he had scored at football, been the best in the team, desperate to rouse a smile, a spark of warmth and interest. He had never succeeded. 'You know this has got to be sorted,' he said quietly, wiping his eyes. 'He needs treatment. He should be locked up! And what about Melanie?'

'Never mind her. What about me?' Margaret glared up at him. 'What about *me*? What about my marriage? I've got a position in this community, and so has your father. I won't tolerate my son and daughter spreading terrible lies about him. If you persist in this, I'll never speak to you again.' She was shouting now. 'I mean it. All I know is that my son has been turned into a lout by the Merseyside Police Force and my daughter is a crazed pathological liar. It's not nice to be ashamed of your own children, not to be able to talk about their achievements.' Angie was always going on about her barrister daughter and the younger daughter with the 'two gorgeous girlies'. 'I won't listen to these appalling lies and neither should you,' she cried. 'I told you, you're not welcome in this house again until you apologize. Even then it will be some time before I feel like seeing either of you. I'm not going to mention this to your father. Now, leave. Go!' She flung out an arm. 'Go! Get out!' she screamed. 'Get out of this house!'

Josie Duffy jumped away from the kitchen door and flattened herself against the wall as Rob stormed past, face contorted with grief. He slammed the front door so loudly that the house shook and a panel of coloured glass cracked. She went into the kitchen. Margaret Flinder sat at the table, clutching an empty wine glass in her white claws with their blood-red talons, staring in front of her at nothing. She looked like a made-up corpse.

'Bloody hell, what was all that about?' As if she didn't know! It was better than the telly. Josie laughed. 'Shall I get you another wine, Margie luv?' she asked cheerfully. 'You look like you could do with it.'

'Don't you touch that bottle,' Margaret said slowly. 'You steal enough as it is.'

'You what?' Josie gaped at her.

'I said, you steal enough.' Margaret stood up, trying to control the awful trembling in her legs. 'You steal, you listen in to phone conversations, I have to listen to your retarded opinions . . . and I'm sick of it. You don't clean the house properly so you're sacked,' she said evenly. 'You can leave now. I'm sick of the sight of you. I don't see why I should have to look at that mole and facial stubble three times a week either. And with hair that colour you should be arrested for causing a breach of the Queen's peace!'

'Oh, I don't think *I'm* the one should be arrested, Margie luv!' Josie stiffened with outrage but kept her temper. Facial stubble indeed! 'I don't think you wanna get shot of me.' She shook her head emphatically. 'No, I've got too much on you and that bloody pervert of a fella of yours. I know what he is. And so do you.'

'What are you talking about, you stupid woman?' Margaret screamed. 'I said, get out! Now!'

'Don't you go calling me for everything, you stuck-up cow!' Josie said loudly. 'Who d'you think you are, issuing your frigging orders? Butter wouldn't melt! Well, we'll see what Bernie has to say about this. I don't think he'll like it.'

She got her coat, picked up her carrier bag with the pairs of pink and yellow rubber gloves inside and popped into the dining room for a few swigs of Drambuie. It was no good stealing the decanter, it would only leak on the bus home. Why didn't they keep their booze in bottles, like normal people? The pair of them thought they were bloody royalty. And God only knew why, with a copper son and a drugged-up slapper for a daughter.

'I'll be back,' she said to the white-faced Margaret, putting her head round the kitchen door. 'You'd better get your apology ready. Stuck-up cow!' she said again. 'This'll cost you. I'll see *you* off!'

Josie went out. In the porch she picked up pots of green leafy plants, tore them out by the roots and dropped them on the floor, scattering moist black soil. She had hated watering the bloody things, and picking up their dead leaves. She laughed with delight at the mess and walked out, leaving the porch door open. Some desperate bastard might walk in and rape Margie. Do her good!

She wouldn't get much joy from Bernie, that was for sure.

Margaret paced the kitchen, then sat down again and leaned her head on the table, her brain filled with whirling images. Plans for a peaceful afternoon's painting were abandoned. How could she paint in this mood? After hearing such terrible lies from her own son? What was the matter with him and Melanie? She swept up the broken glass, took a new bottle of white wine from the fridge and poured herself a big glassful. She went into the lounge and sat on the deep comfortable sofa, gulping wine and staring through the French windows at the wintry garden. The whirling images faded as one took hold – one she had almost succeeded in banishing from her mind.

She was in the long back garden of their terraced house in Birkenhead, the house she and Bernard had lived in before his parents died. Her parents had died shortly afterwards, leaving her the thousands they had been too mean to spend. There was a shed at the bottom of the garden, stinking of turpentine and full of spider's webs, brown paper tacked over the square of dirty window. Bernard kept it padlocked. He was constructing model aircraft, he said, light delicate things that could be broken by a gust of wind. She was to keep out, he would let her know if he wanted tea or coffee or a sandwich. He spent hours there and she hid her annoyance with jokes about boys who never grew up. 'It's only model aircraft,' her friends laughed. 'What about golf widows? Or anglers? How would you like to wipe their wet wellies or gut the stinking glassy-eyed fish they proudly dump on your spotless draining board?'

One Saturday morning in September Father Michael had phoned from the Presbytery, wanting to discuss something 'rather important and confidential' with 'your good man'. Margaret ran to the back door and shouted for Bernard, rushed down the garden and banged on the shed door.

'It's Father Michael on the phone, Bernard,' she shouted impatiently. 'Hurry up.'

The sight when the wooden door unexpectedly swung open was the one she had almost succeeded in forgetting these past ten years. An eight-year-old neighbourhood girl, pert, dark-haired Janetta Smith, lay naked and spreadeagled on Melanie's old urine-stained mattress; the mattress Bernard had told her he had dumped at the tip. He knelt over the child, trousers sagging to show his round white belly and the erect penis springing from his black thatch of pubic hair.

Margaret gasped, screamed and ran back to the house, forgetting Father Michael hanging on the phone, and started to throw dressing gown, underwear and sweaters into a suitcase, not really knowing what she was doing. Bernard followed and tried to calm her. It was Janetta's fault, he'd said, she was precocious for her age. She'd led him on, said she wanted to know what men and women did to make babies. 'Show me, show me,' she kept saying, giggling and pointing to his trousers.

All right, so he'd been weak. Got a bit carried away. He'd never done that before and never would again. It was stupid, stupid, he didn't know what had come over him. She wouldn't leave? They had their life together, he and she and Rob and Melanie. He would soon be promoted to Head of Science at St Fidelma's. Melanie had emotional problems, she needed her mother. A broken marriage would wreck the stable environment she so badly needed. And – he had never told her this before, didn't want to upset her – as a child he himself had been sexually abused by an aunt, now dead.

Shocked and stunned, Margaret sat on the bed and let his words wash over her. Why did *she* feel ashamed? she wondered. She felt tainted by a terrible shame, dirty, like a rape or burglary victim. She wanted to wash her clothes and the children's, clean the house from top to bottom, scrub and polish and vacuum away the tainted feeling. Set a match to that shed, to those boxes of magazines. And what would happen now? Would Janetta tell her parents? The police? She hated herself. How could she have felt attracted to someone like him? How could she not have known? He'd been charming, but she should have seen through it. She was one of those stupid women who always fell for the wrong man.

Nothing happened. She cried – or sulked, as he described it – for a week, avoiding her parents and friends, ignoring Rob and Melanie. Janetta disappeared from home and was never found, despite a frantic police search. Margaret went to her GP and asked for Valium and sleeping pills. She wanted to leave Bernard, but where would she go? She could type, do secretarial work, but could she make enough to support two children? He would fight her for custody. She would end up in some bedsit, alone. And they were Catholics. He would oppose a divorce, make her life hell. Her parents did not want her and two grandchildren on their doorstep. They liked Bernard, who had always been charming to them. Everyone would be on his side. She would be criticized, put in the wrong, accused of being a foolish, selfish woman. So she stayed. They stopped having sex. And here she was now. Ten years on.

She got up, dumped the wine glass on the coffee table and hurried upstairs. She rattled the panelled oak study door. Locked as usual. What had Josie Duffy said? 'I've got too much on your bloody pervert of a fella!' What did she mean? How did she know? What had she seen? And *Melanie*! Had he really . . .

Margaret began to cry and scream and bang on the door. Tears ran down her powdery cheeks. She knew what was in there. She *knew*.

'You've let me down again,' she wailed as she banged and kicked at the heavy door. Unyielding, like Bernard. 'You've let me down. You promised me it'd never happen again. You've let me *down*!'

Chapter Eight

'What the hell have you been doing? You look bloody awful.'

Gavin Steele, senior partner at Steele & Monckton, put his head round the door and stared at Shannon as she sat at her desk, gazing out across Exchange Flags. She hadn't taken off her Calvin Klein black cashmere coat. Her hair and make-up were immaculate, but she looked pale beneath the light dusting of blusher, and her full red mouth trembled. She had a scared look in her eyes. The make-up only partially concealed a bruise on her left cheekbone. He shifted out of Jenny Fong's way as she hurried in, dumped a cup of espresso on the desk and silently withdrew.

'Thanks very much, Gavin!' Shannon sipped the hot sweet coffee and looked at him over the cup's gold rim. 'I appreciate that. Did you have a good weekend?'

Morning sunlight slanted across her cluttered desk, the white walls and powder blue carpet. The Swiss Cheese plant, its yellowed withering leaves pressed against an icy windowpane above a hot radiator, had given up the ghost.

'It was all right.' Gavin glanced at his watch. 'It's ten past nine,' he said coldly. 'You're not in court this morning?'

'No.' The tiny cup clinked on its saucer. 'I thought I'd do some work on the–.'

'Why aren't you?' he interrupted. 'In court this morning?'

She looked at him steadily. 'I told our Mr Phillips he'd be better off if he pleaded guilty so he'd get a lighter sentence for not wasting more police and court time and taxpayers' money. And forcing the victim to testify. He agreed.'

'You did *what*?' Gavin pulled his hands out of his trouser pockets and stood up straight, sunlight flashing on his Nazi doctor wire-framed glasses. He was small and stocky and wore a tweed suit and black bow tie with red spots. The waistcoat strained over his paunch. He ran one chubby pink hand through his sandy hair.

'Look – you know he assaulted that girl,' Shannon went on. 'I know it, he knows it, the police know it. She certainly does.' She shrugged and looked down. 'I just didn't see the point. He was guilty and deserved to be banged up. Now he is.'

'You didn't see the point? Have you gone mad?' Gavin shouted in disgust. 'Since when did guilt or innocence enter the equation?' He stepped into her office, the one she considered too cramped for someone with a partnership offer, and banged the door shut. 'For Christ's sake!' he exclaimed, exasperated. 'What the hell is wrong with you lately? You're losing it.'

Shannon looked at her pale folded hands with their long shiny nails, blinking to control the tears that threatened. 'I'm sorry, Gavin. I–.'

'Your last two clients went down for burglary and GBH.'

'They were guilty!'

'That's not the *point*! And now you're telling this Phillips tosser to plead guilty.'

'He is guilty,' she said quietly.

'What did I just tell you?' Gavin looked at her furiously. 'There was only that silly little cow's statement and that could have been blown out of the water any fine day of the week.'

'Oh yes.' She clasped her hands tighter, feeling the smooth cool gold of her wedding ring. The diamond engagement ring sparkled in the pale sunlight. 'Victims' statements usually are blown out of the water.'

'I'm starting to regret my partnership offer,' said Gavin, hoping threats would make her pull up her lacy black stockings quick sharp. 'Richard and Priscilla were pretty pissed off about that, as you know. They said you weren't up to it. Looks like they're right.'

'Priscilla's jealous.' Shannon glanced up at him. 'She's forty-four and going nowhere. Richard thinks women belong in kitchens and labour wards. Or in the witness box, explaining what colour underwear they favour and how many men they had sex with before the *alleged* rape.' She bowed her head again as tears threatened, determined not to fall apart in front of her boss.

'What's wrong?' he demanded. 'Have you got some sort of personal problem – crisis – going on?' He paused. 'You're not pregnant, are you?'

'No, Gavin.' Shannon blushed. 'I am not pregnant.'

'Then what?'

My loving husband has turned into a hateful stranger who won't look at me or talk to me. He pushes me out of his way when I try to talk to him. He didn't come home last night. I don't know what the hell to do.

Rob couldn't cope with Melanie's revelations, she thought, the fact that his own father was a paedophile who had abused his daughter since she was three years old. The kind of pervert people said should be strung up, chemically castrated, torched out of their home. How could family members protect them? she'd often wondered. Maybe they were too busy living in denial, trying to hold their own lives together. Rob wasn't doing a very good job of that at the moment. But at least he hadn't left home. She couldn't really believe he meant to do that. This was a horrible time, but they'd get through it, wouldn't they? The phone rang and she grabbed it.

'Is that you? I want to know where Robert is,' Margaret Flinder said querulously. 'I've phoned his place of work and his house.' *His* house! 'He's not there. I want him to apologize and to promise me he won't repeat those terrible allegations about his father. I suppose you put him up to it? You're an evil selfish woman, and a terrible wife. You want to turn him against his own family.'

'Good morning, Margaret!' Shannon managed to keep the tremor out of her voice. 'You certainly don't need my help to turn Rob against his family.' Gavin watched her closely and she wished he would go away. 'He's turned against me too. I'm afraid I can't tell you where he is,' she went on. 'He didn't come home last night.'

'Didn't come *home*?'

'That's what I said. He's going through some sort of crisis and it's affecting our marriage – I'm terribly worried about him. Why don't you get angry with the person who's responsible for all this?' she asked angrily. 'Namely, your so-called husband!'

'What do you mean, my *so-called* husband?' Margaret's voice was harsh, too loud. She sounded as though she'd been at the decanters already.

'Well, he can't be much of a husband – and that's putting it mildly. But, as I said, I suggest you save your anger for him. I don't intend to have this conversation. I also suggest you drink tea or coffee at breakfast – all that gin is clouding your already seriously warped judgement.' Shannon slammed the phone down and buried her head in her hands.

'A marital crisis,' Gavin exclaimed, bored and irritated. Being female, of course, she'd brought it to the office with her. Bloody women. She really was losing it. So cool and tough and professional and sexy – and now suddenly all over the shop. Just his luck.

'Gavin, I–.' Shannon looked up at him, blue eyes glittering with tears. 'I'm all right, really. I'll be fine.'

'I'm not worried about you,' he said rudely. 'I'm worried about the bloody firm.' He moved to the window, brushing non-existent dust specks from his jacket sleeve. The smell of her perfume filled the room.

'I mean, I'll be all right to work,' she said. 'If I could just have a day or so to sort this out–.'

'A day or so!' he snorted. 'You can have a week. You're no bloody use to me in this state.'

'I'm not in a state.'

'You're a bloody mess. I don't need this.'

'I want to work,' Shannon protested, stung. 'It'll take my mind off things. I just need a couple of days.'

'I said, you can take a week.' He moved back to the door, fiddling with his ridiculous bow tie. 'It's a bit quiet at the moment and Richard can deal with your stuff. The stuff you've got left,' he added sarcastically. 'Just bugger off out of here and come back next Monday – crisis sorted. Pull yourself together. I'll be watching you. One week!' He opened the door and went out, slamming it behind him.

'Thanks for nothing,' she muttered. 'You miserable bastard!' She reached for a tissue to wipe her eyes. Jenny hurried in.

'Are you okay?'

'Oh, I'm great.' Shannon sniffed. 'Having a sympathetic employer helps no end.' She stood up and gathered her bag and briefcase. 'I'm taking a week off,' she explained. 'Gavin doesn't want my *personal crisis* interfering with my work. He's right, of course. I just need a bit of time to get myself together. I'm in shock at the moment.' She blinked back tears. 'Devastated, actually!'

'Of course you are.' Jenny grimaced. 'I suppose he was his usual wonderful warm caring self?'

'Oh yes. As I said.' Tears and red lipstick stained the tissue.

'Shall I call you a cab?'

'No, thanks. I'll be all right driving.'

'Well, take care of yourself,' Jenny said anxiously. She opened the door and stood back.

'I'll try. See you in a week.'

Richard and Priscilla would have a good laugh about this, thought Shannon, as she left the office and stepped into the lift, avoiding curious stares. Priscilla, a skeletal hardbitten chainsmoker, called her Barbie behind her back. She would be smirking her head off. Shannon had worked twice as hard as the lot of them, and now everything threatened to come unstuck because she couldn't control the terrible events that were ruining her life. All because of Bernard Flinder! She'd never liked him, hadn't succumbed to the oily charm that worked on most people. She'd thought him a phony. But not a paedophile! It was amazing what you didn't see when you weren't looking.

It was strange to come home at ten on Monday morning, to an empty silent freezing house. Shannon switched on the thermostat, took off her coat and ran upstairs to change out of her black suit. A week off might do her good, she thought, give her breathing space to deal with the calamity that had befallen her and Rob. They could spend time together, she might be able to get him to talk. Behave like a human being again.

She stopped outside their bedroom, her heart accelerating at the sound of muffled bumps and metal coathangers sliding on a rail.

He was home. Thank goodness! But where had he spent the night? And did she dare ask? She pushed the door open.

'Rob?' She walked in cautiously. 'I'm so glad you're home!' she exclaimed. 'Please, we've got to talk.' She paused, watching him nervously. 'What are you doing?'

'Why do you always ask stupid questions?'

He wouldn't look at her. He threw sweaters, shirts and trousers into an open suitcase on the king size bed. A bottle of Chivas Regal, nearly empty, stood on the dressing table. 'Isn't it obvious what I'm doing?' he asked impatiently. 'I'm getting out of here. I've had it - with you, with my so-called *family*. I'm leaving. I told you I'd leave.'

'*What*?' gasped Shannon. She stepped forward, half expecting to plunge into a dark bottomless pit. 'But– you said you wouldn't leave yet. It's not a month. You said you'd give me time.'

'I've changed my mind.'

He still wore his grey padded jacket and his jaw was heavily stubbled. His jeans were crumpled, as though he had slept in them. Maybe he had. He finally looked at her, brown eyes cold and hostile. 'I want a divorce,' he said bluntly. 'I should never have married you. I should never have married anyone.'

'Rob, no!' Shannon dropped her briefcase and started to cry. 'Please don't do this. Sit down and let's talk,' she pleaded. 'You don't mean it. You're not yourself. I know this awful business with your father and Melanie has freaked you out. It's freaked me out too. But we can't let it destroy our marriage.' She trembled, overwhelmed with panic. 'He'll have won then. None of this is our fault,' she pleaded. 'You and me and Melanie – we're victims. It's not your fault.'

'You're not a victim, Shannon. That's the last thing you are.'

'We're both victims if you let this thing wreck our marriage. We've got to deal with it. I can't fall apart and you can't leave me and run away. That's no good! I can help you, we have to help each other. You must see that.'

'No. We're finished.' He turned back to the wardrobe.

'What about Melanie?' She struggled to stop crying, cursing herself for weakness. He wouldn't leave her, of course he wouldn't.

'She'll have to sort herself out,' muttered Rob. 'I can't handle anything now.'

'But she needs you. Christ, I never thought I'd hear myself say that! She needs you, Rob,' she said desperately. 'I need you.'

'I've had enough,' he said. 'I've told you, I don't want to be married anymore. I want to go away and start again. That's it. What does it take to get through to you?' He turned and glared at her. 'I want a new life. Without you or Melanie or my bloody parents in it.'

'For God's sake, Rob! That won't work.' She ran round the side of the bed and grabbed him by the shoulders. 'Why are you doing this?' she cried, tears pouring down her face. 'It's as if you blame me for everything. Your bloody mother phoned me earlier – *she* was trying to blame me too. Why? Don't you think you should direct all this rage at your father? *He's* the one who caused this mess, *he's* the one who abused Melanie and God knows who else all these years. What did you say to your mother when you went to see her?'

'Don't question me.' He unpeeled her clinging fingers and pushed her away. She fell backwards across the open suitcase, arms and legs splayed.

'You can't do this,' she cried. She wiped her eyes and licked salt tears from her lips. 'I love you,' she said desperately. 'You're in shock because of what's happened, you can't take it in. I don't blame you. I understand what you're going through. It must be terrible to find out your father's a–.'

'You don't understand what I'm going through. You don't understand anything.'

'Tell me then! I can't take this – this awful coldness. I can't stand it. I want you back the way you were.'

'That's not going to happen. I'll never be the way I was.'

He yanked her arm, dragged her off the suitcase and rolled her over. She fell on the floor. Pain shot through her arm and right shoulder. The rose-coloured carpet scratched her cheek as she curled into a foetal position, sobbing. Rob reached for the bottle of Chivas Regal and swigged from it.

'You think you're a monster, too,' she sobbed, remembering what Melanie had said. 'But you're not! You musn't think that, it's rubbish. Rob, please don't leave me,' she moaned. Her body shook with panic-stricken sobs. 'Please, please don't leave me,' she begged. 'I love you so much. I want to be with you for the rest of my life. You'll get over this. We were so happy.'

'It's finished,' he repeated savagely. He took several more swigs from the bottle, dumped it back on the dressing table and began to pull socks from a drawer.

'It's not finished.' Shannon got to her feet, brushed herself down and undid the tiny gold buttons of her jacket. 'But you're right,' she gulped. It was a struggle to stop herself from screaming with grief and fear. 'You're right, I don't understand,' she panted. 'I don't understand why you're angry with *me*. Why you feel you have to walk out on me, end our marriage. It's crazy! Why you say we,' she fought down another sob, 'can't have kids.'

He had his back to her now, sorting through coathangers in the wardrobe.

'It's your paedophile father who's responsible for all this!' shouted Shannon. 'He's wrecked Melanie's life and God knows how many other girls. Don't let him wreck our marriage, Rob. You should be angry with *him*, not me. Doesn't it make you angry to think we might have had a daughter by now, a lovely little girl, and he could have ...' She stopped, biting her lip. 'No one thought to warn us, did they?' she said furiously. 'That's what freaks me out. Melanie and your bitch of a mother would have stood by and let him hurt our daughter.' She burst out crying again. 'Blame *him*, Rob. Blame *them*!' she sobbed, pummelling his back. 'I'm your wife, I love you. I've never hurt you, I never would. For Christ's sake!' she exclaimed, struck by horror. 'He's a headteacher. He's surrounded by young girls every working day. In charge of them. It doesn't bear thinking about. We have to do something,' she pleaded. 'We can work together, get him arrested. We have to stop him. Rob, listen to me, please!'

She collapsed on the dressing table stool and buried her head in her hands.

'I can't believe this nightmare has happened to us,' she moaned. 'It's not our fault in any way.'

'Well, it has happened.' He threw in a pile of underpants and closed the suitcase. The snap of the locks caused another wave of panic.

'Don't, Rob.' She jumped to her feet and grabbed his arm, clinging to him as he heaved the suitcase off the bed and dumped it on the floor. 'You can't walk out on me because of what your father's done. It's crazy. Look, you're in a terrible state, you're not yourself. It's the shock.'

'Let go, Shannon,' he said quietly. 'It's pointless trying to stop me.'

'No! No, please.' She put her arms around his neck and clung to him, bawling like an injured child. She was outside herself, observing this wild sobbing woman in the black suit who clung to the stony-faced man, blonde hair tumbling down her back. Tears down her face.

'You can't go,' she wailed. 'We've got to talk. I've got a week off work.'

'A week?' He looked down at her, mouth twisted in a painful grimace. 'Christ! How can Gavin do without his female Rumpole of the Bailey?'

'We could get away from here, go to the Lake District for a few days. Be alone together. Decide what we're going to do.' The dispassionate observer smirked at the clichés that spilled from her swollen lips.

'I've already decided.'

'I love you,' she screamed, hanging on to him as he tried again to lift the suitcase. 'Don't go – please don't go. I can't bear it. Don't leave me, Rob.' She felt as though she would choke. 'I can't live without you. I don't want to.'

'You'll be all right.' He stared down at her, mouth still twisted in that awful grimace. His breath stank of whisky. 'You've got money, a career. You can keep this damn house, you've paid the mortgage so far. You don't need me.' He tried to shake her off. 'You've got beauty and intelligence. You can have any man you want.'

'I only want you,' wailed Shannon.

He looked down at her tear-stained face and wild blonde hair, the jacket open to show her full bust in a tight red ribbed sweater. He hadn't touched her for days, had felt revulsion at the thought.

But suddenly he wanted her. She looked into his eyes, read them, started to kiss him.

He shoved her back on the bed and climbed on top of her, one hand holding her wrists above her head while his other hand ripped her black tights and dragged her skirt up over her hips. Shannon gasped. He'd never been rough like this before. His grip on her wrists was painful. She started to struggle beneath him.

'Don't, Rob,' she cried. 'You're hurting me.'

He dragged up her sweater and unfastened her bra. Her nipples hardened as they were exposed to the cold air. 'Stop!' She tried to free her imprisoned wrists, kicking wildly as her tights and pants were ripped off and her legs forced apart.

'Keep still,' he panted. He fumbled with the zip of his jeans then knelt over her.

She cried out and arched her back at the burning pain as his erect penis tore into her. Tears flowed from beneath her closed eyelids and her ears were ringing.

'Look at me,' he commanded, his whisky breath in her face. He leaned on his elbows, imprisoning her arms as he thrust harder and deeper inside her. 'Look at me, Shannon.' He bent his head, sucking and biting at her breasts.'

'Stop!' she sobbed. 'Rob, please stop. It hurts.'

He took no notice. It seemed he would never stop. Finally he shuddered, groaned loudly and collapsed on top of her, his face in her breasts. She could hardly breathe. He raised his head and looked down at her.

'You see,' he whispered in her ear. 'I *am* a monster.'

He climbed off her and went to the bathroom. The toilet flushed. He came back a minute later with his zip done up, water splashed on his face, his hair combed back. He took a last swig of Chivas Regal and picked up his suitcase. Shannon rolled over and curled up, shivering violently. It was wet and sore between her legs and her breasts ached. He looked down at her.

'I'll come back for the rest of my stuff. Don't try to find me. I'll let you know about the divorce when I get sorted.'

He turned and went out, lugging the suitcase, leaving her huddled shivering on the bed, staring at the half open bedroom door. His navy blue bathrobe hung on the hook, the one she had bought him for his birthday in October. The front door banged and he was gone, footsteps crunching down the drive and fading into the distance. She wondered where his car was parked.

'Rob,' she whispered. 'Rob.'

Water gurgled in the radiator. She reached over and pulled the heavy flowered duvet across her exposed body, wriggling out of her torn clothes. Her skin was pale and felt icy. The bedside phone began to ring but she ignored it. She pressed her face into the pillowcase, damp and stained with her blood and tears. The room smelled of his whisky and sweat and her perfume.

'Rob!' she whispered again. 'Don't leave me. I love you.'

The phone stopped ringing and the house was silent. Her head hurt, she could hardly bear the pale winter sun that slanted across the bed. She closed her eyes.

Chapter Nine

'Ladies and gentlemen, welcome to Manchester.' The nasal voice of the stewardess came over the intercom as the 737 landed and bumped down the runway, engines screaming. 'Local time is seven twenty a.m. on Wednesday November 20. Please remain seated with your seatbelts fastened until the aircraft has come to a complete halt, and remember to take all personal belongings with you. Please refrain from smoking until you are well inside the terminal building. Thank you for flying British Airways and we wish you a pleasant onward journey.'

The intercom clunked off. Were any passengers so out of it that they did not know which day of the week it was, Finbar wondered. Possibly, if they had started their journey in Australia. He stared out of the scratched window at the distant lights of the terminal building. Lines of tiny jewelled red, green and blue runway lights glittered alongside the aircraft as it taxied then curved abruptly away, stretching into the darkness as it turned off the runway and headed slowly towards its gate. He sat still, admiring the beauty. Flying was an almost mystical experience for him and he did not despise people who found it terrifying. He never took it for granted, never sat reading a book or newspaper while the cabin crew demonstrated the use of lifejackets and pointed out emergency exits. The take-off run, the thrust as the aircraft lifted into the sky, the beauty of the stars and moon and fluffy cloud layer below, all entranced him. He had spent this short flight thinking about Shannon Flinder. And the deal made with Jan-Willem Hendriks, his contact in Amsterdam. One hundred rocket launchers, RPG-26s from Russia. They would arrive tomorrow and Finbar would sell them on to the gentleman from a certain embassy in London.

The aircraft slowed to a halt at its stand and the engines died to a whine. The few men in Business Class stood up and opened overhead lockers, reaching for coats and briefcases and yellow Amsterdam Schiphol airport carrier bags full of duty free. Bottles and seatbelts clinked. Finbar put on his black overcoat, smiled at the pink-lipsticked stewardess in her convent school hat, and stepped out of the aircraft, breathing in the icy air and the smell of aviation fuel. The terminal building was quiet and deserted. He went through Passport Control and headed straight for the green section, having no luggage to wait for and nothing to declare.

'Excuse me, sir.' A paunchy Customs official with a grey crew cut beckoned to him. 'Over here, please.'

They didn't usually pick on designer suits with briefcases, but concentrated on furtive Economy Class types who looked as though they had bought too much duty free – or something special from their little break in Amsterdam.

'Where have you come from, sir?' The official peered inside his briefcase and examined his passport.

'Amsterdam.'

'What was the purpose of your visit to Amsterdam?'

'Business,' he said quietly. 'And family.'

'Family?' The officer looked at him suspiciously, noting the soft Irish accent.

'My brother lives there. He's First Secretary at the Irish Embassy in The Hague.'

'The Irish Embassy?' The Customs man grinned. 'I see. And what kind of business are you in, sir?'

'Air freight. That was my business in Amsterdam.'

'All right.' The passport was thrust back. 'Thank you, sir.'

Finbar picked up his briefcase and moved on. A few minutes later he collected his Maserati from the multi-storey car park and drove off, carefully negotiating the complicated airport roundabout with its many entrances and exits. The M62 was busy, crowded with lorries heading for the cargo section of the airport, but his side had hardly any traffic. A 747 on final approach cruised low overhead, wing and tail lights blazing into the darkness.

Fifty minutes later Finbar pulled into Speke airport and drove to Linnell Air Cargo. He got out of the car and walked through the deserted hangar to the office. Mariska sat at the wooden desk, huddled in a fur coat, hands clasping a mug of steaming coffee.

'Hey!' She brightened as he walked in, her pale eyes speculative. 'How was Amsterdam? And Jan-Willem?' She held up the mug. 'You want coffee?'

'No, thanks, I got coffee on the plane.' He put down his briefcase and riffled through papers on the desk, checking bills of landing for Customs stamps and signatures. 'Jan-Willem's fine,' he said. 'And your native city's cold. Twelve below zero. The Amstel is frozen, or some of it anyway.'

'I think winter is very sexy, don't you?' She got up and came around the desk to stand close to him. 'Cold and dark. People hide in their homes, sit by the fire drinking wine. Making love,' she added, gazing at him slyly as she twisted long strands of black hair around her fingers, her thin lips slightly parted.

He ignored her and continued to check cargo manifests for agricultural machinery and engine spare parts, some genuine, some containing toys for the gentlemen in Dublin. A consignment of CZ 70 pistols was due late that afternoon from the Former Yugoslavia. He was thinking of sending Mariska back to Amsterdam. He didn't need her anymore and she was becoming a nuisance. He wanted a normal secretary, someone who did not wear fur coats and carry combat knives and undress him with her eyes.

'Is everything all right?' she asked, pushing her chin against his arm like a cat.

'Yep. Everything's in order.' He put down the papers and moved away from her. He couldn't get Shannon Flinder out of his mind. He had tried to call her again, this time to try and persuade her to have lunch with him, but she was either in court or at a police station or God knew where else. She was on leave this week, the giggly receptionist at Steele & Monckton had breathlessly informed him. Her telephone at home rang and rang. Something was wrong, he felt sure. His Merseyside police contact said Rob Flinder was at work as usual, but looking the worse for wear. Rumour was he had wife trouble. The man had chuckled. Not surprising for a copper married to a criminal lawyer.

What was wrong? Finbar stared at a poster of a smiling Dutch girl in traditional dress holding a bunch of violently yellow tulips. It must have been something unexpected – she had seemed so cool and confident the day they met, despite a slapping by that mad mother pissed off by due process of law. He felt protective towards her, wanted her to be happy. Even if she didn't want him. He thought of Majella and felt suddenly guilty, disloyal to her memory.

'You're doing it again,' Mariska said, staring at him.

He started and looked down at her. 'Doing what?'

'That intense look, that frown,' she said petulantly. 'You've found someone to screw, I know it.' She uncurled strands of hair from her fingers. 'Whoever the bitch is, she must be incredible. Tell me!' She pressed against him, smiling lasciviously. 'What's her *special* talent?'

'I wouldn't worry about that, Mariska, because you haven't got it.' He picked up the papers, slipped them in his briefcase and looked at the computer, the screen blank as usual. 'Why don't you get some work done instead of questioning me about my sex life? There's letters–.'

'You've got a *sex life*!' she hissed. 'I knew it!'

'What's the problem?' he asked, angry suddenly. 'Language barrier? Cultural differences?' He grabbed her by the hair and yanked her head back. 'Is that why you don't listen?'

'Stop it, you bastard!' she screamed, her eyes filling with tears. 'You're hurting me.'

'Why don't you listen?' he asked again. He yanked harder and she howled in pain. 'I'm telling you for the last time,' he said slowly, 'that our association is strictly business. That's all it ever will be.' He looked at her agonized face. She kept still, not daring to struggle. 'You only have to do the few simple things you're asked to do – take a plane here and there, oversee the consignments that arrive. Make appointments, type letters. Keep your mouth shut, mind your own business. Remember you're in a position of trust. Is that clear?' he asked quietly. 'Tell me it's clear?'

'It's clear!' she gasped.

'Good.' He let go and shoved her against the wall with the poster.

'You bastard!' she spat, rubbing her sore head vigorously.

'I'm surprised you go around Liverpool or Amsterdam – anywhere – with that thing on.' He nodded at the mink coat, pale grey like her wolverine eyes. 'You'll get paint thrown over it.' Shannon would never wear fur, he thought. Why did he feel he knew so much about her?

Mariska went back around the desk. 'Anyone doesn't like my beautiful mink . . .' she reached inside the coat and drew out her gleaming combat knife, its tip horribly serrated . . . 'they can see how they like *this*!' Her eyes shone as she stared at the blade. How she would love to use it on the bitch Finbar was screwing! He wouldn't want her anymore when Mariska had finished carving creative designs across her face and tits and belly. Who was it, she wondered. Someone from the club? She would have Finbar one day, she thought. No man rejected her in the end. It would just take longer. He was that almost unheard-of creature, a man who didn't think with his dick.

Finbar checked his watch. He'd go to the apartment, take a shower and rest before meeting with the man from Dublin, Lenny Dowd. He'd tell him that Eastbrook was the last job. If he didn't like it, tough. He had married Majella, not her family and the Republican cause; causes and people who espoused them were a massive pain in the arse, source of all trouble in the world. And Majella was dead. This Friday – November 22 – would have been her twenty-eighth birthday. Roiseann would have been running around, laughing, calling them Mummy and Daddy. The big bad wolf nothing more than a fairy tale. Finbar closed his eyes and shivered. March 15 was the fourth anniversary of their death and – incredibly – the date of Eastbrook's visit to Merseyside. Unlike flying, this was meant to be. Rupert would pay for his government's death-dealing policies with his own death. Moral justice. The only kind that mattered. Finbar opened his eyes and breathed deeply to calm himself. Mariska was still gazing at her revolting knife.

'Put that thing away,' he said sharply, and picked up his briefcase. 'Right. I'm off. I'll be at the apartment most of the day. Give me a call when the flower bulbs arrive from Rotterdam.' The 'flower bulbs' were ammunition for hand guns.

'*Ja, Mijnheer*!' she said sarcastically. She slid the knife into its black leather sheath and replaced it in the coat's inner pocket.

'See you.'

He strode out of the hangar where sleepy-looking men in blue overalls were arriving for work, got back in the warm car and drove to his apartment, parking the Maserati in the car park reserved for residents of the dockside apartments. He entered the building, a converted warehouse near the Maritime Museum and the Museum of Liverpool Life, and climbed the three flights of stairs to his apartment. He unlocked the heavy front door, switched on the hall light and strolled into the massive living room, dropping his keys on the rectangular pine coffee table. and walking to the windows to look out across the Mersey.

The lights of Birkenhead glittered across the dark water. Dawn was coming up. There were no ships out. Downstream was the Princes Dock and the remains of Riverside Station, where ocean liner passengers had once embarked for New York, the wealthier ones having spent the night in the Adelphi Hotel, favourite of Charles Dickens and famed for its turtle soup. He watched as the cloud layer parted and the sky lightened. Was Shannon asleep? What did she dream about? He shook his head, as if the impatient movement could shake her out of his brain. He switched on the central heating, threw off his overcoat and went into the big stainless steel kitchen to grind coffee beans.

He had a headache, felt exhausted after a night of drinking with Jan-Willem, in the various Amsterdam bars where he met his contacts. Then in the old house by the canal where the rocket launchers were stored. But the deal was done. He poured water into the coffee machine, switched it on and went back to the living room, pulling off his tie. Rays of pale yellow winter sunshine touched the whitewashed walls and crept across the shiny parquet floor towards the two soft squashy blue leather sofas placed at right-angles to one another. The apartment was vast; he thought the sweet pungent smell of spices still lingered in its old walls. There were no plants or pictures. The only picture he owned, a photograph of Majella cuddling Roiseann, he kept in a drawer in his bedroom. One long wall was lined with bookshelves from floor to ceiling.

The huge austerely furnished space began to warm up and the aroma of Blue Mountain coffee drifted from the kitchen. Finbar poured himself a cup, added a flat teaspoon of sugar and took it into the bedroom. No one but he slept in the king size bed. The quilt and pillowcases were smooth, the way he had left them. The two bedroom windows overlooked the still waters of the Albert Dock. Colourful boats were moored around its sides. At this hour of the morning there were no tourists or visitors to the restaurants, coffee shops and assorted craft, sweets and souvenir shops that lined the dock's colonnades. There was also the Tate Gallery; he'd never been in it. The Russian Navy ship was gone from its berth outside the Maritime Museum.

He drank the coffee, stripped off his clothes and went into the adjoining bathroom with its mirrored walls, jacuzzi and frosted glass shower cabinet. Finbar never used the jacuzzi. He ran the shower and stepped inside the steamy cabinet, lifting his head, enjoying the feel of the hot stream of water on his body. He lathered himself with shower gel, his penis stiffening as he thought of Shannon again. He would love to fuck her – in this shower, in the jacuzzi, in bed, on the sofa. Anywhere. Did she like him, or was that wishful thinking? Testosterone pumping through his bloodstream, filling his brain with delusions? He stepped out of the shower, took a towel and wrapped it round his waist. He shook out his wet black hair. His green eyes in the steamy mirror looked fierce, predatory. Was he a predator? Would he be involved with PIRA had not the Brits murdered Majella and Roiseann? The 'favours' he did them – and himself – guns, drugs, lending cars and aircraft to transport 'active service units' – would be a thing of the past once the balding pinstripe blob was out of the way. His death wouldn't bring back Majella and Roiseann, but it was better than festering away in misery and despair at their loss. Finbar wished he had never set eyes on Shannon Flinder. She made him think all that might not be so important anymore. Again, he felt he was betraying Majella. And Shannon didn't want him, did she?

He put on a thick white cotton towelling robe, went to pour

himself more coffee and was drinking it when the buzzer went, pressed long and hard. He went into the hall and picked up the intercom phone.

'Hello?' he said guardedly.

'It's me. Let me in, you bastard.'

'Come up.' He pressed the buzzer, opened his front door and lounged in the doorway waiting, coffee cup in hand. Slow footsteps trudged up the wide stone staircase and he heard Lenny panting and swearing. The stink of his clove cigarettes preceded him.

'You'd think you were seventy-six, not twenty-six,' he remarked as Lenny Dowd appeared at the top of the stairs, gasping for breath and frowning, cigarette dangling from his beautiful curved lips. He was the same build as Finbar, tall and thin and broad-shouldered, with angry dark eyes and thick tangled dark brown hair that reached to his shoulders. He had the pale complexion of someone who spent most of his time in bars and beds.

'Holy fuck, Finbar!' he panted. Finbar stood back to let him in. 'Can you not get somewhere with a lift, for Christ's sake?'

'It's only three flights, it should be nothing to you.' He looked at Lenny's jeans and combat jacket. 'D'you have to go around looking like you've just come from a shoot-out with the Brits in South Armagh?' he asked coldly.

Lenny laughed. 'What should I do – be like you? Get all dressed up in designer suits? Be the big man?'

'I'm a businessman,' Finbar said shortly.

'Sure you are, Finbar. Sure.' He walked into the stainless steel kitchen and looked round disapprovingly. 'Not very cosy in here, is it?'

Finbar held up his cup. 'D'you want some coffee?'

'No. I'm thirsty. Have you got a beer? Let's have a look.' Lenny opened the big fridge and took out a bottle of Grolsch. 'How about some breakfast?' He eyed the bacon, eggs and sausages.

'You'll have to cook it yourself.'

Lenny banged the fridge door shut and turned round. 'What you need, Finbar my man, is a good woman in your bed and kitchen.' He swigged the beer. 'I can't be bothered to do that myself.' He yawned. 'I'm knackered. Been up all night with that wee blonde who goes to your club, the one with the tits. Christ, she–.'

'Save it, Lenny. We've got something more important to talk about.'

'Whatever you say, chief.'

They went into the sunny living room and sat down. Lenny stretched out his long legs and sighed.

'I'm not used to being up at this hour.' He looked at his watch. 'Jesus, it's only half-eight.' He swigged beer and glanced around the huge room. 'I don't suppose there's an ashtray in the place?' He coughed. 'I wouldn't want to spoil your lovely floor.'

Finbar got up and fetched a saucer from the kitchen. 'The way I see it,' he began, 'there's only one option.' He sat down and picked up his coffee cup. 'There's no point trying to hit him at Salmesbury, we've got no chance there. The best bet is the Maritime Museum.'

'A bomb?' Lenny took another *Kretek* from the red-and-gold pack, lit it and blew out sweet clove-smelling smoke. 'In the Maritime Museum?' He laughed and slapped his knee. 'Send the bastard down with the *Titanic*! Sweet!'

'It can't be done until he's in there. The police and Special Branch will be all over the place, and the car parks will be closed for the day. It has to be done inside, while he's there. We could hit him when he gets in or out of his car but they'll expect that, be watching out for it. And you never know, there might be some have-a-go wanker in the crowd who'd try to wrestle the gun off me.'

'An old Brit war hero with a red beret and wooden leg?' Lenny sucked in smoke, coughed and burst out laughing. "I fought Herr Hitler, you know." He mimicked an upper class English accent. "I can deal with some common little tosser of a Paddy any day of the week, don't you worry about *that*!" The old bastard'll be on the six o' clock news, so he will.'

Finbar drank the rest of his coffee and put the cup down. He wrinkled his nose. 'Those cigarettes stink!'

'I love them. They're Indonesian.' Lenny held up the red-and-gold pack. 'Got them in Amsterdam.'

'So–.' Finbar leaned back on the sofa. 'We hit him inside the Maritime Museum. And it's got to be a one-man job.'

You mean, we won't need an active service unit?' Lenny looked puzzled. 'How's that?'

'On the day – no one'll be allowed in except the security forces, local councillors and business people,' Finbar explained patiently. 'They're having a reception for him after the guided tour. They were going to have it at the Town Hall, but they changed their minds.'

'How do you know all this?' Lenny asked suspiciously.

'None of your business.' His contact in the Merseyside Police Force had been very helpful. 'I'll be invited to that reception, I'll have the run of the place. I can plant the bomb then. It's too risky to do it beforehand, they'll sweep the building.'

'Get away with you! You'll be frisked going in.'

'They'll frisk cleaners and catering staff. They won't want to offend the prominent guests.'

'Where will you plant it? And how d'you know it won't just blow the fat bastard's leg off?'

'Believe me . . .' Finbar started to laugh. 'Don't worry about that. I'll find a good spot near him. Nothing will go wrong.'

'And how will you avoid being blown to kingdom come?'

'I'll get out before it blows, what d'you think? Would you miss me?' Finbar began to feel angry. 'Let me worry about that,' he said. 'What does it matter as long as the job gets done?'

'You're right, Finbar, you're right,' Lenny said loudly. He waved the bottle at him. 'I'm just concerned for your personal safety, that's all.'

'I'm very touched.' He was silent. 'It's important I do this job myself,' he said after a minute.

'Oh, I get it.' Lenny looked at him and smiled. 'Personal, is it?' he asked softly. 'Your own personal *jihad*?' He knew about the wife and baby daughter – and something else. Not something he would tell Finbar. Ever.

'We don't need you, you know, Finbar,' he laughed. 'We're big boys. We can do it all by ourselves.'

'Yeah. You can get invited to receptions for Defence Secretaries. That's the only option in this case, and you know it.

Otherwise it's another operation down the pan. High ranking army council faces splattered with crap. Not good for your image, Lenny. You don't want to mess up on this one.'

Lenny was silent, smoking and thinking. He was one of the youngest commanders. No operation of his had failed and he didn't want this to go wrong. Finbar would do it, but Lenny would get the credit. He finished his beer.

'How much d'you want?' he asked. 'We haven't discussed that.'

'Nothing. I'll do it gratis. It's the last time.'

'The last time what?' he asked, astonished.

'The last job,' Finbar said quietly, and looked at him. 'The end of my association with your organization. In every way.'

'Just like that?' Lenny stared at him. What was he up to?

'Just like that.'

'Why?'

'I've told you. I do this for nothing because it's the last time. Then that's it. All accounts settled. Finish.'

He smiled. Lenny was not pleased, he knew. He would go back to Dublin and discuss this with High Command, and they wouldn't like it either. But they would not want to give up on this. If they wanted the perfect hit, a hit that would strike fear into the heart of the British government, they had no choice. And afterwards they would have to let him go.

Lenny stood up and put his empty beer bottle on the coffee table. 'I've got a plane to catch. Going back to Dublin.' He walked to the front door and Finbar followed. 'I'll look in on the trial of an informer when I get there,' he said casually. 'We've got him locked up in a holiday cottage out of town.' He laughed. 'He thinks he can make a deal with us, but all he'll get is a bullet in the back of the neck. And a priest – if he's lucky.'

'Why tell me?' Finbar opened the door.

'No reason.' Lenny turned and looked at him, his dark luminous eyes full of laughter. 'No reason at all. Talk to you soon, eh?' He clapped Finbar on the shoulder. 'Thanks for the beer. You take care now.' He went down the stairs laughing. 'Take care.'

Chapter Ten

'Excuse me for interrupting, Mr Flinder.'

Bernard glanced up as his fat dowdy bespectacled secretary Irene Watchet came into his panelled office overlooking the school playing fields, carrying a sheaf of letters for signature. Her face looked more pale and drawn than usual and her thin chapped lips were compressed in a tight line. The pockets of her brown wool home-knitted cardigan bulged with scented tissues and eucalyptus mints wrapped in crackly cellophane. He would have preferred a sexy teenage girl as secretary but Irene was extremely efficient and dedicated and her presence guaranteed, if not glamour, the absolute security of his reputation.

'Thank you, Irene.' He took the letters and uncapped his fountain pen. He could smell eucalyptus. 'Friday afternoon again already, eh? Thank goodness for the weekend.' He smiled up at her. 'Are you feeling all right?' he asked. 'You look a bit pale to me.'

'Fine, thank you, Mr Flinder.' She blushed and twisted her rough hands together. 'Well, actually, I do have a bit of a headache,' she confessed. A 'bit' of a headache that two extra strong painkillers wouldn't shift. It was like Mr Flinder to notice she wasn't well. Other people looked forward to the weekend; she dreaded it. Stuck in the cramped little house in Bootle with Mother, run ragged from morning until night, a nasty foretaste of the unpaid, unloved, uncared-for 'carer' existence that awaited her when she retired in two years' time. Retirement, that was a laugh. She went to work to relax. To escape.

'Is everything all right?' he persisted, looking closely at her. How handsome he was, she thought, so tall and well built, such a well trimmed moustache and good head of hair. And that smart tweed suit. He looked like a Victorian gentleman. 'Sit down a minute.'

Irene obeyed. 'Well – it's very kind of you to ask,' she said awkwardly. 'I don't want to keep you from your work.'

'Nonsense! What would I do without you?' He paused. 'The old lady playing up again, is that it?'

'She is a trial, Mr Flinder.' Depression swept over Irene. 'I had a terrible time with her this morning before I got off to work. She screamed at me, called me a–.' She blushed again, compressed her lips and looked down at her clenched hands. 'She threw her tea and grapefruit and bowl of cereal on the floor. That's why I was a few minutes late, I had to clean up the mess. When I went home at lunchtime there was a leak in the kitchen ceiling. She'd let the bathroom sink overflow, there was water everywhere. She's not senile or anything, just . . .' Irene stopped again. 'Well, to be honest, she's just bloody-minded!' she burst out.

Bernard wanted to laugh. It was the first time in twenty years he had heard Irene swear.

'She says I should give up my job and stay at home to look after her,' the secretary went on, kneading her hands together as though she were making bread. 'But I'll have to do that anyway in two years' time. I need to work another two to make sure I get a decent pension. I've no husband to look after me,' she said bitterly. 'Mother saw to that. She was always horrible to anyone I brought home.'

'It must be very hard for you,' said Bernard sympathetically, looking at the straight dry grey hair, worn short and parted to one side like some Thirties' schoolgirl, the flat chest beneath the drab cardigan and the gnarled veiny hands. He wondered if she had ever had sex with anyone; he thought not. She fancied him, of course, had done for years. Not only was she an ugly bitch, though, she was at least fifty years too old for his tastes. His black eyes gleamed with laughter. He leaned across the desk and bestowed his most charming smile on her.

'Like a lot of dedicated ladies, you've got two full-time jobs. Here and at home.'

She nodded tiredly. 'That's *certainly* true, Mr Flinder. You're so understanding!' That stuck-up wife of his didn't realize how lucky she was.

'Take the rest of the afternoon off,' Bernard urged. Miserable old bitch, always down in the mouth and stinking of eucalyptus! He'd had enough of her for one week. 'Start your weekend early.' He smiled. 'Don't go home to the old lady just yet. Take the bus into town and have a wander round George Henry Lee's or Lewis's or somewhere. Get a cup of tea and a cream cake. Look after yourself, give yourself a treat. You need it more than most of us.'

'It's very kind of you, Mr Flinder,' Irene said gratefully. She basked in the warmth of his concern, something she received from no other human being. 'But it's very cold and rainy today, I don't feel like going into town. I think I'll stay here.'

'As you wish.' He leaned back in his chair. 'But don't do anymore work on the computer for the moment, it's bad for your eyes. Won't help the headache either. Take it easy for the rest of the day.' He glanced at his watch and smiled again. 'Why don't you make us both a cup of your wonderful tea? I'd love some. Be good for your headache too.'

'Of course, Mr Flinder.' She got up and went to the door.

'And remember!' he said warningly. Irene turned. 'No more work on the computer today, is that understood?'

'Yes, Mr Flinder.' She smiled and went out, closing the door quietly. What a wonderful man he was, so kind and considerate, a real gentleman. So *charming* to everyone! How would she cope in two years time when she had to retire from St Fidelma's? She hurried into the tiny kitchen adjoining her office, put the kettle on and got out the delicate flowered china cups with their pattern of leaves and wild strawberries. They both agreed tea tasted so much better in china cups.

Could she stay on longer, she wondered, say another five years instead of two? She practically ran the school, he said so often enough. She cheered up slightly. Why should he have to get used to a new secretary? He would hate that. Some silly young girl who cared more for boyfriends and clothes than typing proper reports or drafting the polished articulate letters she was so good at. She took another extra strong painkiller from the packet on the drainboard, swallowed it with fizzy lemonade and stared out of the small window across the deserted rainwashed tennis courts.

Bernard's phone rang and he picked it up. 'Bernard Flinder speaking,' he said quietly. 'Can I help you?'

'It's me.' The man had a thick Scouse accent and his voice was low and cautious.

'Just a minute.' Bernard got up and opened the door. The clink of china came from the little kitchen. He closed the door, sat down again and picked up the receiver. 'What d'you want?' he asked. He cleared his throat, which was dry from central heating and the dusty chalky school atmosphere. He could do with that tea.

'I've got good news for you, Bernie.' The man giggled. 'I called Ron because I couldn't get hold of that other fella I told you about. He'll sell you the videotapes.'

'Tapes? I thought you said there was only one.'

'Yeah, that's what I thought. But now he says he's got five or six. It's fifty quid a tape,' he said, upping the price by fifteen pounds. Bernie could afford it. 'Bloody good value for what you get,' he added. 'You won't be disappointed.'

'Fifty pounds each?' Bernard said slowly. 'That's a bit steep.'

'I told you, Bernie, they're bloody good value. And hard to get nowadays. It's more dodgy – we're not all as lucky as you, never been caught and banged up. Look,' he said, growing impatient, 'if you don't want the bloody things, just say so. I've got plenty of customers who'll pay well over the odds-.'

'I'll take them,' he said abruptly. 'I suppose they're copies. Can they be exchanged when I've finished with them?'

'Maybe,' the nasal voice said. 'We'll see. Right! You want, I've got. I need to get shot of them quick sharp. Where and when?'

Bernard thought. 'I haven't got time now. It's Friday afternoon and I can't leave school yet. And I don't have the cash on me. I'll meet you tomorrow at twelve-thirty. In Sefton Park, by the boating lake. All right?'

'Right you are, Bernie. See you then. Don't worry, you won't be disappointed.'

He put the phone down and sat there thinking, breath

quickening as he thought of what would be on the tapes. Smooth, hairless, immature female bodies, innocent eyes staring at the camera, pupils dilated with Ecstasy – or maybe shock and pain. He jumped as Irene knocked at the door and walked in.

'Here you are, Mr Flinder,' she said proudly. 'One sugar, a bit of milk, just the way you like it.'

He swallowed. 'Thank you, Irene.'

She lingered, hoping for more comments about her efficiency and wonderful tea then left, closing the door maddeningly slowly and quietly. He longed to get home, pour a big Scotch and shut himself in his study. He sipped the hot sweet tea, wishing he could go home that minute. He sighed impatiently as Irene knocked at the door again. The old bitch couldn't leave him alone today. She probably fantasised about him. What a revolting thought!

'I'm sorry to bother you again, Mr Flinder,' the secretary said apologetically. 'But Mrs Flinder, your daughter-in-law, is here. She'd like to speak to you for a few minutes.'

Shannon, here? Amazed, he put down the half-finished cup of tea. She hardly ever visited his home or invited him and Margaret to hers. Now here she was at his school. What could she possibly want? He felt vaguely uneasy, the way he always did when anything unexpected happened. Bernard had a hatred of surprises.

'Well, I suppose I can spare my daughter-in-law a few minutes,' he said with false heartiness. 'This *is* a pleasant surprise,' he lied. 'Show her in, will you, Irene?'

'Of course. Come in, please, Mrs Flinder,' she called. 'We were just having our afternoon tea. Would you like a cup?'

'No, thank you.' Shannon appeared, a Shannon he'd never seen before. Her long curly gold hair was dishevelled, she wore no make-up and her violet eyes were wild and red-rimmed. Her face was pale and she looked very upset, the customary cool confidence gone. Her tight black velvet top, tartan jeans and black leather coat meant she hadn't come straight from her office. What was going on? Irene lingered, smiling stupidly.

'Dreadful weather today, isn't it?' she commented. 'Rain, and that awful icy gale – straight from Siberia, I imagine.'

'I need to speak to you in private.' Shannon ignored Irene and fixed her father-in-law with a glare of such hatred that his unease turned to alarm.

'Thank you, Irene.' He sprang up and walked to the door. 'Why don't you go home?' he said. 'Just go home. Now.'

Something in his voice warned her it wouldn't be a good idea to go on about Siberian gales or Mother or traipsing around George Henry Lee's.

'Well, all right, Mr Flinder. But I–.'

'Have a good weekend, won't you?' The door slammed in her face.

How could he say that? He knew her weekends were never good! She went to collect her coat and handbag, feeling slighted. What did that rude, badly dressed girl want? Irene had never met his daughter-in-law before. She was certainly beautiful to look at, but her manners left a lot to be desired. She was upset, that was obvious. Everyone ran to Mr Flinder with their problems! Suddenly Irene felt like going to a pub, an old-fashioned Victorian pub with mirrors and panelling and coloured glass, and drinking one brandy after another until she slid into a coma and didn't have to worry about anything or anyone again. She switched off the computer, picked up the damp umbrella and left to start her weekend from hell.

In the office Shannon faced Bernard Flinder. 'I know about you,' she said simply. 'What you are.'

'My dear girl, I can see you're upset.' He was seized with panic. His breath came quicker and his palms were clammy with sweat. He took refuge behind his desk. What *did* she know? 'But I'm afraid I don't have the faintest idea what you're talking about.' He fought down panic and burning indigestion.

'Don't waste time denying it.' Her voice rose and he glanced nervously at the panelled door. Had the old bitch gone? He didn't dare get up and look. 'I know what you are,' she repeated, staring at him. 'I know you're a paedophile.'

Bernard flinched and his face turned a sickly white. This is it, he thought. This is what I've been terrified of all these years. What the hell am I going to do?

'You raped Melanie when she was three years old and went on raping her for years,' Shannon said shrilly. 'You got her pregnant when she was thirteen and made her have an abortion.'

'I wouldn't advise you to believe anything Melanie tells you,' he interrupted, struggling to pull himself together, deal with this horrendous shock. He'd never believed his daughter would open her mouth. Just deny it, he thought. She can't prove anything. 'I thought you had more intelligence? Melanie's a very confused individual – she can't tell the difference between fantasy and reality. She has a lot of problems.'

'Caused by *you*!' Shannon flashed.

'Rubbish! I'm afraid all this nonsense is the product of my unfortunate daughter's very warped imagination,' he said weakly. He tried not to show his terror, the panic that made his stomach churn and his heart race. What would she do? He rubbed his sweating hands on his trousers.

'That's what I thought at first,' Shannon said. *'Hoped.* But your reaction just confirmed it – not that I really needed confirmation.'

'My reaction?' he echoed. 'What reaction?' Think straight, he urged himself. Pull yourself together. She's got no evidence. Melanie could easily be dismissed as an alcoholic mental case. Neither of them can do anything. 'I won't tolerate these ridiculous accusations,' he said boldly. 'From you or from Melanie. It's disgraceful. *Hurtful.* If you think you can walk in here and interrogate me like this, you're mistaken,' he went on, easing into the role of outraged innocent. 'I've tried to be a good father to that ungrateful girl, always had her best interests at heart. Now *this*!' he spat. 'This is all the thanks I get for years of sacrifice. Children are supposed to bring joy,' he continued, 'but we don't often hear about the sorrow and misery they can cause.' He stared down at his sweating hands. 'I suppose that's a cross I'll have to bear,' he said sadly.

'Stop it, you lying hypocrite!' Shannon's eyes blazed. 'I don't believe I'm hearing this! I'm not proud of myself,' she said bitterly, 'but I don't actually care that much about Melanie. I'm not here because of her.'

He raised his eyes and looked at her. 'Then why?'

'I've been drinking and crying myself stupid since Monday morning because–.' She stopped, voice cracking. 'Rob's left me!'

she wailed. 'He says he doesn't want to be married anymore – doesn't want children. He wants to go away somewhere, says he's going to start a new life. And it's all because of you, you pervert! Melanie told him what you are, and what you did to her. He's in shock, he's going through some sort of crisis. He won't let me help him. Thinks it's his fault for not protecting his sister. He thinks he could be a monster like you. I want you to talk to him, tell him that's rubbish.' Shannon bowed her head, crying bitterly.

Bernard sat staring at her, stroking his moustache. Slowly his confidence began to return. She was upset, and she had no proof. He could deal with this. She looked very young and very vulnerable, more like fourteen than twenty-six. Almost young enough to . . . So his son had walked out on her, eh? That was a surprise. Not that Bernard gave a damn about it. And she was all alone in that big house.

'You're not going to ruin our lives.' Shannon pulled a handkerchief from her pocket and wiped her eyes. 'I won't let that happen. You're going to talk to Rob, then confess to the police. You must have raped other young girls. Well, you won't do it again! You're going to jail.'

'The police? My dear girl!' he exclaimed again, looking at her, mouth twitching nervously. 'I can understand you're upset because your husband has left you. That's a terrible thing to happen to any woman and I'm very sorry. I believe marriage is for life – even a Registry Office marriage. What Robert's done is wrong, of course, but I'm afraid he'll have to sort himself out. I have no intention of admitting to him – and certainly not to the police! – that any of these ridiculous accusations you've made are true. You can't possibly expect that of me.'

'He's in shock!' cried Shannon. 'He might have a breakdown because of you. Don't you care about your own son?'

'Robert's a grown man, I can't accept responsibility for his actions. Has it occurred to you that you yourself might be in some way to blame?'

'*What*?' She stopped crying and stared at him.

'You haven't exactly been the most devoted of wives, have you? When you marry a man you have to put him first. Not your career.'

'I always put Rob first,' she protested, exhausted and discouraged by his intransigence. 'We love each other – we were happy until he found out about you! Okay,' she said, 'if you won't go to the police, I will. You're not going to hurt anymore young girls, I won't let you. You're going to jail.'

'Don't be ridiculous!' said Bernard sharply. 'You need evidence to put someone in jail. You're a lawyer, you know that better than most. Besides, who's going to believe a hysterical deserted wife?' he sneered. 'A hysterical deserted wife who drinks too much? You can't prove anything.' He sat back, heavy body trembling.

'I'll prove it,' she said icily. 'I'll get evidence. You're not as clever as you think. I'll tell everyone about you. My husband's left me, my life's falling apart because of *you*. I've nothing left to lose. And you've got everything. What will friends and colleagues and the Knights of St bloody Columba think?'

'You won't tell anyone!' he gasped and felt himself blanch again. 'They'd never believe you. They wouldn't believe a pathetic deserted wife who's turned bitter and twisted and wants to blame her husband's family.'

'Don't count on it. No smoke without fire, is there?' she jeered. 'That's what people always think. Enough mud will stick.' She paused. 'I'm going to ruin you,' she said slowly. 'You won't hurt another girl. You're finished.'

'No!' He jumped up, pushing his chair back. 'Think!' he stammered, terrified. 'Think what trouble you could cause yourself! If you go around accusing me you could get yourself into a lot of trouble. It could ruin your career – your life – if people think you're related to a – a–.'

'A *paedophile*! That's the word, Bernie. And I don't *care*!' Shannon blazed. 'You don't get it, do you? You're *finished*. I'll make sure of that. You've already ruined my life, now I'm going to ruin yours. You're going to get what you deserve.'

She meant it. Panic crashed over him. He had to stop her. But how? He jumped in terror as he heard laughter and voices outside. There was a knock at the door. A young, fair-haired man in a green Army sweater came in, followed by two grinning boys in school uniform, heavy bags slung over their shoulders.

'Sorry, Bernard! Am I disturbing you?' the young man asked

anxiously, sensing the atmosphere in the room. He looked at them, embarrassed. Bernard smoothed his tie and coughed nervously.

'What can I do for you, Greg?' he asked weakly. 'Don't worry, this young lady was just about to leave, weren't you?' He glanced desperately at Shannon, not meeting her gaze. Don't let her say anything, he prayed. Please God!

She was silent, breathing hard. The three newcomers looked at her and she knew what they were thinking. She looked upset. What was the matter with her? Bernard's words sprang to mind. Female, hysterical, out of control. Bitter and twisted because her husband had walked out on her. A failure at that most vital of female objectives – holding on to a man. He was right. Who would listen to her? Evidence, she thought. Get that first.

She stumbled out of the office, ran down the corridor and pushed her way through crowds of departing students to the swing doors at the main entrance. In the car park rain and icy wind hit her face. The car, she thought. Search his car. There might be something there.

She darted between the lines of parked cars looking for Bernard's blue Volvo, half blinded by wind and rain. It was by the wall of the Science block, the privileged spot guarded by white lines and a weatherbeaten board marked 'Private: Headmaster'. She peered inside, sweeping raindrops off the cold window.

A soiled yellow cloth, a canister of anti-freeze, a box of blue cardboard files on the back seat. What did she think she'd find? You're breaking into someone's car, she thought. Are you crazy? 'It's not just *someone*,' she whispered.

She banged on the window with her fists then straightened up and glanced round, averting her eyes from a passing middle-aged woman in a black coat and tartan scarf. The woman did not look at her but hurried on, groping in her bag for car keys, head bent and shoulders hunched against the wind and rain. Shannon looked desperately for something to smash the window with, and spotted a pile of bricks at the foot of steps leading up to double doors. She grabbed one, looked furtively around to make sure no one was watching, took a deep breath and crashed it through the driver's window.

She laughed. It felt good. She ducked into the car, closed the door and opened the glove compartment. It contained the Volvo's manual, a street map of Liverpool, a carton of latex gloves, a packet of condoms and a packet of Dolly Mixtures. Shannon shivered as she looked at them. She climbed into the back and scrabbled around on the floor. Her hand strayed beneath the driver's seat and grasped a tiny cold plastic foot. She gasped and pulled harder. Out slid a Barbie doll with long blonde tangled hair and naked plastic moulded breasts, dressed in a pair of dirty pink cotton jeans, a torn pink thread where the top button had been.

'Bianca!' she gasped, horrified, remembering news reports about the doll. She clutched it to her chest. Her father-in-law had murdered Bianca Mitchell, the poor little girl whose body had been found raped, battered and strangled in Calderstones Park. Incredible that he had left the doll there, under the driver's seat in his car. Was he so stupid, so arrogant? So *confident*? Waves of fear swept over her, shaking her body, and she cried, trying to imagine what agony, what fear the poor child must have gone through before her precious beautiful life was so cruelly snuffed out. How could any human being do that to another, especially to a helpless child? She saw Bernard Flinder's black eyes gazing at her. He was not a human being! He was a devil, a demon. Something evil. He should be snuffed out!

'Pull yourself together,' she whispered. 'Stay calm. You have to get out of here, go home. Think what to do.'

Icy fear seized her again. She got out of the car and looked around. He was capable of murder and she'd threatened to expose him. She could be in terrible danger. She ran out of the school gates and got into the Nissan Nomad, clutching the doll to her chest as though it were a precious baby. Or little Bianca. She put the doll carefully on the seat beside her and drove off, blaring the horn at a group of grinning schoolgirls who strolled across the road, bags and scarves trailing on the ground.

'Bitch! Watch it!' They jumped out of the way and Shannon sped down the road, brakes screaming as she slammed to a halt at the junction on the main road, wet cold hands sliding on the wheel.

'Locks!' she muttered, glancing impatiently to right and left at the slow stream of school run traffic. 'Get more locks. Just to be safe.'

Alone in his office, Bernard Flinder picked up the phone and dialled.

'Good afternoon. Steele & Monckton, how may I help you?' Go away, Anita the receptionist felt like saying. I want my weekend.

'Good afternoon. I'd like to speak to Mr Gavin Steele, please. It's rather urgent.'

It always was. 'One moment, please.' She couldn't be bothered to ask his name but he sounded self-important, like most of Gavin's clients. Anita put him straight through.

'Yes? Gavin Steele speaking.'

'Oh, Mr Steele, good afternoon. This is Bernard Flinder, Shannon Flinder's father-in-law.'

There was a pause. 'Yes?'

'Well – I'm very sorry to interrupt you at work but I'm extremely concerned about my daughter-in-law's state of mind.' Bernard clutched the phone. 'She burst into my office here at school a few moments ago, hysterical, and screaming that her husband – my son – had deserted her and she didn't know what to do.' He laughed awkwardly. 'I'm afraid her breath smelled as though she'd been drinking again, although of course she denied it when I questioned her. She's gone now, I don't know where. My wife and I want to help her – help them both – but she swears she doesn't need help. I wondered if she's been under a lot of pressure at work, if you've noticed any changes in her behaviour recently?'

Gavin sighed and played with the tiny Zwarowski crystal teddy bear he kept on his desk, a birthday present from his teenage daughter Olivia.

'She was rather upset on Monday morning,' he said reluctantly. 'I told her to take the rest of the week off, get herself sorted. I thought she'd just had a row with her husband. I didn't realize things were this serious.' Great, he thought angrily.

'I'm afraid they are.' Bernard coughed. 'My wife and I are very concerned that the stress of this marital break up – we hope it won't be permanent, of course – might bring back her depression. I'm sure she's stopped taking her medication . . .

'Medication?' Gavin echoed in alarm. 'Depression?'

'Oh, yes. She has a history of mental illness – depression. I'm afraid her parents aren't interested, they were never very sympathetic. She doesn't see them any more. We've given her a lot of support but . . .' He stopped. 'You didn't know about her depression?' he asked, adopting a surprised tone.

'No,' Gavin said grimly. 'I didn't. She omitted to mention it in her curriculum vitae.' Bloody bitch, he thought. She can forget a partnership.

'Er – if she turns up at work next week and she's in a hysterical state, could you possibly let me know?' Bernard asked. 'She's a free woman, of course, I can't keep tabs on her, but as I said, my wife and I are very concerned. I'm afraid my son's not much use at the moment, he's too upset. He feels betrayed, you see.'

'Betrayed?'

'Well, I understand that there was another man involved. Several men, in fact.' He paused to let this sink in. 'I'll just give you my telephone number.' He read it out slowly. Gavin didn't bother to scribble it down. So she was a slapper as well!

'Thank you very much for your cooperation, Mr Steele. Shannon's very lucky to have you for an employer. Your firm is one of the finest in Liverpool – in the north-west,' he added. 'You have a wonderful reputation.'

'A reputation I intend to safeguard,' Gavin snapped. 'Thank you for calling, Mr Flinder.'

'Goodbye. Have a pleasant weekend with your family.'

'Thanks a lot!' Gavin slammed the phone down and stared at the crystal teddy bear which winked and sparkled in the light from the desk lamp. 'Brilliant,' he murmured. 'Just bloody brilliant!'

Chapter Eleven

'Landing card, ma'am?'

'What?' Melanie opened her eyes and looked into the beautiful, perfectly made-up face of the Singapore Airlines stewardess. Her shining black hair was pulled back in a bun and secured with a lethal looking bamboo stick, and her narrow slit ankle-length skirt and V-necked batik top were tight across her tiny waist and full bust. They all looked like supermodels, she thought drowsily. No wonder this was one of the most popular airlines.

'Do you need a landing card, ma'am?' the girl repeated politely. She flourished the stack of white cards in her delicate hand.

'I don't know. We're not landing yet, are we?' Melanie glanced at the blackness outside the window. 'I thought we only took off about twenty minutes ago?'

'That's right. Is another thirteen and a half hours' flying time, ma'am.' The girl's painted red lips curved in a smile. 'But we always give out landing cards at the start of the flight. Is easier for us and for you. Then you can relax and enjoy. You need landing card if you will stay more than one night in Singapore,' she explained.

'Oh. Okay.' Melanie took the card and picked up her plastic glass. 'Can you get me another drink?' she asked. 'Double vodka.'

'Certainly, ma'am. Ice and lemon?'

'No thanks.'

'Do you have your menu card, ma'am?' She fished the card out of the seat pocket, unfolded it and laid it on Melanie's tray, moving aside the unopened packet of dry roasted peanuts. 'We will start to serve dinner soon. You can choose the beefsteak or the terriyaki prawns.'

She walked gracefully up the aisle to the galley and Melanie sat back and studied the menu. Dinner Manchester-Singapore, Saturday 23 November. Terriyaki prawns or steak in a black bean sauce, served with rice and stir-fried vegetables. There were snacks for between meals and all the drink you could get down your neck in the time available. Her only complaint was that this was a non-smoking flight. Passenger demand, they said. The Megatop was not full – she had the luxury of two empty seats next to her. Even if it was Economy and not Raffles Class. The Ecstasy was in the overhead locker, disguised as cartons of duty free cigarettes in a Manchester airport carrier bag. Guy had given them to her before they set off at lunchtime for the airport. She had to check in three hours before take off, he said. Melanie had never been on a long haul flight before.

Thirteen hours! she thought, swigging the vodka as soon as it was placed gently in front of her. Amazing that an aircraft could stay in the sky for so long. She giggled to herself, feeling bolder and more relaxed. She had got through security checks without any problem. Guy was right, it was easy-peasy. All you needed was nerve or, in her case, a few good bolts of vodka. She was apprehensive about swallowing a stomach full of heroin-stuffed condoms for the return flight in two days' time, but Wady would help her with that, Guy had promised. Hundreds of people did it every day, he emphasized. There was nothing to it. So long as she stayed cool.

Melanie finished her vodka and stopped a passing sex goddess to order another drink. The cabin crew bustled around with clinking, bottle-laden trolleys, and the savoury smell of hot food drifted from the galleys. Melanie sniffed, her mouth watering, and decided to have the steak. At home she ate fish and chips, chicken and mushroom pies, sausages, curry sauce with chips. That would change once she got her hundred grand. She would eat steak and smoked salmon and giant prawns whenever she liked. Get her own luxury apartment, tell Paul the parasite to fuck off out of her life. She might even go back to college and complete her computer studies degree, start her own company. Buy a gun and blow old Bernie away. Now there was a thought!

She giggled again, feeling the drink. The aircraft rose suddenly then levelled out, giving her a fluttery feeling in her stomach. She glanced at the landing card, half concealed by the unfolded menu. Date of birth, gender, reason for visit, length of stay. Passport number. What the hell was her passport number? She opened her bag, took out her new passport and got the loan of a biro from another sex goddess. She pushed the menu aside and froze.

In the centre of the card the words *'Death Penalty for Drug Traffickers'* was printed in large red letters. Melanie drew in her breath and stared at the awful warning. Terror gripped her. She was on her way to a country where death by hanging awaited people like her. If they got caught. From Changi airport to a death cell in Changi prison. It could happen. It could happen to *her*. Stay cool, she heard Guy say cheerfully. Wady'll meet you, take you to the hotel, collect the stuff. All you need to do is stay cool.

It was all right for him, she thought, staring at the red letters. He was not risking a slow choke on the end of a rope, sitting in his poncy office at the Carmen Club. She clenched her hands and began to shake, vodka leaking from every pore. Another smiling stewardess approached.

'Have you filled out your disembarkation card yet, Ma'am?' she asked cheerfully.

'I haven't finished.' Melanie's hand shook as she gripped the biro.

'Okay, no hurry. Are you feeling all right, ma'am?' She looked worriedly at the girl's white set face. 'You are nervous about flying?'

'No.' That was the least of her worries. 'I'm fine. I'm all right.'

'Good.' The stewardess smiled. 'We are starting to serve dinner soon. Would you like the prawns or the beefsteak?'

'Nothing.' Melanie shook her head. 'I won't bother with dinner,' she said abruptly. 'I'm not hungry.' She held up her empty glass. 'You can get me another drink though. Double vodka.'

She drank the vodka when it came, closed her eyes and leaned back, trying to relax. She felt dizzy and panicked. The smell of food made her sick. When dessert was over and the cabin crew circulated with coffee and liqueurs she ordered a large Drambuie and drank it down in one go, coughing and gasping as the strong liquid burned her throat. It helped a bit. How could she get out of this mess? she wondered. Not clear immigration, dump the Ecstasy in some toilet or rubbish bin, stay in transit for two days? Camp on a sofa in the transit lounge until she could catch her flight home? Was it possible to stay in transit for two days? They probably had security cameras all over the airport, spying on passengers. She might be questioned, picked up. And how could she go back to Liverpool not having delivered the Ecstasy and collected her stomach full of heroin? No hundred grand! Guy and Paul might be so angry they would kill her. And Rob! Why did I tell him about Bernie? she thought. Why the hell did I tell him? He was a mess. She'd tried to phone him at work a couple of times but he wouldn't speak to her. It was all such a mess!

She hated her life, felt torn with guilt about Rob. But she didn't want to end it choking on a rope. Dinner ended and the cabin lights were switched off. People settled down to sleep or watch the stupid movie: pale-skinned, red-haired characters in Fair Isle sweaters doing nothing very much against a background of green mountains and white cottages. Melanie looked out of the window at patterns of winking orange lights miles below, and wept silently. She had to go through with it. There was no escape.

She undid her seatbelt and staggered to the toilet, her head whirling. In the small stuffy lavatory she threw up, bending over the steel pan with its funny blue water. 'Get a grip,' she gasped as she ran the tap and splashed lukewarm water on her face. 'It's going to be all right. You'll be set up for the rest of your life. You just have to get through this.' She drew a scratchy beige airline comb through her tangled auburn hair and stared at herself in the mirror. Maybe she should have dressed up a bit more, she thought, looking at the crumpled jeans and heavy black sweater. It was cold on the aircraft, colder than she'd expected.

She wiped away smudged black eyeliner, staggered back to her seat and fell into a heavy sleep – so heavy she felt nothing when the aircraft hit a patch of turbulence and dropped hundreds of feet in seconds, sending books, magazines, glasses, unbelted passengers and Singapore girls flying around the cabin. Melanie awakened as breakfast was being served, and nibbled a mushroom omelette and chocolate muffin. She drank coffee because her mouth felt so dry. Her head throbbed and she longed for a cigarette and more vodka. The sun rose over the Andaman Sea as they approached Singapore and the aircraft began its slow descent, passing through mountainous white fluffy clouds. She was too frightened and hungover to appreciate the beauty.

'Could you get me a double vodka?' Melanie asked a steward in a pale blue jacket who was passing down the aisle refilling coffee cups.

'I'm sorry, ma'am.' He smiled charmingly. 'It's not possible to serve anymore alcohol now. The bar has been sealed because we will be landing in approximately one hour's time.'

She glared at him. 'Can't you unseal it?'

'I'm very sorry, ma'am,' he repeated, shaking his head regretfully. If the lady drank any more vodka she would have to be carried off the aircraft on a stretcher. He held up the coffee pot. 'How about some more coffee?'

'You must be joking!' she said sullenly. He moved on.

A few minutes later the cabin crew went into overdrive, clearing cluttered breakfast trays, emptying rubbish, slamming and locking everything away in galley cupboards ready for landing. An information video about Changi airport came on the screens, showing its two terminals, restaurant and shopping facilities, Customs, duty free allowances ... Melanie did not bother to watch. She stared out of the window, sweaty hands clenched, her heart racing. The aircraft came in low over Singapore harbour, the rippled blue water dotted with ships and small boats, distant skyscrapers glinting in the morning sun.

She wiped her sweaty palms on her jeans. Could she leave the bag of 'cigarettes' stuffed at the back of the overhead locker? Of course not! It was no good, she had to do it. The wing dipped as the aircraft circled and dropped lower and seconds later they were tearing down the runway at Changi airport.

She felt the heat and humidity even through the air conditioning in the terminal building. She followed the other passengers, walking along acres of carpet. She sweated and shook, ears ringing after the long flight and all the vodka she had drunk. Her stomach churned and she longed to go to the toilet, but did not want to get left behind and maybe attract attention. She paused, dropped her green Samsonite bag and the carrier bag and pulled off her heavy black sweater, tying the sleeves around her slim waist. Her bra-less nipples poked through the tight pink T-shirt she wore underneath. Probably get arrested for that!

Changi was a vast airport. She had never seen so many shops, souvenirs, bags and suitcases, designer clothes, sweets and chocolates, books, cameras, vintage wines. Uniformed cabin crews passed by and there were men and women in Muslim dress, European dress, Indian women in colourful glittery embroidered saris. A group of Japanese tourists in shorts, T-shirts and trainers. Three blond tanned Australian men in shorts, thongs and bush hats, laughing loudly and drinking from beer cans. She wished she could carry on to Australia, jump aboard one of the QANTAS flights to Sydney, Adelaide or Melbourne. They were easy there, civilized. There was no death penalty and you could lie in the sun and drink all day. Smells of sweat, spicy food and warm damp earth mingled with expensive perfumes. Huge green leafy plants were everywhere and there was a distant sound of piano music, running water and birdsong. All very pleasant and relaxing – so long as you did not have a bag of Ecstasy clutched in your hot little hand.

Melanie stopped at the top of a wide flight of steps flanked by green plants that led down to Immigration and Arrivals, and held on to the rail. She felt so dizzy she was afraid she might faint. She had never felt so ill and terrified – sick, sweating all over, her head throbbing, heart banging in her chest. She took a deep breath and forced herself to walk down the steps, praying that her trembling legs would not give way. She longed to turn and run. But where to?

There were few people passing through Immigration and Melanie did not have to wait long. She handed her passport and landing card to a grim girl in a black skirt and dark blue military style shirt. The passport was whipped below the counter, scrutinized, stamped and shoved back at her without a word. She could hardly breathe as she walked through Customs unchallenged, no one so much as glancing in her direction, and gained the safety of the bustling Arrivals hall with its shiny floor, rows of seats and more spiky and leafy green plants.

She sank trembling on to a chair and let the bags fall as she leaned forward and buried her head in her hands, moaning with pain and fear. She was supposed to go through this torture again in just two days time.

'I can't do it,' she whispered. 'I just can't.'

'You are Melanie?' a polite voice enquired.

She glanced up and saw a thin young Asian man. He wore jeans, a crisp white shirt and a gold watch.

'Yes.'

'I am Wady.' He removed his sunglasses. 'You are unwell?'

'I'm just – tired from the flight. I've got a headache. And the stress.' She glanced back at the dark blue shirts in Immigration.

'Of course.' He followed her look. 'It is very difficult. But you made it.' He paused. 'You have something for me, I think?'

'Yes.' Her hand strayed to the carrier bag.

'Wait,' he said sharply. 'Later.'

'Could I get a drink?' she asked hopefully. 'I'd feel better then.' She reached in her bag for cigarettes and lighter.

'Later,' he repeated. 'Wait, you cannot smoke in the airport. I have my car outside, I will drive you to the hotel. Let's go.' He picked up the green Samsonite bag. 'Now, please.'

'Wow!' she gasped as they emerged into steamy sunshine. 'It's like a *sauna*!'

'Yes. Singapore is very warm.' She hurried after him as he headed for the car park. 'You can maybe take city tour while you are here,' he said politely. 'See Raffles Hotel, Chinatown, Botanical Gardens, Sentosa Island. Crocodile Farm.'

'Crocodile Farm?' She laughed.

'Yes. It is very interesting.'

'And I could try the famous Singapore Sling,' she said slyly, lighting her longed-for cigarette and breathing the delicious smoke deep into her lungs.

'Of course. Very good drink.'

They reached the car, a black Mercedes, and he smiled as he took the carrier bag from her. She smiled back.

'I like your car.'

'Thank you.' He opened the door for her and she got in. Singapore's method of traffic control was to make it prohibitively expensive to own a car. He must be rich, she thought, and grinned. Of course he was bloody rich!

She'd made it, despite the terror. I must be really strong, Melanie thought proudly. Not many people would have the guts to do what I've done. And now here she was in Singapore, thinking about cocktails and city tours and crocodile farms. She relaxed into the comfortable seat, enjoying the cool of the air conditioning. It began to seem like a normal holiday.

Chapter Twelve

'But I *told* you, I've got vital information about Bianca Mitchell's murder,' Shannon said desperately. 'I know who did it. I've got evidence, I told the other officer when I went to the station this morning – and yesterday afternoon! I really need to see – speak to whoever's in charge of her case. It's *vital*!' She glanced at the chained and locked front door as an icy draught stirred the wind chime in the porch. It was a cold windy November night, rain lashing down.

'Look, love,' the Duty Officer sighed.

'*Mrs Flinder*, if you don't mind! I'm not calling about my husband this time.' She tried to control her anger. 'I know he's told you not to give me an address or phone number. He doesn't want to see me, I realize that.'

No wonder. She was barking. 'Look,' the officer said sharply. 'We've already got a lot of leads to follow up on this.'

'For God's *sake*!' Shannon brushed away tears. 'Why won't you listen to me? I know who did it! It was my father-in-law, Bernard Flinder. He's a paedophile – abused his daughter for years. *He* murdered Bianca. I've got her doll, it was in his car. I showed it to the other officer, but I got the big brush-off. I can't believe none of you will listen to me!'

There was silence. The wind chime tinkled in the porch. 'I can understand you're upset because you and your husband have split up.' What did she expect? The poor sod was devastated after discovering she'd cheated on him with three other men. Came home to find one of them in his bed, rumour had it. Bloody bitch!

'But this is going too far.' His voice hardened. 'This is *well* out of order.'

'What are you talking about?' asked Shannon, startled by his hostile tone. 'Are you saying I'm delusional or something? Bitter and twisted, trying to blame my husband and his *innocent* family?'

'You said it, love.' She needed a good slapping, he thought. Who did she think she was?

Shannon was silent, breathing hard. 'I've heard about the police ignoring vital evidence,' she said finally. 'But this is bizarre. You're treating me as though I'm some mental case. You're all going to be in big trouble over this.'

'I know you're upset,' he said again. 'But you can't be turning up at the station and calling at all hours. We've got work to do.'

'Why don't you bloody well do it then!'

'It's nine o clock on Saturday night now,' he went on. 'You should call a friend. Get someone to be with you. I'll tell your husband you phoned – again.' Too right he'd tell Rob Flinder! Let him know what his bitch of a wife was up to. 'Night, love.' He hung up, shaking his head in disgust.

The dial tone purred in Shannon's ear. She swore furiously and slammed the phone down, ran back to the kitchen and threw the empty wine bottle in the bin. It was hopeless, they wouldn't listen. What had Rob told them? Of course they'd stick together, take his side. She wasn't just a wife, she was a lawyer! It was all hopeless, hopeless. Her life was falling apart and it seemed she couldn't do anything to stop it. But she wouldn't give up. She had to get Bernard Flinder behind bars. Maybe then Rob would come to his senses.

The big kitchen was spotless because it hadn't been used in a week. A bottle opener lay on the scrubbed wooden table. The fridge contained bottles of white wine and champagne, half full bottles of soy sauce and chilli bean sauce and two packs of unsalted butter. Shannon opened a bottle of Australian Chardonnay, poured herself a big glass and sat at the table, pulling her thick towelling robe around her. She wiped her eyes and took gulps of icy wine. 'I'm so tired,' she moaned. She put the glass down and leaned her head on the table. 'I can't think anymore. Rob, what the hell are you playing at!'

She'd get some sleep. Try to, anyway. Then decide what to do next. She had to find Rob, tell him his father had murdered Bianca. Bernard would be banged up. He'd come back. They'd talk, sort out their problems.

She took her wine glass, climbed the stairs and got into the big bed, the bed where they'd made love so many times. The bed where he'd raped her. The quilt felt cold against her naked body. She could smell him on the sheets. She couldn't believe he'd really left her. Wanted a divorce. She hated being alone in the house, couldn't stand it without him. His things were all over the place. It was as if he'd died. She gulped the rest of the wine, lay down and cried herself to sleep again.

Outside Bernard drove slowly past the house, turned and drove back and parked the Volvo on the other side of the road, beneath an ancient oak. Rain drummed on the roof and bonnet. He had to speak to Shannon. Make her see sense. Otherwise he might as well put a gun to his head and pull the trigger. He clenched his gloved hands and trembled with cold and fear.

Shannon jerked awake in the darkness and sat up in bed, her heart pounding. Had she really heard a noise or was it a dream? She pulled the heavy quilt up to her chin and listened fearfully, eyes straining to make out familiar shapes and objects. The central heating was off and the room felt cold. Rain lashed the windows; the clock radio showed ten past midnight. The curtains were open and faint orange streetlight slanted across the pale wall.

'Switch the light on, you moron!' she muttered impatiently. She leaned over and clicked on the bedside lamp, desolate at the sight of the empty space that should have been occupied by Rob. She pictured him alone in some gloomy grimy bedsit, giving in to despair. Tears filled her eyes again. She needed another drink. She got out of bed and put on her apricot-coloured robe. Her mouth felt dry and her head ached. She should stop drinking and start eating. But she couldn't be bothered. She heard voices and laughter outside. The neighbours, probably. Normal people enjoying themselves, their lives happy and secure. She'd already forgotten what happiness felt like. Car doors slammed.

She was going downstairs tying the belt of the robe when the doorbell rang. She froze and gripped the banister. Who would call at this hour? It couldn't be Rob: he didn't want to see her. Bernard! It must be him. She reached the bottom of the stairs and stood in the hall, terrified, uncertain. The bell rang again, twice. Someone thumped on the porch door. The wind chime tinkled furiously.

What did he want? She snapped the hall light on. She unlocked and unchained the front door and stood in the porch, her bare feet cold on the tiles.

'Shannon!' her father-in-law called. 'I want to talk to you. It's all right, your neighbours have seen me. They know I'm here. I won't harm you. We need to talk. Please let me in.'

She stepped forward and opened the porch door, keeping the chain on. Wind, rain and leaves flew into her face, making her gasp. Bernard stood beneath the porch light wearing his heavy black overcoat and a Russian fur hat, shivering with cold. His car keys were clutched in his gloved hand. She looked beyond his bulk through the trees and over the garden wall. The neighbours, Chris and Lorraine Campbell, were unlocking their front door after garaging the car for the night. Nosy Lorraine stared, but didn't call or wave.

'What do you want?' she asked Bernard harshly.

'I told you, to talk. I don't mean you any harm,' he said. His black eyes looked anxious in his heavy florid face. 'I want to talk to you about this awful situation. About Rob.'

'Rob?'

'I've been thinking about what you said.' She looked pale under the strong light, washed-out. 'I want to help my son. I don't want him to have a nervous breakdown.'

She was silent, shivering and staring at him, trying to read his expression. She didn't believe him. But he wouldn't harm her, he wasn't that stupid. Chris and Lorraine had seen him. She closed the door, unchained it and opened it wide. He stepped into the porch and went through to the hall.

'My God, it's cold out there!' He moved towards the sitting room.

'Where are you going?' Shannon felt vulnerable, barefoot and dressed only in a robe. Her unwashed hair hung loose.

'Well, I thought we'd sit down.'

'You can say what you've got to say here,' she said quietly. 'Then get out.' She kept the house keys clutched in her hand. 'I don't invite child murderers to sit down in my house.'

He winced. 'D'you have a small Scotch?' he asked. 'Just to keep out the cold?'

'No.' She longed for more wine, but she'd have to wait until he'd gone. She couldn't bear the thought of him going into the other room, sitting down, drinking out of her glasses. Touching anything with his murderous hands.

'Well, go on!' she urged. 'What d'you want to say?'

He towered over her, tall, bulky and threatening. Shannon felt afraid. He looked her up and down, eyes lingering at chest level. She blushed and pulled the robe tighter. He wasn't interested in her, surely? She was much too old for his taste. But her fear increased.

'When you came to see me on Friday it was a terrible shock,' he began hesitantly. 'I never meant to hurt any girl. I know I've got a problem.' What had she done with Bianca's doll, he wondered?

'A *problem*!' Rage blew up in her. 'You don't think you've done anything wrong, do you?' she said furiously. 'You know other people think it's wrong, but you don't believe it is. I suppose now you're going to tell me your victims provoked you, tempted you, and that you've had a raw deal because some wicked relative abused you when you were little? Well, save it for the bloody social worker!'

Bernard was silent. That was exactly what he'd been going to say. He felt helpless, frustrated. The idea of her having control over him . . . He longed to teach her a lesson, knock the arrogance out of her.

'You said you'd talk to Rob,' she reminded him.

'Yes, I will.' He nodded, hands clenched in his pockets. 'I'll tell him that Melanie and that other girl – they were the only ones.'

'I thought I told you to save that bullshit for the social worker!'

'I'll tell him it wasn't his fault. That he couldn't have done anything. He was just a boy.'

'Is that it?'

'No, of course not.' Her hectoring tone angered him. 'I'll tell our priest.'

'A *priest*?' Shannon folded her arms and shook her head in disbelief.

'Yes, and my GP. I'll get help, treatment. There's places where I can go to be treated. Cured. What's the point of going to the police?' he pleaded. 'Even if I were sent to prison – which is by no means a foregone conclusion – what use would it be? I wouldn't get any help in prison.'

'You'd suffer,' she said. 'You'd be at someone else's mercy for a change. You'd be ruined.'

'I'd be out within a few years,' he said. 'You're a lawyer, you know they don't usually hand out long sentences these days.' He paused, staring at her. 'And I wouldn't forget what you'd done.'

'Are you threatening me, you bastard?' She glanced around the hall, at the telephone table, the white walls, the barometer that hung near the front door. There was nothing she could defend herself with if he attacked her. He won't be that stupid, she reminded herself. Chris and Lorraine saw him! It didn't help.

'I'm not threatening you.' Bernard smiled slightly. ' I'm just trying to point out that my going to prison won't achieve anything.' He stared at her. 'It certainly won't help Robert.'

She was silent. Her head drooped slightly, the desolate look returning. He seized his chance.

'You're afraid for his state of mind,' he said urgently. 'You think he might have a breakdown. What will it do to him if you go to the police and the school governors and my colleagues, spreading this around? He'd be under seige – we all will be! He'd definitely have a nervous breakdown then. You need time to help him,' he went on. 'You won't get that if you go to the police. The tabloids would love a story like this. Yes, my career – my life – would be ruined.' He nodded sharply. 'Of course they would. But so would yours. So would Robert's. Is that what you want? And there's one more thing.'

'What's that?' Shannon asked dully.

'You got that doll by breaking into my car, committing criminal damage. It may not be admissible as evidence, even if DNA tests – which aren't always conclusive, as you must know –

proved I'd handled it. You'd be liable to a charge of criminal damage, could be struck off for that. So you'll have destroyed your career – your life! – for nothing. And lost Robert forever.'

'Go!' she shouted suddenly, terrifed. He was right, damn him to hell! 'Get out of here. I won't listen to this!'

'You know I'm right,' Bernard said triumphantly. 'You won't go to the police or tell anyone because you know it'll hurt Robert. You can forget your marriage if you do. Where's the doll?' he asked suddenly.

'It – they're doing DNA tests on it,' Shannon lied desperately. 'I've been to the police, I've told them about you.'

'Why haven't they arrested me then?' Bernard moved towards her and she backed away. 'They didn't believe you, did they?' He smiled with relief. 'I told you they wouldn't.'

'I said, get out of here!' She dodged away, pulled open the front door and porch door. 'Get out!' she gasped. 'I don't care what you say, I'm going to stop you.' She took a deep breath. 'If you don't leave now, I'll scream the place down.'

'Like a spoiled little girl.' She shrank back as he passed. 'If you've got any sense – and I believe you've got a great deal – you'll leave me alone,' he said, staring down at her. 'You'll leave well alone. Concentrate on holding your own life together.'

'I hope you like prison food!' Shannon banged the doors shut behind him and locked and chained them. She trembled with fear. He'd threatened her. Would he really do something? She had to get him arrested before he harmed her – or someone else. She went into the kitchen to pour more wine, took her glass and checked the chain and mortice lock on the kitchen door, then the locks on the French windows. She switched off the dining room light, parted the curtains and looked out at the dark drive and tree-lined road beyond. Rain pattered on trees and bushes and a car cruised past. Not Bernard's tacky Volvo. Was he still out there? She couldn't see anyone.

'I can't go on,' she murmured. 'I can't take anymore.' She went into the sitting room, gulping more wine. How could she get through tomorrow, let alone the rest of her life? Everything seemed impossible. The bastard was right. The police wouldn't listen to her. She *had* to find Rob, convince him. Together they could win. Rain poured down outside. She lay on the sofa, trying to think, sitting up fearfully at imagined noises. She finally fell asleep as night passed and the sky lightened to a depressing grey.

She awakened hours later, dry-mouthed and hungover. The rain had stopped. Winter sunshine poured through the French windows. The heating had switched itself on. She stood up, pulled the robe around her and switched on the television for company. Her bare feet felt cold. Coffee, she thought. Don't drink anymore wine. She walked out of the sitting room and gasped in fright as the doorbell rang furiously. Someone was at the front door, trying to break in. It was Bernard, come back to kill her.

'Go away!' she cried. 'Leave me alone!' Why wouldn't anyone help her, listen to her?

'Shannon!' Rob shouted angrily. 'Are you there? Let me in. You've left the chain on.' He thumped at the door.

'Oh, Rob! Rob!' She stumbled to the door, terrified that he would leave before she could open it.

'What do you think you're playing at?' He shoved past her and walked into the hall.

He wore jeans, his favourite denim shirt, purple-and-yellow trainers and a black bomber jacket she hadn't seen before. He had shaved and his brown hair was cropped in a crew cut, shorter than she'd ever seen it. His face looked thin and hollow-eyed, like hers. He smelled faintly of the Dolce & Gabbana aftershave she'd given him a few months ago. She'd loved to surprise him with gifts.

'I'm sorry.' She flinched at the contemptuous expression in his eyes. How could it happen, that he loved her one minute and deserted her the next? 'I forgot. I'm scared, being here alone all the time. It's awful without you! Your father came to see me last night. He threatened me. I know he murdered Bianca Mitchell . . .' She grabbed his arm. 'I've got proof – I found her doll in his car. Please, Rob, you've got to help me! We've got to have him arrested before he hurts some other little girl. I phoned the police, went there on Friday and yesterday, but they won't listen to me. Why? What have you told them?'

'I don't know what you're talking about,' he lied. He looked down at his wife, her blonde hair falling around her face and shoulders, the loosely tied robe partially open to reveal her breasts.

Her blue eyes stared at him, filled with panic. She'd been through the mill these past few weeks, he reflected dispassionately. Especially this week. But there was nothing he could do. His father a murderer? What did she mean? He couldn't think about it.

'Don't talk to me about my father.' He shook off her hand. 'I don't want to see him or my mother or you ever again. Or Melanie.' He was surprised that Melanie hadn't phoned him in days to plead for cash or beg him to pay this or that bill. Surprised but relieved. She understood. She wouldn't make it hard for him.

Voices were either in his face or came from miles away. Sometimes he switched off completely. He felt Shannon's hands grab his shoulders, saw her pale lips form words. He would do it, he'd get away. Nothing would stop him.

'You're losing it, Shannon,' he said coldly. 'I don't know what you're talking about, but you're really losing it.' He threw up his arms to shake her off then shoved her violently away. She stumbled against the wall and banged her head. 'You'd better sort yourself out, stop nagging me,' he said tonelessly. 'I won't be around to take care of you any longer. I'm just here to pick up the rest of my stuff.'

'Take care of me?' she cried, feeling the bump on her head. '*You* take care of *me*? Is that what you think you've been doing? You're the one who's losing it,' she shouted, angry and desperate. 'You find out your father's a paedophile who spent years raping your sister – and God knows who else besides her and little Bianca Mitchell! – and what do you do? You blank out, don't want to know, wreck our marriage, let him get away with it. What's wrong with you? He murdered Bianca Mitchell!' she yelled at him, her face twisted with fury. 'He would have raped our daughter if we'd had one. You're the one who's losing it! Where are you living now?' she demanded. 'Shacked up with some WPC, have you?' She gasped at the startled look in his eyes. 'So I'm right. You're really sad, Rob,' she wept. 'I can't believe how sad you are. Your behaviour is pathetic.'

'You said it.' He stepped forward, grabbed her by the hair and hit her across the face. She screamed with pain and shock. He punched her in the stomach and jaw, pushed her to the ground and kicked her as she lay gasping for breath. She curled up, trying to protect herself.

'Stop it! Don't hurt me!' she cried out in terror as he gripped her shoulders, rolled her on her back and knelt between her legs, pushing her thighs wide apart. The robe fell open. 'Don't!' she cried, hugging herself. 'Stop it!'

'Take your hands off your tits,' he commanded. 'I want to see them.'

Terrified, she did as he said. She shut her eyes and lay still. He dragged the robe away from her breasts and stared down at her exposed body, hands gripping her thighs, holding her legs open.

'It's all right.' He laughed harshly. 'I don't want to fuck you anymore. You're revolting to me now, repulsive. I just thought I'd have a last look.'

He couldn't help himself. It was over, he was a dead man. What the hell did Linda see in him? He got to his feet and ran upstairs.

Shannon heard him moving around the bedroom. She dragged herself up, pulled the robe around her bruised and aching body and staggered to the sitting room where she lay curled up on the sofa. She couldn't stop shivering. Her mouth and left eye were swelling, her nose was bleeding and she had pains in her chest and head. The old Rob was gone, his personality wiped out. She had to protect herself – from him and his father. A few minutes later he came running downstairs. The phone rang.

You answer it, she thought. Maybe it's Daddy and you can have a nice chat. She closed her eyes and curled her body tighter. He picked up the phone.

'Hello? Oh, Nick! Hi! I'm fine, thanks.' There was a pause. 'Sunday lunch? Today? Sorry, I don't know anything about that. Shannon didn't mention any lunch invitation. She's a bit out of it lately.' Another pause. 'She isn't here now, I don't know where she went. I'm going to work in a minute, but I'll scribble a message for her to call you when she gets back.' He laughed. 'I'm really sorry about this but as I said, I didn't know. Okay. Give my regards to Caroline, won't you? 'Bye!' He hung up and walked into the living room.

'That was Nick. He wants you to call him. Anyway,' he went on, as if resuming a normal conversation, 'I also came to tell you

I've found a solicitor to handle the divorce. He'll contact you soon.' She said nothing, didn't look at him. 'This house and its contents will have to be sold,' he said casually. 'I know I said you could keep it, but I've changed my mind. I don't see why you should get everything. I want a half share of the proceeds from the sale. And your income is much bigger than mine, I deserve a piece of that too. There's no kids and we're both in work, so it should all be sorted pretty quickly.' He walked to the sofa and stood over her. 'Are you listening?'

'Yes,' whispered Shannon, terrified he'd hit her again.

'And don't bother changing the locks,' he warned. 'This is my home too.'

'It's not your home anymore,' she moaned. 'You left it. You left me.'

'That doesn't mean I don't have right of access.'

She ran her tongue over her cracked swollen lips and looked up at him. His eyes are dead, she thought. Like his father's. She saw a resemblance between them she hadn't noticed before. Or hadn't wanted to notice.

'Starting a new life isn't cheap.' He wouldn't admit it to her, but he'd moved in with Linda, the WPC who'd fancied him for ages. She'd jumped at the chance. He still couldn't bring himself to screw her, but that would work itself out in time. And if not, he didn't care. 'I'm going to make sure I get everything I'm entitled to,' he said grimly. 'I suggest you find yourself a divorce lawyer – when you get a spare moment from keeping scum out of jail. Right, I'll be seeing you.' He turned away.

'It hurts when I breathe,' whispered Shannon, hugging her frozen body. 'I might have a cracked rib. My head hurts. Help me, Rob,' she pleaded. Hot tears slid down her cold cheeks. 'Just call the doctor. Please!'

'You'll have to do that yourself. I'm sorry about what happened back there, but you wouldn't let go of me.' He looked down at her, wondering why he felt nothing, not even pity. It was as if he was outside his own body, observing its actions. Or that someone, something, had taken him over.

'Don't bother going to the police about my father,' he warned. 'I don't want the hassle. I don't want to think about him or hear any more about him as long as I live. And stop calling me at work, making a show of me and yourself. No one believes you. They all think you're a sad mental case and that I left you because you cheated on me. It's probably true. You're a joke. A mess, Shannon. That's what you are.'

He walked out, picked up the bag of clothes in the hall and left the house, slamming the front door. She lay still for a few minutes, tears rolling off her cheeks and dripping on to the sofa cushions. Cheated on him? What kind of bullshit was *that*? She crawled off the sofa, gasping with pain. Had she cracked a rib? She tottered to the phone and dialled Nick's number. The solitary confinement was over. She needed all the help she could get.

'Nick?' she whispered. 'It's Shannon.'

'Hello!' he said coolly. 'Thanks for taking time in your busy life to call your old friend from university days.'

'Nick, I'm really sorry about the lunch,' she gasped. 'Please tell Caroline. I completely forgot about it because–.' She winced with pain and burst into tears. She'd shed more tears during the past weeks than in her life to date.

'Shannon!' he exclaimed. 'What the hell's wrong?'

'Rob's left me,' she wailed. 'My marriage is over.' Saying it to him made it sound final.

'*What*? But he was there, I just spoke to him! He sounded perfectly normal – said you weren't home.'

'He lied. He moved out a week ago – just came back to collect the rest of his things. Something terrible's happened,' she sobbed.

'Jesus Christ!' Nick was incredulous. 'I can't believe it! He sounded fine.'

'He isn't fine. Neither am I. He hit me. Kicked me.'

'*What*?' If his voice went any higher he'd be singing soprano. '*Rob* hit you?'

'He's changed completely, Nick, I don't know him anymore. He told me he'd found a solicitor to handle the–.' her voice rose in panic – 'the *divorce!* I can't believe this is happening,' she cried. 'My life's turned into a bloody nightmare.'

Nick was silent, trying to take it in. 'I thought you were both so happy,' he said wonderingly. 'And you wanted – Caroline and I thought any day now you'd be telling us you were pregnant.'

'Don't, Nick!' she wailed.

'Sorry, that was stupid. Shannon, this is terrible! What can I do to help you?' he asked. 'Now, this minute?'

Pain stabbed her as she tried to breathe. 'Could you come over and bring a camera or camcorder with you?' she asked. Stop crying, she thought irritably, brushing a hand across her eyes and cheeks. It's time to stop being a victim. 'I'll be all right, I've seen a hell of a lot worse. But I need to photograph the evidence while it's fresh. Like I tell all the punters,' she added grimly.

'Jesus *Christ*!'

'Could Caroline come too? Might be good to have a second witness.'

'I don't think so. She's just got Helen off to sleep and there's still one or two people here.' He hesitated. 'I could bring Finbar,' he said awkwardly.

'Finbar Linnell? The Irishman?' Shock coursed through her injured body.

'Yes, he's here. He came to lunch. I'll get him to drive me. I've had a couple of Scotches and a few glasses of wine so I don't want to risk driving.' He stopped. 'Sorry, I'm rabbiting on. This is such a shock. We'll come over now. Let's see – Crosby to West Derby – we'll be with you in about fifteen minutes. I'll hang up now. See you soon, Shannon.'

She put the phone down. Finbar Linnell coming here? He'd think she made a habit of getting herself bashed up! She walked slowly to the kitchen, poured a glass of wine and gulped it down. She poured more wine, went upstairs and sat at the dressing table. The bedroom was a mess.

She swallowed more golden wine and grimaced at her reflection. White face, bruised swollen eye, bleeding nose, bruised cheekbone, unwashed hair all over the place. Her headache was worse. 'Yes, you look suitably terrible for the camera.'

Shannon wanted to shower, give her dull hair a good shampoo and conditioning, get dressed and put on make-up. But that would have to wait. How hollow and staring her eyes had become! She'd lost looks and self-esteem in weeks, because of what Rob had done to her. Or what she'd let him do. Love made people give in, tolerate things they would never accept when not under its insidious spell. I'd better call Gavin, she thought suddenly. I can't go to work tomorrow with a battered face and cracked rib. She went into the computer room where she kept her files and correspondence, got her address book and sat on the bed to make the call. The wine warmed her inside, made her head whirl and throb.

'Is that you, Anna? It's Shannon Flinder. I'm sorry to bother you on Sunday afternoon, but I really need to speak to Gavin.'

'Just a minute,' Anna Steele said brusquely. Shannon Flinder, she thought crossly, the brilliant blonde bombshell Gavin had been so enthusiastic about. Now he was raging about female hormones and deceitful bimbos, ruining her and the girls' weekend. She shouted to him.

Gavin picked up the phone. 'What do you want?'

'Gavin, I–' Shannon began to stammer, taken aback by the hostility in his voice. 'I'm sorry to bother you, but something else has happened.'

'You don't say!'

'I just need another couple of days off. I'll be back on Wednesday and I promise I won't take anymore leave until next June at the earliest.'

'You don't need to come to work tomorrow,' he said coldly. 'You don't need to come in on Wednesday either. You no longer have a future with this firm.'

'What?' she gasped. She gripped the receiver, stunned by another sledgehammer blow.

'I trusted you,' he said angrily. 'I liked your work. I liked it so much I ignored the flak from Richard and Priscilla over the partnership offer. Now I find you've deceived me for the past two years. Frankly it makes me feel a bit of a stupid bastard.'

'Gavin, what the hell do you mean? I *never* deceived you!'

'You might take up acting as your next profession. I *mean*,' he said heavily, 'the fact you omitted to mention in your impressive curriculum vitae, or in the two interviews you had with us, your history of mental illness. Depressive illness, to be exact.'

'Depressive? I don't have a history of depressive illness,' gasped Shannon, stunned by shock and disbelief. 'No history of *any* illness.' She glanced out of the bedroom windows. The sunshine had gone and dark rainclouds were gathering. Mental illness! She felt cold. 'Where did you – how did you get such a crazy–' She stopped. 'Such a ridiculous idea?'

'Listen, Shannon, we can finish this in a dignified manner. You got this job under false pretences and now you've been rumbled. You don't have a leg to stand on. You can pop in tomorrow morning – or Wednesday, if you like – clear your desk and that'll be the end of it. But if you're going to be difficult . . .'

'Who told you I was mentally ill?' she asked furiously. 'It's a lie! A slanderous lie! Who told you? I've a right to know.'

He sighed with distaste. 'Your father-in-law. He phoned me on Friday afternoon, very concerned about you. He said you'd stormed into his office – *drunk!* – and screamed that your husband had deserted you. Sounds like his reasons for doing so were excellent! He said you had a history of depressive illness and that he was afraid you'd stopped taking your medication.'

'That bastard!' she breathed. 'How dare he! What do you mean, *excellent reasons* for deserting me?' she asked suddenly.

'Well – he said you'd betrayed your husband with several men.'

'*What*?' she gasped. 'It's all lies, Gavin!'

She went cold with fright. Bernard Flinder was a lot more devious, a lot more determined to protect himself, than she'd realized. He'd stop at nothing. She'd been to see him on Friday afternoon. It was now Sunday afternoon and she was already discredited as a mental case and an adulterous wife! He'd been one step ahead right from the start. She was naive, dangerously so. He didn't give a damn about Rob and never had.

'I realize you've had personal problems these past few weeks and I do sympathize, Shannon.'

'Like hell you do!'

'But I can't risk the firm's reputation. We'd all be out of a job then.'

'Gavin, please listen to me.' She forced herself to speak calmly. 'Bernard Flinder's told you a bunch of lies. I haven't got a history of depression, that's rubbish! Rob left me because he found out something terrible about his father – about his family. I won't go into that now. But he can't handle it and I'm afraid he might have a breakdown. If I don't keep my job I won't be able to go on paying the bills to keep home and hearth together for when he comes to his senses. If he does. Yes, I've got problems,' she said. 'But that's nothing to the problems you and your precious *firm* will have if you sack me on the basis of slanderous allegations.'

'Now, just a minute–'

'*You* just wait a minute!' she interrupted. 'You can't do this, Gavin. You've no right. I'll be in tomorrow morning,' she said. 'Obviously I'll have to be! I can't force your hand about the partnership, but I do expect to keep my job. I'll make up for the past few weeks. From now on you'll certainly get your money's worth.' She paused. 'I know I'm stupid and naive, but I'm hurt by your attitude. After two years of hard work, results and reliability, I expected some sympathy and trust. Support. Not dismissal the minute someone you've never even met phones and lies to you about me.' She felt like telling him to stuff his job.

A car pulled into the drive and she stood up and looked out of the window. Finbar Linnell and Nick were getting out of a dark green Maserati. Finbar, huddled in a black overcoat, glanced up at the house and into her eyes. She turned away.

'I have to go now, Gavin,' she said calmly. 'I'll see you tomorrow morning.'

She hurried downstairs and flung open the front door.

'Shannon! For Christ's *sake*!' Nick stared at her in horror, his handsome face contorted with shock. Finbar stood close behind him.

'What the hell has he done to you?' Nick put his arms around her and she buried her face in his overcoat, smelling soap and aftershave and cold winter air. 'You've lost weight,' he said. 'Christ, you're like a little bird!' He hugged her gently. 'When did you last eat? Caroline sends her love, and we want you to come and stay with us. We're both terribly sorry.'

Finbar stared down at her, eyes full of shock. He couldn't speak.

'Oh, Nick!' she gasped. 'I'm so frightened!'

'Don't worry, we'll look after you.'

He hugged her tightly. She buried her head in his coat and started to cry and shake again, completely undone by the first human warmth she'd experienced in what seemed like an eternity.

Chapter Thirteen

Bernard spent an exciting Sunday afternoon locked in his study watching the videos he had bought from the man in Sefton Park. Vernon was right, he thought, as he listened to the terrified cries and screams and watched naked immature female bodies being violated in every imaginable way. They were worth the money. The only cloud on his horizon was Shannon, the daughter-in-law from hell, who was determined to destroy him. He'd shut her up for the moment – he hoped! – but it wouldn't last. She'd go back to the police. Next on her list would be the school governors, then God knew who else! What if she enticed Robert back, got him on her side? It was no use, she'd have to be dealt with. He couldn't allow her to destroy him. He liked the idea of killing her. Plus someone else who could give more satisfaction – the icing on the cake, as it were. He was getting restless again.

The screaming girl in the video was being livened up. He closed his eyes, unzipped his trousers and slid his hand down.

He thought of Bianca. Silly little bitch, running out of her house like that. What did she expect? And the parents, not supervising her properly. They never did these days, responsibility was a dirty word.

At six o clock he switched off the television, locked the videos in the bottom drawer of his desk and went downstairs, sniffing appreciatively at the smell of roasting lamb that drifted from the kitchen. He insisted Margaret abandon the accursed microwave once in a while, cook a proper Sunday roast. He had bought two bottles of Burgundy to drink with it.

The kitchen was steamy. Pans of sprouts, peas and carrots bubbled on the cooker. The relentless November rain poured down outside, streaming over the body of the delicate marble nude with the wreath of marble flowers around her hair and waist, his choice of centrepiece for the back garden. Her marble skin glowed in the yellow light from the kitchen and dining room. He strolled to the window and stared out at the statue, remembering Melanie as a little girl, her skin all wet and slippery after a bath. He'd have to talk to her too, threaten to have her sectioned under the Mental Health Act or something. That would put the fear of God into her! At least she was stupid, easy to deal with. Not like Shannon. Margaret sat silently at the kitchen table, gin-and-tonic and her bottle of Valium in front of her. She was quiet these past few days, hardly speaking.

'Having a pre-dinner drink?' he asked jovially. 'Good idea! I'll join you.' He went into the dining room, helped himself to a Scotch and came back.

'Busy day for you tomorrow, isn't it?' He sipped the Scotch. 'Meals-on-Wheels.'

'I'm giving that up.' Margaret twisted the white plastic bottle top, shook out a tablet and picked up her glass of gin-and-tonic. She wore a purple sweatshirt and purple sweat pants, an outfit he loathed. Her dark mass of hair was sprayed rigid and her unhappy bloodhound face covered with thick make-up. Her stubby fingers were stained with pale blue watercolour paint.

'Giving it up?' he echoed sharply. 'Are you serious, Margaret? Why on earth would you do that?'

'I don't like it, that's why.' She washed the tablet down with gin-and-tonic. 'I never did. It's a thankless task. Boring.'

'You sound like Melanie,' he said angrily. 'Stupid and irresponsible.' What was behind this little palace revolution? He felt nervous. Surprises again.

She ignored him. 'Elinor's asked me to put in more hours at the shop,' she went on. 'I said I would. I know it's not December yet, but the Christmas rush has already started. She's very busy.'

He stiffened. 'You agreed to work longer hours without consulting me?'

'That's right, Bernard.' She looked at him. 'And you can stop talking to me as though I were one of your pupils.'

'Well, seeing as you behave like one!' He took a gulp of Scotch. 'You don't expect *thanks* for voluntary work, Margaret,' he said heavily. 'It's something you do as your contribution to the community–.'

'What's the community ever contributed to me?'

'Don't be ridiculous!' he snorted. 'Someone in your position–.'

'What's my position?' Her dark Melanie eyes ringed with ghastly bright blue eyeshadow challenged him. 'What's my *position*?' she hissed.

'I'm talking about your position as my wife, your standing in the community. Your behaviour, what you do. It gets noticed.'

'Just as well your behaviour doesn't get *noticed* then, isn't it?' She looked at him with hatred. He turned hypocrisy into a fine art form.

'What's got into you?' asked Bernard. 'What are you talking about? You don't say a word to me for days and now suddenly you attack me. What about my behaviour?' he persisted, and glanced at the bubbling pans. 'I think those vegetables are about done.'

She gulped her gin-and-tonic. 'How would you know? You never even toast a slice of bread. And I won't have Josie Duffy back in this house,' she said quietly, afraid to mount a direct challenge.

So that was it. 'Now, Margaret, we've been through this.' He sighed. 'She swears she didn't steal anything.'

'She's a liar! You know she is.'

'You were very rude to her. You can't afford to alienate people in that way.'

'You mean, you can't!' She finished her drink and poured another, not bothering to add ice or lemon. He went back to the dining room and helped himself to another Scotch.

'What exactly do you mean by that?' he asked, confronting her in the kitchen again. 'What is it with these insinuations? *My* behaviour, *I* can't afford to alienate people! I want to know what you're getting at.' He tensed.

Suddenly she was afraid. Afraid that the fragile, carefully

constructed existence she had created for herself would shatter, that she would become mad, raving. That the truth would destroy her, not make her free.

'Nothing,' she muttered, backing down. 'You deal with Josie Duffy, pay her whatever wages she's owed. But I don't want her in this house again. I'll do the cleaning myself. I had to do most of it anyway, she was useless.'

She would concentrate on her job, her painting, anaesthetize herself with gin and Valium, try not to think about the memories that disturbed her, the terrible things Rob had said. Forget what might be in Bernard's study. There had been the little lapse the other day, but she wouldn't allow herself to get upset like that again. She couldn't afford to! She would close herself off, concentrate on what mattered to her.

'I think it's about time we had dinner, don't you?' Bernard said, relieved. 'I'll open the wine.'

Josie Duffy would be delighted to continue to receive seventy-six pounds fifty a week – better make it a hundred now – without even having to turn up at the house and make a pretence of cleaning. Margaret was definitely upset though. Had the woman said something to her? His wife had believed him all those years ago when he'd said Janetta was his one and only 'mistake'. Did she suspect otherwise now? Janetta's body, buried in concrete on a building site, had never been found. It never would be. Some unsuspecting home owner, with no idea of what lay beneath the foundations of his brand new house . . . Bernard's lips twitched and he smiled. He was growing more and more restless. It was time.

The leg of lamb was dried out and tasteless, the unseasoned gravy lumpy and the roast potatoes pallid, greasy and not cooked through. The sprouts and peas were like bullets. A piece of carrot shot off his plate as he tried to cut it. At least the Burgundy was good. They finished one bottle and started on the second.

Margaret, silently eating and drinking, glanced down the long dining table, a fantasy of a different Sunday dinner coming to mind. Melanie might have turned out happy and affectionate, a normal girl who wanted to get married and have children. Rob might have had a respectable profession like law or accountancy instead of the Regional Crime Squad. Her children and their spouses would have sat around this table, talking and laughing, a happy close-knit family. She had never had that and she never would. Why not? Why was she denied what other people took for granted?

She drank more wine and looked at the only photograph on the wall above the mantelpiece, a photograph of Rob and Shannon on their wedding day. Shannon was beautiful, there was no denying. She looked like a fairy princess. What a pity the ethereal looks concealed an opinionated feminist hell-bent on pursuing her career instead of giving it up to look after her husband and get pregnant. Margaret herself had a job, of course, but that was different. She looked at Bernard. My husband, she thought sadly. I loved him. I wish I still did. I have to stay with him because I haven't the courage to strike out on my own. I'm too old for that. Too old and too frightened.

'What are we going to do about Robert and Shannon?' she asked, trying to pretend, as she sometimes could when drunk, that they were a normal happily married couple. There had to be some!

'Do?' Bernard poured more gravy over his badly carved slices of lamb. 'There's nothing we can do,' he said. 'We don't even know where Robert is. I phoned Gavin Steele on Friday to ask about Shannon, but he wasn't very helpful. They'll have to sort out their own problems, Margaret. I hope it won't end in divorce, but you know how things are these days – all these selfish working women who put themselves first instead of their husbands and children. That's when they bother to get husbands! I don't imagine Shannon or Robert would welcome our interference.' He picked up his glass of wine. 'Especially her. I suppose I could have a chat with Father Michael,' he said thoughtfully. 'Ask his advice. I'm popping over to the Presbytery this evening. Better walk,' he laughed. 'I've had rather too much of this excellent Burgundy.'

Margaret was silent, thinking of Rob's visit and the terrible things he had said. A visit she would keep secret from Bernard.

'You're going to the Presbytery this evening?' she asked, startled. 'You never said.'

'I did, Margaret.' Gin, wine and Valium were having their

effect. 'I told you after we came out of Mass this morning.' He pushed his half-full plate away. 'I really can't eat anymore of this,' he said irritably. 'It's dreadful. Only you could overcook a leg of lamb and undercook the vegetables. You don't even make an effort.'

'Cooking has never been my forte,' she said distantly.

'What is, Margaret?' He leaned on his elbow and looked at her, thick straggly eyebrows raised, white teeth bared. She thought how evil he looked. 'We've yet to find out, haven't we? After all these years. You can't cook, you can't keep house. Look how Robert and Melanie have turned out – you couldn't bring up our children properly.' She gasped and looked away, fingers clutching the napkin. 'What use are you, in fact, to any living soul?' he went on. 'You're too selfish and preoccupied even to deliver hot lunches to a few senior citizens twice a week. What *is* your forte?' he repeated. 'Those ridiculous daubs you keep in the attic – oh, pardon me, the *studio*? Do you dream about being the star of the Woolton Art Group? Your own watercolour exhibition at the Bluecoat Chambers? I suppose you imagine you're the sensitive artist type doomed to be misunderstood by us lesser mortals. Why don't you join a yoga or meditation class, like all the other neurotic menopausal women with too much time on their hands?' He laughed. 'Or a cookery class would do for starters!'

Margaret got up trembling, her courage gone, unable to speak. His barbs pierced her sense of self, her hope and confidence. It would take time for the wound to heal and form new scar tissue. Bernard laughed louder, enjoying the effect of his remarks, thinking how easy it was to bring her into line. Almost too easy. Shannon was more of a challenge. He'd really enjoy snuffing the arrogance out of her!

Margaret hurried to the kitchen and took another Valium, swallowing it with the rest of her wine. The clearing and washing up could wait until he'd gone to the Presbytery – she couldn't bear to look at him again this evening. Thank goodness they had separate bedrooms. The Edwardian house was built to accommodate housemaids and numerous children, as well as married couples who could no longer bear to occupy the same bed.

The wine was finished. She poured a gin-and-tonic and

climbed the three flights of stairs to her attic studio, a huge bare room with a skylight and rough wooden floorboards, the walls covered with sprigged faded wallpaper. She switched on the light, a 100-watt bulb that dangled from the centre beam directly over her easel.

She shivered. It was always cold up here, except on summer days when sunshine poured through the skylight. An old black velvet sofa was pushed against the far wall and there was a table with jars, paintbrushes, sponges, different size watercolour pads, a half full bottle of gin. Then the little tubes of paint, whose names she loved and spoke aloud for the pleasure of hearing them: ultramarine, permanent rose, viridian green, cerulean blue, alizarin crimson. On the floor by the sofa were a pile of books on watercolour technique. She had taken it up twelve years ago, at forty, when Angie said they both needed a hobby.

Margaret walked to the easel and, sipping gin-and-tonic, studied her latest creation. She was practising her rainclouds technique, inspired by the grey weather that had hung over Liverpool all weekend. The picture was a clump of trees on a hilltop against a sky of heavy dark clouds. She had completed the first wash before dinner, a pale, pale Winsor blue, now dry. She put her drink down and began to mix a wash of yellow ochre in a ceramic dish.

The familiar sense of peace came over her as she worked, soothed by colour and the concentration that shut out everything. Rain battered the skylight. She might be menopausal, but she certainly wasn't neurotic. What a swine he was! She would live her own life, concentrate on self-preservation, shut out what disturbed her. She was stuck with a horrible husband – well, so were most women! She wasn't the first and she wouldn't be the last. Robert and Melanie were adults now. There was nothing she could do for them. She had to protect herself and her life. Jennifer Rothwell was coming to lunch a week on Wednesday and had promised to come up here afterwards and look at Margaret's work. She would do a cold buffet with French bread, smoked salmon and expensive delicatessen things – no cooking! A thrill of excitement ran through her. What would Jennifer think of her work? Suppose she really had talent? She glanced at the paintings stacked against the walls: flower studies, Lake District scenes, country houses, the back garden on a summer day.

'How could you let your husband – her father – fuck her since she was three years old and do nothing about it? Where were you?'

'No!' whispered Margaret, size eight sable brush poised above the yellow ochre wash. 'It's not true. I *will not* think about that! It never happened. It's all lies.'

She took another swig of gin and went on painting.

Bernard finished his wine, poured himself an Armagnac and went up to his study. That would teach her a lesson, he thought happily. Remind her of her *position*. He should have got rid of her years ago, but he'd needed a respectable wife. Her parents' money came in handy too; they couldn't have bought the house without it. Besides, they were Catholic. Marriage was for *life*. He smiled. You didn't get that for murder! Margaret was intellectually inferior, he had left her behind long ago. He frowned, thinking about the Meals on Wheels nonsense. He'd have to get her to take that up again. She should be as busy as possible, so as to leave him free.

He settled in his comfortable leather chair, put another tape in the video. It was all right except that they spoke Dutch and he couldn't understand a word. She was enjoying it really, he thought contemptuously, looking at the girl's agonized tearstained face. It contributed to her sexual development. He watched raptly, mouth open, eyes gleaming. When it was over he rewound the tape, locked it away in the drawer and unlocked another drawer, breathing in the wood smell and the delicious scent of lavender furniture polish. He polished the desk himself. Josie Duffy or Margaret would not have done a proper job. Josie Duffy! He frowned, picked up the phone and punched in the Norris Green number.

'Yeah?' a nasal female voice shouted. She had to shout because of applause and wild laughter from the television in the background.

'This is Bernard Flinder,' he said shortly. 'I'd like to speak to Mrs Duffy, please.'

He winced as the receiver was banged on a table, reverberating in his ear.

'Mam!' the girl yelled. *'Mam!* It's yer fancy man. He wants to know what yer knickers are doing tonight.'

'Gerrout of it, you soft bitch!' Josie laughed, exhaled smoke and picked up the phone. 'Is that you, Mick?' she asked slyly. 'Don't take any notice of that little scrubber.'

'This is Bernard Flinder,' he said stiffly.

'Oh, Bernie!' She laughed. 'Bernie the Bogeyman. What time d'you want me to start work tomorrow?'

'Well – that's what I'm calling about.' He struggled to keep his tone polite. 'I'm afraid my wife says she won't have you in the house again. She's definite about that.'

'I want an apology from that bitch.' Josie's tone was loud and indignant. 'She said I was retarded. Said I should be arrested because of me hair colour. Who the bloody hell does she think she is? Eh? I'm not having that.'

'I know, but she's going through a difficult time at the moment,' he said. 'I'm rather worried about her state of mind. She gets depressed, you see, and at her time of life–'

'Oh, the change, is it?' Josie dragged on her cigarette and coughed in his ear. 'Yeah. We all go a bit mental then – I was climbing the walls! But I didn't go round calling people retarded and accusing them of nicking things.'

'No, of course not.' He swallowed. 'I hope you'll accept my apology on behalf of Margaret?' The words nearly choked him. 'As I said, she refuses to let you in the house again and I can't do much about that. I don't want to argue with her when she's in this state. But I've thought of something else.' He looked at the open drawer which contained masking tape, a carton of latex gloves, a Bowie knife, a combat knife and a coil of orange nylon rope. Common bitch, he thought. I'd like to shut you up once and for all! 'I'm prepared to give you one hundred pounds a week – cash, of course. You could come to my office at school to collect it. Say, every Friday afternoon at one?' Staff and pupils disappeared at lunchtime. Irene usually did some shopping or went for a walk to clear her latest headache.

'It'll have to be three o' clock this Friday, Bern. I'm doing something at one.'

'All right, three o' clock. But in future . . .'

'You'll see me when you see me, all right? Hey, Bern!'

'Yes?' He stared at the knives.

'Watched any good videos lately? I bet they don't sell the kind you like in Woolton Village, eh?'

She hung up laughing. He wished he could plaster her common grinning mouth with masking tape and slash her throat with one of the knives. Should he get rid of the videos and magazines? Maybe it was too risky to keep them in the house. And it was getting risky to access the Internet for what he wanted. He'd pay Josie Duffy the money for now, but if she became more demanding or started to drop hints about going to the police he'd have to reconsider. He was sure she wouldn't go to the police because she was lazy and immoral and would have accepted handouts from Hitler. But, like most women, she didn't think logically. Women were dangerously unpredictable. 'And I know whereof I speak!' Bernard muttered grimly.

He pulled on a pair of latex gloves, picked up the rope and combat knife and went downstairs. Margaret would be stuck in the attic for hours with her gin and paintbrushes. Stupid bitch! Its only value lay in keeping her occupied. He put the knife, rope and gloves in his deep overcoat pockets; pulled on coat, black wool scarf and Russian fur hat. Should he take an umbrella? No. It might prove awkward. Black leather gloves were pulled on over the latex ones.

The rain still poured down and it was very cold. There were reports of flooding in some areas. Orange streetlight glinted in the puddles on the road. He walked down the dark avenue and turned left on to the main road that led to the village. It was still called Woolton Village even though it had long since become a Liverpool suburb. He walked past a row of lighted shops and an old pub, the Half Moon. There was nobody about. He came to St Augustine's church and its adjoining Presbytery. He didn't turn into the drive but walked on to the bus stop. He caught a green double decker bus into town then another bus to West Derby.

Shannon and Rob's detached house was in darkness except for

the porch light. The gates and garage were closed. This road was dark and tree-lined, like his own. The front gardens were big, the houses set well back from the narrow quiet road. He glanced around, opened the wrought iron gate and walked up the drive, breathing out clouds of carbon dioxide. He tried the toilet window down the side but it was locked and double glazed, impossible to smash. He went back to the front door and rang the bell. If anyone saw him – not likely, with all the trees and bushes in the garden and in the road – he would look like an ordinary visitor paying a Sunday evening social call.

He rang the bell four times, but there was no answer. After the fourth ring he swore and thumped the porch door. She must be there! She was probably cowering in her bedroom or the dark living room, too terrified to answer the door. He shouldn't have talked to her, put her on her guard. He couldn't get into the back garden because of the garage on one side of the house and the high bolted gate halfway down the other side.

He looked at the neighbouring house. Light filtered from behind curtained front windows. He crept into their driveway, edged past the parked Range Rover and down the side of the house to the back garden. The brick wall dividing their back garden from Shannon's was ten feet high and had broken glass along the top. He cursed. There was a garden shed that might contain a ladder, but the shed was padlocked.

'Damn and blast!' He stood there wondering what to do. No light came from the upper rooms of Shannon's house; the wall was too high to see the living room and kitchen windows, but no yellow light penetrated the darkness. Maybe the bitch was out. But where? When would she be back? He might have to wait hours. It was no good, he'd have to try again tomorrow. Bloody bitch! He'd come all this way – on public transport! – for nothing. He'd get her next time, that was for sure. He turned, headed back down the drive and was edging past the Range Rover when he was confronted by a dark thickset male figure who ran out of the front door. Chris Campbell.

'What the bloody hell d'you think you're doing?' he shouted.

'Is that you, Mr Campbell?' Bernard gripped the knife in his pocket. 'Thank goodness!' Damn, he thought! Damn you to hell and back, you interfering bastard! 'Did you see him?' he panted.

'Who?' Chris asked warily. 'What's going on?'

'Chris!' a woman's voice called. 'Are you all right?'

'Yeah. Get back inside, Lorraine, it's pissing down out here.' He turned back to Bernard. 'See who?'

'The burglar. At least, I presume that's what he was. I came to visit my son and daughter-in-law,' Bernard said worriedly, 'but they're not in. They must have forgotten I was coming. An intruder was trying to break in.' He paused. 'A young black man in a padded jacket and woolly hat – he looked about twenty. I challenged him but he threatened me with a combat knife then jumped over the wall and ran down the side of your house. I chased him but he got away.' He laughed apologetically. 'I'm afraid I'm not as young as I used to be.'

'Bloody bastard!' Chris spat. 'Lowlife scum! I'll call the police. You'd better come in,' he said unwillingly. The football was just starting; he'd spent the day with eyes and ears shut so as not to know the score.

'Oh no, no!' Bernard said hastily. 'Don't trouble yourself, Mr Campbell. My car's just down the road, I can call them on my mobile phone. And I'll find my son and daughter-in-law, tell them what's happened. They'll need to come back and check the house. I think I know where they are.'

'Look, mate, it might as well be me who calls the police,' Chris said belligerently. 'He's been in my garden. I'll just check the shed, see the padlock's secure. Bloody bastards!' he swore again. Rain soaked his sweatshirt and stubbly head. 'You find Rob and Shannon,' he ordered. Come to think of it, he hadn't seen Rob Flinder in a while. 'That's the first thing. Leave the police to me.'

'All right,' Bernard said reluctantly. He could hardly tell him *not* to call the police. Damn and blast! 'I'll get going then,' he said. 'Goodnight.' Chris ran back into the house for the shed keys and Bernard walked out of the drive and turned into the road.

He hurried along, chest heaving with fury, blood hissing in his ears. This was all Shannon's fault! She'd pay double when he got her. He imagined her staring up at him, those big long-lashed violet blue eyes dilated with terror. He couldn't wait! He glanced over his shoulder and stopped for a breather. There was no one about. Not many people would come out on such a night. Rain soaked his face and shoulders and hat. He came to the bus stop at the end of the road. Act normally, he thought angrily. Don't rush. You're not guilty of anything.

'Terrible night, isn't it?' he said pleasantly to the young auburn-haired girl waiting at the bus stop.

She moved away, eyes averted, and glanced impatiently up and down the road. Bernard felt annoyed. They had no manners nowadays. He stood still, getting his breath. This is ridiculous, he thought, coughing. He should take more exercise, get fit. Too much smoking, driving around, sitting at desks. He was fifty-three, that was nothing.

'D'you know what time the bus is due?' he asked the girl. He smiled. 'It's raining and bitterly cold, so of course it's bound to be late, isn't it?'

She was about five-foot-four and very thin. She wore a long black jacket, dogtooth check trousers, clumpy boots, and like all of them these days, some sort of backpack strapped to her bony shoulders. They came to school looking as if they were about to set off for a week's camping in the Lake District. He noted that the bus stop backed on to a sports field, surrounded on three sides by rows of tall poplars. White goal posts at either end gleamed faintly in the darkness.

'Eh? You *what*?' She looked at him, her lidless eyes blank. She had a small petulant bow mouth and her nose was too big for her narrow pale face.

'I said, do you know what time the bus is due?' he asked impatiently. He glanced at his watch. It was almost nine o clock.

'Dunno. Haven't a clue.' She shrugged and turned away. Stupid old bastard, she thought. What use was a fur hat and a posh accent when you had to go on buses? She smirked as she looked down the road, straining her eyes to see if the distant headlights were the bus at last. What was he doing now, fiddling about? Looking for his old git bus pass, probably.

She screamed and froze in panic as he grabbed her hair and jerked her head back. A cold knife blade pressed the pulsing artery at the base of her throat.

'Don't move and don't say anything, you little bitch!' he hissed.

'Or I'll slash your throat and let you bleed to death right here. D'you understand?'

She uttered a strangled grunt and tried to nod, her terrified eyes staring at the bus stop sign. The approaching headlights belonged to the bus, she could hear its throbbing engine. Gripping her hair, the knife pressed to her throat, he dragged her away from the stop and into the dark field beyond, her head pulled so far back she couldn't see where she was going. They stumbled through dark wet grass, his hot winey breath on her neck.

'I won't hurt you as long as you do what I say,' he muttered. 'I only want to touch you a little bit, that's all. Then I'll let you go home.'

'Oh, God!' she gasped. 'Oh, Jesus. Mum! Mum!'

'Shut up!' He wrenched the backpack from her shoulders and shoved her against the rough bark of a tree. He pulled off her jacket and threw it on the grass. A few hundred yards away a police car sped past the bus stop, blue light flashing, siren blaring.

'Keep still or I'll kill you.'

Her thin body shook with cold and terror as her wrists were tied with orange nylon rope. He'd have to get hold of a pair of handcuffs, he thought, as he struggled in the darkness to tie the knots. He turned her round to face him, pushed her back against the tree trunk and used the knife to slit open her sweater and the T-shirt she wore underneath. He undid her trousers and dragged them down her thighs. She saw the latex gloves and began to cry. He had planned this. He wanted to rape someone. She was in the horribly wrong place at the horribly wrong time.

'Don't hurt me!' she wailed as he slashed at her pants with the knife, ripping the thin cotton. 'Don't! Please!'

'Are you scared?' he asked thickly, choked with the excitement that threatened to overwhelm him. Take it slowly, he thought. Enjoy.

'Please let me go!' she sobbed. She screamed as his gloved fingers probed her crotch.

'You've got hardly any hair. That's nice. Are you scared?' He drew back his arm and hit her twice across the face, pressing his other hand on her naked chest to make sure she didn't fall.

'Yeah, I'm scared,' she moaned, dazed by the blows. Blood

trickled from her nostrils into her mouth. She was prone to nose bleeds.

'What's your name?' he hissed.

'F-Francesca.' She licked metallic tasting blood from her lips.

'That's nice. Have you got a boyfriend, Francesca?' He unbuttoned his coat and unzipped his trousers. In the dim light he could see her heart beating through her white skin. He drew the knife blade over her frozen nipples.

'Yes.'

'How old are you?'

'Twelve,' she gasped. 'Please let me go!'

'Twelve's too young for a boyfriend, Francesca.' He pressed himself to her trembling icy body. 'But you're lucky. You're going to get a real man.'

He groped in his overcoat pocket again and she moaned in terror and struggled frantically as masking tape was wound around her mouth, sticking to and trapping her hair. Warm urine streamed down the inside of her thighs.

'What did you want to go and do that for?' he shouted in disgust. He pushed her and she fell face down on the ground. 'Now I'll have to really hurt you!' He bent, panting, and pulled off her trousers and clumpy boots. She kicked her feet up and wriggled frantically, her face in the freezing wet grass. She could hardly breathe.

'Keep still, Francesca,' he warned. 'I need you to keep very still.' He parted her legs and grabbed her buttocks. 'Otherwise I'll have to teach you a lesson.'

He taught her a lesson anyway.

An hour later Father Michael unlocked and unbolted the front door of the Presbytery, wondering what the caller wanted at ten-fifteen at night. He hoped it wasn't some demented hooligan with a knife to back up his hard luck story. You never knew these days.

'Bernard!' he exclaimed, astonished. 'For God's sake, man! I thought you weren't coming.' He stood back and opened the door wide. 'Mrs O'Connor just locked up and went to bed.'

'Sorry I'm so late, Father.' Bernard stepped into the hall and smiled as he saw the glow of a coal fire through the living room doorway. 'But I've got a confession to make.'

'Ah, yes. What would that be now?'

'I fell asleep in front of the television after Margaret's Sunday roast. With which we enjoyed some excellent Burgundy and Armagnac.'

'Did you now?' Father Michael took off his spectacles and rubbed his eyes. 'Did you now? Well, you're entitled, Bernard. I'll let you off with a Hail Mary. Armagnac, eh?'

He led the way into the big living room and headed for the sideboard with its array of bottles. 'D'you fancy a wee nightcap?' he asked. 'I won't tell if you don't.'

'You're on, Father.' Bernard winked back. 'You can lead me into temptation.'

Margaret, painting rainclouds and swigging gin-and-tonic, didn't know if Bernard had gone out or come back. And she didn't want to know.

Chapter Fourteen

Shannon stirred and stretched in the big bed, pulling the quilt over her bare shoulders. On the Mersey the pilot boat chugged past and a fog horn sounded. Rain pattered the double glazing. She woke, sat up and looked round the dark unfamiliar room. White walls, white Venetian blinds, parquet floor, two big windows, an antique floor-length mirror in one corner, a wardrobe and pine chest at the foot of the bed. Her handbag, briefcase and open suit-case on the floor between the windows. Bianca's doll was in the briefcase, wrapped in two freezer bags. The blinds were open and the river cast rippling patterns of faintly coloured light on the walls and ceiling.

She lay down again and closed her eyes. She had had her best night's sleep in weeks, deep and peaceful and dreamless. She'd accepted Finbar's offer of a bolthole, this huge warm silent apart-ment by the river. She could have stayed with Nick and Caroline, but they had Helen to take care of and she didn't want to disrupt their lives. She could stay with him, Finbar offered, he was out or away a lot. She was welcome to stay as long as she liked. Nick had taken photos of her bruises, the doctor had examined her. The rib was not cracked, just bruised. She would ache for a day or two, the swelling around her eye would go down. Shannon knew she was lucky; it could have been a lot worse. But she didn't feel lucky.

She showered, dressed, packed some things and went to Nick and Caroline's for dinner, a dinner she couldn't eat. Afterwards Finbar had driven her here. He'd made her a cup of tea and showed her the guest room. She had drunk the tea, collapsed into the big bed and fallen deeply asleep.

How did her face look this morning? She'd need plenty of war paint before she faced the office. Exchange Flags was only ten minutes walk from the Albert Dock. She'd take a bus or taxi to West Derby later, pick up the Nissan. Or not. Tomorrow would do. She felt safe with Finbar. She wanted to stay in the warm room, sleep the morning away, not face Gavin. His contempt and lack of support had changed cheerful indifference to deep dislike. To think he believed Bernard! It was outrageous. Anger rose in her. She had to face him. Her future depended on it.

'Shannon?' She stiffened at the sound of Finbar's voice. He knocked softly at the door.

'Come in.' She switched on the bedside lamp and huddled beneath the quilt.

He came in, dressed in dark suit and tie. He carried a tray with coffee, toast, a boiled egg and a bunch of muscat grapes.

'Good morning! You asked to be woken at seven. Brought you some breakfast.' He put the tray on the bedside table and looked out of the window. 'Cold again,' he said quietly. 'Fog on the river.'

'Thanks for the breakfast,' she said awkwardly. 'It looks delicious. I can't eat all that though.'

'Try,' he said. 'You need your strength. You look even thinner than when we met a few weeks ago.'

'How – how does my face look this morning?' she asked, blushing with embarrassment. He turned and bent slightly, studying her, his expression calm and self-possessed. She pushed back her hair.

'Not bad,' he said after a few seconds. 'Honestly. A caffeine fix, vitamin C from the grapes, a lick of make-up and you'll be the business.'

She smiled, relaxing slightly, and he smiled back. He longed to have the bastard husband put in intensive care – hopefully there wouldn't be any beds! – but that would upset her more. She was loyal. She still loved him and wanted him back. Last night she'd said something about the tosser having a breakdown. Finbar was delighted, if surprised, that she'd accepted his offer to stay here.

She was desperate to be out of her house, he could understand that. But he couldn't shake the feeling that something or someone apart from the husband was freaking her out. Something she wouldn't tell him or anybody. He wouldn't ask. Not yet anyway. She needed to rest, to heal. He remembered his shock at the sight of her yesterday.

'I'm leaving in a minute,' he said. 'Flying to London for the day. Business. I'll be back around six, six-thirty.' He hesitated. 'Would you like to have some dinner with me when I get back? If you're not busy this evening.'

She was silent, embarrassed. 'I – I don't want to go to a restaurant.'

'No worries. I'll cook us something here. Use the kitchen for once.'

'Finbar.' She shifted in the bed and pulled the quilt up to her chin. 'Don't you have a wife or girlfriend?' she asked tentatively. Nick had said he wasn't married, but he might be mistaken. 'I mean, it's very kind of you to let me stay, but won't she mind my being here?'

'There's nobody,' he said briefly. He turned away and stared out at the misty river again. 'I was married once,' he said. 'We lived in Dublin. Her name was Majella. We had a baby daughter, Roiseann, she was nine months old. They were killed in a shootout at a checkpoint in the North. My wife had gone to visit a cousin she hadn't seen for years. The wrong place at the wrong time.'

'Oh, my God!' she exclaimed, horrified. 'That's terrible. I'm so sorry!'

He glanced at his watch. 'I'd better go.' He turned away from the window and looked down at her. 'Eat some breakfast,' he smiled. 'Oh, spare keys.' He took them out of his pocket and laid them on the tray. 'That's for the main door downstairs and this is for the front door,' he explained. 'Make yourself at home, do what you want. Don't feel you have to talk to me. If there's anything you need, let me know.' He longed to kiss her, hold her, tell her everything would be all right. *Did* she like him at all?

She smiled, still embarrassed. 'Thanks, Finbar.'

'You're going to work today?' he asked.

'Yes.'

'Sure you're up to it?'

'No.'

'Well-.' He grinned. 'Take care. I'll see you this evening.'

'Okay. 'Bye!'

He went out and seconds later the heavy front door closed. She sat up and reached for the breakfast tray. The coffee smelled wonderful. Butter melted into the toast and the egg was hard-boiled, the way she liked it. The grapes were bursting with sweetness.

How terrible to lose his wife and child like that, she thought. Shot! Would she ever have the child – children – she wanted? She thought about Bernard and what he'd said. Even if he was banged up he'd be out in a few years. He'd fake remorse, tell some gullible psychiatrist or social worker what they wanted to hear. They would find him a job, maybe let him teach again. Nothing would surprise her. He'd be free to rape and murder more girls. Rob, Margaret and Melanie were in denial, they cared only about themselves. She herself was a coward, terrified she might drive Rob to a nervous breakdown and never get him back. She was still in shock from his behaviour yesterday. He was getting worse. She'd never have believed he'd hit her, rape her.

Shannon pushed away the breakfast tray and sat shivering with fear, her knees drawn up. What was she going to do? Neither Rob nor the police would listen to her. She was probably the big laugh of the Regional Crime Squad right now. She carried Bianca's doll around with her, not knowing what to do with it for the present. She couldn't think of anywhere safe to leave it. She still loved Rob and wanted him back, but she had to protect herself. What if he beat her up again? Should she try for a restraining order, an injunction? And there was Bernard. What would his next move be?

Grey light dawned over the misty river as she left the apartment and walked through the Albert Dock complex, up Water Street and on to Exchange Flags. The rain was icy. Shannon hurried through the cold wet streets carrying her briefcase and umbrella. Bernard should be given a concrete overcoat, she thought suddenly. The idea made her laugh. Kill anyone who stood in your way? If only life could be that simple! But there had to be certain commonly held principles, a legal system. Without that there was chaos.

She reached Exchange Flags, entered her building and headed for the lift, shaking raindrops from the umbrella. Anita the receptionist was not at her desk, Shannon noted with relief. She must be in the toilet plastering on more blusher and lipgloss or squeezing a spot on her nose.

'Shannon!' Jenny Fong jumped up from her desk as Shannon passed down the corridor to her office. 'How are you?' She ran after her. 'I tried to call you a few times but there was no answer. My God! What happened to your face?'

'Thanks a lot! Does it look that bad?' Shannon unlocked her door. 'I thought I'd done a good job with the old war paint.'

'Oh, you have. But you can see bruising around your eye and on your cheekbone . . . what *happened*?' gasped Jenny.

'It's a long story, as they say. I haven't the time or the inclination to explain.' She took off her black coat and patted her damp curly hair. 'Is Mini Tampon in?' she asked, and dumped her briefcase on the desk. 'I need a cosy chat.'

'Yes, half an hour ago. He's in a right mood. Anita's crying in the toilet because he just asked her why she spends all her money on make-up and poodle perms when she'd be better off saving it for a nose job.'

'That wasn't very nice.' Shannon ran her hands over her black close-fitting suit with the long tight skirt. She wore clumpy black leather ankle boots.

'You've lost weight,' Jenny looked her up and down. 'I bet you're no more than eight stone. You'd better have a cow pie for lunch.'

'How do I look?' Shannon asked, and whirled round, hands on hips.

'Professional? In control? And yet sufficiently feminine and non-threatening to the masculist ego?' Jenny giggled. 'I say masculist because of course you can have masculist women as well as men. Speaking of which-,' she murmured.

Priscilla stood in the doorway, smoking a cigarette and wearing her saddest tweed coat.

'So you're back, are you?' she said, looking cross.

'Apparently!' Shannon smiled sweetly. 'Good morning, Priscilla!'

'Shame we can't all run off whingeing for a week when work gets on top of us.'

'Work's the only thing that'll ever get on top of you. And I hope you had a *lovely* weekend?'

Priscilla snorted and marched on to her office. Bloody bimbo, she thought angrily, crushing out the cigarette. Gavin would shaft her once and for all. Partnership! At least he'd come to his senses about that, thank God. Shannon Flinder would be kicked out this morning. He'd hinted as much although he wouldn't discuss what had happened. Well, he obviously felt a fool. He'd hired her. Why did she look so cocky when she had no job anymore? Or did she think she still had? Stupid cow! Priscilla smiled gleefully.

'Good morning, Gavin!' Shannon went into his office and sat on the chair opposite his desk. The sofa was reserved for clients and honoured visitors.

'Hmm!' He swivelled round in his chair and dropped *The Times* on the desk. 'What have you got to say for yourself? To *explain*?' He glanced at his watch. 'Make it snappy.'

'I'd like you to read this,' said Shannon, her heart thudding. She unfolded a sheet of paper with her GP's letterhead. 'This is a letter – a certificate, if you like – from my doctor, to say I have no history of depression or mental illness of any kind. You can phone him if you like. He's been my GP for years, has all my medical records since birth.' She laughed nervously. 'Not many people have a certificate to prove they're sane. I bet you don't!'

Gavin looked at her stonily from behind his Nazi doctor glasses and she bit her lip, wondering if she'd gone too far. This wasn't a time for levity. It never was with Gavin Steele!

He read the letter and blushed to the roots of his sandy hair. He'd been having twinges of doubt since her phone call yesterday. Bernard Flinder had made a real arse of him.

'I'm devastated because Rob's left me,' said Shannon quietly, seeing his reaction. 'There aren't any other men involved – that's another lie. It's a big shock to the system when you suddenly discover you don't have a marriage anymore. But there's a vital difference between unhappy and *unbalanced*, Gavin! Rob changed, literally overnight. I don't know him anymore. He says he wants a divorce. That's why I was in such a state.'

She noted the past tense and suddenly realized that something had altered in her since Rob's assault, hardened. Self-preservation kicking in? 'All this has been a terrible shock. But I'm trying to pick up the pieces, get on with my life. I'm dealing with it. If you sack me on the basis of a slanderous allegation, I'll have to sue,' she said, giving him a fierce look. Gavin dropped his eyes. 'There's no legal aid for libel or slander cases – not that I'd qualify anyway – but it's my career, my professional reputation at stake. I'd have no choice. If you sack me I won't get another job in Liverpool, maybe not in the whole of the north west. So I've no choice,' she repeated.

'Why would . . .?' Gavin cleared his throat. 'Why would your father-in-law do what he did?' The little crystal teddy bear winked at him. He felt completely stupid, furious that he'd been made to look such a fool.

'I don't really know,' lied Shannon. She couldn't tell him the truth about Bernard. There was too much at stake. She looked down at her lap and flexed her slim fingers. 'We've never got on - his attitude to women is feudal to say the least. He wasn't much of a father to Rob. I've shrugged off his snide remarks and domineering behaviour and attempts to interfere in our marriage. But this time he's gone too far.'

And so have you, you bastard, she thought. She'd start looking for another job immediately. She could use the withdrawal of the promised partnership as an excuse, make Gavin look the arsehole he was. Time *I* indulged in a bit of slander, she thought grimly. With truth as my defence.

'Well.' Gavin folded the letter and handed it back. 'Obviously this proves you don't have a history of depression,' he said abruptly. 'I won't bother to call your GP. And you say you're getting things sorted. You can go back to work and we'll forget this. Say no more about it.'

'There is one thing you could say.' Shannon took the letter and stood up.

'What's that?'

'*Sorry!*'

'Don't push it, Shannon,' he snarled. 'Okay, I admit I was wrong to listen to your father-in-law. That's as far as I'll go.'

It wasn't good enough. 'What about the partnership?' she asked.

'We'll leave that for the moment,' he said evasively, fiddling with his blue bow tie patterned with gold stars and glancing out across rainwashed Exchange Flags. 'Now, if you don't mind?' He glanced at his watch. 'I have to be somewhere ten minutes ago.'

Shannon went back to her office and sat there fuming. But she still had her job, that was the important thing. Jenny came in with a cup of espresso.

'I thought you might need this. Anita says there's a message for you to call your neighbour,' she said, putting down the gold-rimmed cup and saucer.

'My *neighbour*?'

'Yes.' She uncrumpled a pink post-it note. 'Mrs Lorraine Campbell. This is her work number, some Job Centre in Wavertree. She'd like you to call her as soon as possible.'

'I wonder what she wants?' Shannon sipped the coffee. 'She came round to complain about our barbecue smoke one day last summer and she's hardly spoken to me since. Mmm, lovely coffee. Thanks, Jen!'

Pain took hold as she recalled the hot August afternoon when she and Rob had abandoned cold white wine, chargrilled salmon steaks and giant prawns to make love on the living room floor. Lorraine had disturbed them at a crucial moment, leaning on the door bell until they answered. Jenny went out and Shannon dialled the Job Centre number and asked for Mrs Campbell.

'Lorraine, this is Shannon Flinder,' she said briskly. 'You wanted me to call you?' She visualized her neighbour's heavy body in the baggy jeans and boring home-made sweaters she always wore, her brassy dried-out perm and suspicious blanket hole eyes. She was thirty, but looked ten years older.

'Yes.' Lorraine had a whining nasal I'm-so-badly-done-by voice. 'Chris and I went round to your house three times last night, but you didn't come home,' she said accusingly. 'Didn't your father-in-law tell you about the intruder?'

'My father-in-law?' She froze. 'An *intruder*?'

'Yes,' Lorraine said impatiently. 'Mr Flinder came to see you and Rob last night about half eight, quarter to nine. Chris ran out because he saw someone sneaking down our drive. He thought they wanted to steal the Range Rover. But it was your father-in-law, chasing an intruder he caught trying to break into your house. A black man of about twenty, he said. It was really brave of him to give chase like that, he could have been attacked. He said you must have forgotten he was coming.' She sounded full of disapproval. 'Chris called the police and Mr Flinder said he'd find you and Rob and tell you what had happened.' She paused. 'Obviously he didn't succeed. Have you been away or something?'

'My *God*!' Shannon breathed. Fear gripped her. Bernard! He must have tried and failed to break into her house and crept down the side of the Campbells' house, hoping to climb over the wall and break in at the back. He'd meant to threaten her, hurt her maybe. Feeling safe because neither Rob nor the police would listen to her. How typical that he'd described the imaginary intruder as black!

'Have you or Rob seen anyone suspicious hanging around lately?'

'No. Well, I haven't seen anyone.'

'It's so creepy,' Lorraine said shrilly. 'But that's not the worst of it.'

'No?' Shannon closed her eyes, praying to whatever benign powers might be on her side.

'A young girl was murdered near here last night. Francesca Delaney, her name was. Twelve years old. It was on breakfast news, did you watch that?'

'No,' Shannon said faintly. He's done it again! she thought. I should have stopped him. My God, why didn't I stop him!

'It's the second murder of a young girl within weeks,' Lorraine said indignantly. 'The rest of Britain must think Liverpool's bursting with perverted homicidal maniacs. Some dog walker found her body on the playing field. Practically on our back doorsteps! It's always dog walkers who find bodies, isn't it? The police want to interview everyone in Eaton Road – they'll want to see you about the attempted break-in too. There's an incident van parked a few houses away, you're supposed to go and fill in a form. She'd been raped and strangled and probably other gruesome things they won't make public. It makes you shudder to think of it. They say it could be that intruder who did it, he might have been out looking for a victim. She's – she *was* – the girlfriend of some boy who lives round here, she'd spent the day at his house. Wouldn't you think the miserable little sod would have walked her to the bus stop? I feel sorry for girls nowadays.'

'Yes.' Shannon wanted to cry. She should have stopped him! The nightmare had happened again. She wished Lorraine would shut up.

'I'm surprised Rob didn't phone to tell you about it,' Lorraine said curiously. 'He must have known the minute he got to work. He's probably got inside information. Can you both pop round for a drink tonight?' she asked, eager for gossip. 'We should keep an eye on each other's houses from now on, maybe start a neighbourhood watch scheme.'

'Well, I'm not staying at home,' Shannon said awkwardly. 'Not for a while anyway.' She couldn't get through a single day without having to explain her business to somebody! No one explained anything to her.

'But you're at work.' Lorraine was mystified. She sniffed intrigue, hopefully to be upgraded to scandal. 'What . . .?'

'Look, Lorraine–' Damn! 'To tell you the truth, Rob and I have split up,' said Shannon, closing her eyes. How it hurt to say that! 'At least for now. He moved out a week ago.' The Nissan could stay in the garage. She was too afraid to go near the house after this. 'I'm staying with a friend for a few days.'

'You've split up?' Lorraine was astonished, triumphant. She'd often remarked jealously to Chris how that pair couldn't keep their hands off one another. Now they had problems like the rest of squabbling disappointed humanity. 'You and Rob have *split up*? God!' Her pale lips curved in a big smile. 'Why? What happened?' she asked, ignoring the weary jobseeker sitting opposite.

'I don't want to discuss it,' Shannon said sharply. Your good news pissed people off, your bad news gave them orgasmic delight.

'But it's good to talk about things-.'

'Not with a nosy neighbour who's called round once in eighteen months and then only to complain about something. You've got a bloody nerve, Lorraine!'

'Well, I'm sure I–'

'I'm going to hang up now. I don't work in a Job Centre so I haven't got all day to gas on the phone at taxpayers' expense. *Goodbye!*'

Shannon hung up and buried her head in her hands. So the police wanted to see her! That made a change. It didn't mean they'd tackle Bernard. If she showed them the doll again and had to tell them how she'd got it they might even charge her with criminal damage, like Bernard said. He'd regained confidence, knew Rob and the police wouldn't listen to her. But he was still scared of what she might do. That made him dangerous. What the hell *could* she do?

'Ready to go, Shannon?' Jenny popped her head round the door. 'Magistrates' Court. It's old Eric again. He's nicked a bottle of body lotion and two packets of Super Plus tampons this time, can you believe it? They'll probably defer for a psychiatric report.' She paused. 'Are you all right?'

'I'm fine.' Shannon stood up, pushing her hair back. 'Absolutely bloody fine.'

'Well, you don't *bloody* look it!'

She picked up her briefcase. 'Let's go and defend our bewildered gentleman. Poor old sod.'

Shannon didn't know how she got through the day. The rain turned to sleet, sweeping through the city, catching people unawares. The wind rose. It was dark by four-thirty. She got back from court and sat staring at case books and law reports, blinds drawn on the wet lights of Exchange Flags. Bernard was free, she was the prisoner. Trapped by fear and a cunning bastard whose devious moves left her gasping. She'd thought *she* was so clever! She was half-baked, naive. Knew *nothing*.

Shannon left the office at six. The streets were crowded with office workers hurrying to James Street Station or queueing for buses from the Pier Head. Shiny black cabs swished past, spraying sleet. She hurried through the dark wet streets down to the Albert

Dock, the smell of the river in her nostrils. She ducked into an old wine merchant's, a dim oak-scented cellar full of bottles and wine casks, and bought two bottles of Australian Shiraz Cabernet as her contribution to Finbar's dinner. The bottles clinked in the carrier bag as she walked quickly along, glancing back to check she wasn't being followed. She hated the constant fear, the realization that Bernard might threaten or even harm her. My life has been turned upside down in a few weeks, she thought. Rob rapes me, beats me up. It turns out his father's a murderous paedophile who walks free. No one will help me. It's unreal! Even Finbar Linnell was kind just because he wanted her in his bed. She was alone. Terribly alone.

She stopped and gave a cry of fright as a car door slammed nearby. 'Sorry. Did I startle you?' A tall woman laden with shopping bags smiled at her, streetlight and raindrops glistening on her long dark curly hair.

'It's okay.' Shannon shook her head, smiled back and walked on, physically and mentally drained. Her body ached and she felt sick because she'd eaten nothing since breakfast. Weird to feel sick on an empty stomach. She didn't think Bernard would risk another visit to her house tonight; Chris and Lorraine would be glued to their windows and the area thick with police and forensics in white romper suits. Poor Francesca!

She gripped the briefcase and carrier bag as she hurried across deserted Salthouse Quay. It was freezing. Sleet sprayed the dock waters, stung her face. She couldn't wait to get warm.

Bernard was light on his feet for such a big man. The blow to the back of Shannon's head sent her sprawling on the wet cobblestones and the bottles smashed, spraying Shiraz Cabernet over her legs. She could smell the wine. Dazed, she tried to get up and screamed as Bernard's bulk loomed over her in the darkness. He lashed out again and she fell back, head hitting the cobblestones. She was wet, freezing, paralyzed with terror. Who would help her? Crowds of people one minute, nobody the next. Water slapped against the dock sides. She saw the lights of the Maritime Museum and the old warehouses in the distance. The smell of wine was strong in her nostrils. Bernard grabbed the briefcase and opened it.

'I thought so!' He gave a gasp of triumph. 'I knew my souvenir would be safe with you.' The doll might not be admissible as evidence, but he wouldn't take any chances. Without it she had nothing. Except her big mouth.

He dropped to his knees, straddled Shannon and gagged her with masking tape. She kicked furiously and struggled beneath him. Her arms were trapped, eyes wide and frantic and full of terror, the way he'd imagined. He glanced quickly around. He'd followed her from Exchange Flags, not difficult when screened by darkness and driving sleet and hordes of commuters. He'd intended to follow her home, overpower her, force her to drive to Calderstones Park where he'd taken Bianca. Kill her there. But she'd come here and that meant a change of plan. What was she doing near the Albert Dock? It didn't matter. It was pitch dark, quiet. Shannon couldn't have chosen a better spot to end her bitch existence.

She didn't understand why he pulled open her coat and jacket and shoved his rough hand up her tight sweater, grabbing her breasts. She arched her back and dug in her heels, trying to wriggle her arms out of the coat sleeves.

'Don't worry,' he laughed, gazing down at her. 'It's not what you think. I just want another little souvenir before I choke the life out of you.'

She saw the gleam of the combat knife and her heart jumped with terror. He meant to kill her, mutilate her first. She couldn't breathe. She writhed beneath him, pulling her arms free. He pinched at her frozen left nipple and held the knife poised.

Feet pounded the cobbles and stopped abruptly. Bernard glanced up to find two young boys staring at him. They wore jeans, trainers, baseball caps and black padded jackets.

'Go away!' Bernard hissed. 'Get out of here.' Damn! He whipped the knife out of sight. Shannon freed one arm and tore the tape off her mouth.

'Help!' she screamed at the startled boys. 'Help me!' She hit out furiously at Bernard then turned her head and sank her teeth into his right thigh. He cried out at the pain.

One of the boys turned. 'Mum!' he shouted nervously into the dark. '*Mum!* Come here. Quick!'

'What's up?' a woman's voice called.

Damn and blast! He had to get away. Bernard grabbed the wrapped Barbie doll, her blank eyes visible through the plastic. Shannon struggled to her feet, shaking with fright, adjusting her clothes with trembling hands. She picked up the heavy briefcase and swung it at his head. He groaned and sank to his knees, still holding the doll. The fur hat toppled off. The boys ran off into the darkness.

'You bastard!' she screamed. 'If you come near me again I'll kill you. I'll kill you! You won't hurt anyone else – not ever!'

Suddenly Shannon knew what she had to do. He could keep the doll, it didn't matter anymore. She turned and ran, stumbling over the slippery cobblestones, leaving him behind. He couldn't chase her, he wasn't fit enough. She raced across the car park and gained the safety of the Maritime Museum and Albert Dock, Finbar's spare keys clenched in her fist. Her breath came in sobbing gasps. He wanted to kill her! Well, now she knew. If Chris and Lorraine hadn't seen him the other night he'd probably have tried to do it then. He thought he could get away with anything. She unlocked the heavy entrance door and ran sobbing up the stairs to the apartment.

Finbar's stainless steel kitchen was warm and bright with green leeks and red peppers, and smelled of garlic and fresh ginger. Rice steamed in a pan. He had changed out of his sharp suit and wore jeans and a long loose black top.

'Hello there!' He turned as she came into the kitchen and stared. His smile faded. Shannon looked battered, white-faced, terrified. Her hair and clothes were in a state, soaked and covered with mud. He could smell alcohol. 'What the bloody hell happened to you?' he asked, horrified. He took the briefcase out of her shaking hand.

'I – I fell over.' She sniffed, gulped, tried to get herself together. She wouldn't look at him.

'*Fell over*?' he repeated disbelievingly. 'Did your – was it him? Did he hurt you again?' He took her arm.

'No! Please!' Her gorgeous violet blue eyes stared up at him in panic. 'It wasn't Rob. I was crossing Salthouse Quay and slipped on the cobblestones, went flying. I had two bottles of wine in a carrier bag – they got smashed. It wasn't Rob,' she repeated desperately.

He didn't believe her. 'Why are you so frightened?' he asked gently.

'I'm not! I'm just–. It's been a long day and I'm really tired,' she protested. 'And freaked out by everything that's happened lately. I got a shock when I slipped and fell and the bottles smashed. That's all.' She looked away, close to tears again.

She was lying. It might not be *Rob*, but it was somebody. She didn't trust him. But why should she? He let go of her arm.

'Are you sure you're not hurt?'

'I'm fine.' She struggled against a desire to fling herself into his arms and burst into floods of tears. 'I just need to get a hot shower.'

'Have a drink first.' He poured her a big glass of velvety red wine that went straight to her head and empty stomach, spreading warmth throughout her frozen terrified body. He watched as she drained most of the wine in one go, gasped and closed her eyes.

'Are you really okay?' He took the glass from her and refilled it. 'I mean, apart from the trouble with your husband.' He hated to say the word.

'I'm fine, honestly. It'll take a while for all this to sink in. I can cope, though. I'll be fine.' Shannon looked away, glance resting on the pan of softly steaming rice. 'What's for dinner?' she asked, too brightly, embarrassed by the warmth and concern in Finbar's beautiful green eyes. Rob had once looked at her like that.

'Chicken breast, stir-fried with mushrooms and leeks and red pepper. I hope you can eat a bit?'

'Sounds delicious. Can I do anything to help?' She looked at the array of knives in their wooden blocks and shivered.

'You're joking!' He smiled, following her glance. 'Just relax, and drink your wine. Go and have your shower.' He picked up a lemon and peeled away thin strips of zest. I'll give you a shout when dinner's ready.'

'Thanks.' She turned and left the kitchen.

He dropped the lemon zest on a saucer and sliced mushrooms thinly. If only she'd tell him who – what – frightened her so much. He drank more wine and sighed. He should leave her alone, not put pressure on her. It was crazy to care so much about a woman he scarcely knew, but he couldn't help it. He longed to follow her to the guest room and comfort her. All right – *fuck* her. He'd never wanted anyone so much, not even . . . He gasped as the Sabatier knife almost sliced off the top of his index finger.

The hot shower warmed and relaxed Shannon, easing away aches and pains. It couldn't ease her mind. Bernard wanted her dead. *Dead!* He might have succeeded if the two boys hadn't come along. And he would have . . .! She gasped as her hand flew protectively to one breast. Had he mutilated his other victims? She dried herself, smoothed on body lotion and baby powder and sprayed herself with Obsession. Then she slipped on the heavy thick baby blue robe that went with the baby blue bathroom and towels and strolled back to the adjoining bedroom, rubbing her hair dry.

She sat on the bed. It was pointless to try to talk to Rob. He was like Margaret and Melanie, determined to live in denial, blank out what it didn't suit him to know. Start his *new life*. She had to deal with Bernard herself. She wasn't sure how to go about doing what had to be done. But she'd find out somehow. In the meantime she had to stay alive. Bernard had followed her to Salthouse Quay, but she didn't think he knew she was staying at this Albert Dock apartment. She'd have to be extra vigilant, until she knew she was safe. She jumped in shock as Finbar knocked softly at the door. 'Pull yourself together,' she whispered. 'You have to!' She had to fight for her life.

'Dinner's ready,' he called.

She knew she wanted him the way he wanted her. But it was wrong. She was too vulnerable. There was too much going on. How could she think about sex when her life was in danger? Or did that make you think more about sex?

An hour later she sat curled up on the sofa in the candlelit living room, glass in hand, listening to Annie Lennox. Finbar sat silently on the other sofa, arms folded, long legs stretched out. The river lights glittered through the big windows. He wished he had the nerve to go and sit next to her, take her in his arms. Her hair had dried to a soft golden halo around her head and she looked snug in the fluffy robe. He could smell her perfume. She hadn't said much at dinner, but she seemed more relaxed. She'd had quite a lot to drink. Her beautiful skin glowed with wine and candlelight. He smiled at her.

'Feel better?'

'Much better.' She turned away from watching the river lights and looked at him. 'Thanks for the dinner,' she said in her soft clear voice. 'It was delicious.'

'My pleasure.' He bowed his head.

'Do you like to cook?'

'Not every day,' he said. 'Then it wouldn't be fun anymore.'

He seemed so kind, she thought, so calm and reasonable and humorous and sexy. Like Rob before he'd discovered he was the offspring of a psychopathic murderous paedophile! Would he ever recover from the shock? Would she? She remembered him shoving her, staring down at her naked body. She was revolting to him now, repulsive! She looked out of the windows again, blinking back tears. The phone rang and Finbar jumped up.

'Excuse me.' He went into the bedroom to answer it and she got up, took her wine glass and strolled to the windows, gazing out over the lights of the Mersey. She loved this apartment, it was so big and quiet and comfortable. And *safe*. No one could get in. Only Nick and Caroline knew she was here and they wouldn't tell anybody. The river soothed and relaxed her. She tensed as she thought again of what she had to do. A few minutes later Finbar came back.

'Didn't want to spoil the music with talking,' he explained. He crossed to the CD player, removed the Annie Lennox disc and slid in a new one, The Verve. 'I'll be away for the next few days,' he said moodily. 'Got to go to Dublin.' High Command wanted a 'chat', Lenny had said.

'Dublin?' Shannon whirled round and stared at him. He saw the panic in her eyes.

'What's the matter?' He went to her and took the wine glass from her trembling fingers. 'What is it?'

'Nothing!' she said wildly. 'Nothing's the matter.'

She'd be alone here for the next few days, hiding from a murderer. Until she did what she had to do. Could she do it? The reality of her situation overwhelmed her.

'You'll be safe here,' he said, as if he guessed her thoughts.

'Don't answer the door unless you're expecting someone and don't pick up the phone. Leave the answering machine on. I'll be staying at the Shelbourne on St Stephen's Green, I'll write down the phone number for you.'

'How long will you be gone?' She fought down her panic.

'I'll be back Friday afternoon.' He put her wine glass on the coffee table. 'We could go somewhere for the weekend if you like, get out of Liverpool.'

'Yes. Get out of Liverpool,' she repeated. But running away wouldn't do it.

He looked at her. 'You're a bundle of nerves, aren't you?' he said softly, seeing her tears. 'It's not surprising after what you've gone through.'

Unable to stop himself, he put up a hand and touched her hair then stroked her soft flushed cheek. 'It's not just the husband, is it?' he said. 'You're a strong lady, you won't let him hurt you again. There's something else. Tell me. I can help you.' He put his arms around her and pulled her close. 'I don't judge and nothing surprises me.'

She smiled up at him through her tears. 'I am in danger of losing my immortal soul,' she whispered. Not to mention her mortal body.

'Are you now?' He lightly kissed her nose and lips and buried his face in her neck. He undid the belt of the robe, stroked her breasts and smooth back, kissed her throat and the lobes of her ears. She gasped with pleasure. Her skin was so soft. She smelled wonderful. 'Don't worry about that,' he murmured, holding her tight. 'You won't lose it if it's in a good cause. You're the most beautiful woman I've ever seen,' he said, gazing into her eyes. 'Inside and out. I've been dreaming about you since the day we met.'

'Rob said I was repulsive.' Tears ran down her cheeks and her lips trembled. 'He hurt me! I loved him,' she cried. 'I loved him so much!'

'I know you did.'

She put her arms around him and they kissed, clinging together. He was so hungry for her, wanted her so much! It made a change from being called revolting and repulsive. He lifted her, carried her to his bedroom and pulled off the robe, stroking her breasts and the insides of her thighs. She gasped as he flicked his tongue over her nipples while his fingers probed inside her.

'I shouldn't do this!' she moaned. 'I've got enough worries. Out of the frying pan, into the fire!'

'This is a good fire. It's meant to happen.' He slid out of his clothes. 'I knew it the day I saw you. You're so beautiful!' he whispered. 'Don't ever forget that. And don't worry about anything anymore.' How could that bastard hurt her so much? He kissed and licked her belly. 'That's lovely, the way you get wet so quickly.'

'Because of you.' She closed her eyes and surrendered to violent desire, shuddering as his fingers probed deeper, stroking relentlessly, his mouth on hers. She came once, then again. She felt his touch heal her broken body, undo the hurt caused by Rob. What's the point? she thought. I might be dead any day now. It's like ordering green salad in a famous seafood restaurant then being hit by an articulated lorry outside. She gasped with sudden laughter, arching her back as he withdrew his fingers and knelt between her legs, stroking her inner thighs as he gently spread them wider.

'What's funny?' He leaned over her and kissed her again, tongue exploring her mouth. She loved the hardness of his body against hers.

'I was thinking that not making love with you would be like eating green salad in a seafood restaurant before going outside and being crushed by a lorry.'

He smiled down at her. 'I am extremely flattered by that analogy, Ms Flinder.'

He lifted her buttocks and slid inside her. She screamed and clung to him, tasting his salty skin, smelling his sweat.

'You're so beautiful!' His green eyes stared down into hers. He kissed her again and she brought her legs up as he thrust harder and deeper, the sensation making her weep with excitement and delight. Her body tingled, overwhelmed by pure sensation. The delicious spasms started pulsing through her body, making her cry out, cling to him, bite his shoulders. She couldn't bear them to stop. She wanted to forget everything.

Chapter Fifteen

The heroin-stuffed condoms looked like wonton or the dim sum she'd eaten for lunch, little prawn-and-pork balls. Melanie sat on the edge of the bath and stared at the pile arranged on the marble bathroom counter. In the bedroom Wady sprawled on the bed watching a Western from the hotel's movie channel. When the film ended he glanced at his Rolex, got off the bed and looked out at Singapore's glittering skyscrapers. The hotel's floodlit outdoor swimming pool ten floors below was deserted as the guests ate their dinner. He tapped at the bathroom door.

'How are you getting on?' he called. 'Melanie? You have to check out soon, your flight leaves at ten-thirty. We must leave for Changi in half an hour.'

'Prison or airport?' She opened the bathroom door, trembling, her face streaked with tears and black eyeliner. 'I can't do it,' she wailed. 'I'll get caught. And if I don't get caught, what if they start leaking or burst while I'm on the plane? I'll die of toxic shock at forty thousand feet. I'll be another million dollar stomach, and people will laugh and say it served me right.' She clutched her million dollar stomach. 'I'm going to be sick!'

'No, no,' he said soothingly. 'Everything will be fine. You must relax, Melanie. I told you, this is easy. Wait a minute.' He went to the mini bar, tore the paper wrapping off an upturned glass and emptied two miniature bottles of gin into it. He knew better than to add tonic. He would tell Guy not to use her again, she was unstable, too nervy. Not to mention the fortune she'd cost him in gin and vodka.

'Here, drink this. You will feel better.' He handed her the glass and she gulped the gin in one go. 'I get you another.'

There was no more gin or vodka so he had to give her Scotch. Melanie drank that down and heaved a deep sigh.

'I must be crazy,' she said viciously. 'Why the hell didn't I just stay in Sefton Park and go to college? Why the hell did I let myself get mixed up in *this*? "Because you need the *money*, Melanie! Be a good girl, stay cool!'" She mimicked Guy. 'It's all right for him to stay cool,' she spat. 'It's all right for *him*.'

'Melanie, please calm yourself.' Wady glanced at his watch again. 'You must do this now.' He pointed to the stuffed condoms. 'You must hurry. You are here now, you must do this. You have no choice.' He needed a drink himself. He picked up the bottle of mineral water and poured her a glass. 'Hurry!' he urged. 'You must hurry.'

'All right, all *right*!' She glared at him. 'Don't boss me like that, I'm not one of those bloody Singapore girl stewardesses in a Wonderbra.' Po-faced little bastard, she thought, and began to swallow the condoms, coughing and choking and gagging. Tears filled her eyes at the revolting bitterness of the sperm-zap coating. Wady moved around the room picking up T-shirts, underwear, packs of cigarettes and stuffing them into her green Samsonite bag, removing all traces of her presence. She was a dirty, drunken bitch, he thought disgustedly. He had offered to buy her a dress and good shoes to wear for the flight back, but she insisted on wearing the scruffy jeans and tight pink sleeveless vest that made her look like some backpacker who would carry anything for the right price. Her breasts stuck out like a prostitute's. The girl in *Bangkok Hilton* had worn a dress, she said. It was bad luck.

Twenty minutes later Melanie checked out of the hotel and they started off for the airport, racing down the brightly lit road lined with big palm trees. She looked at the endless lines of huge apartment blocks.

'Doesn't anyone in Singapore live in an ordinary house?' she asked, lighting another cigarette, trying to take her mind off the ordeal that awaited her at the airport.

'Not many. Too expensive.' He glanced in the mirror and overtook a scruffy white van packed with people and suitcases.

'Most families must live together in apartments,' he said. 'Parents, children, grandparents, all together.'

'Grandparents too?' She laughed. 'Bloody hell! Sounds like a real nightmare.'

'Family is very important to Asian people,' he said stiffly.

'Of course it is.' She laughed again. 'Especially when you don't have a welfare system.'

'We have welfare system,' he said coldly.

'Yeah, right. *And* a democracy. Hello-bye-bye!' She leaned back and sucked smoke, trying to get as much nicotine as possible into her bloodstream before they arrived at the ridiculous airport that only permitted smoking in a special room. She wound the window down. 'Christ, it's so bloody warm!' she puffed. 'I don't know how you lot stand it. Ninety percent humidity!'

'You must keep the window closed or the air conditioning will not work.'

'Yes, sir!' She was silent for the rest of the journey. Half an hour later the Mercedes sped up a long low hill, levelled out and the lights of Changi airport came into view. Melanie's heart began to race and her mouth went dry.

'Can I get a drink before I go through Customs?'

'Okay,' he sighed. 'One drink only.' He couldn't wait to get rid of her.

He parked the car and escorted her to the Terminal One check-in area. Crowds of perspiring people swarmed everywhere, pushing trolleys laden with bags, cameras and suitcases. She drank a large vodka at a bar and he accompanied her to Departures. Two armed, uniformed guards in black caps and dark blue shirts stood checking passports. One woman, not allowed to go through, argued frantically with them as they shook their heads. Another guard came up and escorted her away. Melanie shoved her cigarette pack into her jeans pocket then gasped and recoiled as Wady's arms encircled her waist.

'What the hell d'you think you're doing?' she shouted, pushing him away.

'We are friends,' he said urgently. 'We are saying goodbye.' He squeezed her, pressed his cold lips to hers and swiftly released her. His face twisted into a grimace and she grimaced back. She was yet to see an Asian man who really smiled. Her legs were trembling again. Cold pins and needles of sweat broke out on her face and body.

The guard stared at the outline of her breasts beneath the tight pink vest and grinned at his colleague. Western slut, he thought. He flicked through her passport.

'Where are you going?' he asked aggressively.

'England – Manchester,' she stammered. She'd never thought of Manchester airport as a beautiful or desirable destination. Until this moment. He glanced at the date on the immigration stamp.

'You don't stay in Singapore so long.'

'No.' Oh, God! She stuck out her tits at him and smiled inanely. 'I had a row with my boyfriend.' She giggled.

'Okay.' He handed the passport back and gestured brusquely to her to go through.

The next horrible moment, three vodkas later, was at the gate before boarding the aircraft. Her bag was searched by a fat gimlet-eyed woman who looked at her vest, tutted, and shook her head disapprovingly. Melanie felt like telling her to fuck off. But the man in front was being escorted to a curtained cubicle. She didn't set off the metal detector. She longed to be in Raffles Class where champagne was served before take off. You're lucky to be on this bloody plane, she told herself as she settled into her window seat and picked up her copy of *Silver Kris* magazine. Now all you have to do is get to Manchester without dying of toxic shock. As a concession to her stomach she drank mineral water in between vodkas. Two large Drambuies later she fell asleep and dreamed that she was naked, held down on a table while the fat bitch from airport security pulled on condom gloves in preparation for a body cavity search.

Guy met her at Manchester wearing a black leather coat and a big smile on his round ugly face. His head was too big for his body, she thought as she walked towards him. The cold was appalling after Singapore's steamy heat.

'Have a nice flight?' he asked cheerfully. 'You don't look too good.'

'Neither would you if you'd . . .'

'See,' he whispered, 'I told you it'd be easy.'

'*Easy*?' Melanie stood there shivering in her thick black sweater and denim jacket. 'I've aged ten years in the past couple of days,' she said furiously. 'I feel terrible. Sick and bloated. My mouth is so dry! I need a drink.'

'You made it, Melanie, like I told you you would.' He grinned. 'Wady phoned me last night. Said we shouldn't use you again because you were too nervy. But I think you've been a real pro. Good girl!' He patted her on the shoulder.

'Don't 'good girl' me!' She shrugged him off. 'Where's my hundred grand?' she asked. 'When do I get that?'

'All in good time, Melanie, all in good time. Not here in the middle of the bloody airport.' He glanced around the Arrivals Hall, quiet at that time of the morning. 'Christ! Why do these long haul flights always land at five or six in the bloody morning?' he muttered. 'I hope the chemist's open.'

'Chemist?' She looked puzzled. 'Why do you need a chemist?'

'*I* don't.' He smiled at her. '*You* do. Unless you've already bought the laxatives? It's a bit dodgy buying them here but they slipped my mind, if you'll pardon the expression.'

'Laxatives? What for?' She groaned and made a face. 'Oh, yuck!'

'Yeah, right.' He grabbed her arm. 'Come on,' he said briskly. 'Let's get out of here.'

They sped down the empty motorway towards Liverpool and parked in silent Sefton Park Drive an hour later. The dark flat was freezing and filthy and stank of cigarettes and stale chips. Paul was asleep in her bed, thin white arm flung protectively across his rat-like face. He didn't stir. Guy made himself a cup of instant coffee and sat smoking and watching breakfast news while Melanie spent a horrible hour in the bathroom. She emerged, pale and trembling, and handed him a plastic carrier bag.

'They're all in there.'

'You counted them?'

'Yes, I counted them! After I rinsed the shit off.' He stood up and she blocked his path. 'Where's my money?'

'Here.' He reached inside his jacket and took out a folded white envelope. 'Ten grand.'

'*Ten* grand?' She gaped at him. 'You said I'd get a hundred thousand pounds!' she cried, and pushed back her wild hair. 'I'd be set up for life, you said. I want my hundred grand! I want my hundred grand, you bastard! I risked my life for this!'

'Look, Melanie.' Guy shrugged and held up his hands. 'I don't understand it either,' he lied. 'I was told you'd get a hundred grand. But there's been some breakdown in communication. I believed you'd get that much, I told you in good faith.'

'Good faith? You wouldn't know good faith if you fell over it.' Tears of rage poured down her cheeks, mingling with liquid eye-liner. 'I could be chained up in Changi prison right now!'

'But you're not.'

'I could have died of toxic shock on the plane. I could have been arrested at Manchester. And now you have the bloody nerve to tell me . . .'

'Take it easy, Melanie!'

She whirled round to see Paul standing in the doorway, wearing her red-and-black striped dressing gown and smoking a cigarette. His thin wrists stuck out of the sleeves.

'And why are you still here?' she blazed, hating the sight of his pinched face and greasy blond hair. 'This is *my* flat. I want you out. I never wanted you here in the first place. I don't want to see you again. Get out!'

'Melanie, come on! Calm down.' Guy grabbed her arm and held on as she tried to push him away. 'You can do a lot with ten grand.' He couldn't help laughing. Stupid bitch!

'Do me a favour! I can't start a new life with it, can I? I can't tell everyone to go to hell. Be somebody. You promised!' she wailed. 'You promised me a hundred grand.'

'For Christ's sake!' He let go of her arm. 'Look, I'm sorry it didn't work out, okay? If it was up to me you'd get the money. I tried my best. But there isn't a hundred grand to give you this time.'

'This time?' she gasped. 'What are you on about, *this time*?'

'Well.' He grinned. 'Once you've done another little job for us and got a bit more experience and we know we can trust you . . . next time there'll be a lot more.'

'Next time?' she shrieked. And burst into hysterical laughter. 'You must be joking! There's not going to be a next time. I'm never doing that again! I've never seen such a creepy place in my life – it was a bloody nightmare! And that little bastard Wady bossing me around like I was some Singapore girl.'

'Actually, Wady wasn't too pleased with you,' Guy said, his eyes narrowed. 'I told you that. He thought you'd bottle out. He wanted to wait until someone else could bring back the stuff.'

'Oh? And what about me then?'

He was silent as he lit another cigarette and exhaled smoke.

'Use your imagination,' he said slowly. 'You'd be at the bottom of Singapore harbour by now. Wearing a designer concrete overcoat. Or having your brains . . .'

'What brains?' Paul Ashton smiled.

'. . . screwed out in some chophouse in Chinatown.'

'One more trip,' Paul said. 'Or your beloved brother might get a concrete overcoat instead.' He came forward and put his arms around her waist.

'Get off me!' Melanie twisted away, hitting out at him. 'You promised if I did this you wouldn't hurt Rob. I've done it. You owe me.'

'I owe you nothing, Melanie.' He yanked her hair and pushed her hard in the small of the back. She staggered forward and fell against Guy. The orange box coffee table was knocked over, scattering cigarette butts. The green glass ashtray cracked as it fell on the tiled hearth.

'What are you going to do?' Guy laughed as he pulled her upright and turned her to face Paul, holding her arms behind her back. 'Go to the Serious Fraud Squad?' She cried out and sagged in his arms as Paul smashed her across the face. 'Tell them you delivered a consignment of Ecstasy to Singapore *in good faith* and smuggled a belly-full of heroin back but didn't get the money you were promised? They'll be gutted for you. Hey!'

She grabbed the gun from his pocket and held it with both hands, pointing it at them.

'Stay away from me!' she yelled as they came towards her. 'Both of you. Scumbags!' She shook hair out of her dark frantic eyes. 'I hate you – I'll kill you!'

'Don't be silly, Melanie,' Guy said in a bored voice. Give me the gun.' He raised his hands. 'Look, we'll work something out, okay? Maybe I can squeeze out a bit more cash for you.'

'Liar!' She began to cry again. 'I risked my *life*!' Blood trickled from her left nostril.

'Your life's not worth a tenner, never mind ten grand,' Paul said coldly. 'Give him the gun. You won't fire it. You haven't got the bottle.' He threw his cigarette into the hearth. 'Give it back to him,' he ordered. 'Stop messing around.'

'No one's going to hurt me anymore,' she gasped. 'I'm sick of being hurt and pushed around. Everyone thinks they can control me . . .'

'Give him the *gun*!' Paul rushed at her and she fired twice, hitting him in the face and chest, sending him flying back against the wall. The noise of the gun deafened her. Paul slumped to the floor and lay still, blood pouring from his head and chest. She looked at the bloody mess, like raw hamburger, that had been his face. The dressing gown fell open to reveal his skinny bow legs and the tiny wrinkled penis in its thatch of fuzzy blond pubic hair. She gasped, dropped the gun and fell on her knees. She couldn't believe what she'd done.

'Good one, Melanie!' Guy said grimly. 'Terrific. We'll both go down now.'

'I'm not sorry,' she gasped. 'I don't care. It was self-defence.'

They were silent with shock, listening for doors, voices, footsteps pounding upstairs, police sirens, the urgent ring of the doorbell. Nothing happened. Guy switched off the light, pushed up the window and stuck his big head out into the dark freezing air. The park was silent. No cars cruised past. No police cars. He waited a minute then pulled the window down and switched the light back on.

'Maybe we can sort something out,' he panted, looking at the blood spattered wall and carpet. 'I get rid of the body, you do another trip. Then that's it, we don't know each other.' He pointed to the horrible thing on the carpet. 'He's left, moved out, if anyone asks. You don't know where. Okay?'

She nodded, dark eyes huge in her white face. 'I don't care,' she gasped again. 'Paul deserved it. I had to protect myself.'

'All right, all right.' He picked up the gun and stuck it in his pocket.

'It reminds me of *Gone With the Wind*.'

'*What?*'

'*Gone With the Wind,*' she said excitedly. 'Haven't you seen that film? Scarlett shoots a Yankee soldier who wanders into the house and steals some of her dead mother's jewellery. She says she guesses she's done murder but she'll think about it tomorrow.' She laughed. 'It's incredible,' she said. 'I never thought killing somebody would be this easy. I'm free, I don't feel guilty. He's out of my life. Just like that. It's fantastic!'

'For fuck's sake!' Guy stared at her. 'Have you got a screw loose?' Wady was right, he thought, she was a ticking time bomb. Of all reactions to murder, he had never witnessed such childlike delight. It was distinctly unnerving. He looked round the dingy room and grabbed a vodka bottle off the mantelpiece. There was about two inches of spirit left in it.

'Here.' He shoved the bottle at her. 'Get that down your neck. Then, come on. We've got to do this before it gets light.'

'Do what exactly?' She tipped back her head and drained the vodka.

'Shut up. I'm thinking.'

The park lake was too obvious. And shallow. They could dump him in the Mersey. But where? 'Get some bin bags,' Guy ordered. 'And tape or rope, something to tie him with. 'Go on!' he hissed as she stood there uncertainly. 'Get your arse in gear.'

Melanie ran out giggling. Twenty minutes later they were loading Paul's body into the boot of Guy's BMW, parked down the side of the house, hidden from prying eyes by a high wall and dense trees. The body was wrapped in bin bags and trussed up with a roll of red plastic washing line that Melanie had never used.

'The wimp feels light,' she giggled. 'He was only little. Short thin wimps have a complex, they feel they've got to prove themselves.'

'Shut up.' Guy glanced nervously around.

They got into the car. She'd get someone tall next time, thought Melanie. Long and lean and broad-shouldered, like that gorgeous Irishman with the black hair and green eyes and pointy beard, Guy's friend or associate or whatever. She'd seen him in the Carmen Club, standing at the bar. If she hadn't been stuck with Paul she might have chatted him up. She started to laugh.

'Shut it, Melanie!' Guy said tersely. He backed out of the drive and accelerated down the wide bumpy road. He wasn't surprised no one had called the police. If anyone had heard the shot they'd probably thought it was a car backfiring. Or else they didn't want to get involved.

'Where are we going?' Melanie lit a cigarette.

'I said, shut it! I won't tell you again.' His heavy profile was grim in the darkness.

He sped down the road, through the park gates and headed for the city centre. They went through the Mersey tunnel and surfaced in Birkenhead.

'I've hardly ever been on this side of the river,' she said, gazing out at derelict dockland interspersed with streets of terraced houses. 'I suppose it's like London. People spend most of their lives on one side of the river or the other. Which side of the Mersey were you born on, Guy?'

He didn't answer. They drove over a canal bridge and he took a left turn and bumped the BMW along a maze of deserted railway sidings, the rusted rails covered with grass and stones and piles of bricks. He pulled up outside a hut with smashed windows and graffiti-covered walls.

'Come on, give us a hand.' He got out of the car and kicked open the hut's wooden door. The rough concrete floor was covered with broken glass, sweet wrappers, crisp packets, used condoms. Crumpled beer cans gleamed in the moonlight. In one corner was a big pile of moss-covered coal.

'No one comes here except kids,' he said. 'Now and then. We'll bury him under the coal.' He pushed an ancient rusted shovel into her chilled hands and they worked for ten minutes, panting and sweating.

'I'm not used to manual labour,' Melanie gasped, pausing to wipe her sweaty face. 'God, my hands are filthy!'

So was her face. The whites of her eyes gleamed in the dim light.

'Hurry up,' he urged. 'It'll be daylight soon.' He stopped shovelling and looked at her. 'What did you do with the ten grand?'

'It's in my pocket.' She patted her bottom and giggled. 'You didn't think I'd leave it in the flat, did you? Why? What have you done with the *merchandise*?'

'It's in the car. Never mind about that. Come on, keep going!'

'What did your last slave die of?' She dug the shovel into the coal again.

When the space was big enough they heaved the bin-bagged corpse from the boot and dumped it in the corner of the hut.

'You'd better buy yourself a new dressing gown,' Guy said calmly.

She laughed. 'A big thick fluffy cotton towelling robe,' she breathed. 'Apricot colour. I'll buy half a dozen.'

He went back to the car and shone a torch in the boot. It was clean.

'*Don't* rest in peace, tosser!' Melanie gazed down at the wrapped corpse, panting, hands on her hips. 'You never gave me anything but grief. I hope the demons of hell are torturing you right now. I'm going to pop a party!' She laughed and stooped to start shovelling coal back.

The shot in the back of her neck knocked her sprawling. She was killed instantly. The shovel clattered on the concrete floor and she plunged forward on top of the coal heap, dark eyes wide and staring at the moon. Blood and saliva dribbled from the corners of her mouth. Her face and long hennaed hair were coated with sticky black dust.

Guy put his gun away and pulled the envelope of money from the back pocket of her jeans. She might have been good for one more run, but Wady was right. She was unstable, a security risk. She knew enough to cause trouble. She was just in a state, screwed up, and he'd felt sorry for her. But not that sorry. He put the money in the glove compartment and returned to shovel coal.

When both bodies were covered he dropped the shovel, closed the hut door and leaned against the brick wall to rest, taking in gulps of icy air. He would give the stuff to Finbar and keep her ten grand, not say anything about the shooting. Naughty, but a nice little perk. Finbar would never find out.

He got back in the car and drove slowly along the railway sidings to the road, headlights off. Hot and sweating, he kept the window open. The freezing air smelled of soot and molasses. He would go home to his flat above the club, shower, get some sleep.

He started as a bundle of rags wearing a woolly hat and clutching a bottle in its grimy hand appeared from nowhere and flung itself against the car bonnet, bringing with it a terrible stink of stale urine, sweat and decay.

'Hey, lover!' a female voice whined. 'Give us a quid for a cup of tea? Go on, be a gentleman. Be my lover!'

'*Fuck* off!' Guy recoiled and pressed the button to close the window, wishing he had another bullet to spare. What was this, the Dark Ages? They should be wiped out like the scum they were, picked up and disposed of. He flicked the headlights and they blazed into the dawn light as he sped off down the narrow road.

Chapter Sixteen

'I'm fine, Nick. I feel better this last day or two.' Shannon sat on the edge of the bed wearing the baby blue bathrobe, Finbar's key ring dangling from her finger. Her long blonde hair was damp and curling. A bottle of champagne stood on the bedside table. 'No, I haven't seen Rob,' she said. 'I don't actually *want* to see him. I haven't been back to the house. I'm trying to blank him out for now, the way he did with me. Maybe that's why I feel better.'

Finbar was the other reason she felt better. She'd never had such incredible sex. He'd be gone only a few days, but already she missed him terribly. He'd saved her, made her stronger. At least for the present.

'He phoned me this afternoon, asked me where you were staying,' Nick said. 'Of course I refused to tell him – I can't believe he expected that I would! He might try to contact you at work, seeing as he can't get hold of you anywhere else. *Literally* get hold of you,' he added grimly. 'I didn't ask what he wanted.'

'He probably wants to talk about the divorce,' Shannon said disconsolately. 'He certainly doesn't hang about!'

'He really means it then? Really wants a divorce?'

'Looks like it.'

'What the hell is the matter with him?' Nick asked incredulously.

'Oh, Nick!' She sighed. 'I can't even begin to talk about it – not yet anyway. It's too painful. I feel grief, as if he'd died. Well, he has in a way. I'm just concentrating on trying to hold myself together.'

'Yes, you're right.' He paused. 'What if he–?'

'If he attacks me again he'll have injunctions, restraining orders and assault charges slapped all over him,' she said. 'I hate the idea, but I have to protect myself. I'm starting to get angry. That helps. And–.' She stopped.

'What?'

'I think Rob and I really might be finished, Nick.' Tears filled her eyes. She picked up her glass and took a gulp of champagne. 'After what he did. I know what he's capable of now - things can never be the same again. He *raped* me, beat me up! He did it once, it could happen a second, and a third time. I might forgive him, but how could I forget? How could I ever trust him again?'

'I don't know,' Nick said thoughtfully. 'Only you can decide. You're right to concentrate on getting yourself together, coming to terms with what's happened. I still can't believe it myself! What if he suddenly came to his senses?'

'I don't know . . . I just don't know.' She wiped her eyes on the robe sleeve.

'Is Finbar being a gentleman?' he asked suddenly.

'Of course he is.' She laughed, glad that Nick couldn't see her blush. 'Like something out of Jane Austen. Why d'you ask?'

'Oh, no reason.'

'He's not here at the moment. He flew to Dublin for a few days. Business, he said.' She glanced at the bedside clock. 'Listen Nick, I have to hang up,' she said quickly. 'I'm going out this evening.'

'Good on you!' he exclaimed. 'I'm glad to hear it. All that hibernating wasn't doing you any favours. Going somewhere special?'

'Just out for a drink with a couple of girlfriends. The most important people at a time like this!' Except for Finbar, she thought. 'Thanks for the dinner invitation,' she said. 'What time d'you want me on Friday?'

'Get here for seven. We'll eat around seven-thirty, screaming babies permitting!'

'I'll look forward to it.'

'See you, Shannon. Take care.'

He hung up and she poured more champagne and drank it

down. Dutch courage, the best kind. She switched the blow dryer to its highest setting and bent forward as she scrunched handfuls of hair. She started to shake with nerves again, worse than before. Much as she missed Finbar, she was glad he was away. She had to do this by herself, in secret. She smoothed on powder and blusher but no other make-up. How should she dress? she wondered. Behave?

'It's no good,' she muttered, sipping champagne. 'I haven't a clue. I'll have to play it by ear.'

She dressed in black jeans bought from Tesco, a purple sweater, the long black cashmere coat and black ankle boots. She checked her wallet; it contained three thousand pounds in fifty pound notes, plus a few tens. Rob wouldn't find out – for some lucky reason they'd never got around to opening a joint account. She believed it was a subconscious desire on her part to save his male pride by never letting him see exactly how much she earned. She studied herself in the bedroom mirror. She looked younger without make-up, she thought. She picked up the hideous black woollen hat she'd bought at lunchtime and pulled it on, tucking away every curl and strand of blonde hair. She'd considered buying a wig, but had dismissed that as too melodramatic. If Bernard was hanging around he wouldn't recognise her with all her hair tucked under the hat. She hoped. She threw on a black wool scarf of Finbar's, slung her black leather bag over her shoulder and took a last gulp of champagne. She wound the scarf around the lower half of her face and felt in her coat pocket for the small CS gas canister. It wasn't legal, but what could she do against a six foot three psychopath with a combat knife?

It was freezing outside. Mist hung over the river. She left the apartment building and jogged across Canning Dock and Salthouse Dock Quays, the gas canister gripped in her gloved hand. The dock waters were shiny and still. On the Pier Head the Liver Buildings blazed with light. She reached Strand Street and hailed a passing cab to take her into town.

'Where to, love?' the driver shouted as she climbed in.

He dropped her off in Islington Place and she got out and stood looking around for the pub, the Malakand. It was down a tiny street behind a Catholic church, St Mary Magdalen. The cabbie reversed and turned back towards London Road and Lime Street. For a split second Shannon thought of hailing him again, telling him to drive her back to the Albert Dock. She stood there shivering. Next to the church was a school, a big Victorian building with a bell tower.

'Are you mad?' she whispered. 'Are you *crazy*?'

If she hung around much longer she might be taken for a prostitute by the two men heading towards her, cigarettes glowing in their mouths. Despite the sad hat. She turned and walked quickly down the tiny narrow street with tall buildings to either side, reminiscent of the crowded stinking tenements that had covered large areas of Liverpool in the nineteenth and early twentieth centuries. She stopped outside the pub, smelling beer and cigarette smoke, listening to the shouts and laughter.

'Gonna stand out here all night, queen?' She jumped. The two men were behind her.

'You wanna get shot of your fella, making you wait out here in the cold!' They laughed and pushed through the swing doors. Do it, she told herself. Don't think. Just do it.

She pushed open the doors and stepped into a time warp. The pub was small, dim and smoky with rough wooden chairs and benches, a long polished bar with a brass rail, and sawdust on the floor. There were hardly any women. She looked round, ignoring the stares. A battered piano stood in a corner. She pulled herself together and went up to the bar.

'Are you the stripper?' A red-faced skinhead in a black bomber jacket bawled in her ear. 'Get your kit off, let's have a look. What you wearing that bloody hat for?'

'Leave her alone, you soft bastard!' The fat, platinum blonde middle-aged barmaid, underwired breasts bursting out of her low-cut flowered blouse, smiled at Shannon. She wore blue eye-shadow and bright pink lipstick. 'What can I get you, my darlin'?'

'Large gin-and-tonic, please.' She was getting as bad as Melanie.

'Would you like ice and lemon in that, my darlin?'

They had ice and lemon in this place? 'Please.' She smiled. 'Er– is Dean here?' she asked tentatively. 'Dean Carver?' Dean Carver, unbelievable. She felt stupid saying the name. 'I'm supposed to meet him.'

'Oh, him.' The barmaid frowned. 'Yeah, he's over there.' She pointed one sausage finger and dumped the gin-and-tonic on the wet bar, her friendliness gone.

Shannon wondered if she should buy Dean Carver a drink and decided it could wait. He looked her over as she approached his corner table, but didn't get up. He had cropped grey hair, thick straight black eyebrows that met in the middle, and pale stubbly skin. His face was thin, sunken, and his brown eyes calm and reflective. Too calm. He looked about forty-five, but she couldn't tell. She was hopeless at guessing ages, and never that interested. He wore baggy jeans, a combat jacket and a big cream coloured fisherman's sweater. His hands – and for all she knew, the rest of his long skinny body – were covered with tattoos, the usual reptiles intertwined with the usual pneumatic-breasted naked ladies. And of course *'Mother'* was not left out. His dirty nails were too long. She shuddered.

'Mr Carver? I'm – I'm Cheryl Kent,' she lied, heart pounding. She put her drink on the table and he shifted his chair to make room for her. He was drinking Scotch. 'I phoned you last night.'

'Yeah. Where'd you get my name?' He'd been surprised by her call, so surprised he had forgotten to ask. There had been no punters for a couple of months. Winter was usually the busiest time, when the punters were stuck at home spending long dark evenings with their hated ones, all those life insurance policies going to waste.

'My boss was the instructing solicitor for your barrister, Roy Gardner,' she said hesitantly, and gulped gin-and-tonic, certain that platinum tits at the bar had watered it down. Ice and lemon! 'Before your last stretch for burglary and aggravated assault.' Not his speciality. 'I was sort of asking around and – your name came up.'

She recalled the conversation with Roy Gardner. A discussion over lunch about a client accused of murdering his business partner in a computer firm, shooting him at the front door of his country house as he got out of his Mercedes. Shannon herself being the instructing solicitor in question.

'Why didn't he get someone to do the job for him?' she'd asked lightly, trying to make a joke out of something unfunny. 'Who would you go to if you wanted someone murdered, Roy?'

'I defended a despicable tosser a few years ago. Well, they're all despicable tossers.' Roy loved telling stories, especially to beautiful Shannon Flinder over a bottle of excellent Burgundy. 'Dean Carver his name was, would you believe?' He laughed. 'Used to be a combat survival instructor, training navy pilots. Got kicked out. Too much combat and not enough survival. Nearly beat a man to death. Calls himself a contract killer now, quite open about it. That's not what he went down for, though. Times were hard and he indulged in a bit of aggravated burglary to make ends meet. Brained some poor sod of a householder with a length of steel pipe. He's out now. Used to drink and hold court in some pub up Islington called the Malakand. Probably still does. Old habits die hard.'

Fortunately for Shannon, they did. Dean stubbed out his cigarette and picked up his glass of Scotch.

'So you work for Jon Callie?' The calm brown eyes studied her. 'Don't think much of him. Useless bastard, that's what he is. Didn't give a toss about me. Bloody lawyers, they're all the same. What are you, his secretary?'

'I was his secretary,' she said hastily. 'I don't work for him anymore. I'm unemployed now.'

'Yeah. Right.' He looked at her black cashmere coat and expensive leather bag, 'Ungaro' stamped in tiny letters on the black flap. His last client, before he blew up Conal the Irishman, was a young wife – merry widow, now! – whose abusive husband's untimely demise meant she now owned the family home lock, stock and barrel, no more mortgage payments to cough up. Women were his best customers. Men usually preferred to murder their wives and girlfriends themselves, often in very imaginative ways. If caught they pleaded manslaughter and came out laughing in three years. Women who murdered husbands or boyfriends were banged up for much longer, and usually lost their kids if they had any. They had to be much more careful. Cheryl was not this one's real name, he thought. She didn't look or talk like his idea of a Cheryl. Not that Dean cared. It was none of his business.

'So-.' He lit another cigarette. 'What can I do for you? Your old man, is it?' He imagined her married to some ageing rich git who wasn't too lavish with the credit cards and couldn't get a hard-on. Maybe she'd discovered sex with someone her own age.

'Does it matter?' she asked stiffly.

'No, love. None of my business. All I need is a name, address and photo.'

'Is it all right to talk about this here?' Her hand holding the glass shook. 'It's not exactly private.'

'The fellas in here mind their own business. See?' He glanced around the smoky pub as she drained her glass. 'No one's looking at us. They won't bother you if you're with me. Now-.' She recoiled as he blew smoke in her direction. 'Let's talk business.'

'Okay.' Suddenly she wanted to laugh. *Let's talk business*. It was like some stupid gangster movie.

'I need the name, address, photo, like I said. Information.' He looked at her pale face and their empty glasses. 'Let's get another one in first,' he suggested. 'You look like you could do with it.' He stood up. 'What d'you want?'

'Let me get them,' she said. 'I mean, if I give you the money, will you?' She didn't want to brave the bar again.

He nodded and held out his hand. She opened her bag, took out her wallet and gave him a ten pound note. 'Large gin-and-tonic,' she said. 'And tell her to leave out the pretty water this time.'

He grinned. The men at the bar made way for him, their eyes downcast, false smiles on their faces. The platinum blonde barmaid had a scared look. She wouldn't call Dean Carver a soft bastard. This is like a film, Shannon thought again. I can't believe I'm doing it.

He came back with the drinks and her change and she gave him the photograph of Bernard, a tiny head and shoulders square cut from her wedding album. He stood, shoulders braced, looking down his long nose at the camera, thin lips beneath the heavy moustache twisted in a contemptuous grimace. She couldn't think why she'd packed the album and brought it with her to Finbar's, but she was glad she had now. After cutting out the square she'd taken a thick black marker and blacked out all images of him, Melanie and Margaret, turning them into tree trunks among the other wedding guests. After that she'd cried herself to sleep. She'd have to get rid of the album now, of course.

'His name's Bernard Flinder,' she said in a low voice, forcing herself not to glance round the pub again. 'He's a headmaster – headmaster of St Fidelma's. It's a Catholic school in–.'

'I know where that is.' Dean raised his creepy eyebrows. 'Go on.'

'He lives in Woolton. Woolton Village.'

'Nice.'

'24 Tanunda Avenue.' She had no intention of writing it down. 'Can you remember that?' He glared at her.

'I want it to look like an accident,' she said. Shannon picked up her glass and drank more gin-and-tonic. It tasted stronger this time. 'A car crash or mugging or–.'

'Don't tell me how to do my job, love,' said Dean quietly.

'I'm not! I'm sorry, I didn't mean to. It's just that I don't know–.'

'Right!' he interrupted. 'You don't know. I do. Leave it to me. What time does he get to work in the mornings?'

'Eight-thirty, sometimes earlier. He usually stays until five or six. They have staff meetings and clubs and things. Administrative work. He goes out a lot in the evenings,' she said. 'Sometimes with his wife.' She paused. 'He's a child molester – a murderer,' she added, and gulped her drink.

Dean looked at her white face. 'I should do it for free, is that what you're saying?'

'No, of course not. I'm just saying, he's an evil person. He deserves to–.'

'Look, love.' He drank his Scotch. 'You don't get it. I'm like a lawyer, right?' He tapped his hollow chest and she looked at him, startled. 'I don't care if the punter's innocent or guilty. I don't care if it's Hitler or Mary Queen of the Angels, d'you know what I'm saying? I just get the job done. Know what I mean?'

'Yes.' She looked away. 'I know what you mean.'

'Right then.' He lit another cigarette.

'Oh!' She turned back. 'How much?'

He blew out smoke. 'Eleven hundred. Cash. Half now, half when the job's done.'

'Eleven hundred?' Shannon looked at him aghast. Was that the price of a human life? Even one like Bernard's?

'Come on!' He grinned, misunderstanding her. 'You look like you can afford it. Can't you get the cash off your fella? Or your old man?'

'I've got the money,' she said crossly. 'It's mine. When can you do it?'

He shrugged. 'Whenever you want.'

'I'd like you to do it this Friday,' she said. 'In the evening. That gives you time to – I don't know, follow him around, whatever you have to do. I'll be out to dinner with friends, that'll give me an alibi. Should I need it.'

'Okay,' he said. 'This Friday it is.'

'Do it before ten in the evening,' she said. Nick and Caroline went to bed earlier these days.

'Okay. Where's the cash?'

'Just a minute.' Shannon got up and pushed her way through the crowd, heading for the toilet.

Women's toilets didn't usually stink like this. There were brown and reddish stains on the cracked dirty white tiles and the mirror was as clear as vaseline on a camera lens. She locked the flimsy graffiti-covered door and counted out five hundred and fifty pounds, rolling it tightly in her palm. It was just as well she didn't want to use the toilet, because there was no paper. She went out, sat down again and slid the money into Dean's grimy tattooed hand.

'When shall I give you the rest?' Shannon asked breathlessly. She was breathing heavily, almost panting, as if she'd run a marathon. She couldn't believe she was doing this. From criminal damage to murder in one leap! To think she'd agonized over smashing car windows! This was big time.

'I'll meet you on the steps of the Walker Art Gallery on Saturday morning,' he said. 'Twelve sharp. You can give it me then.'

'Okay.' She paused. 'How will you do it?'

'That's my business, love. You'll find out. That's all.'

'Okay,' she said again, got up and slung her bag over her shoulder. 'I – I'll see you on Saturday. At twelve. There's one more thing,' she said. 'He carries a knife. A combat knife.'

'A knife!' Dean smiled for the first time. 'I'm scared!'

He finished his Scotch and got up to go back to the bar. Shannon pushed her way out of the pub and stumbled down the oppressively narrow street towards the lights of Islington Place. What have I done? she thought. She reached Islington Place, hailed a cab and got in.

'The Albert Dock, please.'

She felt sick with guilt and fear. You're a murderer, she told herself. You're no better than Bernard. You'll lose your immortal soul. What's the difference between you and him? Okay, you don't rape and murder young girls. But you think you've got the right to kill? He's going to die on Friday.

The cab raced down London Road and turned left into Lime Street. They drove past the Empire Theatre and the stone Landseer lions that guarded St George's Hall. She remembered walking past them as a child and feeling frightened. What choice do you have? she argued. He's a murderer, a paedophile. He's already tried to murder you. The police won't do anything, you've got no evidence. Who'll protect you? Nobody! You should have prevented Francesca's murder. What are you going to do? Let him carry on? Let him mutilate and murder you? Maybe tonight!

Tears came into her eyes and the streetlights blurred. It was over between her and Rob. She could never go back to him after this. The terrible situation had exposed huge flaws in his character, flaws she knew she couldn't live with. She could never trust him again. And she'd be responsible for his father's murder. How could they live with that between them? She was in danger of her life, forced into this horrendous moral dilemma. She gripped the leather bag strap and stared out of the window. She had to fight. Choose one evil over another. There was no choice!

Safely back in Finbar's warm silent apartment, Shannon didn't switch on any lights. She took off her coat and boots, threw the black woollen hat in the kitchen bin and curled up on a sofa in the living room, sipping more champagne and gazing at the river lights. She got up and paced the huge room as her agitation increased. How would Carver do it? She was supposed to sit through dinner with Nick and Caroline – play with Helen – while a murder she had commissioned was being carried out. It was bizarre. Would Carver try to blackmail her? That was another worry. He must know Cheryl Kent wasn't her real name, and could find out who she was if he really wanted to. If she got away with this, she'd have to go through the rest of her life – assuming she survived the next two days! – with a terrible secret. A secret she could never share with any future husband, lover, daughter, son, friend. Cat even!

Stop it! she told herself fiercely. This is the only way to fight back. You'll get through it, you must. In six months or a year it'll be behind you, you'll have a new life. All this will be a bad dream. But first you have to fight. It's him or you. And it's not going to be *you*!

Bernard must be frantic now that he was unable to find her. He'd be desperate to kill her. She really must watch her back for the next two days. She'd take taxis to and from work, stay in the office at lunchtime . . .

Shannon jumped as the phone rang. The red button on the answering machine glowed red in the darkness.

'Shannon? Are you there?' Her heart raced at the sound of Finbar's soft southern Irish accent. 'I'm in my hotel room. Will you pick up the phone?'

She crossed to the sofa, put down her champagne glass and grabbed the receiver.

'I'm here,' she whispered. She wished he was too.

He let out his breath. 'Hi! How are you?' He missed her terribly after two days. Wednesday night now, and he had to wait until Friday!

'I'm okay.' She leaned back on the soft leather and stretched out her legs. 'It's been one hell of a day – again.' Desolate, she wished she could tell him everything, feel his arms around her, his body against hers. But the subterfuge started here.

He frowned and sat up in bed. 'Has that bastard been bothering you?'

'Oh, no. Not recently, anyway. He couldn't reach me, so he

called Nick to ask where I was staying. Of course Nick wouldn't tell him. He might turn up at the office if there's something he wants to . . . communicate.' She closed her eyes, remembering the feel of Finbar's hands and lips and tongue on her naked body, the concentration in his green eyes, the orgasms that had left her gasping and shaking with their strength. She still felt slightly sore after that incredible night.

'Well, call me if anything happens, okay? Call me anyway.' He was silent for a few seconds. 'I miss you,' he said in a low voice. 'I wish you were here in this bed with me. Will I tell you what I'd do?'

'No!' She laughed uneasily. 'I have to sleep tonight.'

'I called you earlier but there was no answer.'

Dean Carver and the spit-and-sawdust pub flashed into her mind. 'I was out,' she said. 'I went for a drink with a couple of girlfriends.'

'That's good,' he said. 'That's nice.'

'Oh, and I've been invited to Nick and Caroline's for dinner on Friday. I'll go straight from work. I shouldn't be too late, they'll probably start nodding off around ten. They've suffered from chronic sleep deprivation since Babsie-boo came on the scene.'

'Helen's a cute little girl.'

'Yes, she's gorgeous. Those big blue eyes and that lovely smile.'

He needed to change the subject. 'D'you still fancy going away for the weekend?'

'Oh, that's another thing I've got to tell you.' Her heart raced. 'I'm supposed to meet a client on Saturday at twelve,' she said guiltily. She hated lying to him. 'It's a pain, but I have to do it. Shouldn't take long, just half an hour or so.'

'Well, we could go after that, if you want to. Tell you what, we'll talk about it when I get home on Friday. It'll probably be early evening, not afternoon like I originally thought. Listen.' He picked up his glass of Kilbeggan and took a sip. 'Will you stay with me a bit longer?' he asked. 'I mean, another few weeks at least? I think you feel at home. You like the apartment, don't you?'

'I love it.'

'And you like me a little bit?'

'More than a little bit,' she said shyly. 'But Finbar–.'

'Please!' he interrupted. 'Say you'll stay with me? Be nice to a sad old man.'

'Sad is the last thing you are!' Shannon laughed. 'And you're certainly not old.'

'I'm thirty-four. Eight years older than you, but not necessarily wiser. Birthday October 25. When's yours?'

'June 15.'

'Ah, I thought you were one of those complicated Geminis. Will you stay?' he persisted.

'Well, if you don't mind me using up the hot water and towels and drinking all your champagne and coffee-.'

'I don't mind what you do,' he said. 'I love it.' I love you, he thought. He didn't dare say it. Not yet.

'In that case, it would be great to stay another few weeks.' Shannon felt she wanted to stay forever. 'I feel safe here,' she said. 'No one horrible can find me.'

He still had a feeling she didn't mean her husband. Who was she hiding from . . .?

'Finbar?'

'Yes?'

'I – I think I'll get some sleep now.' She longed to tell him everything. But she could never tell anyone about this.

'Of course,' he said. 'Will you do me a favour?'

'Depends what it is!' Shannon blushed.

'Sleep in my bed tonight. I like to think of you sleeping in my bed. Wearing nothing but that gorgeous perfume. Maybe thinking about me a little bit.'

Her face burned in the darkness. 'I'll think about you a lot.'

'Will you?'

'Yes. Goodnight,' she said quickly.

She hung up and he listened to the dial tone for a few seconds before replacing the receiver and lying back in bed. Had he gone too far? He didn't want to put her off. There was enough going on in her life at present. He sighed and turned over. He couldn't wait to see her again, gaze into those violet blue eyes as they made love. Talk, sleep, hold her in his arms all night long. He would get no sleep tonight, that was for sure.

Shannon stripped off her clothes and curled up in his bed,

pulling the quilt around her. She could smell him on the sheets. She stroked her breasts and stretched out her limbs as she imagined him making love to her, but Dean Carver's beetle eyebrows and tattooed hands with their horrible dirty nails kept destroying the delicious fantasy.

How would he kill Bernard? Would he try to blackmail her? Would she get away with it? Was she really afraid of losing her immortal soul, or of being caught? She felt she didn't know herself anymore. Her ideas about life, her so-called principles, the layers that formed the personality she knew – or thought she knew – had been peeled away, exposing a ruthless determined individual who was prepared to kill. The right – or wrong! – buttons had been pressed. She'd been hurt, knocked down, rejected, her life threatened. Now the people who had hurt her would pay. She wanted to survive. Make a new life. What would that new life bring?

Sleep would not come. She went back to the living room, stretched out on the sofa wrapped in the quilt, and spent the rest of the icy still winter night gazing out at the Mersey.

Chapter Seventeen

'What are you bloody gawping at? Miserable old cow!'

Josie stopped outside Bernard's office and glared at Irene as she stuffed two fifty pound notes into her red plastic purse. Bernie's hundred quid would come in handy for the weekend; she could buy herself the red jumper she'd admired in Marks and Spencer's and treat herself and the girls to takeaway pizza and chocolate fudge gateau tonight before Mick arrived to take her down the Cabbage.

'We don't appreciate language like that in here!' Irene blushed, lowered her tired eyes to the computer screen and pulled her grey acrylic cardigan protectively across her flat chest. It was astonishing, she thought indignantly, that Mr Flinder employed such a dreadfully common woman as his cleaner. Irene glanced disgustedly at the awful red hair and shiny black plastic mac. Ridiculous on a woman that age. And why had she suddenly started turning up at school to collect her wages? Money almost certainly not declared to any tax inspector!

'Don't yer? Don't know what you're missing!' Irene gasped and shied away as Josie crossed to the desk and banged one red chapped hand down on the keyboard, turning the section of the report she was typing into a variation of the Enigma code.

'What are you up to this weekend, eh, luv?' she breathed, grinning at Irene's outraged expression. 'Got your dildo and your bottle of sherry? You could come down the pub with me tonight and look for a fella, but there's not many who'd fancy a sad old bat with a face like a cow's arse.' She straightened up. 'Ta-ra, luv! See you next week. If you can't be good, be careful!'

She banged out of the office laughing and Irene sat there breathing hard, her arms folded. Tears of outrage pricked her eyes. That did it! She picked up the phone and hastily put it down again as Bernard opened his office door and stuck his head out.

'Have you finished that governors' report?' he asked brusquely.

'Not yet, Mr Flinder. I–' Irene blushed again. That was another thing. Mr Flinder hadn't called her Irene all week, or asked about Mother once. She wondered what was the matter with him. Pressure of work? Or was that wife of his making a nuisance of herself? 'Mrs Duffy insulted me,' she said, and pointed to the hieroglyphics on the computer screen. 'Look what she did. She's insufferably rude,' Irene went on, aggrieved. 'And why does she come here anyway?'

'Keep your comments about Mrs Duffy to yourself,' snapped Bernard. 'It's none of your business why she comes here. You're the school secretary – you don't own the place. Your job is to get that report typed by Monday lunchtime, not sit there drinking tea and poking your nose into my domestic arrangements.'

'Mr Flinder!' exclaimed Irene, shocked, and rose from her seat. 'I'm not – I'd never dream of interfering in–.'

'Get on with your work, *Miss* Watchet!' His door slammed.

She stared at the closed door for a minute then got up and stumbled to the tiny kitchen for a cry. He had never insulted her like that before! What had she done or not done? Tears spilled from her eyes and she felt shattered with misery. Another Friday, another nightmare weekend to get through. Most nights when she and Mother sat watching television, she felt like jumping up and running screaming into the street. If only she'd ignored her mother and married Hughie all those years ago! She would have a life of her own now, be respected as a married woman. She might have had children. Now she was a despised, ageing spinster of the parish, pathetically pining for her married boss. One who treated her cruelly. Poking her nose into his domestic arrangements indeed! How could he be so unjust?

She stared out of the window. A group of shouting, laughing schoolgirls strolled past the tennis courts in the fading winter sunlight, wearing heavy boots and rucksacks, long thick hair hanging loose. Girls looked so scruffy these days, so unfeminine. Two of them were smoking. But was it four o' clock already? Irene quickly swallowed two aspirins and made herself another cup of tea. She wouldn't ask *him* if he wanted any, the mood he was in! She had her pride. She took the tea back to her desk, sat down and riffled through the telephone directory until she found the Preston number she wanted.

'Good afternoon,' she said nervously. 'I'm not sure if I've got the right number but I want to report a woman whom I have reason to believe is being paid cash for her cleaning work and not declaring it to Social Security. This is confidential, isn't it? She won't be told my name? Good. She's a Mrs Josie Duffy and her address is . . .'

Bernard sat down, drumming his fingers on the desk. He felt tense with agitation. Where was the bitch hiding? He'd hung around outside her office at lunchtime, but she hadn't come out. He'd try again after school, then cruise Eaton Road for a while. Shannon had to go back there sometime, it was her home. When school broke up for the Christmas holidays in two weeks' time he'd have all day to follow her and choose his moment. But it might be too late by then. He had to get her soon – tonight! Perhaps he should go back to Salthouse Quay, the scene of his abortive attempt the other night? She might know someone who lived round there, be staying with them. He was desperate, but he'd have to be careful. Very careful.

He thought of Francesca. He'd done everything under the sun before finally he choked the breath out of her. He'd had to gag her first, of course, or the noise would have alerted someone. He'd been surprised to discover she was a virgin. The power, the thrill of having absolute control over a girl, the knowledge that she was helpless and you could do what you wanted . . . there was no feeling in the world like it. Shannon had experienced fear the other night. But she'd escaped and now she was on her guard. Had the mother of those two boys been to the police? he wondered. He didn't think so. She hadn't even seen him.

Bernard got up and paced the office, feeling hot and restless. It was strange, he thought. In the past he'd gone for months – years, even – without feeling the urge to kill, being content with videos and magazines, fantasizing about young girls, watching them. Suddenly there'd been two killings within a month. He was entering a new and exciting phase of his life. Or would be once he'd got rid of Shannon! He swore as the phone rang.

'Yes, who is it?'

'It's me, Bernie. Vernon. You sound pissed off. Did you like the videos?'

'Oh!' He relaxed slightly. 'Yes, they were excellent. Just a minute.'

He opened his door and looked out. Irene sat at her desk typing away, eyes downcast, an injured expression on her ugly long face. She didn't glance up or smile enquiringly. Stupid bitch, he thought. He closed the door and picked up the phone again.

'Have you got anymore?' he asked in a low voice.

'That's what I'm calling about.' Vernon gave a nervous giggle. 'There's some new stuff come in, from Holland. Not the usual sort. Something extra.'

'What do you mean? I've had Dutch videos before.'

'Well – the girls don't just get shagged and have things used on them. At the end . . . you know what I'm saying?'

Snuff movies! Bernard shifted in his seat, filled with excitement. Sweat prickled along his moustache and under his arms.

'I know what you're saying.' His throat was dry. 'I'm interested.'

'It'll cost you, Bernie,' Vernon hissed. 'It'll really cost you this time. This is dangerous stuff, it's bloody dodgy handling it.'

'How many have you got?'

'Just two at the moment. A hundred and fifty quid each. See you outside the pub at seven?'

'I can't tonight, I'm busy.' He and Margaret were dining at the Presbytery. Before or after that he'd have to try to get Shannon again. 'I'll meet you in Sefton Park tomorrow at eleven,' he said. 'Same place, by the boating lake. I'll have the cash for you then.'

'Right. See you, Bern.'

He hung up, leaned back in his chair and closed his eyes, brain whirling with fantastic images. Maybe he'd make his own snuff movie. Starring Shannon Flinder. There was a knock at the door.

'Come in!' He jerked upright and pulled some papers towards him, composing his contorted face into a semblance of calm. Irene came in followed by a nervous Patricia O'Neill clutching her rucksack in her arms. Her blonde hair was done up in a thick plait and the navy blue school skirt now ended at her knees instead of her bottom. She looked as if she'd lost weight. Her blue eyes avoided his.

'Patricia O'Neill's here for her detention, Mr Flinder,' Irene said tightly.

'Oh, yes.' He leaned forward and stared at Pattie. 'How many times have I told you not to climb over that wall?' he asked angrily. 'You can write an essay about why you think it might not be a good idea to do it in future. Go back to your classroom and get started,' he ordered. 'I'll be in later to check on you. And don't imagine you can write any old rubbish, because I won't tolerate it. You have to take this seriously. D'you understand?'

'Yes,' she muttered sulkily, blonde eyelashes cast down.

'Yes, *what*?' he barked.

'Yes, Mr Flinder.'

'That's better. On your way, now.'

He watched with satisfaction as she turned and trailed out of the office, followed by Irene. Discipline, he thought. That was what those bitches needed. And that was what they'd get from him.

'What are you doing here?'

Shannon dropped her pen and sprang to her feet as Rob walked into her office and shut the door. 'Do you know what an injunction is?' she asked nervously. 'You will, if you try to hurt me again.' What if he caused a scene here? Gavin would be furious, blame her. Not to mention the possibility that she might end up in Casualty.

'Take it easy, Shannon.' Rob held up his hands in a conciliatory gesture. 'I'm not going to hurt you. I just want to talk.'

'Oh, you've decided it's time to talk, have you? As opposed to punching and kicking!' Anger replaced nervousness. 'I haven't time to talk,' she said. 'I'm at work. I don't *want* to talk to you anyway. I've had enough.'

He wore a brown leather jacket, navy blue suit and a grey silk tie, and smelled faintly of Dolce & Gabbana. He looked different, she thought, not blank and unfeeling anymore. Just subdued.

'You're never at home and I don't know where you're staying,' he said quietly. 'I phoned Nick and asked him, but he wouldn't tell me.'

'Are you surprised?' she flared. 'After what you did?'

'No. I don't blame you for not wanting me to know.' He looked down at his shoes. 'I can understand that. This is the only place I could think of. I just want to talk,' he repeated.

'Well, I don't,' she said fiercely. 'You can't just walk in here after what you did and expect to *talk*!'

'I'll never hit you again,' Rob promised. She looked fantastic, he thought, her blonde hair curling around her shoulders, pushed back to reveal those lovely cheekbones. She wore a purple velvet top and a long tight black skirt. 'I don't know what came over me,' he said helplessly, shaking his head. 'I must have been crazy! Of course you're afraid and don't trust me anymore. It'll take time to rebuild that trust. What I did was terrible,' he said despairingly. 'I feel like I've woken up from a nightmare. I don't know what came over me,' he repeated.

She stared at him, not knowing what to think. 'Let me guess,' she said bitterly. 'It wasn't *you*, Rob Flinder, who raped your wife and walked out on her then came back a few days later and beat her up. All the while calling her a bitch, repulsive . . . you name it. It was another person who did those things, wasn't it? Not the *real you*. Oh, come off it!' she snarled. 'I've heard that from too many punters to find it even mildly convincing.'

'I don't blame you for feeling bitter.'

'How very sensitive and New Age of you. You'll be joining some men's discussion group next, wanking on about your *feelings*. Is that a new initiative of the Chief Constable's? Apart from the one about not fabricating evidence?' She blinked back tears of anger. 'You can't just walk in here and play with my emotions like this!'

'Please, Shannon,' he begged. 'I know you're angry, and you've every right to be.' The police social worker had said she was bound to be hostile initially. 'I don't know what happened. I just freaked out, went crazy for a while because of . . .' He stopped. 'What I did to you was inexcusable.'

'You've got that right!'

'But – I don't want a divorce anymore.' Rob looked pleadingly at her. 'I want to save our marriage. I want you.'

'You freaked out, went crazy for a while. That's it, is it? You expect us to get back together, like nothing happened! You raped me,' she said, her voice shaking with anguish. 'You *raped* me, Rob! You punched and slapped me and kicked me while I was lying on the floor. You humiliated me. You said you didn't love me, that I was repulsive to you. You blamed me for what your father did. You even lied to your colleagues about me, said I'd cheated on you. You *hurt* me,' she said, eyes full of tears. 'How do I know that won't happen again? How the hell am I supposed to go back and live with you, trust you? That would take a huge leap of faith, Rob,' she cried. 'Faith I just don't have.'

He flushed. 'Then what do you want?'

'*Time*. You turned my life upside down,' she said sadly. 'I need time to get back on track, think what to do, sort my head out. I can't make any decisions right now. Don't pressure me.'

'But you think we can get back together?' he asked tentatively.

'I don't know.' She looked down, shaking her head. 'You can't ask me that now.' She stared at him again. 'What about your father?' she asked. 'That's the big question. He did it again the other night. Francesca Delaney! What are you going to do about him?'

'*No!*' he exploded, making her jump. 'You don't know it was him!' He walked to the window and stared out across darkening Exchange Flags. 'My father's not on the agenda, Shannon. He never will be. As far as I'm concerned, he doesn't exist. That's final. I won't change my mind.'

'So you won't do anything?' She went cold. 'That means nothing's changed, Rob. He can go on raping and murdering girls and so far as you're concerned he just doesn't exist?'

'Him *and* my stupid mother.' Rob's agitation increased. 'Melanie'll be okay,' he said. 'He won't touch her again. You were right, he nearly ruined our marriage.' He turned to her, face distraught. 'He could still ruin our lives,' he said. 'How could we live, keep our jobs, if everyone found out what he is? You know what people are like! We'd be crucified along with him. I told you, I don't – I *won't!* – think about him anymore. I can't if I want to stay sane.' He clenched his fists. 'We won't have anything to do with him as long as we live. I want you back, but I realise that'll take time. We'll be all right again, Shannon, I know we will.'

They wouldn't be all right. He'd just signed his father's death warrant.

'I think you'd better go,' she whispered. 'Please don't come here again.'

'Will you call me?' he persisted. 'Call me soon, please.'

She turned away, cold with fear and disappointment. He went out and closed the door. She collapsed, shaking, in her chair, hands over her face. She'd agonized all day, been on the point of trying to reach Dean Carver, to call off the hit. But now it had to happen. Rob wouldn't do anything.He wanted her back – just like that! – but he hadn't really changed. Only she could stop Bernard, save her own life as well as others. She glanced at her watch. Six o' clock. Was Finbar back from Dublin yet? The phone rang and she grabbed it.

'Shannon? It's Nick.'

'Oh. Hi!' She tried to sound cheerful.

'Listen, we've got a babysitter tonight, Helen's granny offered to look after her. I thought we could eat out instead and go on to a club afterwards. Give Caroline the real night out she wants. Is that all right with you?'

'It's fine,' she said. 'Great.' Even more of an alibi. 'Except that I won't get to see gorgeous girlie-girl.'

'Well, you might. She'll probably be awake. I'll pick you up from work and we'll go home and have a drink first. If you want to get changed I'm sure Caroline can lend you some sexy little number that doesn't fit her anymore.' Caroline didn't have Shannon's full bust and beautiful curved waist, he thought disloyally. 'Are you finished for the day?'

'Damn right I am!' She yawned and closed her eyes. 'Gavin will probably stay until seven or eight, but I've had enough.' In more ways than one. 'I need a weekend.'

'I'll leave the office now, then. See you in about ten minutes.'

'Okay, Nick. I'll be ready.'

She put the phone down, switched off the computer and tidied her papers away. Tonight's the night, she thought. It's too late to call it off. Even if that were an option. Rob still couldn't accept what his father was, what he'd done to Melanie, Bianca, Francesca. What he'd go on doing if not stopped. Which meant they were finished. She paused and leaned her head on the desk, crushed with sadness. How would Dean Carver do the deed? she wondered for the millionth time. What sort of *tragic* accident would it look like? She might be questioned by the police, she had to psych herself up for that.

She stood up, parted the blinds and looked out across dark Exchange Flags, at the men and women with briefcases hurrying past below. Was Bernard out there, watching and waiting? She was dry-mouthed and shaking with nerves. She longed for a gin-and-tonic or a glass of white wine.

'You're a murderer,' she whispered. 'You're playing God.'

She didn't feel like God. She felt terrified, felt like she was losing it, coming apart at the seams. She had to hold herself together. She had to eat, laugh, talk in the candlelit restaurant, act as though she was enjoying a normal night out with friends. Gavin was right, maybe she should go on the stage. She'd have to live a lie from now on. May as well get used to it.

She put on her coat, picked up her bag and briefcase and left her office, locking the door. At reception Anita had her coat on and was packing up ready to leave. The computer was switched off. Anita's red glossy lips shone and the dark make-up around her bulging eyes made her look ghoulish. Her tightly curled dyed blonde hair looked like little chipolata sausages. She smiled at Shannon.

'Not working late?'

'On Friday? You must be joking! I'm waiting for a friend to come and meet me. I'm going out to dinner with him and his wife. Oh!' She smiled as the lift doors slid open to reveal handsome Nick standing there in his suit and overcoat. 'Here he is now.'

Quarter to six. How late would the bastard make her stay? The cleaners had been and gone. Pattie sat in the empty classroom and looked out of the windows at the bright lights of other empty classrooms across the dark playground. Lots of people climbed that wall. He'd deliberately picked on her. She sighed and looked down at the page she'd written. Bush Boy, or Mr Bushman, her English teacher, said you should be able to write in an interesting way about any subject under the sun. There wasn't much chance with this one. Pattie read it over. She had adopted a sarcastic tone and was quite pleased with the result.

> *It is not a good idea to climb over the wall because of the high risk of personal injury to myself and to anyone who attempted to assist me. If I climbed over the wall and fell I could sustain physical injury, which could necessitate a hospital visit and therefore perpetrate the irresponsible act of further burdening an already overstretched National Health Service. In this culture climbing walls is not considered socially acceptable behaviour for females. I would also cause great anxiety to my mother.*

Fat chance! The only thing that caused her mother great anxiety was not having enough money to go down the pub or to bingo. There would be no tea for Pattie when she got home. Martin would have eaten it. She hated Martin. She hated her mother. Her father visited once a week and they always ended up having a row. She hated silly old Flinder too! He'd saved her from the bullies, but how long was she supposed to go on being grateful?

She looked up and gasped. He was standing in the classroom doorway. Watching her.

'How are you getting on?' He came forward and took the sheet of paper from her. She looked down, playing with her Biro as he read in silence.

'Well, Patricia, I can see you really sledgehammered your imagination on this one,' he said coldly. 'I'm not at all satisfied with your effort.' Good vocabulary, he thought. She must like to read. It certainly wasn't the result of Mr Bushman's teaching talent. 'I suppose you think you're very clever.' He looked down at her nervous sulky face. Anyway, it's late.' He tore up the page. 'You'd better go home.'

She jumped up with relief, put on her duffel coat and grabbed her rucksack.

'Are you ready?' he asked sternly. 'I'll give you a lift.'

'Oh, no. No!' She stared at him in dismay. He'd planned this! 'I can get the bus,' she stammered. 'I'll be all right on the bus. It stops outside our house.' She hated being in his car. She wasn't sure why.

'Don't argue, Patricia,' Bernard said impatiently. 'It's dark now, I've kept you in detention. I can't possibly let you go home on your own, it would be very irresponsible of me. If anything happened to you your mother would never forgive me.'

She would! Pattie gripped the rucksack and looked helplessly around the silent classroom, visualizing the miles of empty corridor beyond. They were the only two people in the school, unless the caretaker was hanging around somewhere. Surely Flinder wouldn't try anything? Her friends and the old cow secretary knew she'd had detention, she'd spent the day moaning about it.

'Come on then,' he said briskly. 'Chop-chop!'

He strode out of the classroom and down the corridor and she followed, trailing the rucksack straps along the scuffed vinyl floor. She didn't want to put it on. He got his coat and briefcase and car keys from his office and locked both doors behind him. They walked towards the main entrance. Pattie wondered if the school lights were left on all weekend.

She shivered as they came out into the icy darkness. The sky was low and cloudy, dull orange around the horizon. The air smelled of smoke and traffic fumes. His Volvo was the only car left in the car park. Everyone tried to get off early on Fridays.

'Get in,' he ordered, unlocking the doors. Pattie obeyed, wedging the rucksack between the gear stick and her feet. She pulled the seatbelt across her body but didn't fasten it, and sat as close as possible to the door. Take me home, she pleaded silently. Just take me home. For once that dirty boring house seemed like an attractive place.

He started the engine, reversed out of the parking space and jerked the car towards the main gates, glancing to right and left. Pattie stared at the dark road ahead, playing fields to either side.

She held her shoulders rigid and her knees jammed together, hardly daring to breathe. She glanced at his jowly profile, thin set mouth, the straggling moustache. He wasn't saying anything, not asking stupid questions or laughing at things that weren't funny. Maybe he would just take her home. She wouldn't go climbing over walls again, that was for sure. She'd be a model of restrained behaviour.

'Patricia.' He drove slowly a little way down the road and stopped the car under the big chestnut tree that had pink flowers in spring. 'Would you like to go for a little drive somewhere?' he asked softly. 'I'll treat you to a milkshake and hamburger first.'

First? She froze. 'N-no thanks,' she stammered. 'I should go straight home. My mother'll wonder where I am. I forgot to tell her I had detention.' She bit her lip, cursing herself.

'Did you now? You see, Patricia . . .' She gasped as he slid his arm along the back of the seat and settled it heavily around her shoulders. He shifted his horrible heavy body closer. His breath stank. 'Despite all your tomboy antics, I rather like you. And I think you like me too. Don't you?' he asked hoarsely. He bared his teeth. It wasn't a smile, she thought, it was like an animal threatening attack.

It was no good. He hadn't meant to touch her, but why not enjoy himself a little? What could she do? Who would believe her if she told anyone? The mother thought the sun shone out of his arse. And Patricia would be all right so long as she did what she was told.

'No,' he heard her whisper. 'I don't like you. I want to go home.'

He grasped her shoulder and pushed his other hand up her skirt, kneading the smooth cold bare thighs, trying to force her knees apart. She cried out and began to struggle wildly, hitting out at him.

'Stop that, you little bitch!' he hissed. 'I'm not going to do anything except touch you a bit. But I'll have to hurt you if you struggle.'

Her eyes were wide with terror, the pupils dilated. Her left hand made a sudden movement, swift, like a small animal. He screamed in outrage as the knife, a sharp vegetable knife, was plunged into the back of his right hand. She'd been keeping it for the bullies. Warm blood poured out, soaking into his coat and trousers. He brought up his hand and stared in shock at the thing sticking into it.

'You little bitch!' he roared as she pushed open the door and scrambled out. 'Get back here!'

But Pattie was out of the car and sprinting down the road, the rucksack left behind. 'Help!' she screamed. 'Help me!' She collided with two women strolling along, one of them dragging a big Alsatian on a leash. The dog growled.

'What's up, love?' the older of the two asked. They wore trousers and big fat padded anoraks. 'What's wrong?'

'That man attacked me,' she sobbed. She turned and pointed. 'The man in that car.'

'What car?' the younger woman asked. 'The Volvo or that Jeep down the road?'

'The Volvo, the Volvo. Help me!' Pattie screamed again. She grabbed the woman's arm and held on.

'All right, love, all right,' she said comfortingly. 'You stay with us. You'll be all right, don't worry. Call the police, Maureen, there's a phone box at the end of the road. Bloody perverts!' she spat. 'Kids aren't safe anywhere these days.'

'The man who attacked me – he's the headmaster!' Pattie sobbed, looking up at her. 'He's the headmaster! I've been scared of him for ages, I knew he'd do something.'

'Jesus Christ!' the woman breathed. 'What's his name?'

'Flinder – Bernard Flinder.'

She grabbed Pattie's hand and held it tight. 'Get the police, Maureen!' she shouted. 'Go on, hurry up! Look, he's still there.'

Terror had lent Pattie strength. It took a big effort for Bernard to pull the knife out of his hand. He thought a bone was splintered. He gasped and swore at the pain. Dark sticky metallic-smelling blood was everywhere: on his trousers, coat, the seat. All over his hands. It spurted out. Was an artery severed? Get after her, he thought. There were only two women with her, he could handle them. Make up some story. He had to get her back. He pulled a handkerchief from his coat pocket and wrapped it around his bleeding, shaking hand, reached for the car keys and started the engine.

Pattie and the two women jumped back, arms flailing, as the Volvo suddenly burst into flames. The dog ran to and fro, straining at its leash, barking furiously. A shattering bang followed as the petrol tank exploded, sending orange and yellow flames shooting into the darkness. Glass and twisted metal flew through the air, and a big ball of dense black oily smoke ballooned against the dull sky. The stench of burning rubber hit their faces. The tyres exploded. Maureen whirled round and dashed for the phone box. No one noticed as the Jeep lurking further down the road did a swift U-turn and sped off in the opposite direction, tyres screeching.

In the burning car Bernard lay dying of massive trauma and blood loss. Both legs and arms were blown off and there were third degree burns over what remained of his body. His last conscious emotion was that of surprise.

Part Two

Chapter Eighteen

Finbar drove slowly along the Dock Road, high old stone and brick walls to one side, pubs, warehouses and offices to the other, a clash of ancient and modern. Brick walls and dilapidated fences gaped to reveal huge brightly lit car ferries, the Irish boats or the Isle of Man one. The Dock Road was creepy at night. Parts of it looked as though they had barely recovered from wartime air raids, particularly the May Blitz of 1941. The Liverpool Overhead Railway, the 'Docker's Umbrella', had run along here, providing close-up views of docks goods stations and berthed Atlantic liners. Pier Head was the busiest station. The railway had closed in 1957. Had it survived, it would have been a great tourist attraction now.

He flicked the indicator and turned left between the huge round fortress stone gateposts of Clarence Dock, parked the Maserati on the wet overgrown cobblestones and switched off the engine. This part of the dock was deserted, fallen into disuse years ago. He took a torch and got out of the car. The dark mass of the clock tower loomed above, and the river slapped gently at the quay where no ships were berthed.

'There's a rumour that French prisoners were kept there during the Napoleonic Wars,' Ken, Guy's father, had told him over a drink at the club one night. 'I didn't believe it because the tower was built in 1845, long after the Napoleonic Wars. Then one day when Arthur and me were mending the clock, old Green frigged off to his fancy woman for a cup of tea and a bit of how's-your-father and I decided to look under the trapdoor in the middle of the floor. Arthur jumped down and slammed it on me head, the bastard! Pitch black it was. *Pitch*. Never known blackness like it. It was below water level, I could hear the river sloshing about. I banged on the trapdoor, shouted at Arthur to let me out, called him for everything. He was pissing himself laughing. When he lifted it and let the light in I saw that the walls down there were much older than in the rest of the tower. There were rusted chains hanging from them. I looked down and saw a skull and a ribcage, other human bones. I screamed, I was that bloody terrified. They'd kept prisoners there all right! They'd built the tower over it. Must have demolished whatever was there before and just left that dungeon as the foundations. Imagine dying in a place like that, chained up in the pitch black with the Mersey sloshing around your ears. Doesn't bear thinking about!'

'No, it doesn't.' Finbar had been intrigued by the tale. 'Would have made a good air raid shelter during the Blitz,' he remarked.

'Aye, you're right,' Ken said thoughtfully. 'I've never been back since – wouldn't want to – but you'd have been safe down there.'

As safe as the handguns, Semtex, Ecstasy and suitcase full of cash were now. Finbar had examined the tower, fitted new locks and padlocks on the studded iron door and trapdoor and started to use the dungeon as a temporary arms dump and storage place for other sensitive items. It was a wonderful hiding place, no one would ever find it. He made sure he was never followed there. The only worry was that it was below water level and the old walls and floor were damp. But the stone walls were thick and strong, and everything was well wrapped.

He took the box of Ecstasy that he'd brought back from Dublin on the Linnell Air Cargo plane from the boot of the car and unlocked the heavy iron door, shining his torch on the gleaming padlock. Inside the tower the air was dank and smelled of spices and molasses. And fear. He stooped to unlock and unbolt the trapdoor, lifted it back and jumped down, the box in his arms. There wasn't much space between floor and ceiling, just eight or ten feet. People were shorter in those days. He shone the torch on the cases and boxes of guns, and on the skull and ribcage that had terrified a teenage Ken. Who was it? he wondered. A young Frenchman who'd left his native land to fight in shortarse

Napoleon's wars? At which pointless battle had he been taken prisoner?

'*Bonsoir, Monsieur,*' he whispered. Madame had been left behind in France, wondering if and when her husband would return. Not knowing that he'd languished in a Liverpool dungeon, spending his last hours chained up in the pitch dark with the River Mersey sucking and slapping around his ears. His body thrown on the floor to make way for the next unfortunate.

Finbar wondered how he would spend his own last hours, and shook his head impatiently. He heaved himself up, closed and locked the trapdoor and brushed damp dirt off his suit and overcoat. He needed desperately to see Shannon, touch her, talk to her. He locked the tower, shone the torch around and got back in the car. It was only ten, she wouldn't be back from Nick and Caroline's yet. Had she missed him? She liked him, he thought, felt safe with him, enjoyed the sex. But did she feel anything more? He loved the way she lost control, gasping and crying out, clinging to him as she slid over the edge into one orgasm after another, violet blue eyes dazed with desire. Her heart and soul were in it, there was no doubt. He felt that Majella had sometimes held back, he didn't know why. He banished the disloyal thought from his mind. Rupert Eastbrook was still a marked man, would still pay. Finbar had the backing of the High Command. They seemed to accept that this would be his last job. There had been no argument. That was why he was worried.

He slid the car through the massive gateposts and only switched on the headlights when he was well along the Dock Road, heading towards St Nicholas's church and the old Cunard building. Ten minutes later he was pushing his way through the sweaty dancers in the Carmen Club. He ran up the back stairs to his office.

'Good evening!' The blonde Former Yugoslav with the tits sat on his desk, her bare scarred back to him, legs spread, flimsy dress bunched around her waist. She and Guy jumped as he opened the door and strode in.

'You – out!' he ordered. She jumped off the desk, pulled up her dress straps and ran out, eyes lowered. He closed the door. Guy zipped up his trousers and straightened his tie.

'Sorry about that, Finbar,' he muttered. 'Got a bit carried away there.'

'Get carried away in your own time.' Guy stood up to make way for him and he sat at the big polished mahogany desk and switched on the computer. No one else in the place knew how to use it or dared touch it.

'Haven't seen you for a couple of days,' Guy said nervously. He never knew when Finbar would turn up. He picked up his glass of Coke and drank.

'Did Melanie bring back the stuff all right?' Finbar opened an account book and leafed through receipts. He began to type.

'Yeah. No worries. It's upstairs.'

'Van den Berg'll be here at nine tomorrow night to pick it up, okay?'

'Okay.'

Music boomed through the walls but the plush dimly lit room was silent except for the tapping of the computer keys. Guy watched scornfully. He hadn't a clue how to use those bloody things and cared less. They were a waste of time and money. You couldn't hack into police or bank files or the Pentagon anymore, or so he'd heard, so what was the point?

'Can I get you a drink?' he asked.

'No, thanks. I'm not staying.' Finbar stopped typing and switched off the computer. 'So it went all right?' he asked again.

'Yep.' Guy sat in a leather armchair near the polished table with its collection of bottles and glasses. 'As I said.'

'Will she do another run?'

'No. No chance.' He coughed and shook his head. 'She nearly lost it. Wady phoned me while she was there – he wanted to dump her and get someone else to bring the stuff back. Said she was too nervy and freaked out, spent the whole time panicking and drinking the mini bar. I don't know how she got through.' He shrugged. 'She was in a terrible state when I picked her up from the airport. Said she'd never do it again.'

Finbar stood up, hands in his pockets. 'That's odd,' he said thoughtfully. 'Beginners normally get cocky after the first run. Makes them feel they've achieved something, been pushed beyond their personal limits and triumphed. Like executives on a survival weekend.' He laughed and Guy joined in. 'Well, what about Nietzsche?'

'Who?'

The Philosophy student, her boyfriend. Paul something. Can't we use him?'

'Paul Ashton?' Guy paused. 'Haven't seen him for weeks,' he said, rubbing his chin. 'Don't know where he is.' He laughed nervously. 'Did you hear about Melanie's old man? Bernard Flinder?' he asked, wanting to get off the subject. 'Weird, isn't it?'

Bernard Flinder? Melanie's father. Shannon's father-in-law? Finbar stiffened. He hadn't realized. 'What about him?'

'He was murdered tonight. Made the nine o' clock news. "Liverpool headteacher in car bomb attack". Got blown up outside his school around six. Motive unknown. Bet it's some little tosser with a grudge and a chemistry set. Kids nowadays, eh?' He laughed. 'No respect.'

'I'm off,' Finbar said briefly. Guy got up, relieved.

'Sure you won't stay?' he asked. 'Dad might drop in later. He likes you.'

'Give him my regards. His drinks are on the house. Tomorrow night at nine, okay?'

'Okay. See you, Finbar.' Guy hoped the boss would forget about Paul Ashton and Melanie. He'd have to find someone else to do the next run. He waited until Finbar left the club, then went out of the office and beckoned to the blonde girl sitting at the bar. She looked up, smiled gleefully and pouted at him as she slid off the bar stool.

Shannon was not home. Finbar showered, wrapped himself in his bathrobe and took a bottle of champagne from the fridge. Demi-sec. She hated Brut, said it prickled her mouth and gave her a headache. He smiled as he opened it and poured himself a glass. He thought of the murdered father-in-law. Who would car bomb a headteacher? Teachers were assaulted sometimes, but rarely murdered. And never like that. A car bomb! Did she know yet? Probably not, if she'd spent the evening having dinner with Nick and Caroline. They would eat, talk, listen to music, play with the baby if she was awake. Not watch television.

He took the bottle of champagne and two glasses into the living room, switched on a lamp and lit the floating candles in the Waterford crystal bowl. Shannon loved candles. Candles reminded him of Christmas, not far off. Would she spend it with him? He had no intention of visiting his parents in Dublin, or either of his brothers.

The river lights winked through the mist. It had to be a professional hit, he thought, gazing at the chilled champagne bottle. Not many people had the resources – the nerve – to rig their own car bomb. Someone had wanted Flinder dead. But who? Why? It was a mystery. Not one he cared to think about right now.

He built a fire in the grate, put on the Annie Lennox CD and stretched out on the sofa. It was a relief to get back from Dublin. It had been at the back of his mind that they might want more than a chat, especially after Lenny's talk about shooting informers. Did they suspect him of being one? They were paranoid enough. But there was nothing to inform about, he wasn't a member. They must realize that. If the Branch ever decided to pay him a visit he'd be between the devil and the deep blue sea; he'd lose everything, probably his life. He *had* to finish after the Eastbrook job, Majella and Roiseann avenged. He sighed and closed his eyes, wishing Shannon would come home. He needed her desperately.

The slam of the front door woke him. Finbar sat up and glanced at his watch. One-forty. He'd slept for two hours. In the hall something thudded to the floor and he heard Shannon gasp and laugh. A minute later she opened the living room door and came in, walking unsteadily on high heeled black velvet shoes with velvet ankle ribbons. Her eyes were bright and her cheeks flushed. Her curly blonde hair was wild.

'Since when do you wear gear like that to the Magistrates' Court?' he asked, taking in the tight sleeveless crimson crushed velvet dress and the sheer black stockings that matched the shoes. She had beautiful legs and the tiniest waist he had ever seen. He could smell her perfume. Her soft skin gleamed in the candlelight.

'It's Caroline's.' She giggled. 'The shoes too. She said I could keep them. She bought the dress to make herself go on a diet after Helen was born, but it didn't work. She said the shoes were a momentary aberration.' She crossed to the other sofa and sat down, feeling nervous and shy at the sight of him. She'd longed for this moment and now that it was here she didn't know what to say.

'We got dressed up,' she said breathlessly. 'Caroline's mother babysat Helen, Nick took us to a posh restaurant. I had lobster. After that we went to a club.'

'Did you have a good time?' He reached for the champagne.

'It was great,' she lied. 'We danced, talked a lot.' She laughed. '*Drank* a lot.'

'I hope you're not too fluted for some of this?' He poured two glasses of champagne and slid one in her direction.

'What's fluted?' she asked. 'Irish for arseholed?' She picked up her glass, gulped champagne and put it down again.

'That's right,' he said slowly. 'Dublin, to be precise.' He picked up the bottle again. 'A refill?'

'Yes, please.' She held out the glass, her glittering eyes avoiding his gaze. Her red lipstick was licked off except for the outline, and there was a smudge of gold eyeshadow on one cheek. He wanted to tear off the dress and fuck her in one minute flat. 'Did you have a good time in Dublin?' she asked politely.

'Not particularly,' he replied. 'It was business, that's all.'

'What kind of business?'

'Air cargo.'

'What kind of cargo?'

'Anything.' He shrugged and drank. 'Engines, machinery, spare parts, flower bulbs . . .'

'Flower bulbs?' She choked on her drink and laughed. 'Tulips from Amsterdam?'

'Well, not from Dublin. Did you miss me?' he asked. She glanced at him in alarm. 'Don't worry,' he smiled, disappointed. 'I was just kidding.'

'Finbar–.' She put down her glass and clasped her hands together. She was shivering slightly. 'I think I should move out.'

'Why?' he asked, trying to hide his disappointment. 'When we talked on the phone the other night, you said you'd like to stay.' What a night that had been! He'd lain awake tortured by frustrated desire, and finally fallen into a doze around seven o' clock.

'I know, but–.' Was Bernard dead yet? And how? 'Rob came

to see me today,' she said, and picked up her glass and drank more champagne. 'He wanted to talk.'

'Talk?' Anger shot through him and he sat up straight. 'With his mouth or his fists? Talk about what?'

She laughed again, but didn't sound amused. 'I told him to go.'

'Good,' he said grimly.

'He wants me back.' Shannon said. She looked down at the tiny bubbles bursting in the glass. 'Just like that. Unbelievable, isn't it? He said he'd changed his mind about the divorce and that he realizes it'll take time to regain my trust. He said he doesn't blame me for being *bitter*!' Tears came into her eyes. The evening had been a terrible strain. Gavin was wrong about the acting.

'What's brought this on?' He felt furious at Rob, torn with anxiety.

'I don't know.' She shrugged. 'He said he felt like he'd woken from a nightmare, that he'd been crazy and didn't know what came over him. I think he's moved in with some WPC, but I didn't ask him about that. It didn't seem important compared to–.' She stopped, biting her lip. 'He thought he could just walk into my office and *talk* to me!' She gripped the glass. 'After what he did.'

'D'you want him back?' He held his breath. 'Or is it too soon to tell?'

'I don't – I can't have him back,' she whispered.

'No?' He felt a surge of hope.

'No.' She looked straight at him for the first time. A tear rolled down her cheek. 'Not after what he did. I don't believe he's really changed,' she said. 'It's too late. I could never trust him again.' Her lip trembled. 'Not now.'

'Why d'you think he did what he did?'

'I don't – I can't talk about it!'

There was so much he didn't know. Maybe never would know. He could live with that. So long as she still wanted him. He got up, sat beside her and refilled their glasses. 'Why do you want to move out?' he asked. He put up one hand, stroked her hair away from her face. It crackled with static electricity. 'Wow!' he exclaimed, and stroked the back of her neck. 'You're live!'

'I really like you, Finbar.' She gazed up at him. 'More than *like*. But with everything that's happened, everything that's going to happen, it can't be good for me to jump straight from one relationship to another. It's not fair to either of us. Maybe I need to be alone for a while, sort my head out. That's what I told Rob.'

'Normally I'd agree.' He kissed her lips, teasing her with his tongue, and slipped his fingers under the dress strap, easing it down over her shoulder. 'But not in this case. Shall I tell you what I think you need? If you want the opinion of a mere male?' The other strap came down and he kissed her neck and shoulders, breathing in the wonderful smell of her body.

'Go on,' she gasped. 'I mean, tell me.' She felt a surge of desire as he leaned back on the sofa, his arms still around her. He was so sexy, his touch so sure. She felt she could come just listening to his voice, looking into his eyes.

'You need champagne, sex, laughs, relaxation, plenty of lobster, and the Dublin man who–,' he hesitated – 'fell in love with you outside the law courts one fine autumn day.'

'You've kissed the Blarney stone,' she said shyly, and slid her arms around his neck.

'I'd rather kiss you. Will we take off the dress?' he murmured, feeling for the zip. 'It's beautiful, but I've always wanted to make love with a woman wearing nothing but black stockings. It's one of my sad old fantasies.'

'Don't tell me you've never fulfilled it?' The soft leather sofa felt good against Shannon's bare skin. He deftly unfastened her bra and slid off her pants.

'I haven't.' She gasped as he put his hands on her breasts, squeezing the nipples slightly. 'It's so bloody good to see you again! Touch you.' He laughed as he leaned back and lifted her astride him. 'I've been like Jesus in the wilderness for the past few days,' he groaned. 'Wanting you, worrying if you were all right. Couldn't eat. Couldn't sleep.'

'You look a bit like Jesus,' she giggled. 'Without the long-suffering expression, of course. I don't think he had your fabulous green eyes though. Do it now!' she gasped, leaning over him as his fingers explored her wet warmth. 'Please! I don't want to wait.'

'You're an impatient young lady.' He pulled her down, kissing her hard. 'I'd do anything for you,' he said. 'You know that, don't you?'

'Yes!'

He thrust upwards and inside her, his hands on her breasts, fingers gently squeezing the nipples. She screamed with delight. His expression was intense as he stared up at her, lips slightly parted. A minute later he lifted her off him, turned her over and slid into her from behind, thrusting so hard she thought she would faint. She came twice, crying out, loving the feel of his hands on her breasts and buttocks, moving inside her. It had been good with Rob – in the old days! – but never like this. Or did she just want Finbar more? She'd never felt such overwhelming, all-consuming desire. He shuddered and cried out, holding her tight as he came. They collapsed on the sofa and lay wrapped in each other's arms.

'I can still feel tremors inside me,' she whispered a minute later. 'Like after an earthquake.' She laughed, hugging him. 'I wonder what that was on the Richter Scale?'

'God, I missed you so much!' He leaned over her, kissing her mouth and breasts, stroking his hand up and down her smooth curvy body.

'I missed you too.' She kissed him back. 'It was terrible in that bed without you. I could smell your body.'

'I missed your face and your hair and your beautiful eyes and gorgeous body and your voice and your laugh and the things you say. I want to fuck you all night. I love you!' He paused, looking down at her. 'You don't mind if I say I love you?'

She hesitated. 'I don't mind. It scares me, that's all.'

'You don't need to be scared.' He kissed her again, exploring her mouth. 'Will we go to bed?' he asked. 'It's getting cold in here. You can open your presents in the morning.'

'Presents?'

'Over there. I forgot about them, I was so desperate to have my wicked way with you.'

She raised her head and glanced at the pile of green-and-gold wrapped parcels in the middle of the floor. She'd been too drunk and nervous to notice them when she came in.

'Presents,' she murmured sleepily. 'You brought me presents. You're so sweet and kind to me all the time.'

'I always will be. You can have that in writing.' She closed her eyes and held him tight as he lifted her up and carried her to the bedroom. He was like a drug, an addiction. She was way beyond the point of no return.

The morning was clear and sunny with a cold wind blowing off the river. Shannon woke at ten, slid out of bed and went to her room to shower and dress. She put on the black jeans, ankle boots, a long heavy black sweater decorated with red satin bows, and her black leather coat. She made coffee and took Finbar a cup.

'Good morning!' He lay back and smiled at her. 'You look beautiful. Hey, thanks for the coffee!' he exclaimed. 'I'm not used to being spoiled like this.'

'You're welcome.' She kissed him. 'I've got to go in a minute,' she said. 'The client, remember? It shouldn't take long.'

'Don't worry about it. Take all the time you need. And be careful,' he warned. 'Make sure he's not following you around. He might be lurking outside your office.'

She stiffened. 'Oh! You mean Rob. I'll be careful,' she promised. 'But I don't think he'll follow me around. I think he'll respect my privacy.'

'Don't count on it. D'you want my car?' he asked. 'Shall I drive you?'

'Oh no,' she hastily. 'I'll walk. I want to walk, it's a lovely day. Freezing but lovely. Drink your coffee, get some more sleep. You need it after last night.'

'Last night.' He grinned and stretched his arms above his head. 'Holy fuck!'

'It was.' She kissed him again and stood up. 'I've got to go,' she said reluctantly. 'I'll see you later, okay?'

'I'll be waiting.' He sipped the coffee. 'D'you still want to go to the Lake District?'

'Yes, why not? It'll be good to get away.' Out of reach. 'I'll see you later,' she called as she ran into the hall.

A few tourists were already inspecting the Albert Dock colonnade shops and strolling around the Maritime Museum. Shannon ducked out of the way of an elderly American man with a camcorder. Seagulls screamed overhead. She glanced up at the Liver Buildings as she left the dock and crossed the car park, heading for Water Street and Exchange Flags. The cold clear weather made her feel confident, invigorated.

If only Rob and Bernard didn't spoil her peace of mind! Of course Bernard didn't exist any more, assuming Dean Carver had done his job, but his existence had poisoned hers, destroyed her marriage. The fear, the tortured guilt of last night had faded like Mersey mist. It would certainly return. You took a life, she thought again. You're a murderer. But it didn't feel like murder. It felt like self-defence.

Anger rose in her as she walked. It should never have come to this. To save herself and future victims she'd been turned into an outlaw, confronted with a horrendous moral dilemma. She thought of Margaret and Melanie and Rob. Looking the other way, living in denial, letting him rape and murder undisturbed. Rob said he wanted her back, but expected her to accept that Bernard wasn't 'on the agenda'. He wanted to call the shots. And Margaret, acting so holier-than-thou! How the hell had she stayed married to him all those years? Drink and pills, probably, keeping herself permanently anaesthetized. She looked like she'd lost it long ago. A dysfunctional family! Was there any other kind?

Fifteen minutes later Shannon was climbing the steps of the Walker Art Gallery, the wind whipping her hair. Dean Carver stood at the top of the steps, smoking behind one of the huge stone pillars. He was dressed in the same clothes he'd worn at their meeting in the Malakand. He nodded to her, looking nervous but excited.

'Good, wasn't it?' He grinned at her as she joined him. 'Did you see it on the telly?'

'See what on the telly?' she panted, pushing her hair out of her eyes. 'What are you talking about?' She glanced around. There were few people on the pavement below, and no cars parked on the double yellow lines.

'The job,' he said proudly, and threw the cigarette away. 'My car bomb. Good, wasn't it? Made the nine o' clock news.'

'A car bomb?' She stared at him in horror. 'You killed him with a *car bomb*? And it was reported on television?'

'Right.' He nodded gleefully, rubbing his tattooed hands together. 'Good, eh?'

'You stupid bloody psycho!' she shouted, furious and panicked. 'I told you to make it look like an accident. Are you *crazy*? How could you be so thick? Take your hands off me!' she shouted as he grabbed her wrist and pulled her behind the pillar.

'Shut it!' he hissed. 'Christ's sake, *shut* it! Now listen, love.' He let go of her wrist and moved closer. She smelled his cigarette breath. 'What was I supposed to do? Walk into the bloody school or his house and say "excuse me" while I shot the bastard?' he asked angrily. 'The police don't know it's not an accident.'

'The police don't know a car bomb's not an accident?' Shannon echoed. 'Do me a favour! Even they aren't that brain dead! Oh, my *God*!' she moaned. 'What have I done?'

'He had a kid in the car with him,' Dean said urgently. 'A girl. I let her get away before I detonated it.'

'So you're an amateur bomb maker?' she sneered. 'Why don't you get a job with the IRA?' She seized his arm. 'He had a *girl* in his car? Was she all right? Did he–?' She couldn't speak.

'I dunno. She got away. Ran off down the road.' Dean held out his hand. 'Look, love, I've done what you wanted. He's dead, he won't bother you again. We just have to keep our mouths shut. Now give us the rest of me money and let's get lost. We don't want to be hanging round here.'

Shannon opened her bag, cold fingers trembling, and gave him the white envelope with seven hundred pounds in it. 'I put in an extra hundred and fifty as a bonus,' she muttered. 'Don't know why I bothered.'

'Thanks, love.' He nodded. 'Maybe we can do business again sometime.'

'Yes, if anyone else pisses me off I'll give you a bell. Christ!' she said scornfully. 'Where *do* you get your lines? Goodbye!'

She turned and hurried down the steps, her mind in turmoil. Fear gripped her. A car bomb! On television! For God's *sake*! Would Dean keep his mouth shut? He was proud of what he'd done. His *job*! What am I going to do now? Just keep your head down. Keep calm. No one can connect this with you. You don't have a motive – an obvious motive. Carver doesn't know your real name. Stay cool. If you panic now you've had it.

She'd called the police, told them she had evidence about Bianca's murder, said Bernard had done it. Would they remember? How the hell could she explain *that* if his paedophile activities came to light? They might suddenly forget they'd dismissed her as an adulterous embittered deserted wife!

Finbar came out of the gallery entrance and watched as Shannon reached the bottom of the steps and ran across the wide road into St John's Gardens. He wrapped his scarf around his face and strode rapidly after Dean Carver.

'Carver!' he called. 'A word in your ear.'

Ten minutes later Dean was dead, shot in the back of the neck as he lay curled up in the boot of his Ford Cortina in a nearby underground car park. Finbar ran back to his Maserati, parked by St George's Hall, and was back at the Albert Dock before Shannon returned. So she'd had the headmaster hit because he was a paedophile! Was it him she'd been frightened of? There was still a lot he didn't understand. He put the envelope with the seven hundred pounds into a drawer in his bedroom. He'd return it to her gradually, slip a hundred into her wallet now and then. The phone rang.

Shannon felt calmer by the time she reached the Albert Dock. No one can connect Bernard's death with you, she kept telling herself. No one's going to suspect you. He must have attacked the girl in his car and somehow she'd escaped. Good on her! If it came out that he was a paedophile, so much the better. Suppose the police did remember her allegations and questioned her about them? She'd say she'd made up the story out of a desire for revenge and by a horrible coincidence it was true. Rob wouldn't contradict her! Whoever had taken her calls would probably keep quiet, knowing they'd have major egg on their faces if their incompetence was revealed. People would be outraged that Bernard had been a head teacher with authority over young girls. There would be no public sympathy for him. It would make headline news for a while, the police would launch an investigation – or appear to – and that would be the end of it. She'd just have to sweat it out. Who really wanted to find the killer of a paedophile anyway? Bring them to *justice*? That thought made her smile.

She let herself into the apartment and stood in the warm hall, taking off her jacket and ankle boots. It's over, she told herself. It's over. You're safe.

'Are you all right?' Finbar came out of the living room and took her in his arms, kissing and hugging her. Shannon responded, her tension melting.

'Your nose feels cold,' she said. 'Have you been out?'

'Just on the balcony, smelling the air. Looking at the river. Are you all right?' he repeated anxiously.

'Of course I'm all right,' she said slowly, looking into his green eyes. 'Why shouldn't I be? Rob wasn't hanging around Exchange Flags. I'm absolutely fine.'

He let go of her. She was a cool one, he thought admiringly. Very, very cool. It made him sad that she didn't feel she could confide in him. Maybe one day.

'Nick phoned while you were out,' he said hesitantly. 'Rob called him again because of course he can't get in touch with you. He asked Nick to tell you that his father's been murdered. By a car bomb, apparently. It was on the news last night. Of course we missed it.'

'Murdered? By a car bomb?' Shannon breathed out, a long breath. They stared at one another. She didn't know what to say. 'I – I'm no longer part of that dysfunctional family,' she said at last and shook her head. 'It's nothing to do with me.'

'D'you still want to go to the Lake District?' He laughed nervously. 'I keep repeating that like a mantra.'

'Yes, I do. But first . . .' He watched, desire rising in him as she slowly stripped off her sweater, jeans, pants and black bra and stood naked in front of him. He smelled her perfume and the baby powder she liked to smooth on her gorgeous round high breasts. She stood on tiptoe, put her arms around his neck and he lifted her, holding her tight. She kissed him and wrapped her strong slender legs around his waist.

'I want you,' she whispered in his ear. 'I really want you, Finbar.'

'You can have me,' he whispered back.

Chapter Nineteen

Detective Sergeant Cindy Nightingale swore she'd change her name when she reached thirty. You couldn't grow old with a name like Cindy. Her mother asked what made her think she'd grow old anyway, the job she did? Today, Saturday December 16, was her twenty-ninth birthday and she had no time to visit her mother to eat frosted creamy cake so sweet it made her teeth itch. Or listen to whinges about how she wasn't getting any younger and wasn't it time she found herself a husband and got pregnant before her womb and ovaries seized up? If they hadn't already. The Bernard Flinder case was ballooning faster than a bouncy castle.

'So you've no idea where Melanie might be?' she asked the silent widow and her son who sat together on the chintz-covered sofa. Margaret looked neat in red polo neck sweater, pleated navy skirt and black patent court shoes with a tacky gilt buckle, the contents of a make-up counter on her strained set face. Rob was on compassionate leave that he didn't want. He didn't want time to himself, time to think. He couldn't believe his father was dead, murdered. Who was responsible? He felt no love for the man who'd never done anything but criticize, look at him with contempt. It was a huge shock just the same. His initial reaction was one of relief; his father *literally* didn't exist anymore. Shannon might come back to him sooner now. He was also terrified. The police would dig into his father's background. Find – what?

The morning sun poured through the patio windows and the stiff breeze bent the slender silver birches in the garden. Bird droppings disfigured the flower-wreathed head of the nude marble girl. It was odd, Cindy thought, that the comfortable room – hideous with its flowered wallpaper *and* flowered sofas, but nevertheless comfortable – contained no family photographs.

'You see, we have to interview all family members, his friends, anyone who knew him,' she went on. They weren't being very helpful. Of course they were in shock. 'And you don't know where your wife is, Rob?'

'I told you,' he said stiffly. He scratched his chin and rubbed his tired eyes. 'We've split up. I don't know where she's staying at the moment. But it's just temporary, we'll be back together soon.'

'How come you don't know where she's staying?'

I raped and beat and threatened her and she doesn't trust me. He shrugged. 'We had a row,' he said irritably. 'We haven't made up yet, that's all. Just a stupid row, nothing serious. Look, you – or I – can get in touch with her at her office. She's a solicitor, works for a firm called Steele & Monckton in Exchange Flags.'

'Right. Er.' Cindy shifted on her chair and pulled down the hem of her grey skirt. 'There's something else.' She glanced at her colleague, Detective Constable Eddie Merton, who sat there in his jeans and leather jacket, a vacant expression on his face. He looked beyond thought but she knew he was just longing to smoke the single cigarette he carried around in his pocket. 'It appears that Mr Flinder had a young girl in the car with him just before the explosion,' she said, looking hard at Rob and Margaret. 'A first-year pupil at St Fidelma's. Her name is Patricia O'Neill. She said she'd been in detention and Mr Flinder insisted on driving her home. She claims he stopped the car and sexually molested her. She escaped and ran down the road towards two ladies who were walking their dog. One of them called the police.'

Rob flinched and looked away. Margaret twisted her hands tighter, massaging them as if rubbing in soap or hand cream. She looked at the confident young policewoman, smart and slim in her grey suit, straight brown hair falling to her shoulders, her brown eyes watchful. Watching her.

'Excuse me a minute.' She got up and went to the kitchen where she splashed cold water on her wrists and forehead and poured herself a gin-and-tonic. Oddly, she didn't need a Valium.

Her mind was blank, her body numb. It was impossible to believe that Bernard was dead, that he would never walk into this house again, run up the stairs, throw wounding remarks at her over badly cooked meals. Lock himself in his study . . . She jumped as the phone rang again. Another newspaper wanting an interview! A group of reporters were camped at the front gate and there was another lot outside St Fidelma's. The paedophile headmaster from hell who'd molested a young female pupil – a tabloid editor's dream! She and Bernard had become public property overnight. She couldn't understand how the story had got out so quickly. But that was the media for you – rumour ruled. She stood at the counter sipping her drink, wondering whether or not to pick up the ringing phone. She dared not switch on the television.

'Mrs Flinder?' Cindy appeared in the kitchen doorway. 'Can we get on?'

'Yes.' She decided she did need a Valium after all. 'Yes, of course. I'll just–' She picked up the bottle, shook out a tablet and washed it down with gin.

'Don't you want to answer that?' The phone was ringing off the wall!

'All right.' Margaret picked it up. 'Hello?'

'Mrs Flinder? There's a rumour that your husband was responsible for the rape and murder of two young girls? What have you got to say–?'

She hung up and gulped her drink. Cindy watched. Margaret Flinder wasn't the archetypal grieving widow, or not in her experience anyway. Most of them collapsed, started crying and screaming, and didn't stop for weeks. But 'archetypal' was a mistake; people reacted differently. Responses deemed inappropriate by society were not always evidence of guilt. This woman could just be in shock, not able to grasp the enormity of what had happened. Being splashed all over the newspapers and television wouldn't help the sense of unreality either. The son was defensive, sulky, downright unhelpful. Was he worried about his job, afraid he'd be vilified because he was Flinder's son? Feeling guilty? They might have known about Bernard for years and done nothing. Margaret followed her back to the living room and they sat down again. Ed lit his cigarette without asking if anyone minded.

'We had a phone call from a Mrs Josie Duffy,' he began.

'I sacked her,' Margaret interrupted sharply. 'She was insolent – extremely rude. She was a bad worker and she stole things. Food, drink. Even soap and shampoo and shower gel.'

'She told us she was sacked because she saw videotapes and magazines in Mr Flinder's room upstairs–.'

'The study.'

'The study.' Ed glanced at Cindy. 'She said they contained pornographic material. Child pornography.' Margaret stared in front of her and said nothing.

'Don't listen to her!' Rob said aggressively. 'She's just a vicious old bat who's got the hump because she was sacked. And she was sacked because she was bloody useless as well as a thief!'

'Rob, your father was murdered,' Ed broke in. 'We think it's a contract killing. Someone wanted him dead, we don't know who. Everything in this house is evidence. We'd like to take a look upstairs, if you don't mind?'

'I bloody do mind!' he flashed. 'Got a search warrant, have you?'

'We can get one.' There wasn't much left of the car; it was burnt out. Not much left of Bernard either. Patricia O'Neill was one lucky young lady.

'Go and get one then!' Rob loathed being dragged into this; wanted nothing to do with it. It would only lead to more trouble. What would it do to his life, his career, if the truth about his father came out? Who was he kidding? It *was* out. Rob wished Shannon was with him, supporting him. He was better now, he'd come to his senses. Only a few weeks ago she'd begged him not to leave her, said she couldn't live without him. She must still love him, despite her misgivings. His father couldn't stand in their way anymore. If it wasn't for this bloody investigation! And where the hell was Melanie? He'd go round to her flat later. It was no use going before twelve, she'd be in bed.

Ed was about to give his little speech about doing things the hard way or the easy way when Margaret spoke up unexpectedly.

'You can look upstairs if you want to.'

'Mum!' Rob looked at her in alarm.

'I said, they can go and look. This is my house, not yours, and I say they can go and look. You might have to break the door down,' she said to Cindy. 'My husband kept it locked. He was the only one who had a key. I wasn't allowed in there. I've no idea where he kept the key.'

So that was her angle. The innocent wronged woman who played the loyal unquestioning wife, blissfully ignorant of her husband's deviant sexual tastes and murderous propensities. She wasn't ignorant, Cindy thought. She had known or suspected for years. And stayed silent. The policewoman fought down the hostility that rose in her. Paedophiles, child murderers, couldn't function without people like Margaret Flinder who lived their lives looking the other way, pretending nothing was wrong, ignoring what it suited them to ignore. Shutting their eyes and ears to victims' agony. Who had murdered Bernard Flinder, or had him murdered? Some outraged parent who didn't want to put their daughter through the trauma and farce of a trial where she rather than her assailant would be judged? Assuming it ever got to trial. If Margaret Flinder wanted to live in denial that was her right. But her silence had put others at risk. She'd had no right to do that.

She and Ed stood up. He found a little Delft Blue ashtray on the sideboard and stubbed out his cigarette.

'Thank you, Mrs Flinder,' Cindy said briefly. 'You said you don't know where the key is. Do you have something we could use to break the lock?'

'My husband had a tool box, I don't know where he kept it. In the shed, perhaps. Just a moment.' Margaret got up, opened the patio doors and went into the garden. An icy draught invaded the warm stuffy room. A few minutes later she came back with a claw hammer and crowbar.

'The shed wasn't locked then?' Ed gave her a bright smile. He took the hammer and crowbar. 'Thanks. Come on, Cind.'

Rob waited until they were out of the room and on their way upstairs before he turned on his mother.

'Are you mad?' he asked furiously. 'Why did you let them look? Suppose they find something? What do you think my – your – life will be like from now on if they prove he was a–?' He stopped, face working. 'He's dead, for Christ's sake! Everything could be all right now. Why can't they just leave it?'

'They *can't* leave it. You know they can't.' The phone rang again and Margaret got up. 'I'll answer it.' She went into the kitchen and picked up the receiver.

'Margaret? It's Angie. Hello, how are you?' She didn't wait for an answer. 'I'm afraid I've got to cancel our lunch date on Monday,' she said, her booming voice filled with false brightness. 'Stupid of me, I completely forgot Jane's coming round with the girls.'

'I see.' Margaret glanced at the bottle of gin on the counter, just out of reach.

'And Jennifer Rothwell phoned. She asked me to tell you she won't be able to come to lunch after all. She's teaching a class on Wednesday, she forgot to note it in her diary.'

A class at which she and Bernard, not raincloud technique, would no doubt be the main topic of conversation. Dare she brave the art group again?

'Amazing,' Margaret said mildly. 'This sudden outbreak of amnesia.'

'What did you say?'

'I said, this sudden outbreak of amnesia is amazing. If you want to drop me, Angie, just say so.'

'Margaret? Did you know about Bernard? Did you know what he was?'

She was silent, not knowing how to reply.

'You must have known,' Angie said accusingly. 'You must have suspected. Men like that can't have normal sexual relations.'

'Read that in this morning's tabloids, did you? I thought Meals-on-Wheels was your speciality, Angie? Not sexual psychology.'

'You've been living a lie all these years, Margaret. You must have known what he was yet you did nothing. Just stayed with him, pretended you had a normal marriage.'

'Like you did after your husband's affair with that bimbo?'

'Hardly the same thing!' Angie sounded furious. 'Do you think we'd have been friends with Bernard, had him as a guest in our home, if we'd known what he was?' she shouted. 'You're despicable, Margaret. As bad as he is – was. I've got two little granddaughters!'

'So lunch is off? All right. And do give Jennifer my regards, won't you? I hope she gets herself organized. Goodbye, Angie.'

Margaret hung up and poured another drink. She knew she sounded hard, callously indifferent, and that wasn't good for public relations. But she didn't know how to act, what to say. She only knew she had to stay in control. Whatever the cost.

'Who was that?' Rob stood in the doorway, staring at her. She thought how smart he looked in that dark blue suit and colourful patterned silk tie. His brown hair was neatly trimmed and he was clean shaven. His brown eyes, so like hers, looked angry, scared.

'A friend of mine. Ex-friend now.' His mother held up the gin bottle. 'Would you like a drink?'

'At this time of the morning? Oh, all right, go on then.' He frowned and walked into the kitchen, hands in his pockets. 'Shannon should be here,' he said angrily. 'I need her, I've got to talk to her. I said I wouldn't bother her, but now that this has happened– Jesus Christ!' He wrenched the ringing phone off the wall. '*What*?' He shoved the receiver at her. 'It's for you.'

'Good morning, Margaret! It's Elinor from the flower shop.' She laughed shakily. 'Er – this is slightly embarrassing–'

'Don't tell me. Your Christmas rush suddenly came to a complete standstill.'

'Well, I–' She was ready to feel sorry for Margaret, but this cool sarcasm annoyed her. 'I just wanted to tell you that after what I saw on the news last night – and in the papers this morning – I think it's best if you don't come to work anymore. I've got my business to consider, I'm sure you understand? Of course I sympathize with you but – well, actually I don't!' she said angrily. 'How you could live with a man like that and let him–.'

Margaret hung up and turned to her son.

'Have you got a cigarette?' she asked, ignoring the ring at the doorbell.

'A cigarette?' He stared at her. 'I don't smoke. *You* don't smoke!'

'I think I'll take it up again. I stopped years ago, at your father's insistence. I used to enjoy a cigarette. Those long thin menthol ones. I must make a note to buy some when I go shopping.' She paused and looked at him. 'Will you come with me, Rob?'

'No,' he said shortly. 'I've got things to do. Like get my wife back. This bloody mess should never have happened.'

'Shannon didn't care about you before. What makes you think she'll come back now?'

'She *will* come back!' he flared. 'I love her. She loves me. You wouldn't know what that means, would you?' Margaret had no answer.

Upstairs in Bernard's study Cindy Nightingale and Ed stared, frozen with horror, at a video of a young girl being raped and sodomized by two masked men. The desk drawers were open. Pale sunlight shone on the combat knife, orange nylon rope and carton of latex gloves. The wrinkled shrivelled thing in the clear plastic envelope looked like it might be Francesca Delaney's missing nipple.

'I can't believe it!' Irene wept. 'I simply can't believe it. Mr Flinder dead, blown up by a car bomb. *Murdered!* And you say he molested that girl? I don't believe it,' she repeated fiercely. 'She's making it up. She was angry about being given detention.'

'Don't be ridiculous, Irene! I always thought there was something odd about that man.' Joan Watchet sat up straight in her armchair, hands folded, her blue-white curls permed and sprayed rigid. She wore a brown cardigan and flowered dress. 'My stupid daughter was in love with him,' she said indignantly to the young fair-haired detective. 'Carried a torch for him for years, worshipped the ground he walked on. A married man. Pathetic!'

'Mother!' Irene hissed. And blushed furiously.

'Don't "Mother" me, Irene,' she said harshly. 'You're an absolute fool where men are concerned, you always were. It's a good thing you never married, that's all I can say. God only knows what sort of character I would have been forced to acknowledge as my son-in-law! Now, pull yourself together and answer this young man's questions. He hasn't got all day to sit here and listen to your snivelling.'

Gary Leitz cleared his throat and flipped over a page of his notebook. The stuffy little net-curtained room stank of eucalyptus.

'Can you think of anyone who would have wanted to murder Mr Flinder, Miss Watchet?' he asked gently.

'No, of course not.' Irene shook her head, handkerchief pressed to her mouth. 'He was a wonderful man.'

'Was he well liked by the staff and pupils at St Fidelma's?'

'Irene, take that handkerchief away from your mouth!' Joan snapped. 'It's very embarrassing to witness a woman of your advanced age carrying on like one of those schoolgirls.' She turned to Gary. 'She's fifty-eight, you know!'

Irene obeyed, hating her mother. 'He was well liked,' she said hesitantly. 'Very strict, but fair. He wouldn't stand for any nonsense.' Read different opinions, thought Gary. 'But a headmaster has to maintain a certain distance, doesn't he? There are difficult decisions to be made, he can't always worry about being popular.' Joan snorted.

'Did you notice any differences in him lately? Anything at all?'

'He wasn't himself lately,' Irene said slowly. 'Not his usual charming self.' Her mother snorted again.

'What do you mean exactly?'

'He called me Miss Watchet instead of Irene, and he was very critical of my work. He never used to criticize my work. He used to say I ran the school and that he didn't know what he'd do without me.' She bit her lip. 'I thought maybe he had trouble at home. That he was under pressure. Then there was the afternoon when that girl came to see him . . .'

'What girl?' Gary looked up.

'His daughter-in-law. She's in her mid-twenties, very pretty. Blonde, striking dark blue eyes. She arrived one Friday afternoon and asked if she could see him for a few minutes. She looked rather upset.'

They both stared at her. 'What happened?' Gary pressed.

'I don't know. Mr Flinder said he'd deal with her. He took her into his office and told me to go home. Then he shut the door. He was immediately on edge, I could tell. I assumed she had some problem and wanted to consult him, ask his advice.'

'Anything else?'

'No.' She looked down, twisting her handkerchief. 'Except, I can't imagine anyone wanting to murder him. And those accusations, those terrible rumours! They're not true? They can't be. Mr Flinder was a pillar of the community.'

'They always are,' Joan said wearily.

'Well, thanks very much, Miss Watchet. Mrs Watchet.' Gary stood up and put his notebook away. 'You've got the Regional Crime Squad number, give us a ring if anything else comes to mind.'

'I will. What do I do?' Irene asked. 'Go to work on Monday as usual?'

'I'm afraid I wouldn't know. That's got nothing to do with me.' She followed him to the front door and opened it. 'I should warn you that the media are camped outside the school and the Flinder house,' he said. 'You shouldn't speak to them. Even if they offer you money for a story.'

'I've no intention of speaking to them,' Irene said sharply. 'Do you know when the funeral will take place?'

'Again – nothing to do with me. No idea.' There wouldn't be much left to put in the coffin, he thought. They'd had to scrape Flinder off the road. 'Thanks,' he repeated. ''Bye, now!'

Irene shut the front door, went back to the sitting room and collapsed on the lumpy sofa, red-rimmed eyes shining with tears.

'Pull yourself together, for goodness sake!' Joan said sharply. 'Why don't you go and make us a cup of tea? I could do with one. That *disgusting* man!' she hissed. 'To think you worked for him all those years. People might believe you're an accessory.'

'*Accomplice*, you mean. I'm not a handbag or a pair of gloves! And don't be silly, Mother,' she said wearily. 'They haven't even proved he committed those two murders. It's just vicious rumour. You always want to believe bad things about people.'

'I wanted to believe good things about you, but I never had the chance. Of course I've given up now. You're useless, always were. You may as well hand in your resignation on Monday before you're sacked. His successor – whoever that is – won't want an old frump like you hanging around, making the place look untidy.'

Irene heaved herself off the sofa and went into the kitchen. Her world might have come to an end, but she still had tea to make.

Gary Leitz headed straight for Cindy Nightingale's desk.

'The secretary's gutted,' he said excitedly. 'Couldn't stop crying.'

'More gutted than the widow then.' Cindy grimaced.

'The mother made a right show of her. Told me she'd fancied Flinder for years.'

'Amazing,' Cindy said briskly. 'Mrs Flinder let us look in his study. You'll never guess what we found? Knives, rope, latex gloves. Videos and magazines – kiddie porn. Not very pretty. We looked in his diary, but he wasn't stupid enough to write down phone numbers of contacts. We'll have to wait for the DNA, of course, but it looks like he could be responsible for Bianca Mitchell and Francesca Delaney.'

'Jesus!' Gary breathed, looking round the busy incident room. 'And that girl in his car last night – he would have done her too. Imagine it, your bloody headteacher putting his hand up your skirt!'

'He's done a lot more than that, Gary.' Cindy thought of the shrivelled nipple, now being examined in the lab.

'Yeah, but . . . *Jesus!*' He shook his head.

She picked up her ringing phone. 'Melanie Flinder was what?' she asked in consternation. 'She's really disappeared? Okay, let me know.'

'What?' Gary asked.

'Ed just went to Melanie Flinder's flat with Rob because he said she hasn't answered her phone for days. Her things are there, including a sink full of scummy dishes. There's blood on the walls and floor in the living room. Something's happened to her. Rob got upset when he saw the blood. Broke down. I think all this is a bit much for him. I don't think he knew about his father.'

'Might be an act. He might have killed him. It's usually one of the nearest and dearest.'

'Yep. I don't think it is Rob, though. And no other pointers so far. We need to find Shannon now, talk to her. I could phone her on Monday at her office. No, we'll go round there.' Cindy smiled. 'She's a lawyer, she'll hate that. Wonder how she came to marry a copper? Bet she wishes she hadn't bothered now!'

'I'm going to kill you, you bitch! You destroyed me.' Bernard ran after her, stumbling through the woods, glinting knife held aloft.

'I'm going to kill you!' he screamed. 'You and all the others. You won't get away with what you did. I'm going to kill you!'

'Leave me alone!' The trees and bracken ended at the edge of a drop to a thundering waterfall far below. Water, shiny as glass, gushed over jagged rocks. Shannon stopped and looked down, gasping for breath, bare feet sliding on loose soil. She had to jump or be stabbed to death, mutilated. She slipped, swung on a branch and it cracked. The sound reverberated through the forest. Rob appeared, staring down at her. He looked frightened, helpless.

'Rob, help me! Help me!'

'I will, Shannon. I love you, you're my wife.' He stretched out a hand and she tried to grasp it, but it was too late. The branch gave way and she fell.

'Shannon! Wake up.' Finbar's voice penetrated her dream. 'Stop it. You're safe. Wake up!'

She woke up, panting and crying, wrestling him. His head and shoulders loomed over her in the darkness.

'Put the light on!' she sobbed.

He clicked on the bedside lamp, put his arms around her and pulled the quilt over her bare shoulders. Shannon stared around the room. Flowered wallpaper, oak beams, a four poster bed with cream lace bedspread thrown back. Curtains partially open, moonlight shining on distant fells. His warm hard body, heart pulsing against her cheek.

'I had a nightmare,' she gasped.

'I gathered that.' His face in the lamplight was grim. She'd called out to Rob.

'I thought I was dealing with this but–'

'Dealing with what?' He looked closely at her.

'The – everything that's happened. Oh, God!' groaned Shannon. 'I'm so scared!'

'There's nothing to be scared of,' he said gently, and held her tight. 'You're in Borrowdale with me. It's a beautiful icy winter night and the moon's shining on the fells. Look.' He paused. 'You're not sad about your father-in-law being blown to kingdom come?' He wished she would confide in him.

'Oh, no. No! I told you, I don't care about him. It's nothing to do with me. He was a bastard.'

This wasn't a good time to tell her that the police would want to interview her at length about the deceased and his family. Her private life. She knew it anyway.

'You just have to stay cool,' said Finbar quietly, gazing anxiously at her flushed sweaty face. He kissed her and smoothed damp blonde tendrils off her cheeks and forehead. 'You know that, don't you? You're good, you can do it.'

She stared up at him. It was as if he knew and approved of what she'd done, wanted to protect her. But he *couldn't* know. That was impossible. 'I know you can cope,' he went on. 'But you've been through a terrible ordeal, you've got to go easy on yourself. You've got me now, I love you. Just try to relax.' He massaged the nape of her neck and stroked her back, long comforting strokes that soothed her and made her feel sleepy again. He wished she'd called out to him in her dream! She still had feelings for Rob, of course. She couldn't stop loving him just like that. However much he hated the idea.

'No one's going to hurt you,' he murmured, kissing her. 'Christ! You freaked me out. Roaring and punching me in the middle of the night! Must have been that Stilton you ate at dinner.' He clicked off the lamp. Moonlight slanted across the bed.

'I didn't punch you,' Shannon said sleepily. 'Did I?' She closed her eyes.

'Hey!' he laughed. 'Don't go to sleep just yet!'

He lay down, lifted her on top of him and kissed her hard. She spread her legs and her blonde hair fell over him, tickling his face and chest and shoulders. She bit his lips and pushed her tongue in his mouth, soft breasts pressing against him. He groaned with pleasure. His penis stiffened, rising against her belly.

'I was thinking,' he whispered. He stroked her breasts, flicked his tongue across her hardened nipples. 'I was thinking–'

She cried out and arched her back as he surged into her, his hands gripping her buttocks. She loved the feel of him inside her, wanted him all the time.

'Will you marry me?'

She opened her eyes in the moonlight.

Chapter Twenty

The blue sky was reflected in the dock waters and the red brick warehouses glowed in the afternoon sunshine, the blue of the water reflected in their square windows. Inside the Maritime Museum Finbar walked to a window and looked out across the Albert Dock, its waters whipped into little waves by the icy wind. The model of the *S.S. Titanic* was a few feet away, enclosed in a glass case. He liked it, didn't want it to be blown up by his bomb. He hated the thought of planting explosives anywhere in this building, with its beautiful models of old ships and its exhibitions about Liverpool history, ships and the sea. The Battle of the Atlantic exhibition had been his favourite. Lots of children came here. Roiseann would have loved the model ships, he thought, would have tried to get her baby hands on them.

He looked at Lenny standing below, feet scuffing the cobblestones, pulling down the scarf that covered his face to take drags of foul clove *Kretek*. Finbar was losing interest in the assassination, losing it day by day, hour by hour. But he couldn't back out now. And he still needed to avenge Roiseann and Majella. He couldn't fool himself - Majella would have wanted this. She would have hated Shannon simply because she was English. He realized that Lenny was waving at him, making cupping motions with his cigarette-free hand.

If he wanted to go for a drink they could find a pub. Finbar didn't want him in the apartment again. He wondered how Shannon was getting on at work. Had the police questioned her?

Had Rob turned up again? He took a last look at the *S.S. Titanic* and strolled out of the room and down the wide staircase.

Shannon loved him, she said, but she couldn't think about marriage. Finbar understood. He'd been too hasty. He wished she would trust him completely, though. Why had she wanted Flinder dead, for instance? Dean Carver had told him it was because Flinder was a paedophile. That wasn't the only reason, thought Finbar. She'd been terrified – Flinder must have threatened her in some way.

'What the holy fuck have you been up to?' Lenny asked irritably when Finbar joined him outside. He leered at a young girl with long black hair, dressed in tight jeans and a short fake fur jacket, pushing two toddlers in a pram. 'Hey, love! I wish I'd been at that party!' She ignored him. 'So!' They walked around the side of the building and he pointed to the Maritime Museum entrance. 'His car'll come in over there. You and the other distinguished guests are waiting inside. Where'll you drop the thing? I thought down that big funnel thing by the door.'

'Too obvious,' Finbar said briefly. 'I haven't decided yet.'

'For Christ's sake!'

'There's plenty of time.'

'Ah, well . . .' Lenny took a last drag of his cigarette and threw it on the cobblestones. 'That's where you're wrong.' He shook back his luxuriant brown curls, dark eyes gleaming. 'That's what I came to tell you. It's been brought forward.'

'Brought forward?' Finbar felt a shock of dismay. He shoved his hands into his coat pockets. 'Why's that? Since when?'

'Change of plan, old boy.' Lenny put on an upper class English accent. 'Our source informs us that the visit to the poor sad bastards on Merseyside, some of whom really can work, so they say - don't believe it myself! – has been brought forward. To January 15, to be precise.'

'January 15?' Finbar stared at him, shivering with cold. 'That's just weeks away.'

'Right. Let's go back to your place and have a drink. I'm freezing my bollocks off out here.'

'We'll go to a pub.'

'Why? What's wrong with your place all of a sudden? Got a

woman at last?' Lenny nudged him. 'A naked lady cowering between your satin sheets, wondering what filthy perversions you're going to subject her to when you get home?' He laughed.

'Why didn't you tell me this before?' Finbar demanded. 'I was in Dublin last week, nobody said anything. What are you playing at?'

'Security, old boy. We have to be very careful about that sort of thing. Come on, let's get out of here! I told you, I'm freezing my arse off.'

The Dock Road pub was small and fogged with smoke. Blue tiles on the lower half of the walls made it look more like a public toilet. At four in the afternoon it was crowded. Lenny sipped his Scotch and looked at Finbar, his eyes narrowed.

'If I didn't know better,' he began, 'I'd say your personal *Jihad* was becoming less important and less personal by the bloody minute.'

'I don't care what you'd say, Lenny,' Finbar answered shortly. 'You mind your own business. This isn't the only thing I've got going down at the moment. You're exceeding your brief as messenger boy.'

'I wouldn't describe myself quite like that.' Lenny's smile faded.

'Of course you wouldn't, Lenny. People have to maintain their self-delusion, don't they? Otherwise there'd be mass suicide.'

'You can't back out now,' Lenny said warningly. 'Even though you're doing it out of the goodness of your heart! You know that, don't you?'

'Don't threaten me.' Finbar stared at him, his green eyes chilly. 'Don't ever threaten me.'

'Sure, I'm not!' Lenny laughed. 'No one can do that, we all know it. Hey, come on, lighten up! Look!' He nudged him. 'Look at the state of that. Gagging for it, wouldn't you say?'

The teenage girl with wild auburn hair and purple glossy lips smiled at them then turned and bent low over the snooker table, her round bottom straining in tight jeans. Lenny grinned and whistled. 'Over here, love!' he shouted. 'Fancy a drink?'

Finbar got up, leaving his Scotch unfinished. 'We know the date, time and place then. I'll contact you in a week or so to finalize everything. And watch it!' He laughed as the girl undulated towards them. 'She probably works for MI6. Happy Christmas!'

'You goin?' The girl looked at him, disappointed. 'I've got me mate over there, we can have a laugh. Go on, get us a bevvy!'

'Ask him.' Finbar waved at Lenny and walked out. Fifteenth of bloody January, he thought as he walked back to the Albert Dock. Why hadn't they told him earlier? It could just be security. Distrust, paranoia. He hoped that was all it was.

He got home to find Shannon drinking white wine and pacing the living room. She wore a tight black suit with a velvet collar, and long black suede boots. Her curly hair floated over her shoulders. She stopped pacing as he came into the room.

'What are you doing home so early?' he asked, delighted. Thank Christ he hadn't brought Lenny back! They could go to bed or get into the jacuzzi and he'd take her out to dinner later. Or not. Whatever she wanted. He threw off his coat, loosened his tie and went to take her in his arms.

'What's wrong?' he asked. 'What's upset you?'

She pulled away from him. 'The police came to harass me at the office today,' she said angrily, avoiding his kiss. 'They didn't bother phoning first, just turned up. I told them I knew zero about Bernard bloody Flinder's murder, but they still insisted on asking me loads of personal questions.' She gulped back some wine. 'They even wanted me to go to the police station, like in some stupid detective series. Of course I wasn't having that. You'd think they'd know better! Some bitch of a detective sergeant named Cindy Nightingale – she *hated* me. I took one look at her and knew she had it in for me. And a sleazy greasy-haired creep in a leather jacket who sat there holding an unlit cigarette and didn't raise his eyes above nipple level.'

The sunset over the Mersey turned her hair to flame. Finbar sat on the sofa. 'I know it's not exactly pleasant, but they can't touch you,' he said calmly. He was hurt by her rejection. 'They're just interviewing anyone and everyone who knew him. It's standard procedure, you know that. They'll leave you alone now.'

'I don't think so! They said if I wasn't living in the *marital home,* what was my address in case they needed to get in touch with me? I said that was none of their business, that I didn't have to make a statement because I had nothing to do with it. I gave Nick and Caroline as my alibi for the night he was murdered. But they said I had to give my address, had to make a statement because I was Rob's wife. I had to do it, it would have looked weird if I'd refused. They asked me why we'd split up. I said that was none of their business either.' She finished her wine and picked up the bottle from the coffee table.

'Let me do that.' He jumped up and refilled her glass.

'They seemed to think I was being too hard on him,' she went on, pushing back her hair, distraught. 'I mean, what's a few slaps and kicks and punches and the odd rape!' Finbar flinched and stared at her, shocked. She took another gulp of wine. 'Oh, and something else – Melanie's disappeared, can you believe it?'

'Disappeared?'

'Rob and the sleaze went to her dump of a flat and found all her things there and blood on the walls and carpet. Obviously something's happened to her. They're examining the place for clues. Her so-called boyfriend's missing too, Paul something. Maybe Melanie murdered her father, they said. Did I think she or Rob capable of murder? Maybe Melanie's boyfriend did something to her. Maybe, maybe. What a bunch of lowlifes!' she exclaimed furiously. 'Rob called me again, promising he wouldn't pester me. Says why won't I come back now that his father's out of the way? He thinks it's that simple! I can't stand it,' she went on wildly. 'I don't want anything to do with this whole sordid mess. I want my life back!'

'You'll get it back.' She seemed totally unnerved, on the verge of panic. 'Take it easy, Shannon,' he warned. 'You've got to stay cool.'

He stood up and tried to take her in his arms again but she swerved out of reach and carried on pacing. Wine slopped on to the shiny floor. The sun's rays faded from the room. Finbar switched on the lamps.

'So how come I get the big brush-off?' he asked. She didn't answer, wouldn't look at him. He felt anxious. If she panicked, lost it now, she was finished. He couldn't save her. Why did she push him away?

'You musn't let them rattle you,' he said, feeling seriously rattled himself. 'They can't do anything, you should know that. Listen.' He longed to touch her, try to calm her. 'I can understand you're upset. Nervous. But you musn't let them get to you. Finish your drink, take a shower. Have a rest. We'll go out to dinner later. You'll feel better.'

She turned and faced him, the glass trembling in her hand. 'I don't want to go out to dinner with you,' she said slowly. 'I don't want to go out to dinner with one of Liverpool's biggest drug dealers. Air cargo!' She laughed at his shocked expression. 'Is that what it's called nowadays?'

He stared at her, unable to speak.

'I had to give the police this address, tell them where I was staying,' she said, anticipating his question. 'Like I said. Apparently your club is just a front for drug trafficking and God knows what else. They said it's only a matter of time before you get arrested and that it won't do my reputation or legal career any good to be associated with you. I don't care about that, but–' She finished her wine and put the empty glass on the coffee table. 'Drugs!' She looked at him, tears in her eyes. 'For Christ's sake, Finbar! How could you? Is it true?'

He was silent, thinking hard. So Melanie Flinder and Paul Ashton had disappeared? It seemed as though Guy hadn't been entirely straight with him. What the hell was going on?

'It's true,' he said finally. 'But I never intended to get involved with that. I'm giving it up.'

'Oh, do me a *favour*!' She turned away. 'You sound like the tossers I represent every day.'

'Let me explain. Please, Shannon,' he begged. 'Sit down and let me talk to you.'

'There's nothing to talk about.' She felt crushed with misery and disappointment. She thought of his presents; the designer clothes, the diamond earrings, the delicate sapphire necklace. Paid for with drug money. Money from desperate people, people without hope. He was responsible for their misery.

'How could you do it?' she shouted. 'You had a daughter. How would you have felt if she'd ended up dying from some bloody party pill? You bastard!'

Pain gripped him, a suffocating pain. For a second he struggled to breathe.

'I suppose – as bad as I felt when that Brit's bullets slammed into her.' He saw only fear and bitterness in Shannon's violet eyes, the eyes that only that morning had looked at him with love and desire. He couldn't bear it. And she'd mentioned Roiseann! 'I don't think–' He stopped momentarily. 'I don't think you're really in a position to take the moral high ground, are you?' he asked softly. '*Cheryl*.'

She gasped and put her hand to her throat. 'What did you call me?'

'Cheryl,' he repeated. 'Miss Cheryl Kent. Former secretary to Mr Jon Callie. That's what you told Dean. He said you didn't look like a Cheryl and he was right.' He gripped her arm and steered her towards the sofa. 'Now, let's sit down and talk,' he said. 'Wait while I get myself a drink. I need it.'

He poured himself a Kilbeggan, replenished Shannon's glass of white wine and sat next to her on the sofa. She stared at him, her face pale in the lamplight. The sky outside was dark blue, the colour of her eyes.

'How the hell did you know?' she whispered. 'How did you find out?'

'I followed you last Saturday,' he said. 'I was worried about you. I thought Rob might be hanging around your office, that he'd hassle you. But you didn't go to your office. You went to the Walker Art Gallery and met Dean Carver. I eavesdropped on your enlightening conversation. I was just a few feet away, inside the entrance. Why did you pick him anyway? He's got a mouth as big as the Mersey tunnel. You took a hell of a risk.'

'Well, how would I know where to find a contract killer?' Unnerved, she gulped her wine. 'One of the barristers told me about him. We were having lunch, I was the instructing solicitor in a murder case. He mentioned Dean Carver, said he hung around a pub up Islington called the Malakand. I phoned, went to see him–.'

'You went to the Malakand?'

'What else could I do?' she asked as Finbar shook his head

despairingly. 'I told him what I wanted and–' She shrugged. 'You obviously know the rest.'

The Kilbeggan burned his throat. 'Why did you want Flinder dead?'

'Rob and I were so happy,' she said tearfully. 'I thought we'd be together for life, I really did. I loved him, thought I knew him completely.' She stopped, gripping her glass. 'Then he changed suddenly. Wouldn't talk to me, wouldn't look at me, stopped being caring and loving and affectionate. Didn't want to have sex. He was like a zombie. I couldn't get through to him. Remember that night you phoned?' He nodded. 'I tried again to make him talk to me. He pushed me away – shoved me so that I fell over. I couldn't believe what was happening.

'Then he said he didn't want us to be married anymore, that he wanted to leave and start a new life. He wouldn't explain anything.' She paused to wipe away tears. 'To cut a long story short, as they say, I found out his bloody father had abused Melanie, been raping her since she was three years old. She finally told Rob on Bonfire Night. He was completely freaked out, couldn't deal with the shock of it. He even thought he might be a monster like his father. He felt guilty, thought he should have protected Melanie. He was in shock. That's the reason he treated me the way he did. I didn't know what to do.' She was weeping now.

'He just blanked me out, wouldn't tackle his father, do *anything*. He just wanted to leave me. I thought he was heading for a breakdown. He moved out – raped me beforehand! I felt so . . . I can't tell you! I went to see his father, I was desperate. I told him I knew about him, begged him to talk to Rob, tell him none of it was his fault, that he couldn't have protected Melanie. Bernard was terrified I'd expose him. I searched his car and found the doll – the one that belonged to Bianca Mitchell, the little girl who was murdered in Calderstones Park.'

'I know. I heard about her.' Finbar nodded, his face grim.

'*He murdered her*! I was going to go to the police, but I was too scared at first. I would have had to admit breaking into his car, causing criminal damage. I could have been struck off for that. The doll wouldn't have been admissible as evidence. I thought Rob might really go over the edge. Bernard didn't talk to him, he was just trying to delay things. He didn't give a damn about his own son. I went to the police but they thought I was another vengeful deserted wife. Rob lied to his colleagues about me, said he'd left because I'd cheated on him. Bernard phoned my employer, lied about me having a history of alcoholism and depression. No one would listen to me.'

'I would have listened. What happened then?' Finbar's face was pale, grim.

'Rob beat me up. Then Bernard tried to kill me.'

'*What*?' He stared at her in horror.

'I was alone,' she went on. 'Terrified. Rob didn't want to know. Bernard tried to break into the house but I wasn't there and the neighbours saw him so he made up some story about chasing a burglar. After that . . .'

'The night you came back in a state. You didn't slip on the cobblestones, did you?' he interrupted.

'No.' Shannon took a long shaky breath. 'He followed me, pounced as I crossed Salthouse Quay. He was going to cut my nipple off as a souvenir.' Finbar gasped. 'Before he strangled me. Two boys ran up and I got away. I was incredibly lucky! I knew then it was either him or me.'

'Jesus *Christ*!' Finbar exploded, staring at her in shock. 'Why the hell didn't you tell me? I could have helped you!'

'I couldn't tell anyone.' She looked down. 'I had to do it by myself. And he killed that other girl,' she whispered. 'Francesca. I should have prevented that. It's too late now.'

'You couldn't possibly have prevented it,' Finbar said quietly. He felt suffocated by shock. 'You musn't blame yourself for that, for God's sake!'

'I told myself he wasn't human,' she said dully. 'That he didn't deserve to live. I didn't want to do it . . . have someone murdered. But I kept thinking of Bianca. Even if he'd been caught he would only have been banged up for a few years then let out on the recommendation of some brain dead psychiatrist. I know I'm a murderer. That it's wrong to take a life. But he was going to kill me and there was no one I could turn to. I didn't know what else to do.' She looked at him. 'Do you think Dean Carver will tell anyone?' she asked nervously. 'The police?'

'Don't worry about him.' Finbar finished his drink. 'He won't tell anyone anything.'

'You mean you . . .?' She looked away, not wanting to ask. Not wanting to know. 'Oh, my God!' she gasped and put her head in her hands.

'Of course it's wrong to kill someone,' his soft Irish voice went on. 'Under normal circumstances. But Shannon, this was self-defence. The police wouldn't help. Rob let you down and that's an understatement! What were you supposed to do? Lie in your bed and wait for that pervert to break in and murder you? You did what you had to do – to survive. That's how I got involved in what I'm doing now,' he said. 'I didn't choose it. I didn't wake up one morning and think, Hey, I'll become a drug dealer! It happened because of circumstances. I want to stop,' he said earnestly. I *will* stop. The police can't do anything to either of us, it's bullshit what they say.'

'I told them about Bernard! A couple of duty officers anyway. I didn't get to speak to whoever was in charge of Bianca's case. What if they remember?'

'D'you think whoever you spoke to will want to admit information they didn't pass on could have broken a murder case?' He smiled. 'I think they'll keep their mouths well shut!'

'I hope so. All this is freaking me out so much! I can't believe my life lately. And now you . . .'

He shifted closer so their thighs touched. 'I'm going to stop,' he said. 'I need you to believe that.'

Shannon looked at him, her eyes cold. 'You've admitted you're a drug dealer,' she said. 'Am *I* safe? How do you know I won't tell the police?' She laughed bitterly. 'Supposing they'd listen!'

'I'm in your hands,' he said gravely. 'I trust you with my life. You can do anything you want. I'd never hurt you.'

Finbar longed to touch her but she obvioiusly didn't want him to. He got up and poured himself another drink and stood gazing out at the dark river. A brightly lit ferry was crossing to Birkenhead. 'Tell me something.' He turned to her. 'Do you regret what you did?'

She was silent for a while. 'No,' she said in a low voice finally.

'I regret that I *had* to do it, that I was forced into such a situation. But I'm not sorry he's dead.'

'But you're afraid?'

'Yes, I'm afraid.'

'Of being caught.'

She dropped her eyes. 'All right, yes! Of being caught. That's what scares me most. I don't think I'll lose my immortal soul. Like you said, it was in a good cause.'

He strolled back to the sofa, glass in hand. 'You've got nothing to worry about. Dean's not a problem anymore.' He paused. 'And d'you think this is a killing the police *want* to solve? Bernard Flinder was a paedophile, he murdered two young girls, maybe more. They're not great at solving crimes like his murder, even when they try.'

'That bitch of a Detective Sergeant has got it in for me.'

'She's probably the jealous, resentful, chip-on-the-shoulder type. Don't worry about her. Look, I really am a businessman,' Finbar insisted. 'Most of my interests are perfectly legitimate – ask Nick. This drugs thing – I told you, I never meant to get involved with it and I'm going to stop, You had enough to worry about, that's why I never told you. Can't we deal with it?' he pleaded. 'Put it behind us? I couldn't bear to lose you, Shannon. Our relationship.'

'We don't have a relationship,' she said brutally. 'We just have sex.'

'I can't agree with you there,' he said, stung. 'You don't mean it.'

She gulped wine. 'We just *fuck*, Finbar!'

'I wouldn't describe it like that,' he said. 'What I feel for you, I've never felt for any woman.' He paused. 'Not even Majella. Of course I loved her – I still love her. But with you it's different. We understand one another, we're made for each other. It's not just the sex! Am I crazy?' he asked. 'Is this all in my head?'

'No,' said Shannon in a low voice. Her golden hair shone in the lamplight. She looked down, face in shadow. 'I've never felt like this either. But I loved and trusted Rob, look what happened! He's honest, decent, he joined the police because he genuinely wanted to help people. You're a drug dealer!'

'Pity that model of upright manhood wasn't motivated enough to save his wife from his psychopath father!' said Finbar softly. 'He let you down when you were in terrible danger. He wouldn't listen to you. He still won't. He wants you back, but only on his terms. Don't tell me you can go back and live with him again and put all *that* out of your head.' He hated, was tortured, by the thought that she still might return to Rob. 'Don't tell me that because I don't believe it, Shannon.'

'I can't go back to Rob. I had his father murdered, for Christ's sake!'

'It was him or you,' Finbar reminded her. 'It's called survival.'

'I'm a murderer.'

'Shannon!'

'What makes me any better than you?' Her head whirled from the wine and the effort of thinking. 'You make me laugh,' she said. 'I feel safe with you. When we make love it's from another world. I want to be with you all the time. But this isn't right! I have to get away.'

Finbar went cold. 'You don't mean that?'

'I do. How did you get into drug dealing?' she asked tiredly. 'God, I sound like a social worker!'

'I told you, I was married.' He sat down on the other sofa. 'And I had a daughter. As you reminded me.' She glanced away. 'Majella, my wife, came from a Republican family. I didn't care about that, wasn't into causes of any kind. And I was a lazy bastard. I had my car hire business, I had Majella. She got pregnant, we both wanted a child. We were happy. She asked me to do a few favours for her brothers and uncles – lending cars to transport active service units, guns, drugs, whatever. I didn't like it, but it paid well and it kept her happy. It was no use arguing with her, she'd been brainwashed since she'd learned to walk and talk. I was worried about the baby, didn't want Roiseann to grow up in that atmosphere. I saw a struggle ahead, but I didn't want to think about it. I sounded Majella out about moving to England, but she was against it. I didn't really mind. The business was doing great, we were in love.' He stopped. 'When Roiseann was born, I was so happy. I felt more *human* somehow, I can't explain it. It was like she humanized me, took me out of some ivory tower. She was so beautiful! I couldn't wait to get home to see her. I'd spend hours playing with her, feeding her, getting her off to sleep. Took her everywhere I could. I loved her so much! She had a personality already, you could see . . .'

He stopped. Shannon wiped away tears.

'Go on,' she said softly. Finbar drank whisky to ease the choking feeling in his throat.

'When she and Majella got shot by that Brit, I just couldn't believe it. I didn't believe it. I went mental.' He looked at her, hand clenched around the glass. 'Have you lost anyone you loved?'

'My husband,' she said in a low voice. 'I lost my husband.'

'Sorry,' he said. 'I'm sorry, Shannon.' She shook her head. 'I wanted to die,' he went on. 'Wanted to be with them. I don't know what stopped me. There were enough bloody drugs and guns I could lay my hands on. I stopped working, lay in bed all day. The business went to hell. I didn't see anyone, didn't care about anything.'

'What about your family?' she asked. 'Or Majella's? Didn't they help you?'

He grimaced. 'Majella's family were too gutted. I didn't get on with my family, hardly saw them. My mother was a diplomat. Nothing grand, just a consul. That's what my elder brother does now. They only do passports and administrative work.' He smiled. 'Visit people in foreign jails and tell them what they *can't* do for them! My father lectured at Trinity College – Irish literature. They're retired now. They were quite old when they had me, in their forties. Old for having children, I mean.'

'My parents too,' she said wonderingly. 'Strange.'

'I never got on with them. I wouldn't go to university, I started my business. And they didn't like Majella. When she and Roiseann were shot I had to get out of Ireland. I'd been in Liverpool before, liked it. So I came here. Majella's brothers had contacts who helped me set up the air cargo business. On condition I–'

'Did favours for them?'

'Right.' He paused. 'It's all mine now, I've paid them back ten times over. But they helped me and they'll never let me forget that. I told them this would be my last job but . . .'

'What would be your last job?' she asked, looking intently at him.

'The – I –.' Shit! he thought. Get a hold of yourself, man. 'A consignment of Ecstasy,' he lied. Well, it was partly true. 'Smuggled from East Germany.'

'Don't tell me anymore. The less I know, the less they can torture out of me!' Shannon smiled suddenly. 'If they question me again, I'll plead soft girl. They're only too willing to believe a woman's got no brain of her own. I'll say you cast a sexual spell over me.' She stared at him. 'Which wouldn't be a lie.'

'Shannon – do you still want me?' His heart raced and his palms sweated.

'I still want you,' she said in a low voice.

'But you're going away?'

'Yes . . . I don't know!' She pushed back her hair. 'You're right, of course, when you say I'm in no position to take the moral high ground. I had someone murdered!'

'So you keep telling me.'

'I just can't stand the thought of your being a drug dealer! I know it's hypocritical. I'm like those prisoners who beat up paedophiles. *They* might have bashed up some poor old lady in the course of a break-in, but that's different! It's not fair, the way I feel. I know it's not.'

He came to sit beside her. 'I'm giving it up. I told you.'

'Just like that?'

'Just like that.' He took her hand. It felt cold. 'Don't split us up, Shannon,' he pleaded. 'I love you, and I think you love me.'

'It won't last,' she sighed.

'How can you say that?' He put his arms around her. This time she didn't pull away.

'Because it's true. Sex never lasts. Love never lasts! I still want you, even though I know now you're a drug dealer. That's how much I want you! All the moral principles I thought I had have fallen by the bloody wayside. But one day we'll be fed up with each other. That's *life*.'

'Don't you think we have something special?'

'Bullshit!' she said angrily. 'Everyone thinks they've got something special. They haven't. It's just the same sordid tedious pathetic rubbish every time. Nothing and no one is special.'

'I don't believe that,' he said. '*You're* special.' He pulled her close. 'I've never met anyone like you.'

'Of course you haven't. They haven't got around to cloning humans yet. Or so they tell us.'

'You're not human,' he said, kissing her neck. 'You're a goddess. Let me worship at your shrine.'

'Oh, bloody hell!' she sighed. 'Now I'm being put on a pedestal!'

He began to undo her jacket. She didn't resist. He slid his hands up her soft back and unfastened her bra. 'I love you,' he said again, massaging her breasts. 'I'm crazy about you!' Her nipples hardened instantly under his touch.

'How can I believe what you say?' she groaned as he eased her down on the sofa and pushed up her skirt. 'How do I know you're not a pathological liar?'

'You're a fine one to talk about lying,' he murmured, kissing and sucking at her nipples. 'God, your tits are so beautiful! Your skin is so soft.' He leaned down and dragged off the long suede boots then pulled gently at her black tights and pants. 'A liar by omission, as the nuns would say. Going through all that trauma and not telling me. Not letting me help you. I told you, I love you. I'd do anything for you, I want you forever.'

'This is purely a physiological response, you realize that?' She gasped as the tights and pants came off and his fingers found the sensitive place inside her.

'I can live with that. I love your physiological response.' He kissed her hard. 'I know I keep saying this, but I love the way you get wet so quickly. Makes me feel fantastic!' He stroked harder.

'Don't!' she moaned as she came, her eyes half closed. The spasms of her orgasm quivered around his fingers. He unzipped his trousers and slid between her legs, spreading her thighs wider. 'Stop it!'

'Ah, come on, don't be mean!' he whispered. 'D'you really want me to stop?' He stared down at her. 'Shannon?'

She said nothing, just looked into his eyes. 'I'll take that as a no.' He smiled. 'We have to be politically correct in these matters, don't we?'

He plunged inside her and she cried out and put her arms around him, holding him tight. Later they moved to his bedroom, stripping off the rest of their clothes as they went. He made her cry, gasp, shout his name. He needed her desperately, wanted to bind her to him forever. Her long shiny nails made little scratches on his shoulders, dug into his back and buttocks like cats claws.

He woke up hours later in the dark, the dock waters casting rippled patterns of pale yellow light across the ceiling. He turned and reached for her. Shannon was gone.

Chapter Twenty-One

'Look at this!' Rob burst into the kitchen where Margaret sat sipping bitter instant espresso and smoking a long thin cigarette, the morning's hate mail on the table in front of her. 'Shannon's divorcing me,' he cried. 'She's really doing it!'

'What did you expect?' His mother glanced indifferently at the divorce petition before it was whipped from under her nose. She flicked ash off the sleeve of her black wool coat and looked out of the window. The morning was gloomy, cold and windy with thick low grey cloud. Perfect funeral weather.

'The undertakers will be here in fifteen minutes,' she said mildly. 'And the police, probably. I don't see how we're going to get to the crematorium without a police escort. It doesn't look like Melanie will turn up,' she added. 'Not that I want to think about her at the moment.'

Rob took no notice. 'Unreasonable behaviour!' he exclaimed, staring at the petition. '*Adultery*! "Respondent has committed adultery with a woman whose name is unknown to the petitioner,"' he read out. '"Petitioner finds it intolerable to live with the respondent"'. She knows I won't hurt her again!' He clenched the papers and shook his head in despair. 'How can she do this to us?'

He rushed to the hall phone. Margaret got up, poured herself a gin-and-tonic and dumped the hate mail in the bin. There was one condolence card, from that sad old virgin Irene Watchet. Every day hate-filled voices on the telephone and grammatically disastrous letters scribbled on cheap lined writing paper expressed hopes that she would be killed in a horrific accident, die slowly and agonizingly of cancer, be lynched, beaten, burned alive. The front windows, smashed several times, were boarded up. She couldn't leave the house without microphones and flash bulbs being shoved in her face. She was vilified as the wife who'd kept silent about her murderous pervert of a husband. It would get worse, they said, if she didn't give her story. Silence would be interpreted as arrogance, complicity, stubborn defiance. She put the phone down, stopped answering the door. Swilled gin, comfort-ate crisps, chocolates, vol-au-vents, sandwiches, cream cakes. She'd gained weight. Widows were supposed to lose it. She couldn't do anything right. Her husband had been an evil pervert, but she was supposed to mourn him, lose weight, look suitably devastated while at the same time denouncing him. They wanted too much. She couldn't think, couldn't feel. Didn't want to feel.

Nine-thirty. Margaret got up and put on her black hat with the silk ribbon. It looked nice, the kind of hat Spanish dancers wore, although it didn't complement her heavy face and square jaw. She heard Rob talking wildly in the hall. It would have been good to have a supportive daughter-in-law on the scene. She didn't ask herself what she'd done to deserve Shannon's support.

'Don't do this, Shannon, please!' Rob begged over the phone, his voice breaking. 'I don't want a divorce. I can't believe you do either.'

Shannon glanced up at her client, the sulky teenage daughter of rich parents. She was charged with stealing a T-shirt from Marks & Spencers. 'Amanda, could you step outside while I take this call?' she asked brightly. 'Anita will give you a cup of coffee.' The girl sighed heavily, got up and went out.

'Listen to me, Rob,' she continued quietly. 'Just listen, okay?' There was silence at the other end of the line. 'We're finished,' she said. 'I'm really sorry, but we are. We have to accept that. I don't like it anymore than you do.'

'No!' he groaned. '*No*, Shannon.'

'I never wanted this.' Her throat tightened. 'I know it wasn't your fault, about your father. I hope *you* know that now. But the way you reacted to it, the way you hurt me, tried to blank me out, pretend it wasn't happening . . . *raped* me! If he weren't dead you'd still refuse to do anything about him. You want me back, but on your terms.'

Finbar's words. A terrible pang of loss shot through her. 'We can't live together anymore,' she cried. 'I put adultery and unreasonable behaviour on the petition because they're the most common grounds. I thought we could do this quickly, get it over with. I'm really sorry, Rob,' she repeated. 'You were my best friend as well as my husband. I hate to lose you. But you haven't changed. You think we can get back together just because your father's dead – you actually think it's that simple! Are you still living with the WPC?' she asked suddenly.

'That's nothing!' he said furiously. 'It's just somewhere to stay. I don't give a toss about her. I want you!'

'I'm sorry.' Shannon brushed away tears. 'I hoped she'd make you happy.'

'I'll never be happy again.'

'A clean break is best.' She tried to sound practical. A clean break of their hearts! 'You'll get your share of the house – I won't buy you out, I've got no desire to stay there – and a lump sum that I'll pay you. We've got no children.' Grief swept over her again.

'I don't want a bloody lump sum!' he shouted. 'You can't just buy your way out of our marriage, Shannon.'

'Rob, please be reasonable. Don't make this any more ghastly than it has to be.' She felt exhausted, hopeless.

'I am unreasonable, remember? That's why you're divorcing me.'

'Your solicitor will confirm that it's in both clients' interests to cooperate,' she said patiently. 'If you refuse to accept my offer you could be penalized for stubbornly increasing costs without merit, as it's called. Defended divorce petitions are strongly discouraged by the courts. You can let the legal details drag on indefinitely, or you can be sensible.'

'*Legal details*!'

'I'm sorry. That sounds awful, I didn't mean–'

'It's my father's funeral this morning,' he interrupted.

'I know. I'm sorry you're going through such a rough time.' He wasn't the only one. She ached for Finbar, physically ached.

'I've got to go,' he said. 'The cars are here. I'll talk to you again soon.'

He hung up and she went to find Amanda. Eleven days now since she'd left Finbar and the beautiful Albert Dock apartment where she'd felt so secure. Where they'd made love so many times. In the bedrooms, the jacuzzi, the candlelit living room with the river lights glittering outside. She'd spent Christmas with Nick and Caroline and Helen. The police hadn't bothered her again. So far. She missed Finbar so much she could hardly bear it. She had to sort herself out, move on. *He* had to sort himself out. She was a murderer, but she couldn't live with a drug dealer! Did he mean it about giving up the business? He hadn't tried to contact her.

'Amanda!' she called. 'Had your caffeine fix?'

Amanda, playing with Anita's computer, looked up and smiled, the sulkiness gone.

'I like it here,' she said. 'I really fancy being a babe lawyer like you!'

'Better make sure you don't get a criminal record then, hadn't we?' Shannon said briskly.

The crowd outside the house booed as the two big black funeral cars drew up, the first containing the coffin with Bernard's scant remains. There were no flowers. Journalists, police and hostile spectators jostled one another for a look at the hardfaced bitch of a widow. There was a chorus of boos and shouts as Margaret emerged from the house, followed by Rob in his black suit, and got into the second car. Her face was heavily made up, leathery cheeks glowing with blusher. The Spanish dancer's hat looked too jaunty for a funeral, even that of a child rapist and murderer.

'Evil bloody cow!' Josie Duffy screeched, shaking her fist. 'Look at the state of her!'

Margaret collapsed on the soft grey leather seat, trembling with fear. Rob sat beside her, hands clenched in his lap. None of this was his fault. He was the victim. He was about to lose his wife – his job could be next! He hated his mother, never wanted to see her again after today. And where the hell was Melanie? She should be here, sharing this ordeal with him. He remembered the crack of fireworks on Bonfire Night, the pagans dancing gleefully around the fire, the awful shock, revulsion, numbness as she related her hideous story. It had destroyed his life, literally overnight. But she was his little sister. He'd forgive her.

Bernard, as a Catholic, would have wanted a Requiem Mass and burial in the consecrated ground of a churchyard. He was getting a short service before being consigned to the flames. This was Margaret's revenge. She didn't miss him, didn't care that he was dead. Her life was hell now because of him. It wasn't fair. Was it true what Rob said? Had Bernard abused Melanie? She recalled Janetta and that awful scene in the shed. She'd persuaded herself it was a one-off incident, that he really loved her, that they had a normal marriage. Whatever that was. People these days whined for help, tolerance, counselling, understanding. She'd never whined for anything. It wasn't fair.

She opened her handbag, took out the hip flask she'd given Bernard for Christmas six years ago, and took several swigs of brandy. She lit a cigarette and puffed on it, ignoring the disapproving glances of the driver and the undertaker.

What could be said? That Bernard had been loved, liked, admired? There was herself, Rob, Irene, the police and the crowd of ill-wishers. She couldn't even paint anymore, the only thing that kept her sane. All she could think of was Bernard sticking his thing into Melanie, into the innocent girls the Press said she should have protected. No one would speak to her, unless to shout abuse. Her windows were smashed, the police just smirked. In the supermarket people hurled bread rolls and cans of soup along with abuse.

Why was *she* to blame? Why was it her fault? She'd been a good wife, given birth to X number of children, supported her husband, kept her mouth shut. She hadn't raped or murdered anyone. The coffin disappeared between the curtains, she listened to the meaningless words. There was one wreath, from the adoring Irene. She came out of the crematorium and opened her mascaraed eyes wide in panic. The crowd surged towards her, flashbulbs blinded her. Police linked arms, straining to hold back the tide of fury.

'Help me, help me!' she gasped. She clung to Rob's arm. 'Please, get me out of here!' It was like a scene from the Middle

Ages. She felt as though she were sitting in a cart on her way to the gallows tree.

Finbar couldn't believe how much he missed her. But he wouldn't call. Shannon might get irritated, bored, grow to hate him. Everything depended on what he did – or didn't do – now. He'd bide his time. Instead he went to the Clarence Dock tower, got the Semtex and gave it to Lenny for the active service unit. Then there was Guy to deal with. Finbar went to the club every night now. Guy was pissed off, he could tell. He was used to having the run of the place.

'Anything wrong?' he asked on New Year's Eve. Finbar had sat brooding in the office all afternoon, huddled in his overcoat, drinking coffee or Scotch and staring into space. It was now ten at night. Dance music throbbed through the walls.

'Why should there be anything wrong?' He stared at the computer screen, seeing nothing. Thinking of Shannon. What was she doing? Was she all right? He knew he should leave her alone. But for how long could he bear to do that? Did she miss him? He felt angry, confused, miserable. Out of his depth.

'I don't know.' Guy shrugged. He sat in an armchair and picked up his glass of Coke. 'You seem different lately, that's all.'

Finbar switched off the computer. 'What happened to Melanie Flinder, Guy?' he asked quietly, leaning back in the leather chair. 'And her boyfriend?'

'I don't know.' The manager stiffened. 'They've disappeared, haven't they? The police can't find them. Nobody knows what's happened.'

'Don't fuck with me.' Finbar pulled out a gun and levelled it at Guy's fat deceitful face. He stared at him. 'I said, what happened to Melanie Flinder and her boyfriend?'

'Hey! Take it easy, Finbar.' Guy got to his feet and backed away in alarm, his arms up. 'What the hell are you doing?' Shit, he thought. Shit, shit, shit.

'I'm waiting for your explanation. Don't waste my time.'

'Listen! It wasn't my fault, okay?' How did the bastard know? 'I picked her up at Manchester,' he stammered. 'She was drunk, freaked out. I told you. We got back to her flat and she went mental when I told her she'd get ten grand.'

'Why? She was lucky to get ten.'

'I told her she'd get ten times that. It was the only way we – me and Paul – could get her to do it.'

Finbar smiled and lowered the gun slightly. 'You told her she'd get a hundred grand for one run and only gave her ten? No wonder she went mental!'

'You said you wanted someone with no form.' Guy shrugged. 'She didn't have a clue.'

'Go on.'

'I tried to shut her up. Paul came in, she started raving at him. She wouldn't shut up. He gave her a smack. She fell against me, got the gun. Shot him. Started laughing, saying how she'd never thought killing someone would be so easy. She was mental, Finbar, I swear! I helped her get rid of the body, we dumped him in a shed in some old railway sidings in Birkenhead. I had to get rid of her too, she was a nutter, a security risk. So I shot her. They're buried under a pile of coal,' Guy said. He wiped his sweaty face. 'No one goes there except dossers or kids looking for a place to shag. No one'll find them.'

Finbar let out a long breath. 'What about the ten grand? I suppose you took it?'

'Come on, Finbar!' Guy protested. 'Ten grand's a piss in the Mersey to you! I killed them, okay? I did it for you. She was a nutter, she'd have blown it for us. Her brother's a copper, for Christ's sake! Come on!' he pleaded desperately. 'Give me a break. I did you a favour. I'll give you the ten grand back,' he offered. 'I haven't got all of it right now, but I'll get it. Give me a couple of days.'

Finbar pressed the red button under the desk. 'You can keep the ten grand,' he said calmly. 'What's left of it.'

'What?' Guy stared at him.

'I said, you can keep the ten grand. I don't want it back. You lied to me. That's the problem. Betrayed my trust. You know how I feel about that.'

'Come on!' Guy backed further away, trembling. 'Give me a break, Finbar!'

'Shut up. You get to keep my ten grand. And your life. You've been given one hell of a break.'

'Yes, Mr Linnell?' Two bouncers appeared in the doorway.

'I want you to take Guy here to the Royal Liverpool Hospital. Use the back stairs. He'll need urgent treatment for his injuries.'

'No!' Guy shouted. The bouncers grabbed him as he ran for the door and tried to shove past them.

'Come on, Guy.' Finbar got up and came around the desk, his gun levelled. 'Be a man, now. Are you going to drop your trousers yourself or do we have to do it for you?'

'No!' Guy shouted, struggling violently. Sweat poured down his face. 'Don't, Finbar! Don't!' he shouted. 'I'll work for nothing, I'll give you the ten grand back. I'll make it up to you.'

'You're being pathetic, Guy. Don't make me despise you any more than I already do. Drop his trousers,' he ordered.

Guy groaned with fear as his trousers were unzipped and dragged down his white hairy thighs. Finbar held the gun at arm's length and shot him in the backs of both knees. He screamed in agony and sagged in their arms. Blood poured on to the red carpet, forming dark stains.

'I might come and visit you in hospital if I've got time.' Finbar raised his voice above the choked screams and curses. 'You take care, now.' He looked at the bouncers. 'Get him out of here.'

The screams faded as Guy was carried down the back stairs and lifted into the waiting car. Finbar put the gun away and sat at the desk again.

So Shannon's sister-in-law was dead. The police still thought she was missing, of course. Or that she might have something to do with her father's murder. Did they know he'd raped her for years? He thought of Majella's elder brother, Eamonn, who'd always seemed a bit too fond of little girls. Perverts like that were all over the place. You were more likely to find them in your own family than anywhere else. He admired Shannon for having Bernard Flinder killed. He would have done the same. Suddenly he couldn't bear it anymore. He picked up the phone and dialled her number.

'This is Shannon Flinder. I can't come to the phone just now, but if you leave a message I'll call you back as soon as possible.'

She wouldn't call *him* back. He slammed the phone down and closed his eyes. What was she doing now? Was she at home, not answering the phone? Out clubbing, celebrating the New Year? Enjoying herself, not missing him? He decided to stay all night at the club. The apartment was horrible without her, unbearably lonely. It smelled of her perfume, the baby powder. Her shampoo in the bathroom, a black lacy Wonderbra draped over the radiator. The novel she'd been reading lay spine-cracked on the floor by the sofa. The fridge was full of bottles of champagne. He felt devastated, without hope. He would make changes in his life. But would she care? Would she see him again?

The door opened and Mariska came in lugging a suitcase. Her black hair shone and her pale eyes glittered. She wore her mink coat. Irritation rose in him at the sight of her.

'Happy New Year!' She dumped the suitcase on the floor by the desk and went to pour herself a drink.

'Not yet it isn't.' Certainly not for him. He got up, opened the suitcase and looked at the neat stacks of US dollars, the proceeds from his last deal with Jan-Willem. He had millions now, tucked away in offshore trusts. It was time to stop. He looked at Mariska, sipping vodka, and she looked back, pouting at him and running her tongue lasciviously over her thin lips.

'You can go back to Amsterdam,' he said. 'You're through here.'

'But, *schat* – darling – I just came from Amsterdam!'

'There won't be anymore deals between me and Jan-Willem. I phoned him earlier.'

'*What*?' She gaped at him. 'But why? Did he do something wrong?' She pointed to the suitcase. 'The money's all there. What's the problem?'

'No problem. I'm going away for a while. Making changes. This is one of them. That's all there is to it. I don't have to explain myself to you.'

'But we were doing great together.' She drained the vodka and put down the glass. 'I just don't understand this.'

'You're not required to understand. All you need to know is that you're through here. You've been paid. You can get out now.'

Mariska looked wildly around the office. 'I don't want to go! I like it here. I'm your courier. You can't do without me.'

He started to laugh. 'I don't want a debate about this, Mariska. I told you, you're through. Get out. Go back to clog land, to your windmills and tulips and coffee shops. Find yourself a cheesehead to shag.'

'You're crazy, you know that?' Her eyes narrowed. 'Crazy! I'm not going anywhere,' she hissed. 'I like it here!'

Finbar was up and round the desk so quickly that she didn't have time to move. The blow on her head knocked her sideways and she stumbled and fell to her knees, her head spinning. His gun pressed the pulsing vein below her ear. She heard his soft voice very close.

'I've just sent Guy to hospital, Mariska. You won't get that far. I want you out of this town now. Right now. If you're here this time tomorrow you'll be dead. That's a promise.' He got hold of her hair and dragged her to her feet. She screamed. 'Get out. Goodbye!' He gave her a great shove in the direction of the door. 'Out!'

She stumbled down the steps, the blow and the throbbing music making her head ache. She was out, finished. He didn't want her. He never had. That hurt more than the blow. She believed him when he said he'd kill her. Guy in hospital? What had *he* done to annoy the Great Man?

She peered through the crowd of dancers to the bar beyond. The music pounded in her head. Guy's girlfriend got off a bar stool and clumped unsteadily towards her, tits hanging out of her silky low cut red dress.

'Hi, Mariska!' she said breezily. 'He still doesn't want you, eh? That's because you have nothing here,' she cupped her breasts, 'or here.' She pouted.

'Did you shag Finbar?' Mariska stared at her, breathing hard.

'Of course I did,' the blonde lied. 'Right there in the office.' She giggled. 'He went crazy. And he's so big...oh!' She rolled her eyes. 'I was sore for two days. But it was worth it.'

Mariska reached inside her coat and the blonde was left staring in shock at the long deep criss-cross slash over her breasts from which dark blood welled. She felt a sting on her cheek and put up her hand. That too was covered with blood. She began to scream. Mariska dodged between sweaty dancers and ran out of the club. She hailed a passing taxi.

'Speke airport,' she panted. 'I'm in a hurry.'

Margaret sat on her chintz-covered sofa drinking gin-and-tonic and watching a New Year's Eve television offering, a compilation of embarrassing moments in the lives of celebrities. The curtains were drawn across the patio windows in case a photographer got into the back garden. The room stank of cigarette smoke and the little Delft Blue ashtray on the coffee table was crammed with crushed stubbs. She didn't know where Rob was. Of course he wouldn't spend this evening with her. The police thought Melanie had something to do with her father's death, but that was just speculation. It was all too unreal. She was still shaken by the public hostility towards her at Bernard's funeral; she'd been too frightened to go out since. She'd have to go shopping, the fridge and freezer were almost empty. No one would help her. She felt tremendous fear and hopelessness, didn't know how she could get through the next day, let alone the rest of her life. It was too hard. She was cast adrift from society, from the company of decent people. Forever. Pity she didn't prefer animals, like some. But she hated dogs and cats, thought them dirty, messy nuisances. Which was how she'd thought of Rob and Melanie when they were children, she realized.

She swallowed two Valium, drank her gin-and-tonic and stared dully at the screen, ignoring the ringing phone and doorbell. All right, they hated her! Fine. Why couldn't they leave her in peace?

'Are you going deaf?' She twisted round to see Rob standing in the doorway glaring at her. 'Why don't you answer the door? Good job I had a key.' He had to shout to make himself heard over the television.

'I'm with Cindy and her colleague,' he explained. 'They're outside, want to speak to us. I don't know what about, they said it should wait until we were together. Here!' He dropped his key on the coffee table. 'I won't need this anymore.' The phone stopped ringing.

Cindy and Ed walked into the living room, false smiles on their faces. Margaret sighed with boredom. What on earth did they want now? Ed sniffed the smoke and took out his solitary cigarette.

'Good evening, Mrs Flinder.' Cindy wore black trousers, black sweater and a three-quarter length red leather coat with a gilt buckle. Her cheeks were pink with cold. Margaret thought how common the coat looked, how unsuitable for someone who called herself a police officer. 'Sorry to bother you on New Year's Eve,' she said. 'But we've got some important news for you.' She paused. 'I'm afraid it's not good news. Er – shall I make you a cup of tea?' she asked awkwardly.

'No.' Margaret raised her glass and drank. She wasn't going to offer them one either.

'May we sit down?'

'If you must.' She picked up the remote control and turned the sound down. 'I hope this won't take long?'

'What's the news?' Rob asked, hands stuck in his jeans pockets. His hair stood up stiffly and he wore his brown leather jacket and an old maroon sweater. Linda wanted him back in time for the party. He wasn't exactly in party mood, but where else could he go? 'Another murder? *He's* dead now,' he said aggressively. 'No point questioning us about it.'

He was hugely relieved by the reaction at work. Keep your chin up, Rob, take care. We're your mates, no one blames you, lad. Of course your job's safe! It made a pleasant change from taunts about being married to a lawyer.

'It's nothing to do with your father.' Cindy glanced at him and they sat in the armchairs. 'Well, we don't think so. We – we've found Melanie's body,' she said gently. 'In an old hut by disused railway sidings in Birkenhead. The body of Paul Ashton, her boyfriend, was there too, buried beneath a heap of coal. They'd both been shot at close range. A tramp who uses the hut found the bodies.'

'Shot? Melanie shot?' Rob collapsed on the sofa, white-faced. Margaret heaved a long sigh. 'Who shot her?' he gasped. '*Why*?'

'We don't know.' Cindy hated seeing his shock and desolation, felt helpless. 'There's no apparent motive.'

'It must have been because of him – Ashton,' Rob said. He

rubbed his face as if he'd woken from a long sleep. 'He was a scumbag. I'm sure he was dealing.'

'Our enquiries haven't revealed anything so far. We found a boarding card in Melanie's flat,' Cindy said. 'It was for a Singapore-Manchester flight. Have you any idea what she was doing in Singapore?'

'*Singapore*?' Rob leaned forward, head in his hands. He felt dazed, couldn't take in this latest terrible blow. Melanie *dead!* 'I didn't even know she went to Singapore,' he said hoarsely. 'She never said anything to me. Are you sure it was her boarding card?' he asked stupidly.

'Yes. There was a brand new passport too. She stayed only a couple of days. Immigration stamped the dates on her passport. You've no idea why she was there?'

'I told you, I can't think where she'd get the money,' he said wonderingly. 'I paid her bills, she was always strapped for cash. Melanie *dead*!' he repeated, staring at them. His eyes filled with tears.

'Can you possibly throw any light on this, Mrs Flinder?' Ed asked.

'No.'

Cindy sighed as Margaret reached for the gin and tonic bottles on the coffee table and poured herself another drink. The woman was quietly freaking out, was in dire need of counselling or the support of a friend. But she had no friends left. She remembered Francesca's withered nipple in the plastic envelope. This bitch could have prevented that poor girl's gruesome murder.

'Melanie!' Rob began to cry, loud choking sobs. 'She's my little sister,' he cried. 'I should have protected her. She never stood a chance! This is all *his* fault,' he sobbed. 'He ruined her life. He ruined *my* life. It's your fault too!' he yelled at Margaret. She gasped and flinched. 'Why didn't you stop him? Why didn't you say anything?' Tears flowed down his cheeks and dripped off his jaw. 'You wouldn't stop him screwing your own daughter!' he sobbed. 'Did you send him to her, tell him not to bother you? I would have helped her,' he moaned. 'Why didn't you let me help you, Melanie?''

What was he on about? Ed got up and patted his shoulder. 'Sorry,' he said quietly. 'Sorry, Rob.'

'She's my little sister.' His shoulders heaved.

'I know she is – was.'

Margaret stared at the television screen. 'I suppose you can't release the body for burial yet?' she said matter-of-factly. 'I suppose there has to be a post mortem?'

'That's right, Mrs Flinder.' Hostility welled up in Cindy again. *The body*. 'We'll let you know when we get more information. 'But first we need one of you to come and identify Melanie. Perhaps you'd like to do that?' she asked. Seeing as you don't seem to give a damn.

'No.' Margaret shook her head and drank more gin. 'No, I don't want to.' Seeing was believing.

'I'll do it,' Rob muttered, wiping his eyes. 'I'll identify her.'

'Sure you're up to it?' Ed asked. 'It can wait until the morning.'

'No. I'll come with you now.' He stood up and looked at his mother. 'You're to blame for all this,' he said brokenly. 'You and him. I never want to see you again. If I remarry and have kids I won't let you see them. You'll be alone. You'll die alone.'

'Oh, yes,' Margaret said calmly. 'I'll die alone. I know that, Robert.'

The three of them left the house, unmolested by reporters, photographers or angry spectators. They were all at home, celebrating New Year with their families and friends. Something she would never do again. Why did anyone celebrate New Year? she wondered, gulping gin. She loathed it. Another year down the toilet, one year older. No wiser, no richer, no happier, no dreams realized. No wars ended. She switched off the television, went up to the attic and looked at the watercolours stacked against the walls.

'Waste of time,' she murmured. 'At least they made me forget for a while.'

She went to her bedroom and got the two bottles of pills, her latest Valium prescription and the strong sleeping tablets Doctor Sutton had immediately prescribed on learning she was newly widowed. He hadn't asked if she wanted them. A stressful time, he'd commiserated. They'll tide you over.

They would tide her over, but not in the way he envisioned. Margaret also took the bottle of Paracetamol from the bathroom shelf. She went downstairs and turned up the television, hating the awful silence. You're a fool, she told herself. What does it matter?

So Melanie was dead. Murdered, like her father. And Rob hated her. No one wanted to know Margaret anymore. She was cast out from society, from normal life. She'd never had a normal life, only the appearance of it. But that was better than this terrible exile. She had nothing now.

She sat on the sofa and emptied gin into one of Bernard's pint glasses, adding a few splashes of tonic to make it palatable. She opened the bottles and shook out the pills, mixing them up. They rolled and clattered over the coffee table. She sat gazing at them while she smoked a cigarette. The television audience laughed and applauded. She stubbed out the cigarette and began to swallow mouthfuls of pills, hoping she could get them all down without being sick. She didn't feel drunk. Just overwhelmingly tired.

She kicked off her brown leather court shoes and stretched out on the sofa, smoothing her hands over her skirt and sweater, pushing back her hair. She pressed a finger lightly against the artery in her throat, feeling it throb with life, pulse with energy. For what? Useless!

It was twenty minutes to midnight. I never had an orgasm, she thought suddenly. Not with Bernard, not with myself. Not with anyone. She shut her eyes and breathed deeply. She felt perfectly calm, calmer than she had done for years.

Drowsiness weighted her limbs as *Auld Lang Syne* began to play. People clapped and cheered. She wouldn't leave a note. She had nothing to say. That would annoy and perplex psychologists, who said genuine suicides always left notes because they wanted to explain. Margaret had no such desire, felt no obligation to explain anything. She was tried, judged, condemned. No one wanted to listen. If they got curious after her death, tough! The gin-and-tonic made her belch and she swallowed hard a few times as her mouth filled with saliva. Don't vomit after you've gone to all this trouble, she told herself. Her lips parted in a smile. I'm lying on my back, maybe I'll drown in my own vomit. Who cares? So long as I'm asleep.

* * *

Rob identified Melanie's decomposed, coal-dusted body, was given a sedative by a police doctor and spent the night at Ed's house after a fruitless attempt to phone Shannon. He couldn't face Linda's party. New Year's Day dawned grey and icy. Margaret's curtains stayed closed and the downstairs lights on. A celebratory Mass from Liverpool Cathedral came onto the television. The New Year's Day concert from Vienna was belting out a Strauss waltz by the time the police broke in.

Chapter Twenty-Two

'We think it's suicide, but we can't be sure. She didn't leave a note.' Cindy wished Ed would stop slobbering over Shannon Flinder. Especially when he had the nerve to accuse women of being ruled by their hormones! She looked round Shannon's small office with its pleasant view of Exchange Flags. Morning sunshine slanted across the walls and desk. Shannon sat there looking bored. Her desk was covered with files and papers, and the computer was on. 'They usually leave a note,' Cindy said. 'Suicides. Psychologists say they want to explain everything.'

'Is that right?' Shannon smiled. 'Touching, your faith in psychologists.' Cindy flushed angrily. 'If I wanted to kill myself, I'd just *do* it,' she said lightly. 'I wouldn't bother to explain. Maybe write "piss off".' Her gaze rested on Cindy. 'Or something.'

Ed started to laugh and Cindy shot him a furious glance. 'Anyway, we're almost certain it was suicide,' she said sharply. 'There are no suspicious circumstances. No signs of forced entry. She was obviously depressed. Your husband was very upset about Melanie,' she said. 'He spent the other night at Ed's house.'

'Cosy.' Shannon looked at Ed, whose gaze was still fixed on her chest. What a creep, she thought. In a minute he'd start dribbling down the front of that clean but crumpled blue shirt. Why can't they be just a *bit* cool? Like Finbar. Life was terrible without him. She felt physically drained, psychologically exhausted. This latest police visit wasn't helping her nerves either. She tried to banish him from her thoughts.

'So would you mind just telling us your whereabouts on New Year's Eve?' Cindy's hostile brown eyes bored into her.

'I spent the evening with my friends, Nick and Caroline Forth,' she said. 'We played with the baby, ate dinner. They had some people round. I got home about one in the morning, took a cab. My neighbour, Lorraine Campbell, can probably confirm that,' she said sarcastically. 'She's recently started her own one-woman vigilante neighbourhood watch. She's more of a nuisance than the local wildlife.'

Ed laughed again. What an incredible shag she would be! He stared hungrily at her beautiful face and the full bust that the soft clingy black sweater with glittery silver bits couldn't quite conceal. She wore a short black leather skirt, but she was sitting behind her desk and he couldn't see her legs. The sun shone on her curly gold hair, illuminating it like in some old-fashioned prayer book picture of a saint. Rob Flinder was a lucky bastard. *Was!* Ed caught Cindy's angry glance and blushed. He was making an arse of himself.

'And you've no idea why Melanie Flinder went to Singapore?'

'I've told you already, I had hardly any contact with Melanie. We didn't get on.' Shannon yawned and massaged her temples. 'I have no idea why she went to Singapore. I'm surprised she could afford the air fare. Rob paid most of her bills. She was always begging him for money.'

She looked out across sunny Exchange Flags, wondering how much more of her day these two clowns thought they had the right to take up. It was nearly lunchtime. Thank goodness Gavin was in London for a week! He'd go ballistic at the police coming here. In fact she did have an idea why Melanie had gone to Singapore, but she wasn't going to share it with them. Let them work it out for themselves, if they could. Someone had paid her to smuggle drugs. She'd probably travelled there and back with a stomach and vagina stuffed with heroin or cocaine. She was lucky to have made it back without dying from toxic shock or being arrested at Changi and sentenced to hangi! Or not, as it turned out. Her killer was almost certainly the person who'd employed her to smuggle the drugs.

A sudden horrible thought flashed into Shannon's brain and she coughed hastily to smother a gasp of fear. She picked up her cooling coffee and took a sip. 'It's incredible,' she said. 'The three of them in such a short time. I can't believe it! But it's pointless asking me to speculate. We didn't get on, as I told you. I've had barely any contact with them since I got married. Now I'm getting divorced. I really can't help you any further.' She shrugged impatiently. 'I've told you all I know.'

Now piss off! She got up and walked to the window, arms folded. Ed stared at her slim legs in the black stockings. Her spicy perfume wafted towards him. The phone rang and she frowned and crossed back to her desk.

'It's Rob,' Anita sounded nervous. 'Shall I put him through?'

'Yes, all right. Hello, Rob,' she said tiredly. Ed and Cindy glanced at each other.

'I'm downstairs,' he said. 'On the Flags. Can we have lunch? I need to talk to you.'

'I wish you'd stop phoning me at work,' she sighed. 'I'm really busy, Rob. We can't have lunch, I'm afraid. If it's something regarding the divorce petition you can always ask my solicitor. Although I don't see what. I thought it was all perfectly straightforward.' In your dreams! she thought.

'It's not the petition. Please, Shannon!' he begged, squinting in the sunlight as he looked up at her office window. 'I need to talk to you.'

'You've got to stop calling me like this. We have to get on with our lives, Rob.'

'That's what I want to do,' he said urgently. 'My father's dead, he can't hurt us anymore. I don't care about my mother either. But I'm freaked out about Melanie!' His voice rose. 'I've got two funerals to organize. I can't do all this by myself, I need your support. You're my wife, for Christ's sake! Please, Shannon, don't go through with the divorce. Let me move back. We can be like we were before, I know we can. Please!'

'No, Rob.' She sighed. 'I'm sorry about Melanie,' she said. 'And I'm sorry about Margaret. It's a terrible time for you, I realize that. But we're finished,' she repeated. 'We can't be like we were before.'

She looked out of the window and saw him standing in the

middle of the Flags, sunshine glinting on his brown hair. He wore the heavy leather jacket, navy blue suit and grey silk tie. He lowered the mobile phone and waved. She didn't wave back. She was agonized, irritated by his frequent calls. They were finished! When would it sink in?

'Shannon–'

'You're making this really difficult, Rob. For both of us. I want you to stop.' She paused. 'I'm going to hang up now. I've got work to do. Please don't call back.'

She put the phone down. He waited a minute then shoved the mobile phone in his pocket and strode angrily across the Flags, disappearing down a narrow side street. She turned away from the window. The office looked crowded with the two police officers sitting there like spare parts. Cindy looked like a car seat in her horrible red leather coat. Shannon felt fed up, suddenly furious with them, with Rob. Why the hell couldn't they leave her in peace!

'If you'll excuse me,' she smiled politely, 'I've really got a lot of work to do.'

'Are you still associating with Finbar Linnell?' Ed asked.

'*Associating* with! What is this?' Shannon stiffened. 'That's none of your business,' she said coldly. 'I've changed my address, if that's what you mean. I now reside in the *marital home* again. Alone. Until it's sold and I find a new place to live. Not that that concerns you either.' She looked at them angrily. 'I don't expect to be bothered by you again.'

'Did you know Bernard Flinder was a paedophile?' Cindy asked.

'I–' *Shit!* 'I know he abused Melanie for years,' she stammered, and felt herself blush violently. 'She only told Rob – just a short time ago. At the beginning of November. He told me.'

'So you dumped him because of his father?'

Shannon glared at Cindy. 'It wasn't quite like that!'

The detective picked up her red leather bag and slung it over her shoulder. Ed was gasping for a cigarette. 'Well, thanks a lot for your cooperation,' she said sarcastically. 'We might want to talk to you again.'

Shannon's heart sank. 'I'll look forward to it.' They were

playing with her. What did they know? Probably nothing. Stay cool, she warned herself.

Shannon Flinder knew more than she was letting on, Cindy felt certain. But what could they do? There was no evidence to connect her with the deaths. She had no motive – no *apparent* motive. It might be true she knew nothing and cared less, just wanted out of her marriage. And, okay, there was a personal element to her suspicion: she didn't like Shannon. She was jealous, felt hostile towards her, resentful. Shannon was beautiful, sexy, bold, the type who never had to struggle to get what she wanted. Cindy hated people like that.

'Jesus Christ!' Ed groaned as they got into the lift. 'Ohh!' He leaned against the wall and laughed.

'Fancy a sandwich?' she asked. 'I'm starving.'

'I know what I bloody fancy! Jesus Christ!' he said again. 'Those eyes, those legs, those tits, that mouth . . . the blonde hair! Good job you don't look like that, Cind. We'd never get any work done.'

'I'll bring you a bib next time,' she said coldly. 'Then you won't spoil your nice shirt and tie. Forget the sandwich, why don't you just pop home for a wank?'

He reached for his cigarette. 'Time of the month, is it?' he laughed. 'You're jealous, that's your trouble.'

'Oh, well, I would be, wouldn't I? We girls love to scratch each other's eyes out. I'm sure she knows stuff about Finbar Linnell,' Cindy said angrily. 'We've been after him for years and never got anything on him. I bet she knows a thing or two. I wonder how friendly she is with him?'

'Stop it, you torturer!' Ed blew out smoke.

'Melanie had no friends, she'd dropped out of her college course. She only had Paul Ashton. They were found dead together, must have been shot in that flat. I wonder what people round there are on! A gun goes off twice and no one hears a bloody thing!'

'They never do these days. Don't want to get involved.'

'And who the hell killed Bernard Flinder? It was a professional hit, we know that. That's about all we do know! I bet *she* knows it all.'

'I doubt it. And do you really care who killed him?' Ed asked lazily. The lift doors opened and they walked out of the building. 'He was a bloody pervert, it could have been anyone. Probably some parent who knew there was zero chance of his being banged up for raping their daughter. You'd do the same if it was your kid. I know I would.'

'So you approve of people taking the law into their own hands?' Cindy asked tightly. She shivered and pulled her coat around her. The winter sunshine held barely any warmth.

'I don't *approve*.' He laughed. 'I'd be out of a job. But in these circumstances, I can understand it. Even if he'd been banged up, some psychiatrist or social worker would have got him released. They take too much notice of bloody psychiatrists, they've got more power than judges. It's not politically correct to believe in evil. No – there's only one thing to be done with his sort.' Ed drew a finger across his throat.

'Well, I think Shannon Flinder and Finbar Linnell just might be at the bottom of this,' Cindy said firmly. 'I don't know how, but I'm going to find out.'

Shannon watched as they walked across Exchange Flags and through the arch to their waiting car. She picked up the phone and put it down again. Jenny knocked at the door and came in.

'I'm going for my lunch,' she said. 'Can I get you a sandwich or a cow pie?'

'No, thanks.'

'Shannon, you hardly eat a thing nowadays!' Jenny looked worriedly at her. 'You'll get sick if you go on like this. Why don't you come out with me?' she asked. 'A walk would do you good. Might even give you an appetite?'

'No.' She stared out of the window. 'Jenny, I need to be alone,' she said abruptly. 'If you don't mind.'

Jenny looked disappointed. 'I hope you get back to your old self soon,' she said. 'I miss you, Shannon. You might be turning into the hottest lawyer in town, but you're such a hardknock these days! I know you've been through a lot lately, but . . .'

Shannon flinched and swung round. 'You're right,' she interrupted. 'I have been through a lot. I *am going* through a lot.

It's called trying to survive. Although sometimes I don't know why I bother. I certainly don't need a stupid bitch like you telling me I'm a hardknock. If I want your retarded opinion, I'll ask for it!'

Jenny's sallow skin bloomed pink. She went out, slamming the door.

'Oh, God!' Shannon sighed. 'Jenny! I didn't mean–' She ran to the door, opened it and looked down the corridor. Jenny was gone.

Shannon put on her black coat, took her bag and keys and left the office. It was freezing outside. She lifted her face to the sun, trying to feel some warmth. It was one o' clock. The Flags were crowded with office workers on their lunch breaks, heading to and from the various bistros and coffee shops in the surrounding streets. She walked past Derby House, where a few tourists hovered around the entrance to the Second World War Western Approaches headquarters, now a museum, and down Water Street, heading for India Buildings.

No one was manning the offices of Linnell Air Cargo. She pressed the buzzer a second time. He must be at the airport. Or in Dublin, Amsterdam, God knew where! She was about to walk away when a tall figure loomed behind frosted glass. Keys clicked in the lock and the door opened.

'Shannon!' Finbar stared down at her. His face was pale and gaunt, his eyes hollow. Was he all right? She felt alarmed. Her heart raced, her legs weakened and her nipples hardened as desire for him overwhelmed her. She stood there, dismayed at her body's betrayal.

'Come in.' He stood back. 'It's great to see you.'

'I need to talk,' she said briefly. 'Well – to ask you something. But not here.'

'It's quite safe, I can assure you.' He smiled. 'I sweep regularly!'

'Not here,' she repeated uneasily and backed away, cold hands clenched in her coat pockets. She longed to kiss him, to feel his arms around her. How could she live with this terrible desire that overrode everything she believed in? *Had* believed in! She didn't care what he was, what he'd done. She only missed him and wanted him desperately. Wanted to feel his hands and lips and tongue on her bare skin, feel him moving inside her, turning her body to sensation and light.

'What's wrong with you?' she asked harshly. 'You look terrible. Are you on your own drugs now?'

'I was on a drug.' He smiled down at her, searching her eyes for some sign of warmth or desire. She just looked angry. 'But she left me. Now I'm suffering withdrawal symptoms. Life seems pointless, I feel old and sad. Thanks for the crumb of concern. What do you want to ask me?'

'Let's walk.' Shannon turned away. 'I'll tell you outside.'

'It's freezing outside. There's a terrible wind blowing off the Pier Head. My car's downstairs, I was just leaving.' He glanced at his watch. 'Come back to the apartment and have lunch with me. We can talk there. There's champagne, caviar and smoked salmon. Irish.'

'Irish caviar?'

'Irish smoked salmon.' He grinned. 'The caviar's Iranian. Persia, land of the nightingale and the rose.'

'I don't want champagne,' she said. 'I've got to work this afternoon.'

'Just the salmon and caviar then. You look like you could do with something to eat. Come on, don't glare at me like that.' What did she want? he wondered. Not to fall back into his bed, that was obvious.

Shannon thought. It was probably better to talk privately in his apartment than walk around the streets where anyone could see them together. Rob might still be hanging about. And it was freezing!

'Okay,' she said guardedly. 'Just for half an hour. I only want to ask you something.'

He nodded. 'I'm all yours. Hang on while I get my coat.'

The apartment was deliciously warm, the huge living room flooded with midday sunshine, dancing wave patterns on the walls and ceiling. Through the windows the River Mersey sparkled. The ferry boats were out. He took her coat.

'Sit down. I'll be with you in a minute.'

Finbar disappeared to the kitchen and she heard a cork popping. She strolled to the bookshelves and glanced again at the titles:

Primo Levi, James Joyce, Anthony Burgess, Marquez, the Brontes, Sean O'Casey. Biographies, travel books, history. No thrillers. Who needed thrillers when your life was the real thing! She sat down, sinking into the soft leather, stretching out her slender, black-stockinged legs. She kicked off her shoes, feeling exhausted, wanting to curl up and sleep. I shouldn't have come here, she thought. I've missed this place so much. Not to mention its owner. He came in with a chilled bottle of champagne and put it on the coffee table in front of her.

'I've changed my mind,' she said suddenly, sitting up. 'I will have some.'

'Okay.' He fetched two glasses, silently poured the champagne and went back to the kitchen. Shannon sipped, tiny bubbles pricking her nose and cheeks, the chill liquid spreading warmth through her body. He came back with a platter of smoked salmon, tiger prawns and caviar resting on a bed of curly biondi lettuce and thinly sliced lemon.

'Won't Gavin mind your drinking champagne before a court appearance?' he asked, smiling. 'Or does that improve your performance?'

'I'm not in court this afternoon, thank God! And Gavin's in London all this week. I'm so tired of this job,' she sighed. 'You see the same idiots come up time after time. It's *exhausting*!' she said petulantly, feeling like crying.

'So it's not exactly an intellectual challenge?' Finbar dug a spoon into the caviar.

'More psychological.' She sipped her champagne. 'I was bored before, but I hate it now. Gavin thinks he deserves to be canonized for keeping me on after I freaked when Rob left. Not to mention my dear departed father-in-law phoning him and lying about me being an alcoholic manic depressive.'

Finbar put down a forkful of smoked salmon. 'Jesus!' He shook his head. 'No wonder you had him–'

'*Don't!*'

'Sorry. So what would you like to do?' He lifted the fork and ate the salmon. 'For a job, I mean.'

'Write novels, of course.' Shannon laughed again. 'Crime novels. Like lots of lawyers.' She swallowed a spoonful of salty caviar and reached for her glass of champagne. 'I don't know,' she sighed again. 'I had a chat with someone the other day, but I don't know if anything will materialize.'

'Shannon-.' He sat back on the sofa, out of the sun. 'I'm under no illusion that you want to move back here and live with me. Or get into my bed for the afternoon.' He watched her blush, enjoying it. 'So what do you want to ask?'

She stared at him. 'Did you kill Melanie? And her boyfriend?'

He smiled slightly. 'No, I did not. I take it this means you've had another visit from the police?'

'Do you know who shot her?'

'Yes, I do.' He leaned forward and refilled his glass. 'I won't give you anymore, okay?' He put the bottle down, sunlight flashing in its watery green depths. 'You'll want to leave in about ten minutes.'

'Who shot her?' she asked fiercely. 'I need to know!'

'It was Guy, my manager at the club. He recruited her to take some stuff to Singapore.'

'I thought that's why she went there! For you, was it?'

'Well – sort of.'

'All roads lead back to you, don't they?'

'It's not like you think.' Finbar took a gulp of champagne. 'I told him to find *someone*, had no idea he'd picked her. I didn't even know he knew her. I only found out afterwards who she was. Guy didn't intend to kill her. He picked her up at the airport, drove her home. Her boyfriend came in and–'

'Her boyfriend was there?' Shannon asked. 'Paul hit her, stole money Rob gave her to pay bills. Rob told him to get out.'

'Well, he was still there.' Finbar shrugged. 'They were arguing in front of Guy and Ashton hit Melanie.' He paused, seeing Shannon flinch and hug herself. 'Are you all right?'

'Yes.' She nodded. 'Go on.'

'Melanie fell against Guy, got hold of his gun–'

'Oh, that's normal, is it?' she flashed. 'To walk around with a gun?'

'I'm telling you what happened. Will you let me finish?' Finbar said calmly. 'Melanie shot Ashton, started freaking out. It was seven in the morning, but she was drunk. Thirteen hours on the aircraft – high altitude combined with all that complimentary booze. Guy helped her get rid of the body. Then he shot her because he thought she might not keep her mouth shut. He kept her money. I didn't know anything about all this until very recently. I didn't even know she was missing until you mentioned it the other week. That's the truth, Shannon.'

She was silent, thinking. She could imagine Melanie behaving exactly like that. Rob was right, she'd never stood a chance after being abused by Bernard for years. Bernard! He'd tried to mutilate and strangle *her.* The scene on dark Salthouse Quay flashed through her mind. If the two boys hadn't disturbed him she'd be dead now. Dead, like poor Melanie. She felt cold, despite the sunshine and central heating, and hugged herself to try and stop shivering.

'Okay. Thanks for telling me. I – I think I'll leave now.' She stood up and sat down again fast, her head spinning. Her heart pounded furiously then seemed to miss a few beats. The warm sunny room went black round the edges.

'What is it?' Finbar leapted up, his voice full of concern. 'Shannon, what's wrong?'

'Don't feel well!' she gasped. 'Dizzy.' He lifted her up, carried her to the guest room and laid her on the bed, pulling the quilt over her.

'Jesus!' he said worriedly. 'Your hands are frozen.' He tucked the quilt around her shoulders. 'Have you eaten anything recently?' he asked. 'Apart from a spoonful of fish eggs?'

'Not hungry.' Tears slid from beneath her closed eyelids.

'Listen to me, Shannon.' He sat down and laid a warm dry hand on her clammy forehead. 'Are you listening?'

'Yes,' she whispered.

'You've got to give yourself a chance – go easy on yourself,' he said. 'You're doing too much. You'll make yourself ill. You've had a terrible time recently. The divorce, your work – the thing with Bernard. I know you're strong, but everyone has their limits. You've got to eat, sleep, relax, let your body heal. Don't tear yourself apart.' He paused, gazing down at her. 'I'm sure your mother would tell you the same.'

'She wouldn't.' Shannon turned over and buried her face in the pillow. 'She doesn't care about me. Neither does my father. They never wanted me, I disrupted their lives. The last time she phoned was eight months ago – she was upset because the bloody cat died. Maybe she'll phone again when my father dies!'

He was silent for a minute. 'Have you seen your doctor?'

'What for?' Her voice was muffled. 'He'd only try to stick me on Prozac or refer me to some boss-eyed *counsellor* who'll tell me she knows how I feel and say I'm seriously disturbed when I tell her to piss off.'

'I didn't mean that.' He smiled. 'You don't look after yourself, you could be slightly anaemic – you might need iron pills for a month or so, that's all.'

'I don't need iron pills,' she muttered. 'I need a break.' The pillow was wet with her tears. 'I need something good to happen in my life for a change.'

'It will.' He patted her shoulder through the quilt, resisting the urge to lie down and put his arms around her. She obviously didn't think meeting him was 'good'. He felt depressed again. 'Why don't you sleep for a while?' he suggested. 'I'll call your office, tell them you're ill and won't be back this afternoon. I'll make you some dinner when you wake up and drive you back to West Derby afterwards. It's Friday tomorrow, you can take it easy. Get a good rest this weekend. Don't go into work on Saturday morning. All right?'

'All right,' Shannon whispered, too tired to argue. She snuggled down and pulled the quilt over her head. He stood up and closed the blinds against the noonday sun. She was asleep before he left the room.

She awoke hours later in darkness, gasping for breath, the room spinning. It was the same dream – Bernard pursuing her to the edge of a ravine, glinting knife clenched in his hand. Her bare feet sliding on loose soil. Rob, his ineffective hand stretched out. Too late, too late. Then she remembered where she was and lay down again, breathing deeply, trying to relax. Light came through the half open door and there was a faint savoury smell of cooking.

It was hot lying fully dressed under the quilt. She got up, opened the blinds and looked out at the river for a moment. The moon, reflected in the water, rose in a sky full of stars. She wanted a shower but had no fresh clothes to change into. There was only the heavy blue towelling robe, newly washed and neatly folded on the chest at the foot of the bed. She combed and fluffed her hair and sprayed on some perfume.

Candles burned in the living room and dining room. The table was set with white plates, green linen napkins and sparkling wine glasses. Finbar stood in the kitchen stir-frying green and red peppers, mushrooms and baby corn. He wore his dark blue bathrobe and his black hair was damp and shiny.

'Hello there!' He turned and smiled at her. 'I looked in on you when I got back, but you were still fast asleep.'

She yawned and leaned on the counter. 'What time is it?'

He glanced at his watch. 'Eight-fifteen.'

'My God!' she exclaimed. 'I've been asleep nearly seven hours.'

'You obviously needed it. Here, have one of these.' He handed her a cracker topped with butter, smoked salmon, caviar and a peeled tiger prawn. 'And don't tell me you're not hungry!'

'Thanks.' It was delicious. She ate it and reached for another. He pointed to the grill pan on which two fillet steaks lay, topped with olive oil and slivers of garlic.

'I'll wait with doing these if you want a quick shower?' he offered. She often liked a shower at night as well as the morning. Evening showers often ended in sex. Not that there was much hope of that now.

'I can't,' she said regretfully. 'I've got nothing to change into.' He looked at her and she blushed and glanced away. She took a third cracker and bit into it. 'Anyway, I'm starving.'

'Good.' He put the steaks under the grill. 'Promise me you'll eat?'

'I am eating!' she mumbled, mouth full of prawn and smoked salmon.

'I mean, when you're not here. When we're not–' He couldn't finish. 'Fancy a glass of wine?' he asked, picking up the bottle. 'Red. More iron. A good excuse, should you feel you need one.'

She took the glass he poured her and sipped. 'That's lovely,' she breathed. 'You're the only person who gives a toss about me,' she said disconsolately.

'Rubbish! Don't get morbid, Shannon.' The steaks hissed and spat beneath the grill. 'The way you feel now is just a reaction to everything that's happened. There's lots of people care about you.'

'Everyone hates me.'

'That's rubbish. You know it's rubbish.'

'I even called Jenny a stupid bitch today.'

'She probably deserved it.'

'No. She said I'd become a hardknock and I told her I didn't want to hear her retarded opinions. She was just concerned about me. We used to get on great. People think I'm a bimbo who's never had to graft for anything. I don't know why! That's what Rob thinks too. That's what Cindy the detective thinks.'

'Since when do you care what people think?' He switched off the gas under the wok. 'Especially the likes of them?'

'The likes of them can destroy me.'

'No one's going to destroy you,' he said calmly. He picked up a pair of tongs and turned the steaks. 'Medium-rare, right?'

Shannon took no notice. 'They can destroy me,' she said miserably. She gulped wine. 'I've got a bad feeling. Something terrible's going to happen, I know it is!'

'For Christ's sake!' He took the wine glass from her and dumped it on the counter. 'Stop talking like this! No one hates you and no one's going to destroy you. Nothing terrible will happen. Nothing bad's going to happen, d'you hear me?' He stared angrily down at her. 'You're safe now! D'you think you can stop this morbid introspection long enough for us to eat our steak?'

'Okay,' she said quietly. She'd never seen him angry. 'You're right. I'm not doing myself any good.'

'She talks sense at last! Come on, let's eat.' He put the steaks on a platter. 'Can you bring the vegetables?' She put on a pair of oven gloves, picked up the wok and followed him to the dining room. They sat at the table and he reached across and took her hand. She didn't pull away.

'I know it's hard,' he said gently. 'But you'll get through this. Try not to worry.'

His eyes shone in the candlelight. He let go of her hand and picked up a knife and fork to slice the steak.

'Why don't we go out tonight?' he suggested. He put steak on their plates and refilled the glasses. 'Just as friends, of course.' Better than nothing!

'Where?' She ate a mouthful of tender steak. 'This is delicious.'

'We could go to a club. Not my club, of course, that'd be like work. Drink, dance, have a laugh. I think we could both do with it.'

'I don't feel like going to a club.' Shannon smiled. 'Sorry to be morbidly introspective again, but I can't imagine having a normal night out, like other people. I feel that they could do it but if I did it something terrible might happen.'

'Shannon, Shannon!' He shook his head. 'You've got to stop this.'

'All right.' She burst out laughing, feeling her wine. 'Let's go to the Malakand!'

'They found a body in that street once.' He smiled.

'I'm not surprised!'

'The police couldn't spell the name of the street so they dragged the body round the corner and wrote on the report that it was found there.'

'How could they not spell the name of the *street*?'

'God knows.' He smiled. 'Here, have some more steak.' He put another piece on her plate.

'I can't believe it!' she whispered, staring into the candle flame. 'I can't believe I did that.'

'Did what?' His heart sank. 'Ate a proper meal for once?'

'You know what!' Her eyes glistened. The silvery bits on her sweater looked gold in the candlelight.

'You're not going to tear yourself apart over him now, are you?' he said roughly. He told her to eat; he couldn't swallow another mouthful. He put down his knife and fork and picked up his glass of wine. 'He was a rapist, a child murderer, for Christ's sake! He didn't deserve to live.'

'Who am I to decide who deserves to live?'

'It was *self-defence*, Shannon! You did what you had to do to stay alive. To save other lives. We've been through all this. If you hadn't done it, he would have murdered you.' He shuddered. 'You barely escaped with your life!' he exclaimed. 'Don't forget that. You did what you had to do,' he repeated fiercely. 'Don't torture yourself over this.'

'I suppose you're right.'

'I know I'm right! You've got to put it behind you. Don't let it destroy the rest of your life.'

Dark shadows flickered over the walls and the wine in the glasses glowed ruby red in the candlelight.

'I just can't get over – I can't understand how anyone can protect people like him. Stay silent for years.'

'Self-interest,' he said. 'Denial. They block out what it doesn't suit them to know. That's what his wife did. After his death and Melanie's, the publicity, she couldn't block it out any more. That's what tipped her over the edge. And Rob . . . *well*!' He looked grim. 'Have you seen him lately?' he asked, not sure that he wanted to know.

'He phones me a lot, keeps begging me not to go through with the divorce. That's another thing tearing me apart! It's going to be horrible anyway, and he's making it more horrible.'

'But you are going through with it?'

'You know I have to. If it hadn't been for Bernard Flinder I'd still be happy,' she said miserably. 'Rob and I would be happy. I might have been pregnant by now.' She picked up her glass of wine. 'I wanted two babies.'

'I know you did.' He leaned back. 'Imagine two baby girls who looked like you. You'd have taken them to visit Granny and Granddad. Granddad would have kindly offered to babysit while you went shopping. We know what would have happened then, don't we?' She flinched. 'Do you wish you were still happy with Rob?' he asked. 'Do you want him back?'

'You asked me that before.' She finished her wine. 'I could forgive but not forget,' she sighed. 'He let me down when I needed him most. He forced me into a horrendous situation. Because of all that I'm now responsible for his father's death. We can't live with that between us. We could try, but it wouldn't work. I wish he'd just let it go. I hope he does soon – for both our sakes.'

'I suppose you wish you'd never met me?' Finbar swallowed nervously. 'Don't you? I've got something to tell you,' he said,

'I've been winding down my – operations. I said I'd stop and I meant it. I can get by fine with the club and the air cargo business. So the rest's over. That's the truth. Even if you never want to see me again.'

Shannon looked at him. 'I do want to see you again,' she said slowly. 'You're wrong. I am glad I met you. I love you, Finbar.'

A jolt of joy shot through him. 'Do you mean that?' he asked incredulously. 'Shannon?' He sat up and grabbed her hand.

'I mean it.' She smiled at him.

'What's brought this on?' He could hardly believe he'd heard right.

'I missed you so much!' She hesitated. 'I was afraid of what I felt for you – I still am. I just know I want you more than anything. Don't ask me to explain.' She stood up, pushing her chair back. 'I think I will take a shower after all,' she said. 'No.' She laid a hand on his shoulder. 'Stay here, finish your wine. We'll go to my house later and I'll pack a few things.'

He kissed her hand. She went to the bathroom, quickly showered and sprayed herself with Obsession. She combed out her blonde hair and smiled at herself in the bedroom mirror, smoothing her hands over her breasts. She walked back to the dining room, naked, and sat astride him. He groaned as she kissed him, pushing her tongue into his mouth, pressing her soft breasts against him. He pulled open his robe and she felt his erection against her belly.

'Say it again,' he murmured. He ran his hands over her breasts and buttocks and held her tight. Say, "I love you".'

'I love you!'

'Don't ever leave me again, Shannon.' He stroked her breasts and kissed her nipples. 'I'll be a dead man. Jesus!' he breathed. 'Sorry, but I can't wait.'

He pulled her down and entered her. She gasped and cried out, hands gripping his shoulders. 'I love you!' she moaned. He stood up and laid her gently on the table, pushing aside the plates and glasses. A plate crashed to the floor. Her hair fanned out. They stared at one another for a second.

An hour later they left the apartment. In the cold car park they stopped to kiss again. Stars glittered above the city lights. The river was still.

'Let's hurry it up.' Finbar smiled. 'I can't wait to get back here.'

'I thought you said I needed rest?' she teased.

'It's a kind of rest. Lots of wasted time to make up for.'

'I love you so much!' She hugged him. 'It was terrible without you.'

'Tell me about it!' They walked towards the car, his arm holding her close. 'How would you like to have your two babies with me one day?' he murmured. He buried his face in her hair, loving its softness, smelling the delicious perfume. She loved him, he thought joyfully, winding a curl around his finger. Finally, he knew she loved him! They had each other. That was all that mattered.

'Shannon Flinder! Mrs Shannon Flinder!'

They jumped in shock as Cindy materialized out of the darkness and shoved her warrant card in their faces. Ed lurked behind. 'Thought I might find you here,' she said coldly. 'We want to interview you in connection with the murder of Bernard Flinder.'

Chapter Twenty-Three

A spiral of smoke rose from the battered metal ashtray in the brightly lit interview room that stank of sweat and disinfectant. The walls had dirty white tiles; easy to hose the blood off, thought Shannon. She was seriously frightened now.

'Why did you go to see your father-in-law that afternoon?' Cindy demanded. 'Irene Watchet said you looked upset.'

'Is that a crime?' Shannon glanced at Ed. 'I suppose I can't ask you not to smoke in your own home.' She should have been lying naked in Finbar's arms. Instead, she was here in a police station. Life was full of nasty little surprises. Calm down, she told herself again. They've got nothing. They have to let you go soon.

Who was she kidding? They could keep her here, shut away from the outside world, for as long as they liked. If she tried to leave they'd probably arrest her. She'd seen it happen many times. To other people.

'You don't like me smoking?' Ed asked, startled. '*Sorry*!' He immediately stubbed out the cigarette.

Cindy stood up. She had taken off her red leather coat and wore jeans and a black sweater underneath. 'Did you murder your father-in-law?' she asked angrily. 'Did Finbar Linnell help you do it?'

'Oh, please!' Shannon sat back, smiling and shaking her head in disbelief. 'Is that the best you can come up with?'

'Just answer the question. Is that a denial?'

'Of course it's a denial,' she said angrily. 'I deny killing anyone.'

'Are you sleeping with Linnell?' Ed asked.

'That's none of your business!'

'We'll take that as a yes,' Cindy snapped. 'What do you know about his drug dealing?' she asked. 'Has he told you about that?'

'He runs an air cargo business,' Shannon said shortly. 'As well as his club. Perfectly legitimate enterprises, so far as I'm aware. That's all. I don't know anything about alleged drug deals.' They were just fishing, she thought. They knew nothing.

'Tell us why you went to see your father-in-law that Friday afternoon,' Cindy repeated. 'Irene Watchet said you were in a distressed state. What was all that about?'

'My marriage had just broken up,' Shannon said coldly. 'I think it's normal to be in a distressed state under those circumstances. Don't you?'

'Answer the *question!'* Cindy thumped the table and Ed glanced up at her. 'Why did you go to see him?'

Shannon sighed. 'I blamed him for the breakup. Rob freaked out when Melanie told him his father was a paedophile. He blamed himself, thought he should have protected Melanie. It changed him completely, he wasn't the same person anymore. He'd walked out on me a few days previously. Said he wanted a divorce. I was terribly upset. I wanted to talk to Bernard Flinder, try to reason with him. I thought maybe he could talk to Rob, tell him it wasn't his fault, that he couldn't have protected Melanie. I wanted him to give himself up to the police. I realize now how stupid that was!' she said in a low voice. 'Stupid to go there, stupid to expect he'd do what I wanted. But I was devastated, in shock. I couldn't think straight.'

'What happened then?' Ed asked gently. She looked tired and upset. He wanted to comfort her, shield her from Cindy who had it in for her, there was no doubt.

'He told *Miss Watchet* to go home. She looked a bit surprised, it must have been earlier than her usual departure time. I told him Rob had left me, that I was afraid he was heading for a breakdown. I threatened to expose Bernard. He said I had no proof and what use would it be if he was imprisoned? He'd get no treatment and he'd be out in a few years. He promised to talk to Rob, but a few days went by and nothing happened. Bernard didn't give a damn about him, of course, about what he – we – were going through.' Of course she wouldn't mention the failed break-in at her house, Bernard's attempt to murder her on Salthouse Quay. That would be seen as motive for retaliation. Women weren't allowed to retaliate.

'Why didn't you tell the police?' Cindy demanded, infuriated by the ring of truth in Shannon's story.

'Do me a favour!' she said scornfully. 'Don't you dare tell me you would have believed me and arrested him! I couldn't prove anything. Who are you going to believe: an embittered deserted wife or the highly respected headmaster?'

'So you would have been delighted to hear about Mr Flinder's murder?' Cindy sat down and glanced at the tape recorder. Shannon wondered if the video camera was switched on.

'I certainly wasn't gutted with grief,' she said. 'I don't think anyone was. Except that demented secretary.'

'Who do you think murdered your father-in-law then?'

'Will you stop calling him that?' Shannon said irritably. 'He wasn't a father in any sense of the word. I don't acknowledge in-law relationships anyway. I've no idea who murdered him,' she answered. 'Now that we know about his spare time activities, it could have been anyone. Maybe a parent who wanted revenge and knew there was no point in going to the police.' She laughed. 'Maybe his wife did it!' She pushed back the chair and stood up. 'Can I leave now?' she asked. 'Or do you intend to charge me with something? Being a lawyer? Going around with an Irish businessman?'

She pulled her coat around her. She hadn't taken it off, feeling too vulnerable. It was strange to be in a police station as a helpless suspect instead of the helpless suspect's solicitor. It was a horrible feeling. In future she'd be more aware of how they felt.

'Just a minute, Mrs Flinder!' Cindy stared at her. 'Have you ever heard the name Dean Carver?' she asked.

'Dean *Carver*?' She trembled and went cold, didn't know how she managed to laugh. 'No.' She shook her head. 'Of course I haven't. I'd certainly remember a name like that. I know a doctor named Butcher.'

'Do you now? This Dean Carver was found dead in the boot of his car a few days ago,' Ed said. He picked up a cigarette and sniffed it. 'He'd been shot. In the back of the neck. Clean, professional. The underground car park attendant noticed a nasty smell from a Ford Escort that had been parked there a long time. Dean was a bit of a prat.' He grinned. 'Went around calling himself a contract killer. Used to hang out in a pub up Islington, the Malakand.'

'Well, I'm sure that's very interesting, but what the hell's it got to do with me?' Shannon felt her face turn white.

'The landlady of the Malakand–' Cindy paused for effect. 'She says a woman answering your description had a meeting with Dean in the pub,' she lied. No one in that place would say anything! But it was worth a try. 'A few days before Bernard Flinder was murdered. Sit down, Mrs Flinder.' She grinned. 'How about a cup of tea? It could be a long night for you.'

Detective Superintendant John Sweet pulled into the driveway of his house in Childwall and sat in the car for a minute, brushing stray red hairs from his jacket. He leaned his head back and sighed. His face and bald head were sweaty, his heavy body limp with exhaustion. He closed his eyes and saw Diane's melon tits hanging over his face, felt her wet mouth sucking him to the kind of climax he never experienced with his wife, Karen. Karen thought oral sex was dirty, disgusting. He liked Diane, enjoyed the sex, but if she thought shagging his brains out would get her promoted to Detective Sergeant she could forget it. He didn't mix business with pleasure. Not like that anyway.

He got out of the car, locked it and went into the house. Karen was pacing in the hall, an anxious look on her face. She wore her red wool dressing gown which made her look even fatter, and her shoulder length grey hair was dishevelled because of her irritatingly childish habit of twisting strands around her fingers and licking them.

'Oh, John, thank goodness you're home!' She came towards him and he recoiled slightly as she put her hands on his shoulders and stood on tiptoe to kiss him. She smelled of lavender talc and Camay soap. She never used perfume, hardly wore make-up. He thought of the array of greasy fingerprinted bottles and jars on Diane's dressing table.

'Gabrielle's not back yet,' she said worriedly. 'She promised she'd be home by eleven and it's after midnight now. I told her she can stay out later when she's seventeen, but she won't listen. I hate to think of her out somewhere in Liverpool at this hour.'

'Right,' he said grimly. 'That's it.' He went into the warm lamplit sitting room and took off his jacket. 'Is she with soft lad again?'

'Ross? I don't know. Probably.'

'*Ross!*' he mocked. 'Well, when she does get in she's grounded for a month. I'm bloody sick of this carry on.' He smiled down at her. 'Make us a cup of tea, will you, love?'

'Of course. Oh! Someone keeps phoning,' Karen said. Her round red face was shiny with some sort of cream. He didn't know why she bothered. 'They must be dialling 141 because when I try to find out who it is, it says "caller withheld number".'

John frowned and sat on the sofa. A film was starting, an ancient cold war thriller, but he was too tired to stay up to watch it.

'I'll put the kettle on.' She hurried out and he jumped up as the phone started to ring.

'I'll get it!' he shouted. He strode into the hall and grabbed the receiver.

'John?' It was an Irish voice, low and urgent. 'I've been trying to reach you.'

'Finbar,' he said uneasily. 'Was it you who phoned earlier? The wife was a bit worried.'

'Two of your clowns – one's Cindy Nightingale, a Detective Sergeant – have pulled in a friend of mine, a Mrs Shannon Flinder. They've been harassing her for weeks, questioning her about me, trying to make out she or I might have something to do with the murder of that pervert Bernard Flinder. She was his daughter-in-law. Nightingale seems to have a big chip on her shoulder. They've got no evidence against her.'

'Got nothing to worry about then, has she?' Sweet laughed nervously.

'Don't get smart with me, John. Since when did lack of evidence bother you lot? I want this dropped,' said Finbar. 'I want her left alone. She's had a rough time these past few months. She's been through enough. Whoever murdered Flinder did society a big favour. But it wasn't her. I want this dropped,' he repeated. 'For good.'

'It's not one of my cases,' Sweet protested. 'I can't interfere.'

'Don't fuck with me.' Finbar's voice was cold and angry. 'Just do it.'

'All right,' he muttered after a second. 'But it'll cost you.'

'Whatever it takes. How's that girlfriend of yours?' Finbar asked. 'Diane's her name, isn't it? How's your career going?'

'It's done, all right? It's done!'

'I want her out of there. Now! I'm waiting.' The phone went dead.

'Here you are, darling.' He turned and took the mug of tea Karen handed him, milky with three sugars. 'Was that the person who phoned before?' she asked crossly.

'Thanks, love.' He took the tea. 'Er – yes, it was. Someone from work.'

'Well, tell him I think he's got very bad manners.' She paused in the sitting-room doorway. 'Are you coming to watch the film?'

'In a minute. I've got one or two calls to make first.'

'After that you sit down and relax,' she ordered. 'You've had a very long day – again!'

She had that right. John grinned to himself. Karen settled in front of the television to eat her hair and he made his calls. As he replaced the receiver the front door opened and his fifteen-year-old daughter, Gabrielle, came in giggling. She wore dark eye make-up, a fringed leather jacket, black boots, and the kind of short tight leather skirt that made him wish he had the legal right to keep her locked in her bedroom. Or make her wear a *chador*. Her thick chestnut brown hair hung down her back. A lanky boy in a leather jacket stood behind her.

'Oh, Dad!' She stopped giggling. 'I thought you and Mum would be in bed by now.'

'And where the bloody hell have you been till this time?' he shouted.

They had gone out to let her sweat, pathetic bastards! And so that Ed could smoke a cigarette. But it was working. She'd refused offers of tea or coffee and a sandwich, but if they kept her here much longer she'd have to eat and drink something. Shannon stared at the tiled wall, avoiding the hostile gaze of the blonde thin-lipped WPC in attendance. No doubt she hated Shannon because she was a lawyer, longed to give her a good kicking. It was hot in the room and she'd finally taken off her coat. What next? A night in a cell? An identity parade for the benefit of the Malakand landlady? They had nothing; even if the landlady identified her there was still nothing. Flimsy, circumstantial *nothing*. But it wouldn't be the first time someone had been convicted on that. It was amazing how people could believe what they wanted to believe.

This is unreal, Shannon thought furiously. I'm going to go down for that pervert's murder. I'll get a much longer sentence than any man. I'll be a Category A prisoner – women who kill men are the most dangerous of all! Women's prisons are worse than concentration camps. I'll be raped by lesbians, turned into a drug addict, end up hollow-eyed and malnourished. There'll be rats, cockroaches, buckets of urine, strip searches. Dr White's non-disposable sanitary towels. No Finbar. Out of his arms and into a police car. Don't worry, he said. How the hell could she not worry?

Exhausted and frightened, she leaned her head on the desk and closed her eyes. The policewoman grinned. She'd break soon. Footsteps sounded along the corridor and Shannon jerked upright. Footsteps along corridors made her think of people being taken for interrogation, torture, execution, informed that there were ways and means of causing them agony . . . She shivered in the stuffy room. Cindy burst in and glared at her.

'You can go,' she said abruptly. 'We won't need you anymore.'

'What?' gasped Shannon.

'I said you can go! We've finished with you.' She was furious, but dared not question the order that had just come through from on high.

'I should bloody well think so!' Shannon glared back. She stood up and pulled her coat on, determined not to ask how or why in case the bitch changed her mind. She swept past Cindy and out of the room. Ed, smoking another cigarette in the corridor, smiled at her ingratiatingly. Shannon ignored him.

'But why?' she heard the WPC whine. 'What's going on?'

'. . . friends in high places, like all scumbag lawyers!'

Shannon walked out of the police station, trembling, avoiding stares and leers from passing policemen. Imagine coming here to report a rape! She ran down the steps of the horrible stark modernist building and looked up and down the dark street, hoping a taxi would cruise past. A horn beeped, headlights flashed and she gave a sob of relief as she recognized the Maserati. She ran across the road, got in and flung herself into Finbar's arms.

'I thought I'd never get out of there!' she cried, her head on his shoulder. 'Oh, my *God!* I can't take anymore of this.' She clung to him.

'You won't have to.' He kissed her and buried his face in her hair, hugging her tight. 'You're safe now, I promise you,' he whispered. 'Those bastards can't touch you. They won't bother you again.'

She drew away and looked at him. 'That's what that bitch Cindy said. "We won't need you anymore." I thought I was in terrible trouble,' she said breathlessly. 'They had nothing, but since when did that stop them? She had it in for me, she would have done anything. Then they suddenly let me go.'

'Are you all right?' he asked worriedly.

'I suppose so. I don't think my system can stand anymore shocks for the present, though!'

'It won't have to. You'll be all right now, there's nothing to be afraid of.'

'I don't understand why they suddenly let me go. I thought they were going to charge me.' She looked up at him. 'Did you . . .?' She started to laugh. 'Don't tell me! You've got a senior police officer by the balls – someone owed you a *favour*!' She put up a hand and caressed his face, felt the roughness of his beard. 'MI6 would say you were a threat to democracy.'

'That'd be the pot calling the kettle black, wouldn't it now?' He grinned and started the engine. 'Where to?' he asked, glancing in the driving mirror. 'West Derby? Or why don't we just go home and you take tomorrow off? We could get your things then. It's late, you must be exhausted.'

Shannon thought for a second. 'Okay. I will take tomorrow off.

Sod Gavin. You know, I might not be working for him much longer,' she said. 'Remember I told you I'd had a chat with someone?'

'Yes?' He drove down the street, heading for the centre of town. A gang of drunken skinheads jeered at the Maserati as it sped past.

'Her name's Mi-Hae Kam. She's starting a new firm, criminal work. We had a good laugh. She's looking for an associate. I think I'll give her a call tomorrow, tell her I'm really interested. I'm so tired of that bastard Gavin,' she sighed. 'Being in that place tonight made me realize how the punters must feel. Especially if they're innocent. It actually made me more enthusiastic about my work. I want to help people again. What are you smiling at?' she asked, taken aback.

'You wouldn't be saying that if they'd charged you,' Finbar said. 'Stuck you in a cell for the night.'

'No, that's true. I probably wouldn't.' They pulled up at traffic lights and she looked away from him out of the window, biting her lip. Her eyes blurred with tears. What else can happen? she wondered.

'Hey!' He grabbed her hand and kissed it. 'I'm sorry, Shannon! I'm sorry, okay? Oh, Christ!' he moaned. 'That was really stupid. I didn't mean it. Don't cry,' he pleaded.

She pulled her hand away and bent her head. The lights changed to green and he let in the clutch. 'I'm sorry,' he repeated desperately, trying to glance at her and keep his eyes on the road at the same time. 'Forgive me, please? I'm inadequate. I've got great gaps in my emotional make-up, you know?'

'I have to go to my house,' she said, wiping her eyes.

'Oh, no!' He groaned and slowed the car. 'Oh, come on. Please!'

She looked at him and grinned. 'I've got no clean knickers for tomorrow. That's what scared me most about spending the night in a cell.'

He laughed with relief. 'I'll go to Marks and Sparks in the morning and get you all the knickers you want. You have a lie-in. I'll go to the office and we'll head for West Derby later in the afternoon. Is that all right with you?'

'It's perfect.'

* * *

She awoke next morning at ten to find a pile of carrier bags at the foot of the bed and a yellow post-it note stuck to her pillow.

> *You look beautiful, very peaceful. I don't want to wake you. Here's a few things I picked out, hope you like them. I got some strange looks at the cash desk! Have some coffee, eat breakfast. I'll see you around two. Thank you for last night and for all the other nights. There'll be many more. I love you. Finbar, xxxx*

Shannon smiled and kissed the note. I never thought I'd love anyone again, she thought. It's incredible. It was a beautiful day, blue sky, sunshine glittering on the Mersey. The driest January since records began. It was always the driest month since records began. She opened the bags. There were pairs of pink, white, black and flowered cotton briefs, stretchy bra tops, two pairs of jeans and a big sweater in a rose pink shade. There was also a bottle of Obsession and a delicate gold and diamond bracelet in a box lined with white satin. She held it up, watching the tiny diamonds wink in the sunlight. It was beautiful. She fastened it on her wrist and went to the kitchen to make breakfast.

She watched a cookery programme while she drank coffee and ate hot buttered toast and a boiled egg. It was wonderful to have a lazy day for once. She hadn't felt so relaxed for ages. After breakfast she went into the living room and phoned Mi-Hae Kam's office.

'Mi-Hae?' She pictured the skinny woman with porcelain skin, long shiny straight black hair and humorous black eyes. Mi-Hae was thirty-five, nine years older than her. Same as Finbar. 'Good morning! It's Shannon.'

'Shannon! Hi! I phoned your office but you weren't there. I was about to make you an offer you can't refuse.'

She laughed. 'You're right. I can't refuse it.'

'Fantastic! We'll make a great team. When can you start?'

'I have to give that bastard Gavin a month's notice,' she said thoughtfully. 'At least. But I can talk to him. Or threaten him, more like.' They giggled. 'It'll have to wait until Monday, though. He's in London this week. I'll talk to him on Monday and get back to you.'

'Fantastic!' Mi-Hae repeated. 'I'm very happy about this, Shannon.'

'Me too. I've been dying to get away from the miserable, low life, bow-tied bastard with his Nazi doctor glasses. I don't know why, but you can practically guarantee that men who wear bow ties will be twenty-four-carat wankers. I should never have gone to that second interview.'

'Nothing is wasted, darling!' Mi-Hae laughed.

'By the way, I've got a new address from today. And phone number.' Shannon read it out.

'Wow!' Mi-Hae scribbled it down. '*Nice*. Bit Eighties, though.'

'I know. It's not my place, it belongs to my boyfriend.' She felt shy, acknowledging Finbar. He wouldn't be a secret any longer.

'Oh, well, you can't have everything.' Mi-Hae laughed. 'Right, I've got that. I'll wait for your call. Have a good weekend.'

'You too, Mi-Hae. 'Bye!'

Shannon hung up, feeling happier than she had for months. Her life was coming together again. She'd have Finbar, a more interesting job with people she liked. Cindy Bitchville would leave her alone. The divorce would be finalized. Rob would get his head round the fact that they were finished. Bernard couldn't rape and murder anymore young girls. In an imperfect world this was as perfect as it was going to get.

She was stepping out of the shower when the hall buzzer sounded, pressed long and hard. She stiffened and stood still, water droplets running off her skin. She reached for a towel and wrapped it around her. Finbar had said not to answer the phone or the door when he was out, and she had no desire to. At least not until she'd told everyone who mattered that she lived here now. She went into his bedroom and looked out over the sparkling waters of the Albert Dock towards the car park. No police cars. Who was it? She was surprised the apartment building didn't have closed circuit surveillance. She walked into the hall, her bare feet slippery on the polished floor. The buzzer sounded again. A minute later the phone rang and the answering machine in the living room whirred and clicked into action.

'Finbar? It's Lenny. Where are you, you bastard?' The harsh voice filled the silent room. 'Get the phone, man! Are you there?

I'm downstairs.' He waited. 'Okay, you're not there. I got your message about your new idea. I'll be in the Phil tonight, eight-thirty. Don't be late.'

She stood in the doorway holding the towel around her, staring at the phone. What new idea? Who was Lenny? Irish, obviously. The IRA? Fear ran through her, doubt and distrust reawakened. She knew nothing about Finbar except what he told her. Being in love with someone and wanting to fuck the lights out of them day and night didn't mean you trusted them a centimetre. *What* new idea? She paced the living room, happiness and peace of mind gone. He'd stopped drug dealing – so he said! – but what else was he involved in? She gasped and whirled round as the front door slammed.

'Shannon?' he called. He came into the living room wearing a black suit, collarless white shirt and his overcoat. He smiled when he saw her. 'Coffee smells good,' he said. 'Just got up?' He came towards her. 'You look beautiful.'

'What are you doing here so early?' She backed away. 'I didn't expect you until after two.'

'There's nothing much going on today. I missed you. Aren't you pleased to see me?' He came up to her and stroked her cheek and her bare wet arm. The golden hairs stood up. 'What's wrong?' He smelled fresh, of the cold outdoors. He laughed. 'Didn't you like the things I brought you?'

'Don't treat me like some bimbo! Who's Lenny?' she asked angrily, staring up at him. She shivered slightly. 'I know he's one of your compatriots.'

'Compatriot!' he repeated mockingly. Anxiety seized him. 'What's that, English for Mad Mick? Paddy the turf-cutter from the bog? Yes, he's my *compatriot*. I did some business with him–.'

'I bet you did!' She replayed the phone message. 'What new idea?' she asked when it ended. 'What's he talking about?'

'Not drugs. Don't you trust me?' asked Finbar, playing for time. The midday sun shone behind her, turning her golden hair to a halo, making her soft skin glow. 'I've finished with that, I told you. I thought you believed me,' he said. 'This is just work.'

'I wouldn't call being a member of the IRA *work*!' she hissed. 'What are you doing – planning a new offensive? Blowing a few women and children to kingdom come? That'll advance your cause, won't it?'

He grabbed her wrist and she gasped in pain and surprise. 'I am not a member of the IRA!' he said slowly, staring into her eyes. He pulled her towards him. 'It is possible to grow up in the Republic of Ireland and not be a member of the bloody IRA.'

'Let go of me!' Shannon pulled away, clutching at the towel. 'Let *go*!'

'Majella's family were Republicans,' he said quietly. 'Not *me*. I hate causes. I told you! I didn't want that for Roiseann. Don't you believe a bloody word I say to you? You tell me you love me and I finally start to believe I mean something to you, and now this!'

He let go of her wrist and turned away, looking out over the river. He couldn't tell her. She couldn't know. For her own safety. Once the hit was over he'd be finished with Lenny and his 'superiors'. Two more weeks and they could start a new life. He had to hold things together until then. After two weeks there would be no more secrets.

Shannon was silent, standing there. I'm getting paranoid, she thought. After everything that's happened. I really will end up bitter and twisted if I don't watch out. Why be so ready to believe bad things rather than good?

'I'm sorry,' she muttered, rubbing her wrist. 'Of course I believe you.' She looked down. 'I'm just scared. Finbar, I'm really sorry!'

'It's all right. Don't be.' He turned, came back and took her in his arms. He felt torn with guilt. 'I'd do anything for you,' he said. 'I told you that. I love you. Don't be scared! All we care about is each other and the two babies we're going to have one day. Right?' He lifted her hand and kissed her wrist, then her lips. She gazed up at him. She wasn't sure whether she believed him or not. But she didn't care. She wanted him, couldn't resist him.

'I came home because I missed you,' he said softly. 'Like I said. Now, why don't you let the towel drop?' He kissed her again, biting her lips, gently probing with his tongue. 'I'll never have enough of you!' he murmured.

She did as he said.

Chapter Twenty-Four

'Such a terrible tragedy, Mr Flinder! I'm so very sorry. I don't have words–'

Rob came out of the crematorium, the same one where his father had been incinerated, and collided with Irene Watchet. Her watery eyes beneath the black spotted veil were red rimmed and bloodshot. She clutched a white cotton handkerchief in her black gloved hand. He could hardly make out the words she said she didn't have. Margaret, Bernard and Melanie were now consigned to the flames, hopefully not together for eternity. He couldn't believe the events of the past weeks. He was alone now. Melanie dead! He still couldn't take it in.

He brushed past Irene, Cindy and Ed close behind him. Shannon hadn't turned up, but he hadn't expected she would. She didn't want to see him. He'd left several messages at her office and two on the answering machine at home, but there had been no word. She didn't want him anymore. She was having a fling with that Irishman, Finbar Linnell. Cindy's eyes had gleamed when she told him. She'd hoped it would wind him up, provoke him to something. But Rob was resigned. Shannon didn't want him back. It was his own fault. She could have her divorce – and her Irishman. From a copper to a big time '*businessman*' with PIRA connections! She certainly liked a contrast. It wasn't worth his while, financially or emotionally, to contest the divorce. She'd been generous, his solicitor pointed out, amazingly so. He could have half the value of the house and all its contents, a lump sum, and no claim on his income.

There would be a lot of money from the sale of his parents des-res in Woolton Village and she didn't want a penny of that. He'd come out of the marriage a lot richer than he went in, his solicitor laughed. And no children. A clean break was best. Rob had to accept it, get on with his life. Such as it was. But it hurt. It really hurt. He started and looked down. Irene Watchet was clinging to his arm.

'Your father, mother and sister all in the space of a few weeks!' she mumbled. She blew her nose and he glanced away in disgust. 'It's too terrible, too tragic. You were such a wonderful family. Your father was a marvellous man.'

She was the only mourner, apart from himself. She hoped he would invite her back to the house for a cup of tea or a glass of sherry, so that they could talk about Mr Flinder. She'd never been inside his house, never been invited for lunch, dinner, afternoon tea. A drink of water!

Rob shook himself free. 'We weren't a wonderful family,' he said dully. 'My father wasn't a marvellous man. He was a paedophile who raped and murdered young girls. You wasted your life fancying him. Get out of my way!'

Irene stepped back, shocked, and stared after him as he walked to his car, white handkerchief pressed to her chapped lips.

'Rob!' Cindy and Ed caught him up. 'Have you thought about what we discussed?' she asked hopefully.

'No, I haven't. It's bloody *insane*,' he said, hand on the car door. He shook his head. 'Shannon's not the type to murder anyone. She hasn't got it in her. I know, I'm her husband.'

Cindy rolled her eyes. 'Not for much longer!'

'Shannon hasn't got it in her,' he repeated angrily. 'No way! I know that much. She's too sweet, too softhearted. I used to tease her about it. She wanted to have a baby before we–' He swallowed. 'Before we split up. That was my fault,' he added bleakly. 'I'm to blame. I put her through hell.'

Cindy glanced at Ed, disappointed. He shrugged. What did she expect?

'Just leave me alone!' Rob unlocked the car door and got in. 'I don't want to hear any more half-baked, round-the-twist crap about Shannon being a murderer. You must be desperate!' He glared at Cindy. 'Leave *her* alone, too,' he warned. 'If you hassle her again, you'll have me to deal with.'

He slammed the door, stuck the key in the ignition and started the engine. He'd ruined their marriage but he could at least stick up for Shannon now. Had she really hired someone to kill his father? If so, that was his fault too. She'd been terrified, desperate, in danger. He'd let her down.

'Drop it, Cind,' Ed said firmly, as the lilac Vauxhall Astra drove down the long tree-lined crematorium drive, speeding past the shuffling black-clad figure of Irene Watchet. 'Just bloody drop it, okay? You've worked hard to get where you are now. Don't blow it.'

'Men take one look at that bitch and their tongues drop out! It's pathetic. She murdered Bernard Flinder!' Cindy stared after the departing car. 'I know she did. I've got a feeling.' She shivered in the icy wind. Dirty white clouds bunched low overhead.

'Feminine intuition, eh?' he laughed scornfully.

'It's called *intelligence*!'

'Feelings won't stand up in court,' he said impatiently. 'There's nothing. You won't get another go at her. Forget it. Come on, let's have a drink.'

'I don't want a drink. I want Shannon bloody Flinder banged up.'

'Come on, Cind! I'm getting seriously pissed off with this. You've got nothing on her, you know that. There's a lot of other stuff we could be doing. You've got it in for her. You hate her. What's she ever done to you?'

She had blonde hair, gorgeous sexy humorous dark blue eyes, tits, a minuscule waist, a brilliant career and a lot more money, that's what. Finbar Linnell was the luckiest bastard on the planet, Ed thought enviously. He was definitely in the wrong job. Drool over but don't touch! That was his fate.

Rob drove back to Woolton Village and let himself into the cold empty house that still smelled of his mother's perfume; he couldn't remember its name, but the smell reminded him of stale cat piss. The awful decanters ranged along the sideboard were covered with dust. He poured himself a large scotch, took it into the living room and sat on the sofa. Something white just under the valance caught his eye and he picked it up. It was a paracetamol tablet.

The shame, guilt and taint that had savaged him since he found out about Bernard had faded, replaced by the more terrible feeling that he was a total failure. If only he could have protected Melanie! He'd let Shannon down too. Why had he blamed her? Hurt her so much? It wasn't her fault. Nothing was her fault. He tossed back the Scotch and went to pour himself another.

It was too late now. She couldn't live with him, couldn't trust him anymore. He was a fuck-up, a mess. And Melanie – poor little Melanie! Shot in the back of the neck by some bastard drug-dealer! He drank the Scotch and started to cry. 'Melanie!' he wept. 'I'm so sorry. I love you! I'm sorry I let you down.'

He groaned with pain, with the anguish of loss. He got a fresh glass, poured more Scotch and went upstairs to the attic. Margaret's paintings were stacked against the walls, some of them curled at the edges. There was a glass and a bottle with about an inch of gin left in it. It was as if she'd gone to answer the phone and would be back any second. But she wouldn't be back. Bernard's study was empty.

He grabbed armfuls of paintings, tossed them down the stairs and went back for more, swigging Scotch as he worked. He carried them into the garden, piling them up, using loose bricks and plant pots to stop the icy wind scattering them. He took a sledgehammer from the shed and knocked off the head of the marble nude. The woman next door stared truculently over the garden wall before going back into the house. Her husband sat at the kitchen table drinking tea and doing a crossword.

'Looks like that lad next door's going mental,' she remarked. 'He's starting a bonfire.'

'A bonfire?' He glanced up. 'That's not allowed. It's a smokeless zone round here.'

'Well, will you tell him or shall I?' she asked aggressively. She poured herself a cup of tea. 'I'm not going to tell the son of a murderer that he can't start a bonfire. He's all dressed up in a posh suit,' she went on. 'It was *her* funeral today. There's been so many I've lost count.'

'D'you think it's hereditary?' her husband asked. 'What he did to those poor young girls?'

'Wouldn't be surprised. They tell you it isn't, but they'd say anything. That wife, how could she keep quiet all these years? Looked like butter wouldn't melt!' She sighed. 'I just hope he moves out and sells the place before the value of our house goes down the toilet.'

'Might go up.' He grinned. 'You never know. Might get sightseers wanting to look around, take photos and videos.'

'You're sick, Colin! God!' she sighed. 'I keep thinking, if we'd had a daughter!'

In the garden Rob was burning Margaret's paintings. There were a lot of them and they were so dried out they caught fire easily. Bits of charred paper flew around the garden, whirling in the icy wind, and there was an autumnal smell of smoke, like Bonfire Night. Bonfire Night, when the trouble started. When Melanie told him! He started to cry again. He stared into the flames, tears pouring down his pale cheeks. 'Shannon!' he sobbed brokenly. 'Come back! I could deal with all this if you came back.' But she wouldn't.

He went back in the house and was in the dining room pouring more Scotch when the doorbell rang. He ignored the intrusive chime. His head spun. He banged the glass on the sideboard, slopping Scotch. Shannon! It might be Shannon! He ran into the hall and flung open the door.

'Hi there!' Linda stood in the porch smiling up at him. She wore her uniform, without the hat. She hated the hat. 'I miss you since you moved out,' she said shyly. 'I thought you might like some company today.'

He stared at her, breathing hard. She was the rhinestone to Shannon's sharp-cut glittering diamond. The heavy hair was dull, badly cut, the eyes a watered down blue, her figure pear-shaped. She giggled too much. She wanted to giggle now, but realized it might not be appropriate.

He stood back and she sidled past, twisting her hat in her hands and grinning up at him.

'Nice house,' she commented, looking around. 'Big.' She sniffed the air. 'I can smell bonfire smoke.'

'I've been burning a few things,' he said evasively.

Watered down versions were all he'd get from now on. Later on he might take her upstairs and try to fuck her, close his eyes, pretend it was Shannon moaning and writhing beneath him. But she didn't sound like Shannon. He'd have to tell her to keep quiet.

Finbar walked into the Philharmonic pub at twenty-to-nine and found Lenny sitting in a quiet corner, large Scotch in front of him. The Philharmonic was one of Finbar's favouite Liverpool pubs, with its round bar, Edwardian panelling and stained glass. He ordered white wine for himself and another Scotch. Lenny stared at the wine as he sat down, but made no comment. He wore jeans and that ridiculous combat jacket. His long hair was tied back in a ponytail. They drank in silence for a minute.

'So what's this new idea?' Lenny asked finally.

'We do the job with a rocket launcher.' Finbar glanced round the pub. It wasn't crowded and no one sat near them, but he felt nervous. Not the best place to discuss a hit on a senior cabinet minister.

'A bloody rocket launcher? Why?' Lenny looked at him in amazement. He pulled out a cigarette and lit it. 'What's wrong with a bomb?' he asked critically. 'Not flash enough for you?' He laughed.

'Blowing up half – or all – of Merseyside Maritime Museum won't be very good PR, Lenny. There'll be lots of people there. Kids.' That would cut no ice with Lenny, but he didn't care.

'Going soft in your old age?'

'They'll sweep the place a few times on the day – they might find the device. If that happens there won't be another chance anytime soon.'

'I suppose not.' Lenny thought for a minute. 'I was worried about that myself,' he admitted. 'So – it's 8 January now. How do we get one of those things by the fifteenth? It's only a week away.'

'I've got one.' Finbar grinned. 'It's a Russian RPG 26, one of the latest. Heat-seeking. Cost me two grand. And there's plenty of heat to seek in that fat bastard.'

'Russian? That's a bloody excellent euphemism for "dodgy",

Finbar, my man! Are you sure it'll work?' Lenny finished his Scotch and began on the second.

'Of course I'm sure. You can only use it once, but it'll work. No worries. I told you, it's heat-seeking. It's got a range of over two hundred metres. It's an anti-tank weapon, for Christ's sake! It'll go through his car like a blow torch through ice. Haven't you seen those Afghan farmers on the telly using them?' Finbar laughed, surprised by Lenny's ignorance. 'A bomb is what they'll expect and be looking out for. This thing fired from a disused office building in Water Street – no way!'

'Where did you get it? It could be booby trapped.' Lenny stubbed out his cigarette. 'Courtesy of the Brits.'

'It's not booby trapped.'

'I need to see it. That and the building.'

'Okay.' Finbar drank his wine. 'Meet me at Derby House tomorrow morning. Ten o clock.'

'Why can't we do it now? And where the hell's Derby House?'

'We can't do it now, Lenny, because I've got an important appointment.' He thought of Shannon waiting for him at home. 'And for the security reasons you're always so concerned about. We walk out of here, I take you to see the rocket launcher, it's going to be some Branch or MI5 bastard's lucky night, isn't it?'

'They haven't put a tail on me,' Lenny said angrily.

'So far as you know. You won't if they don't want you to. And to answer your second question, Derby House is the former World War Two Battle of the Atlantic headquarters, now a noted Liverpool tourist attraction. At ten in the morning there won't be many tourists. There's a few rooms marked "No Entry" and parts of it still aren't open to the public.' He laughed. 'It's a great place to show you the *weapon*.'

'You think this is all a big joke, don't you?' Lenny smiled at him, trying to conceal his anger. Arrogant bastard, he thought. But he'd have the last laugh. He would definitely have the last laugh.

'I've got to go.' Finbar stood up and shoved his hands in his pockets. 'I'll see you tomorrow morning,' he said abruptly. 'Don't be too early or late. Goodnight, now.'

He walked out of the pub and stood looking across the road at the brightly lit Philharmonic Hall. A concert was going on, he could hear violins, an orchestra. He didn't trust Lenny. The only person in the world he trusted was Shannon.

He glanced up the street, got into his car and drove to the Albert Dock. It was freezing and misty. He couldn't imagine warm weather, not having to wear scarf, overcoat, layers of clothing. The icy wind had dropped and the dock waters were calm. He thought it might snow.

'Shannon?' The kitchen and living room were dark and for a second he panicked. He ran down the hall to his bedroom and stopped in the doorway.

Candles flickered over the white walls and ceiling and on the floor by his bed on which she lay sprawled, naked except for a pair of sheer black stockings with lacy tops. The warm air smelled of her perfume and the jasmine-scented candles. There was a bottle of champagne and two glasses on the bedside table.

'Hi!' she said softly. 'I hoped you wouldn't be too long. I've unpacked my things. I thought maybe you could help me really feel at home.'

He started to laugh. He gazed at her beautiful face, her full breasts, the tiny waist and flat belly. One slender stockinged leg was draped over the other. Her thick, curly gold hair shone in the candlelight and her soft skin glowed honey. She smiled at him, sipped her champagne and dipped a finger in the glass, slowly massaging raspberry nipples. She'd put darkish make-up around her eyes.

'I love you!' he said. 'I love you!'

She moved her hand down her belly and slipped it between her legs. 'I'm waiting for you,' she whispered.

He stripped off his clothes in the hall, and got the tiny box from the inside pocket of his overcoat. He felt the heat of the candles on his bare ankles as he walked to the bed.

'I got something else today.' He climbed on to the bed and handed her the box. 'I was waiting for the perfect moment. Looks like this might be it.'

The diamond and sapphire ring sparkled in the candlelight. She caught her breath as she stared at it.

'It matches my eyes. Oh, Finbar, it's beautiful!' he teased. He leaned over and kissed her, his hand cupping her left breast. 'Say something, for Christ's sake!'

Shannon looked at him, her eyes wet. 'I'm scared,' she whispered. 'I'm terrified. It is beautiful but . . .'

'But what? What are you terrified of?' He kissed her again and wrapped his arms around her.

'Of us.' Her long eyelashed tickled his chest. 'Of the future.'

'Are you afraid you'll change?' he asked gently. 'Or that I will? Do a Rob on you?' He hugged her. 'I won't. Ever!'

'But how do you know? How do I know?'

'Shannon.' He kissed her and stroked her soft hair. 'I knew I loved you that day we met outside the law courts. I'd never been so sure of anything in my life. I was gutted when I found out you were happily married. Gutted for myself, not for you. I just wanted you to be happy, even if it wasn't with me. I'll love you forever,' he said calmly. 'That won't change. I want to marry you, spend the rest of my life with you.'

'I do love you,' she said, looking up into his eyes. 'It's just that it's so overwhelming, so unexpected. Especially after all that's happened. My life's been turned upside down in the past few months. A comet must have passed through my sign!' A candle hissed and spat, its flame wavering. He poured them champagne.

'Here's to us!' He handed her a glass. 'To an everlasting love that transcends space, time, matter – you name it!'

'To us!' She swallowed champagne and smiled at him, her eyes bright. 'I want you more all the time,' she whispered. 'You're always there for me, I can express myself with you, just be myself. You accept me the way I am. That's what so many men don't do. They have an agenda, expectations. They want you to play a role – they don't treat you like a fellow human being. You're not like that,' she said. 'That's what bothers me!'

'There's just no bloody pleasing you, is there?' He leaned over and kissed her breasts.

'I mean – it's too perfect,' she persisted. 'You don't lay any of that rubbish on me, you're too subtle.' She slid the ring on the third finger of her left hand. 'Look!' She laughed. 'Even this fits perfectly.'

'Shannon, my darling, for Christ's sake, stop worrying!' He

lifted her hand and kissed it then brought it down and closed it around his erection. 'I'm going to lay something on you right now,' he smiled. 'You like the ring?'

'I love it!' she said fervently. 'It's so beautiful. It's exactly the one I would have chosen.' She put her arms around him and kissed him. 'Thank you.'

'You're very welcome.' He laid her down and ran his hands over her breasts and belly and thighs. 'I love you so much,' he said. 'I love the things you say. I love the way you look at me. I love your tits and your legs and your beautiful blue eyes and your golden hair falling all over the place. And your glorious arse.' He pulled her on top of him and stroked her buttocks. 'And the way you come. Every fuck with you is like a religious experience.'

She gasped with laughter and desire. 'How do you know what a religious experience feels like?'

'I'm Irish. Come on, give me another kiss.' Her mouth closed over his, kissing him, her tongue in his mouth. 'You're my religion,' he groaned. 'You're my cause. You're my life!'

Chapter Twenty-Five

'During the Battle of the Atlantic in the Second World War Combined Headquarters Western Approaches was situated in this building 1941–1945.'

Fucking Brits. Lenny glanced contemptuously up at the slate plaque with gold lettering stuck on the front wall of the massive grey stone Thirties office building that was Derby House. Parts of the stone looked whitish, as though someone had washed the building and not done a proper job. Swirling snowflakes stuck to his ponytail and shoulders and he cursed, smoking a *Kretek* and stamping his feet for warmth. The ponytail felt frozen. He walked further along the street to the entrance where there was a sign; *'Top Secret Wartime Underground HQ'*. The narrow street of tall buildings had single yellow lines, and there were no cars parked. What a dump, he thought. It was two minutes to ten. He turned and frowned as he caught sight of Finbar walking towards him, wrapped in his black overcoat, a black canvas bag slung over his left shoulder.

'D'you know this place?' he asked as Finbar came up to him.

'I've been here once or twice. I like it, it's interesting.' He smiled.

'The only thing I'm interested in is what you've got in there.' Lenny nodded at the bag. 'How much does it weigh?' he asked. He dropped his cigarette on the icy pavement.

'In firing order – three kilos. Come on, let's go inside.'

Finbar paid their entrance money. They walked past books, videos and leaflets detailing the history of the building and its part in the Battle of the Atlantic and went down a dark sloping corridor. Two elderly men in scarves and padded anoraks sat in a dimly lit room to their right where a video was playing, the sound very loud. Black convoy ships heaved up and down in a mountainous grey sea, oilskinned figures lurching and stumbling over storm swept decks, the boom of gunfire in their ears. The place was cold and dank.

'Jesus!' Lenny exclaimed as they walked on, following green arrows that pointed out the tourist route. 'It's like a bloody tomb in here. It's like going down into the bowels of the earth. I'm claustrophobic, you know.'

'Shut up. You'll be all right.'

They went further down through narrow corridors of whitewashed brick walls and came out in the operations room, an enormous space with huge wall and table maps of the north and north-east Atlantic, black and red arrows marking convoy positions. Two long blackboards covered the far walls. On the blackboards was chalked information about aircraft state and convoy escorts, weather reports, what time the moon would rise and wane. Wrens had climbed the terrifying wall ladders to chalk up details of convoys and aircraft positions; the place was even supposed to be haunted by a Wren who had been killed in a fall from a ladder. After that they had worn safety harnesses. Old-fashioned red, white and black telephones with thick cords, little blue, yellow and red wooden ship shapes and dusty black headphones were ranged over the glassed-in table maps.

Finbar paused, breathing in the dusty atmosphere, imagining the sense of quiet urgency that must have prevailed, the sadness at having to remove torpedoed convoys from their map positions. They were the only two people in the place so far, except for the old men upstairs in the video room.

'Come on. Where to now?' Lenny nudged him roughly.

'Up here.' They went up a short flight of stairs to a row of glassed-in offices where people working could look down on what was happening in the operations room. Past the telephone and naval teleprinter station, down another corridor to a small room whose shiny red door stood half open for visitors to peer in.

'L37, Decoding,' Lenny read out. They went in and shut the

door, Finbar propping an old rusty-coloured office chair under the handle. Like the chairs in the telephone exchange and teleprinter station, it had a metal ashtray attached to the back. Imagine that in offices nowadays! He put the canvas bag on the dusty wooden table, shoving aside an ancient decoding machine and a pile of clipped papers with 'Post Office Engineering Instructions' printed on the front in big black letters.

'Don't!' he hissed as Lenny stuck a cigarette in his mouth and felt in his pockets for a lighter. 'Someone might smell it.'

'Down here?'

'They've got air ducts – otherwise they'd have all suffocated!'

'For Christ's sake!' He pointed to the chair. 'I've even got me own private ashtray.' He stuck the cigarette back in the red-and-gold packet. 'Right,' he said grimly. 'Let's have a look at this bloody thing.'

'The RPG 26 is an improved version of the RPG 22,' Finbar explained as Lenny lightly touched the cold army-green metal of the tube.

'You don't say!'

'It's got a telescopic launcher and a shaped-charge rocket with jack-knife fins that unfold after launch. It'll defeat five hundred millimetres of armour at two hundred and fifty metres, and it'll also defeat one metre of reinforced concrete. There's a scaled-up version of the RPG 26,' Finbar went on, 'that'll defeat all types of tanks. But this here'll do the job fine. And the scaled-up version's heavier, it weighs eight kilos. This is perfect for our needs.'

'Right.' Lenny nodded. 'That's okay. Now let's get out of this bloody tomb and you can show me the building.'

Finbar put the rocket launcher back in the bag and they went out of the decoding room and back up winding narrow corridors in to the weak winter daylight. He wondered if Shannon was awake yet, drinking a cup of coffee. He'd left her curled beneath the quilt, sleeping off their night of love. She musn't find out about this, he thought again. For her own protection.

The middle-aged woman at the cash desk glanced at him and blushed. More people arrived as they left, muffled in scarves, gloves, quilted coats and anoraks. It wasn't much warmer in the subterranean Second World War passages beneath their moon-booted feet. There would be few visitors today, even though it was Saturday.

They tramped down Water Street towards the river, heads lowered against whirling snowflakes, feet sliding on icy slush. Finbar stopped outside one of the tall elegant Victorian office buildings.

'This is it.'

'How will we get in here on the day? Without being seen?' Lenny looked at the arrow carved into the blackened stone wall. 'Christ!' he sniggered. 'Get a load of that! '*This way to air raid shelter*'. He grinned at Finbar and lit a *Kretek*. 'Hope it's still there – the Brits in this street might need it again next Wednesday.'

'Drop the cigarette. Put these on.' Finbar handed him a pair of latex gloves. 'We don't want fingerprints anywhere.' He unlocked the heavy glass and wrought-iron door and they went into the entrance and up a flight of red marble steps to a big hall. 'The third floor's not used,' he explained. 'I've got the keys to an empty office there.'

'How'd you get them?'

'Mind your own business.' He had a set of burglar's masterkeys, bought for a hundred quid in a pub in Upper Parliament Street, and had tried them on the building's locks a few days previously. They were worth the money.

There was a lift, but they took the back stairs to the third floor. There was nobody about on Saturday morning.

'That's what's good about these old buildings,' Finbar remarked, their footsteps echoing on the marble. 'Heaps of staircases all over the place.'

'Built for the Irish skivvies to run up and down!' Lenny panted. 'It's all stairs, stairs, stairs with you, you bastard!' he complained. 'I can never see you without having to go up and down millions of bloody stairs.' He paused, coughing and clinging to the wrought iron balustrade.

'You should thank me. You won't get a heart attack when you're forty.'

They came to the third floor and Finbar unlocked a door with a dull brass plaque reading: '*Star & Packard, Shipping Merchants*'. 'Wooden floors up here,' he commented. 'Not so grand. They're supposed to start renovating this floor and the ones above, but that won't happen for another few months.'

The empty rooms had yellowed walls with chipped and cracked plaster, dirty sash windows and ancient plug sockets and light fittings. There was an alcove with a granite sink and wooden draining board, the wood bleached by years of wet cups and plates. They went to the windows and looked down into Water Street.

'I'll take him from this corner window,' Finbar said. 'His car with the police escort will turn down here at about ten-to-three in the afternoon. We'll be here from seven a.m., we want to get settled before the office workers turn up. After it's done they'll be too busy looking for body parts to work out where the missile came from. And they'll be caught on the hop, they'll have expected any trouble at the Maritime Museum, not here. We pack up the launcher, get out via the back stairs, nice and calm. If anyone's coming we use the fire escape. I'll dump this.' He pointed to the bag. 'There'll be no trace. We've worn gloves the whole time. And that's it.' He stared at Lenny, his face pale in the wintry light. 'No more favours.'

Lenny smiled and nodded. 'No more favours, Finbar. You'll be a free man. Now let's get out of here, I need coffee and a Scotch. And another fag.'

'Better make it six on Wednesday morning.' Finbar thought for a second. 'We don't want to be bumping into some hotshot lawyer or accountant who turns up to work at the crack of dawn.'

'Six!' Lenny groaned.

'Six. And make sure this place is clean before we leave. Don't touch anything you don't have to. Wait!' he said sharply, as Lenny started to pull off the gloves. 'Leave them on until we're out of here. We'll go out the back way.'

They went down to the first floor, climbed on to the old rickety fire escape and descended to a courtyard full of damp cardboard boxes, bins and shiny black garbage bags. Lenny pulled off the gloves and stuffed them in his pocket. He lit a cigarette and took a swinging kick at a ginger cat who came miaowing up to them. They unbolted the courtyard door, went down a narrow alley and came out into Water Street.

'What are you doing for the rest of the day?' Lenny asked.

Finbar shrugged. 'Go home and get some more sleep. Watch the snooker. Go to the club tonight, have a few drinks.' He thought of Shannon. 'I'll see you Wednesday,' he said briefly. 'Six sharp. Corner of Fenwick Street.'

Lenny nodded. He turned and walked off to catch a bus to Sefton Park. Finbar drove to Clarence Dock, checking that he wasn't being tailed, and stowed the rocket launcher in the French prisoner's dungeon beneath the clock tower. The heroine, Ecstasy and suitcase of cash were gone, the drugs sold, the money deposited by Nick in the Isle of Man bank account. Torchlight flashed on the Frenchman's skull. He drove back to the apartment. Seagulls screamed over the icy grey Mersey. A ferry boat was out, no one standing on deck to admire the view. The passengers would be huddled below, in the warmth of the saloon.

He didn't think about what would happen if things went wrong. That meant they would go wrong. Murphy's Law. After Wednesday he'd be free. Free to live the rest of his life with Shannon. He thought of the two children they wanted. Would they be girls, boys? One of each? Which parent would they resemble? Roiseann had had Majella's blue eyes. The pain returned, strong as ever. Love for his little daughter and agony at her death, her brutal senseless murder, would never go. He'd feel that loss forever. No matter what happened on Wednesday.

The apartment was beautifully warm after the subterranean passages in Derby House, the icy grey streets and unheated office building. There was a smell of freshly brewed coffee. He poured himself a cup, added a scant teaspoon of sugar and took it into his bedroom. Shannon lay in bed drinking coffee and watching an old black-and-white film on television. Bits of candlewax were stuck to the parquet floor and the jasmine perfume from the candles lingered.

'Hi!' She smiled at him as he kissed her. 'Everything all right at the office, *dear*?'

'Fine.' He sat on the bed and sipped the coffee. 'God, that tastes good!' he breathed. 'It's snowing out, bloody freezing.' He cradled the cup in his hands, enjoying its warmth. 'Must be nine or ten below zero. I wouldn't be surprised if the Mersey freezes over.' He looked at the television. 'What's this?'

'Oh, some old war film about the Battle of the Atlantic. I'm not really watching it.' She finished her coffee and he took the cup and put it on the bedside table. 'That wartime underground headquarters is just up the road from here, isn't it?' she said. 'The Western Approaches. I walk past it nearly every day but I've never been in there. Have you?'

'No,' he said, staring at the television screen. 'No, I've never been there.' He drank the rest of his coffee. 'Is there anything in particular that you'd like to do this weekend?' he asked.

She knelt up in bed, naked, and put her arms around him. 'Only what we usually like to do,' she said teasingly, kissing him. 'I have, however, got a resignation letter to write at some point. I hope my computer and printer have survived the journey from West Derby.'

'They should have. You locked the hard disk?'

'Of course.'

'Use mine if yours doesn't work,' he said. 'But I'm sure it'll be all right.'

'Let's go out shopping first,' she said. 'Get lots of lovely food and wine.'

'Yes.' He stroked her smooth bare back. 'We'll go out to dinner tonight. Go to a club afterwards.'

'Not your club. You won't be able to relax and enjoy yourself. Neither will I.'

'Not my club.' His hand slid down over her buttocks. 'By the way, I've got to go to Dublin again,' he said. 'On Tuesday morning. I'll be back Friday afternoon. It's just business, I swear,' he said, looking into her violet eyes. Their colour was intensified by the grey winter light. 'Legit business. You can come with me if you like.' He knew she wouldn't.

'No,' she sighed. 'I'd love to see Dublin some time, but I can't go yet. I've got to go to work, have more discussions with Mi-Hae. Sort Gavin out. Oh!' She wriggled out of his arms and jumped off the bed. 'Let me show you what I'll wear tonight.' She laughed. 'I'll model it for you.'

'I can't wait.' He pulled off his slate-blue sweater and began to unfasten his jeans. She ran out of the room and came back a few minutes later wearing a sleeveless stretch velvet tiger skin dress, the hemline trimmed with delicate black lace.

'What do you think?' she giggled, striking a pose. 'It's a bit tarty, but it's good fun for a club.'

'Good fun? It's lethal. Jesus Christ!' He leaned back in bed laughing. 'You don't show any mercy, do you?'

'You don't deserve mercy.' Shannon gazed at him. 'You're leaving me for four days next week. Four days and three long, *long* nights.'

'Come here.' He held out his arms and she walked slowly to the bed, lifting the black lace hemline. She stopped, her golden fuzz on a level with his face. He pressed his lips to it, grabbed her and pulled her down on the bed.

'Don't worry, madam,' he said as he slid between her legs. 'Trust me, I'm a doctor. This won't hurt a bit.'

She laughed and lay back, closing her eyes. His tongue probed her, his hands stroked the insides of her thighs. She arched her back and pulled the dress up over her breasts.

'I love you!' she gasped.

Lenny sat at the iced-up living-room window of the flat, looking out over the snowy expanse of Sefton Park. Bare black branches brushed the low grey sky. Between the trees a girl in a scarlet coat threw sticks for a barking terrier. The boys had gone out for a drink. They weren't pleased at the last-minute change of plan. It was no fun making bombs that would not be exploded to devastating effect. They'd fly back to Dublin tonight, weather permitting. He hoped the hit would go off all right. He didn't trust Finbar. But he'd have the last laugh. Lenny drank his Scotch and stared at the gun in his lap. The television was on, the sound turned down. He was waiting for the snooker. He raised the gun and levelled it, imagining bullets slamming into the body of the girl in the scarlet coat. He longed to shoot the yapping little bastard of a terrier. He grinned. If Finbar thought he could walk away after this he was making a mistake. A big mistake.

'Just coffee, please.' Shannon handed the menu card back to the waiter. 'And a Cointreau with crushed ice.'

'What's wrong with you?' Finbar smiled and took her hand. The diamond and sapphire ring glittered on her finger. 'It's not like you to say no to a luscious creamy chocolate dessert, or a mountain of ice cream, strawberries and meringue.'

'I'm stuffed after that lobster.' She patted her stomach. 'Feel a bit queasy, actually. The Cointreau will help me feel less full.' She looked round the candlelit restaurant. A middle-aged man at a nearby table smiled and glanced away as she caught his gaze.

'We don't have to go to a club,' Finbar said. He lifted her hand and kissed it. 'We can just go home after we've had the coffee.'

'No. I feel like going to a club,' she said. 'Honestly, I feel like dancing.'

'You look beautiful,' he said. 'You look fantastic in that dress. You look fantastic in anything. In nothing.' His grip on her hand tightened. 'Are you sure you want to go to a club?'

'I'm sure!' she laughed. 'I really, really want to!'

The club was small, dark and very hot, smelling of perfume, cigarette smoke, sweaty bodies and excitement. Shannon fainted on the dance floor.

Chapter Twenty-Six

The Linnell Air Cargo plane from Dublin landed at Speke airport at five on Wednesday morning, red and yellow lights flashing through the icy mist as it taxied towards the hangar. Finbar jumped out, said goodbye to the pilot and headed for his Maserati, parked anonymously in the car park instead of in its usual place close by. The plane had nearly had to be diverted to Newcastle because of snow and fog. He'd fly back to Dublin later that afternoon, lie low for a couple of days and return to Liverpool on Friday. He was booked in at the Shelbourne. No one had seen him sneak out to catch the green airport bus from O'Connell Street, his face muffled in a scarf. He had a false passport in the name of James McCracken.

He drove along deserted, misty roads towards the city centre and parked the Maserati in the underground car park near St George's Hall. The car park where he'd shot Dean. He took the canvas bag containing the rocket launcher from the boot, and a carrier bag of crisps, cheese-and-ham sandwiches, chocolate biscuits and a flask of black coffee, in preparation for the hours of waiting that lay ahead.

Finbar walked all the way to Water Street. The cold was unbelievable. He wore his overcoat, scarf, two T-shirts, two heavy wool sweaters, boots and leather gloves, but the freezing mist seemed to cut right through them. He walked along, gasping and shivering. Probably nerves, he reflected. Lenny was standing on the corner of Water Street and Fenwick Street, blowing out clouds of carbon dioxide along with smoke from his last *Kretek* for at least ten hours. He wore heavy boots and a dirty sheepskin coat over the combat jacket.

'Good morning!'

'Let's go,' said Finbar. 'Are you ready?'

'Let me finish the bloody cigarette, all right?'' He sucked sweet clove smoke deep into his lungs, as though it were pure mountain air. 'Christ knows when I'll get the next one!'

'About four o' clock, if everything goes according to plan. Which it will.'

Lenny said nothing. He looked down Water Street towards the river. The foghorn blared. Lights were on in the office buildings; only the ground and first two floors of their building were lit. A black cab turned out of a side street and headed for the docks. Lenny threw the glowing stub onto the snowy pavement.

'Okay.' They walked to the building, glancing around as they went, and paused outside to put on latex gloves.

'I hate these things!' Lenny complained. 'They make my hands itch. My wee sister had to give up nursing because she got allergic to them. Why don't we go in the back way?' he asked as Finbar fiddled with the lock.

'It's full of garbage bags and cats to fall over in the dark,' he replied. 'Not to mention the caretaker. And the door to the alley's bolted on the inside, remember? We can get out that way, but we can't get in.'

He opened the door, locked it behind him and they went quietly through the hall and up the back stairs to the third floor. Streetlight slanted across the walls and ceiling of the room. The cold took their breath away.

'Should have brought a blanket or sleeping bag,' Lenny muttered, shivering and stamping his feet. 'We'll be frozen solid by three o clock.'

'Don't stamp!' Finbar said sharply. 'The heating should come on downstairs soon.' He walked to the window, lifted the sash and peered out into the street. 'The heat'll rise, warm us up a bit. We'll be all right.'

He unpacked the rocket launcher, assembled it and laid it on the floor beneath the corner window. Shannon would be asleep, he thought, cosy beneath the quilt in the warm silent apartment by the river, just ten minutes' walk away. Did she dream about him? He missed her, longed to be with her. She'd seemed better since Saturday night, but he was still worried. She needed rest, proper rest, to get away from everything. She'd been through so much. He'd take her on holiday soon, to a Caribbean resort with their own private beach, lie by the sea all day. Eat, drink, sleep, swim, talk. Make love. He sat on the dusty floor, his back to the wall, and took out the flask of coffee. Lenny settled down opposite him.

'Want some coffee?' he asked. Lenny shook his head. He reached inside his coat and took out a bottle of Scotch.

'This is my breakfast,' he said. He swigged and held out the bottle to Finbar.

'No, thanks.' He poured himself a cup of coffee and sipped it, breathing the steam, savouring its warmth and smell.

'So!' He sat back, cradling the cup in his gloved hands. 'Now we wait.'

He sighed. He wished he could go home, get into bed with Shannon and forget the whole thing.

'Not in?' Shannon echoed, staring at Anita.

'He's not in *yet*. That's what I was going to say if you'd let me finish.'

'It's Wednesday, I expected him on Monday morning.' Her resignation letter lay gathering dust on Gavin's desk. 'What the hell is going on?'

'Well, I'm the last person to know, aren't I?' Anita flushed and patted her brassy blonde sausage curls. 'I'm just the receptionist everyone yells at. You in particular! He said he'd be in this afternoon,' she said crossly. 'That's the best I can do for you. I'm not psychic. I only know what people tell me.'

'Not even that sometimes.' Shannon marched down the corridor to her office and Anita exchanged an exasperated glance with Jenny Fong before picking up the ringing phone.

'Good morning, Steele and Monckton, how may I help you?' Gavin went mental if she said 'can' instead of 'may'. 'Oh, God!' she mouthed, cupping her hand over the receiver. 'It's her husband – or ex-husband-to-be. She'll have my guts for garters if I put him through. But if I don't he'll just keep calling.'

'Put him through.' Jenny smiled maliciously. 'Make her day. It's not your problem.'

'You're right.' Anita pressed another button and Shannon picked up the phone.

'Yes?'

'Call for you!' Anita giggled and slammed the phone down. 'As if it's not bad enough trying to get to work in this arctic weather without having to put up with her as well!' she complained. 'What the hell's wrong with her? She's a real bitch lately. She used to be so nice.'

'It's called marriage. Observe and learn.' Jenny walked into her office. Shannon could get stuffed, she thought. She'd been impossible lately. Hadn't apologized for last Thursday's insults. A broken marriage and dysfunctional in-laws – were there any other kind?– didn't give her the right to treat everybody like dirt.

'Shannon? It's Rob.'

She closed her eyes. 'What do you want?' she asked tersely. She'd slept well, despite missing Finbar, but still felt exhausted. Maybe he was right and she did need iron tablets or something. She'd phone her GP, make an appointment for the following week.

'I'm just calling to let you know that I've told my solicitor I'll accept your terms,' he said. 'I won't contest the divorce. It'll be a clean break, the way you want.'

'Do you mean that?' she asked sharply.

'I mean it. He'll tell your solicitor today. You'll probably get a phone call this afternoon.'

'Thank you,' she said simply. 'Thanks, Rob. I really think this is the best way.'

'I won't bother you again unless there are any further points that need to be clarified. What happens now?' he asked hesitantly. 'Do we just wait until it comes through?'

'Yes, more or less. Might take a few months.'

'Right. Shannon?'

'Yes?'

'I'm sorry,' he muttered. 'I'm sorry I hurt you. Sorry for everything.'

'I'm sorry too,' she said wearily. Memories of their wedding day flashed into her mind and she felt immense sadness. They'd been so happy, so full of hope and confidence. And it had ended like this! Her eyes filled with tears.

'Good luck for the future,' he said. 'Maybe . . . I hope we can be friends one day.'

'I hope so too.'

'Goodbye, Shannon.'

'Goodbye,' she whispered.

He hung up and she replaced the receiver and leaned her head on the desk. 'Please let me get through this!' she whispered. 'Let me be happy again.'

'Shannon–' Jenny burst into the room and stopped, embarrassed. 'Sorry!'

'What is it?' She reached for a tissue and dabbed her eyes.

'A Ms Kam phoned while you were talking to – to Rob. She wants you to call her back.'

'Right. Thanks.' She glanced at her watch. She had ten minutes before she had to leave for court. Jenny lingered, her anger and resentment fading.

'Are you okay?' she asked shyly. 'Can I do anything for you?'

'No.' Shannon smiled and stood up. 'Thanks. Oh! Is there any coffee?'

'I'll get it.' Jenny ran out and came back a minute later. 'You've still got a few minutes,' she said, placing the cup in front of Shannon.

'Thanks. Jenny, I'm so sorry for the way I spoke to you last Thursday,' she said. 'I was in a state about something, but it was inexcusable.'

Jenny looked at the blue carpet. 'Those police officers were here. And I know Rob's been calling nearly every day, hassling you. You've had a lot to put up with.'

'That doesn't give me the right to speak to you the way I did.' Shannon paused, looking down at the steaming coffee. 'We used to be friends.'

'We will be again,' Jenny said briskly. 'If you behave yourself! Now drink the coffee, make your call and we'll get going.'

'Thanks, Jenny,' she said gratefully. Alone, she sipped her coffee and dialled Mi-Hae Kam's number.

'Are you still alive?' Mi-Hae laughed. 'And Gavin? How did it go?'

'You won't believe it, but the bastard hasn't turned up yet. If I didn't know better I'd think he was doing it deliberately. The receptionist says he'll be in this afternoon.'

'Want to have lunch? Or leave it until tomorrow?'

No. Lunch today will be fine. You can help psych me up – again!'

'I'll meet you outside the Town Hall at twelve-thirty. You're not going to turn out to cheer our very important visitor later this afternoon then?'

'What visitor?'

'Rupert Eastbrook, the Defence Secretary. He's at Salmesbury this morning having a look at military aircraft, and he'll be at the Maritime Museum this afternoon.'

'Sounds thrilling. Cheer that arrogant fat bastard?' Shannon laughed. 'You must be joking! I completely forgot about him. Shows how *au fait* I am with what's going on in Liverpool these days.'

'I'll see you later,' Mi-Hae said. 'And as regards Gavin, just keep the image of a mini tampon fixed firmly in your brain.'

'I'll certainly do that.' She hung up, gulped her coffee and grabbed her coat and briefcase. She would buy flowers or wine after lunch, a peace offering for Jenny and Anita. Two more days and nights without Finbar! She decided to cook a special dinner for when he got back from Dublin on Friday. He'd done all the cooking up to now, although usually they ate out. She wanted to surprise him. She'd never been to Dublin. Finbar didn't seem to like it much, she thought, as she and Jenny headed for the lift. Painful memories. She herself didn't want to go on living in the house in Eaton Road after what had happened there. Not to mention what *could* have happened!

She did not get back to the office until after two-thirty. Anita and Jenny were delighted with their 'sorry' cards and beribboned bottles of Australian Chardonnay.

'Gavin's back,' Anita warned, rolling her kohl-lined eyes. 'He's in a right mood! He wants to see you.' She snapped her fingers. *'Now!'*

'He must have read my resignation letter. At last.'

'Resignation?' They gaped at her.

'He was horrible to me when I had my crisis.' Shannon grimaced. 'And there's no sign of any partnership, he's just stringing me along. Not that I'd want to go into partnership with him anyway. I've had enough, his attitude stinks. I'm going to join up with Mi-Hae Kam,' she said. 'She wants a partner, associate, whatever.'

'I know her,' Jenny said. 'She's good.' She smiled at Shannon. 'You can headhunt us. You're not the only one who's had enough of Spotted Dick in there.'

'I'll bear it in mind.' She laughed. 'It's crazy, but I feel as if one of the nuns at school just caught me in the toilets with a condom. If I'm not out in five minutes, come and rescue me.'

She knocked at Gavin's door and walked in. He stood by the window, her brief, perfectly typed resignation letter clenched in his hand. Today's bow tie was black with red spots, matching his flushed face.

'Hello!' she said brightly. 'Been to London to see the Queen?'

He looked at her furiously and shook the letter. 'What the bloody hell is this?' he shouted.

'Wake up, Lenny!' Finbar glanced at his watch. 'Lenny, come on, wake up. Move your arse!' He nudged him with his foot. 'It's quarter to three.' He went to the window and looked down into the street. It was snowing again, big soft floaty flakes.

'I can't move my arse. It's bloody numb.' Lenny groaned and stretched on the dusty floorboards. His dark shiny hair was covered with yellowed bits of wall and ceiling plaster. He got up slowly, brushing dust off his jeans and sheepskin coat, and bent to pick up the half full bottle of Scotch. Finbar checked again that the rocket launcher was in firing order. His palms were sweaty despite the cold, and his stomach felt like an iron ball inside him. He could have done with a slug of Lenny's Scotch, but alcohol would have to wait until the job was done. Lenny was pacing now, rubbing his stiff limbs, swigging more whisky. Getting twitchy.

'You all right?' Finbar looked at him and he averted his eyes.

'I could do with a pee.'

'Not long now.' He raised the stiff sash window. Flakes of green paint came off on his gloves and snowflakes whirled in.

'What if the bastard doesn't turn up?' Lenny asked suddenly. 'Look at the state of the weather. They might cancel it.'

'They won't. He'll turn up,' Finbar said flatly. He couldn't be that lucky. He turned back to the window, wishing again he could go home and forget the whole thing. Go back to Dublin, check out of the Shelbourne, tell Shannon his business had finished sooner than expected. It was incredible that he'd reached this point in his existence, waiting in this freezing room to kill a senior member of the British government. How had it happened? The whole thing was bizarre.

Down below policemen on motorbikes roared into the street and began to set up red-and-white striped cordons, marshalling curious people behind them.

'He's coming,' said Finbar. Lenny joined him at the window and looked out.

'Yes!' He put up a hand and smoothed his ponytail, dark eyes gleaming with excitement. 'Yes!' He took a last swig of Scotch and screwed the cap back on the bottle.

Minutes passed. Groups of people gathered behind the police cordons, most of them wondering what was going on. At twenty-past three Finbar lifted the rocket launcher and settled it on his right shoulder, levelling it out of the corner window down at the street. Roiseann's baby face flashed before his eyes. Majella cuddled her, laughing at him, blonde hair streaming in the wind. He flexed his finger and peered through the sight. Snow was falling steadily now. The city would be covered.

'He's here!' Lenny shouted. 'The bastard's here!'

Motorbikes and two cars swept into the street, headlights blazing. Finbar steadied the weapon, got the second car in his sights. Suddenly he lowered it, stooped and laid it on the floor.

'I'm not doing it,' he said. Roiseann wouldn't want him killing anyone else. Shannon definitely would not. 'I'm not bloody doing it,' he said quietly. He felt perfectly calm.

'*Fuck* you!' Lenny screamed at him, enraged. He brought up his hand and the blow from the gun butt knocked Finbar sideways. Another blow followed. He fell, unconscious, sprawled on the dirty floorboards.

Lenny picked up the rocket launcher, steadied it on his shoulder and got the second car in his sights. He took a deep breath and pulled the trigger. There was a flash and a huge bang as the missile exploded, scattering glass, twisted metal and the body parts of the Defence Secretary and his entourage over the street. A ball of flame and black smoke billowed into the air. The buildings shook. Office windows were blown out. People screamed, shouted and dashed for cover or stared in shocked disbelief.

Finbar stirred, opened his eyes, sat up. It was too late! Lenny laughed and dropped the rocket launcher.

'I knew you'd bottle out, you bastard!' His gun was levelled at Finbar's heart. 'I knew it! I warned them but they wouldn't listen.'

He was dazed and his ears were ringing from the blast. His head hurt where the gun butt had struck. Sirens sounded below.

'What the hell are you doing?' he asked, although he knew.

'You're going to die,' Lenny said. 'Sorry you can't go out in a blaze of glory, but that's your fault. You didn't think you could just walk away, did you? And before I kill you I've something to tell you. The icing on the cake, as they say. Kneel!' he ordered.

'For Christ's sake . . .'

'I said, kneel!' screamed Lenny. 'Kneel, you bastard! Keep your hands up!' He stepped back and levelled the gun, a 44 Magnum, at Finbar's head, pointing it between his green eyes. His own hands trembled slightly though he was smiling as he stared at the kneeling man.

'It wasn't the Brits shot your wife and the wee girl. It was us.'

'*What*?' gasped Finbar. Sirens rang in his ears and acrid smoke drifted into the room, the choking fumes making him cough.

'It wasn't the Brits,' Lenny yelled. And started to laugh, enjoying the sight of Finbar's dazed mystified expression changing to shock. And understanding. Terrible understanding.

'But why?' He couldn't take it in. '*Why*? I don't–' He put his hands to his aching head. His fingers were wet with blood.

'She saw something she shouldn't have seen on her way to West Belfast. Keep your hands up!' he screamed. 'Not too clever, eh? She saw our arms dump, ran straight by as we were unloading mortars. We should have done it at night but we were in a hurry. And the Brits have their infra-red anyway. They were watching us – tried to warn her. One of them fired at us so we fired back. She got hit. In the shoulder, it wouldn't have killed her. But she'd seen too much. And we couldn't leave the wee girl sitting strapped in her baby seat, could we? Leave her to grow up, learn to talk? It was great propaganda – innocent mother and baby brutally slaughtered by Private Joe Bastard! It was their word against ours. No one believed their official fucking enquiry. You included.'

'Roiseann!' he gasped. 'Majella!' Tears spilled from his eyes, dripped on to the cold green metal tube.

'Shame to lose your family like that, Finbar.' Lenny laughed again, loving the pain, the anguish he'd created. 'But it was all in a good cause. You're not a great one for a cause, are you? You thought it was all a big bloody joke,' he went on. 'But the joke's on you now, eh? D'you want to say a swift Hail Mary? Sorry there's no priest.'

'Was it quick?' Finbar sobbed. 'Did they suffer?' The terror, the pain, the helplessness they must have felt! Why hadn't he gone with them? Why?

'I don't know.' Lenny glanced out of the window then stepped back and levelled the gun again. 'You'll be dead in a minute, you can ask them. Hey!' He grinned. 'Will I give your wee girlfriend a memorial shag?' he taunted. 'Oh, yeah!' he said, as further shock registered on Finbar's pale face. 'I've seen the pair of you coming out of your fancy apartment. No wonder you didn't want me there anymore. You were too busy snogging her to notice me. I know where she works, too. A lawyer, eh? Done well for yourself. Your wee Majella was a bit bimboid, wasn't she? A nice little shag, but not really your type. You'd have got bored with her eventually. This one's got class and brains as well as tits. Beg!' he commanded. 'Beg me for your life.'

'Go fuck yourself!' Finbar hissed, glaring up at him through his tears, his chest heaving. 'You pathetic little tosser!'

'I take it that means you won't beg?'

'Just do it!' Finbar shouted. 'Do it!' Warm tears poured down his face. He wanted to die. Wanted oblivion, no more pain. But Shannon! He couldn't let this psychopath hurt her. Still Lenny dithered. The Scotch was having its effect.

'I wish I could let you live,' he panted. 'You'd be more tortured that way. But knowing what you know now . . .'

Finbar threw himself flat and lunged for Lenny's ankles, bringing him down. The gun went off and the bullet slammed into the wall. Lenny let go of the gun and it flew out of his hand and skidded against the dusty skirting board. He screamed in agony as Finbar grabbed his ponytail, twisted it and smashed his head against the floor several times. Blood poured from his nose and mouth, staining the wooden boards. He coughed and choked.

'Shouldn't drink on the job, Lenny.' Finbar turned him over and punched him around the head before staggering to his feet and kicking him. 'Slows the reflexes.' He picked up the gun and stood over the fallen man, tears streaming from his eyes.

'Don't!' Lenny moaned. He rolled over and wiped a hand across his bloodied face. 'Don't, Finbar! Please!'

'You're right, Lenny,' he said softly. 'I'm not a great one for a cause. Why should I get all excited because of what a few silly little bastards did or didn't do hundreds of years ago? What does it matter? It's *now* that matters! I'm going to make you a martyr because I know you'll like that. You'll be buried with full military honours and a line of prats in black balaclavas'll give you a gun salute. You'll be the big man, the hero, you'll have died for the cause. That's what all this crap is about, isn't it?'

He wedged a foot beneath Lenny's back, rolled him over and shot him twice in the back of the neck. Blood pooled over the floor. Lenny twitched and lay still, eyes staring, salivating, bloodied mouth forming his last plea. Finbar put the rocket launcher and gun in the canvas bag, picked up the plastic carrier bag with the flask, sandwiches and empty crisp packets and walked out of the room. He took a last look behind him. The Provos hadn't ordered his death. That was a private initiative of Lenny's. He was safe. Sirens screamed through the open window as he ran down the back stairs and climbed out on to the fire escape. The courtyard was quiet, deserted.

He looked as though he'd just been to work. Except that he was crying and shaking, torn with grief and shock. The ginger cat was miaowing in the alley. Finbar stooped, stroked its chin until it purred, and fed it the remains of his cheese-and-ham sandwich.

Chapter Twenty-Seven

'I'm going to resign, Gavin,' said Shannon, for what seemed like the millionth time. 'That's final. I won't change my mind. I'm not happy with the way I'm treated here and haven't been for some time. You must realize that. Only a few weeks ago you were ready to kick me out on the basis of one slanderous phone call from someone you'd never even met. How do you expect me to feel about that? I thought you'd be glad to be rid of me – I don't understand why you're so upset now.' Little bastard, she thought. It was snowing again, big flakes drifting down past the windows.

'I insist you work out your notice,' he said furiously. 'Every bloody day of it. There's no question of letting you go early.' She wore a purple leather trouser suit instead of her usual black clothes; he took this as a gesture of defiance. Her blonde hair floated and curled around her shoulders and her violet blue eyes stared contemptuously at him. 'How dare you do this!' he shouted.

'Who the hell do you think you are, Gavin?' Her lips curved into a smile. 'I'll stay another week, tops. Then I need a little holiday before I start my new job.'

'New job? And where's that going to be?' he demanded. 'Woollies, if I had any say in the matter!'

'Fortunately you haven't. If you give me a hard time about working my month's notice, I'll make your life as miserable as you've helped make mine these past months,' said Shannon, ignoring the question.

'Don't you try to blackmail me!' Gavin shook his fist at her. 'You have a duty of care to your clients.'

'I wasn't talking about the clients,' she said coolly. 'I don't believe your attitude! And you can drop that tone of voice right now or I walk out immediately. How would you like that?'

He was silent, gazing out at the snowflakes. 'Listen, Shannon.' He turned back to her and smiled the insincere smile she hated.

'One week, Gavin,' she said firmly. 'Then I'm out of here. I've had it with you and the disappointed virgin and cro-magnon man in there. Oh, and don't worry, I don't expect a farewell party. You can keep your dry roasted peanuts and pissy sherry to yourself.' She laughed. 'I wouldn't mind that cute little crystal teddy bear as a goodbye present though. It's not really you, is it? Much too . . .'

She gasped and spun round as an enormous bang suddenly shook the windows and reverberated across Exchange Flags. A cloud of black smoke rose above the Town Hall. In the distance sirens began to wail. The floor shook with the after effects of the explosion.

'What the hell was that?' Shannon rushed to the window and yanked the handle to open it, Gavin close behind her. 'It sounded like a bomb.'

'The bloody IRA,' he said. 'I bet it's them. The Defence Secretary, Rupert Eastbrook, is in Liverpool today.' He glanced at his watch. 'He must be here right now actually,' he said slowly. 'He's due at the Maritime Museum . . .'

'My God!' Shannon exclaimed, staring at him in horror. 'A bomb?' she cried. 'There might be people hurt. It came from nearby.' She looked out of the window again. 'Round the corner, in fact.' Finbar! Was he safe?

'Where are you going?' he shouted as she ran to the door and flung it open. 'We've got things to discuss. Don't go out there! Are you mad?'

She dashed into the corridor and collided with Jenny and Anita. Richard and Priscilla were in court.

'Did you hear that?' Jenny looked shocked.

'Of course I bloody heard it!' Shannon ran into her office and grabbed her coat and bag. They followed, confused and afraid.

'D'you think it's a bomb?' Anita asked, twisting her hands with their long nails painted bright pink.

'Yes, Anita. I think it's a bomb!'

Shannon rushed down the corridor, pulling on her coat, and was through the glass doors and going down in the lift when she remembered Finbar was in Dublin. She gasped with relief and closed her eyes for a second. Of course he was all right. He wasn't out there, caught in the explosion, maybe lying dazed and bloodied on some pavement. But other people might be.

She came out into Exchange Flags and stopped uncertainly, suddenly afraid. Snowflakes stuck to her hair and melted on her tongue. She bent her head and hurried across the Flags, trying not to slip on the icy stones. People were walking or running in the direction of Water Street, calling to one another as they went. She stopped and sniffed the air. There was a strong smell of burning rubber. Car tyres? She started to walk again, faster. Round the corner, past Derby House, turn right into Water Street. She stopped again, hand clapped to her mouth.

Two heaps of blackened twisted metal were cordoned off. Policemen on foot and on motorbikes shouted at everyone to move back, move away. People stood around or sat on the edge of the pavements, shocked and dazed, some of them bleeding after being cut by flying glass or metal. There were screams, cries and angry shouts. Glass covered the blackened road and pavements. Two ambulances turned into the street, blue lights flashing. Paramedics jumped out and began to attend to the wounded.

A fat bearded man in a green padded jacket stared at the scene of chaos, his face contorted. Shannon saw blood on the road. Fingers. A severed leg in shredded pinstripe trouser, horribly vulnerable. She gasped and turned away, feeling sick. How many were dead? she wondered.

'Move back, please, love!' A passing policeman in boots and crash helmet shepherded her away, holding on to her arm.

'What's happened?' she asked. 'Was it a bomb?'

'Probably. Can't say for sure, love.' He let go of her arm and walked on. 'Move back, please.' He raised his arms. 'Come on, move back! Move away from the area now, *please*. There may be other devices.'

'It's like the bloody Blitz!' A shocked old woman stared wildly around her. She wore a beige coat and carried a brown leather shopping bag. 'It's the May Blitz in January!' She started to laugh.

'Come on, Mum. You'll be all right.' Her middle-aged daughter took her arm. 'We'll go home and get a cup of tea. Come on. They'll stop the buses if this snow gets any worse.'

Shannon couldn't see any children. Thank goodness! She stared at the horrible chaotic scene for another minute then turned and headed back to Exchange Flags, shivering with cold and fright. How could human beings do that to one another? For what twisted 'reasons'? People were dead, mutilated, blown to bits. And for what? Was this the IRA's work? She felt sick, exhausted and frozen. Wanted only to go back to the apartment, drink a cup of hot tea and rest. Enjoy the warm silent space, look out at the river. She would go home at five-thirty, that was for sure. No more working all hours, at least not for the next few weeks. They might evacuate the area soon anyway. She glanced back unwillingly, to make sure there was nothing she could do, no one she could help.

She gasped and her body went rigid with shock. Finbar was walking up the street in her direction. He hadn't seen her. He pushed his way through dazed and curious groups of spectators, staring straight ahead of him as if at some horrific apparition. Snowflakes stuck to his hair and shoulders, and tears glittered on his pale cheeks. Her mouth formed words that wouldn't come out, like in a bad dream. She began to walk then run towards him. He caught sight of her, his eyes focused and he stopped.

'What are you doing here?' she shouted above the sirens. 'Why are you here? Did something happen to make you come back earlier? Why didn't you tell me?' She grabbed his arm. 'Are you hurt?'

The pure white snow turned his eyes to a brilliant emerald green, and it was so cold she thought his tears would freeze if he didn't wipe them away. He stared down at her.

'The bastards killed Roiseann and Majella,' he said, voice cracking. 'Murdered them! Murdered my baby girl. She was nine months old. I loved her. I love her!' He bowed his head, sobbing. 'I love her!'

'I know you do.' Tears came to Shannon's eyes. 'But what's

happened?' she asked. 'Why are you saying this now?' A feeling of foreboding swept over her. Something terrible was going to happen, she didn't know what. 'British soldiers killed them,' she said, torn with pity for him, for the people around her. 'It was a horrible tragedy. What are you doing here?' she asked again.

'It wasn't the Brits!' he burst out. He glanced round then looked at her again. 'Help me!' he sobbed. 'Help me, Shannon. I can't go on anymore.'

'What do you *mean*?' she asked desperately. 'Of course I'll help you, but you've got to tell me–'

'You all right, mate?' A policeman stopped and looked at Finbar. 'It's the shock,' he said. 'You'll be okay.' He patted him on the shoulder. 'Go home, get warm, get yourself a cup of tea. Talk to someone.' He moved on. 'Get back, please, everyone,' he shouted. 'Now!'

'Help me, Shannon!' Finbar sobbed, and put his arm around her. 'I love you. Please help me!'

She pulled away, staring at him in shock. 'You did this, didn't you?' She looked wildly around. 'You never went to Dublin. You lied to me. You planned this. You must have planned it for weeks – months! Before we met. Didn't you?' she screamed.

'I didn't kill him, I swear. I didn't do it. Shannon–' He stretched out a hand. 'Come home with me now. Let's go home. I'll tell you everything.'

'I won't go anywhere with you!' She stepped back. 'Don't you touch me! Leave me alone. I never learn, do I?' she shouted. 'I never fucking learn!'

'Shannon!' he cried. 'Don't go!'

She turned and ran back towards Exchange Flags, snowflakes stinging her face, blinding her. She collided with a group of men.

'Get out of my way!' She pushed and hit out at them. 'Move!'

They looked stunned with surprise but did as she said, silently parting to let her through.

'Shannon! Shannon!' Finbar shouted despairingly. 'Come back. Please!' He slipped on a patch of ice and fell, twisting his ankle. Pain stabbed through him. He watched helplessly as she ran across the Flags and under the arch, blonde hair flying.

She ran to the side street where the Nissan was parked and got in, scrubbing furiously at the frosted windscreen.

'Start!' she yelled at the frozen engine, beating the steering wheel. 'Come on, start!' She began to cry.

The engine whined, coughed and started. She reversed out of the parking space and accelerated down the road. She had no idea where she was going. Except that it wouldn't be the Albert Dock. Where *could* she go? She felt alone, overwhelmed with misery and disappointment. Betrayed. Finbar loved her and she loved him, but he'd lied to her, done this terrible thing. Why? How could they go on? Live together, get married, have children, lead a normal life? It was impossible. She had been drugged by sex, desire, caught in the classic trap that everyone thought they were much too clever to fall into.

'You're not even interesting,' she muttered to herself as she drove. 'Not original in any way. You're just completely pathetic. You're a fuck-up.' She laughed through her tears, stuck at traffic lights in a crowded street, lighted department store windows to either side. More sirens blared, police cars and ambulances rushed past. The town was going crazy.

'Two murderers,' she said aloud. A horn beeped behind her and she saw that the lights were green. She let in the clutch and drove on. 'Sharing each other's lives. Knowing each other's dark dirty secrets. Got everything in common. *Cosy!*'

She'd never felt such misery, not even when Rob deserted her. She left the city centre and sped along, window wipers doing battle with snowflakes. Tail lights glowed red, traffic lights green. The mist was thickening. She drove out of the city and along a dual carriageway, heading for nowhere in particular. She slowed as she hit a patch of dense fog, peering frantically into the whiteness ahead. A symbol of her life to come! She turned off the dual carriageway on to a narrow twisting country road, hedges and bare fields to either side.

Go home, she told herself. You're crazy, driving around in this fog. But where was home? West Derby? The Albert Dock? Her parents' cold, dingy Victorian house in Little Crosby?

'I've got no home,' she wept. She wanted a drink. I'll go somewhere and get drunk, she thought. Blinded by tears and mist, she put up a hand to wipe her eyes – and cried out as a small figure stepped on to the road from behind the hedge, waving at something or someone she couldn't see. It was a child in shiny red wellington boots and navy blue duffel coat, hood pulled up to hide its face.

She screamed, swerved to the right and stamped on the brake. But it was too late. The wheel spun and she lost control of the steering. This is it, she thought, as the Nissan skidded across the road. I'm going to die. I had Bernard killed and now I have to pay.

The van went off the road, plunged down a bank and rolled. Bushes and branches flashed past the windows and she felt a tremendous pounding and shaking and battering. After what seemed like ages it stopped. There was only silence and white mist.

Shannon opened her eyes. I'm alive, she thought. How can I still be alive? The van was upside down but somehow she was upright, trapped by her seatbelt. The windows were smashed, icy air all around. Cautiously she moved her limbs. Nothing seemed broken, but she felt bruised, battered. Her body ached all over. The seatbelt dug into her ribs. Otherwise there was no pain. Was that good or bad?

She felt perfectly calm and wondered if she would die here. I'm not having an out-of-body experience, she thought. Lots of people have those. Typical that I don't get one. Or maybe I'll be out of my body for good in a few minutes. She wished she could start the engine and just drive away, but the van's roof – now the floor! – and sides were crumpled like an empty Coke can. The window frames were twisted and jagged. She put up a hand. Her hair was full of glass and grit, and sticky with blood. Smashed glass lay all around. She could smell blood and taste it on her front teeth. But where was the blood coming from? She ran her tongue around her mouth. Her teeth were intact, as far as she could tell. She couldn't understand why she had no pain.

She looked down. Her purple suit had a huge dark spreading patch down the jacket and trousers, and her coat and jacket sleeves were ripped open. Her left arm and side felt warm and wet. She moved slightly. She realized that the throbbing feeling was blood pumping out of her arm, literally pumping. That meant an artery must be severed.

'Oh, God!' she whispered. And closed her eyes. She hoped she would die here, not in hospital. If dying was this easy, there was nothing to be afraid of. What was all the fuss about? She felt calm, protected, accepting. She didn't care about anything. She imagined police breaking the news of her death to Rob, to her parents. Going to the Albert Dock apartment to inform Finbar. She smiled. He would think they'd come for some other reason! She clicked the seatbelt open, crawled out of the driver's window and collapsed shivering on the frozen ground.

Footsteps scrambled down the bank, cracking twigs.

'I've called the ambulance from the phone box down the road,' a child's voice called. 'It's coming. Are you badly hurt?'

The voice belonged to a girl of about twelve, with thick straggly brown hair tied in a ponytail, a round freckled face and China blue eyes with long lashes. She wore jeans, a grey duffel coat and a blue-and-yellow school scarf. She knelt beside Shannon.

'Your arm's bleeding a lot,' she said breathlessly. 'Your face is very white. They'll give you oxygen when they come. You've cut your forehead.' She paused, looking down at Shannon. 'I think you're in shock,' she said. 'That was my little brother who ran out in front of your car. He's crying now.'

'Tell him not to cry,' Shannon murmured. 'Tell him it's just an accident and he musn't be upset. He musn't blame himself.'

'I will in a minute. I'm going to put a pressure bandage on your arm first,' she said. 'To stop the bleeding. It'll feel tight, I've got to press hard. I'll use my handkerchief, it's clean.' She had a sweet clear voice, like an angel. 'It's all right,' she said. 'I've done a first aid course. I want to be a doctor,' she added.

'I'm sure you'll be a great doctor,' Shannon whispered. 'You're very good. Very kind. Tell your brother not to cry,' she repeated.

'I will. I promise.'

'Don't let him see me. He might get a shock.'

'He won't come down here. I told him not to.'

'Good.' She closed her eyes. 'What's your name?' she asked faintly.

'Katherine. What's yours?'

'Shannon.'

‘That’s a pretty name. *You’re* pretty. You’ve got gorgeous eyes.’

Something was wound tightly round her upper arm, so tight it made her gasp. She stopped shivering, stopped feeling cold.

‘Don’t go to sleep,’ Katherine said urgently. She pulled off her coat and scarf and draped it over Shannon. ‘You’ve got to talk to me until the ambulance gets here,’ she said. ‘I wish they’d hurry up. Please don’t go to sleep!’ she begged.

‘Will you hold my hand?’

‘Of course I will.’

In the distance a siren split the silent winter air. Katherine, holding on to Shannon’s hand, stared at the congealed blood on the frozen earth.

Chapter Twenty-Eight

'The IRA has claimed responsibility for the murder of the Defence Secretary, Rupert Eastbrook, and two members of his staff in Liverpool earlier today. Mr Eastbrook had visited the military aircraft division at Salmesbury this morning and was due to attend a reception at Merseyside Maritime Museum this afternoon. Two men carried out the fatal attack by firing a rocket launcher from a disused floor of an office building in Water Street. One assailant, whose identity is unknown, shot dead the other and escaped. The dead man has been identified as a member of the Provisional IRA . . .'

'I thought this television was for the benefit of the patients!' a loud indignant female voice exclaimed. Someone switched channels.

'You've woken up!' The slim red-haired nurse in a navy blue uniform smiled down at Shannon as she fixed a new saline drip to the metal stand. 'I thought you would soon.' She had an Australian accent.

Shannon stared round the small hospital room. White walls, pastel green sheets, oatmeal curtains half drawn against the darkness outside. A hideous oil painting on the wall opposite: a fishing boat tossed on huge bright blue waves, lurid green hills in the distance. There was a smell of disinfectant and school dinners. Silly white gown that fastened at the back and would leave her rear end exposed when she got up to go to the toilet. Shannon raised her head slightly. Her right arm was hooked up to the drip and her left, heavily bandaged, was propped on two pillows. Her head ached and her body felt battered. As indeed it had been. She remembered rolling over and over in the van. How had she survived that?

'What time is it?' she asked.

The nurse glanced at her watch. 'Ten minutes to midnight. My name's Red, by the way,' she said. 'I'm looking after you this evening. I'll be on duty until eight tomorrow morning.'

'I realize this is probably a stupid question,' Shannon began weakly, 'but how am I supposed to go to the loo with my arms like this?' She raised her head again and sank back.

'You don't. We get you a bedpan, sweetie.'

'Oh, my God!' she groaned. 'Humiliation as well as pain.' Red laughed.

'How are you feeling?' she asked. 'You're one lucky girl.'

'What?' Shannon said faintly.

'You've been very lucky.'

'Let me get this straight.' She turned her head and looked up at the nurse. 'I just nearly got killed in a car crash and you have the nerve to tell me I'm *lucky*! And how do you think I'm feeling?'

Red finished adjusting the drip. 'The brachial artery in your left arm was severed,' she said cheerfully. 'They had to operate to repair it. You lost about one and a half litres of blood, the paramedics said. Someone at the crash site put a pressure bandage on. Otherwise . . .' She stopped.

'I'd have bled to death,' Shannon finished slowly. 'Katherine,' she said. 'Her name was Katherine.' She recalled the solemn freckled face, the china blue eyes. 'I need to find her, thank her. What else?' she whispered.

'We don't think you'll need a transfusion. We'll keep an eye on you for a couple of days, watch out for signs of anaemia. You've got a cut on your forehead, that'll heal soon. There'll be a small scar, nothing noticeable. All that lovely curly blonde hair will hide it anyway. We can take out the drip as soon as you start drinking. If all goes well you could be out of here by the weekend.' She picked up a plastic jug full of weak orange squash. 'Standard hospital drink!' she laughed. 'Can you swallow some now? The more you drink, the sooner the drip comes out. D'you feel sick or anything?'

'No. Can I have a cup of tea?' she asked as the nurse poured orange squash into a plastic beaker and held it to her lips. 'I'd love some tea. Even hospital tea.'

'Sure. Wouldn't mind a cuppa myself. I'll get you one.' Shannon drank the squash, made a face and lay back on her pillows. 'Oh, and-.' Red smiled broadly and patted her shoulder 'Don't worry, sweetie. The baby's fine.'

'What baby?' Shannon asked weakly. 'What are you on about?' Slowly she raised her right arm and looked at the plastic tag on her wrist. Her name and date of birth were correct, neatly written in blue ink.

'Your baby, sweetie!'

'There must be some mistake.' She wished she could sit up, lean on her elbow, perform movements she'd always taken for granted. 'I haven't got a baby.'

'You certainly have! Or you will have in a few months' time. Sweetie, you're seven weeks pregnant.' Red laughed at her expression. 'Didn't you know?'

'I can't be! Seven weeks? Are you sure?' she asked incredulously. 'You must have got me confused with some other poor sod in here. There's a lot of cock-ups go on in hospitals. Wrong baby, wrong mother, wrong leg chopped off!'

'Tests and examinations show you're seven weeks pregnant,' Red said patiently. She picked up a file lying on the end of the bed. 'Read this if you don't believe me. There's no mistake, darling. Congratulations!'

'Pregnant!' murmured Shannon. 'I can't believe it. It's incredible. What do I look like?' she asked suddenly. 'Is my face a terrible mess?'

'No way. Your car's a write-off, though. It's amazing you walked away from it. People in a roll-over usually get killed outright. It's good news and bad news all at once, isn't it?' she said, seeing Shannon's expression change. 'It's difficult, I know,' she said gently. 'But you'll feel better in a day or so. You need to accept what's happened, come to terms with it. Maybe you'd like to talk to a counsellor in the next couple of days?'

'No!' Shannon said fiercely. 'Don't you dare let any of those demented bastards near me! I don't give my permission for that, do you hear? I don't give them permission to look in my file – anything.'

'Okay. No worries. Calm down, darling.'

'And don't tell me to calm down! I nearly got killed and I've just found out I'm pregnant. Don't tell me to calm down!'

'Sweetie, listen.' Red sat on the edge of the bed, taking care not to disturb the pillows propping up Shannon's left arm. 'You've been through a terrible ordeal,' she said soothingly. 'You need a lot of rest now. Let your mind and body heal. You can't do that if you're carrying on like a pork chop!'

Shannon was silent, gazing at the fishing boat being tossed on the blue waves. She realized she'd missed two consecutive periods. And there was the exhaustion, the queasiness, the two dizzy spells that had freaked Finbar out but that she'd put down to stress and not eating properly. Seven weeks. That meant Finbar was the father! Despite everything, a thrill of joy and triumph ran through her sore body. All that passion, she thought. All the mornings, evenings, afternoons, nights of lovemaking when they couldn't get enough of each other's bodies, couldn't stop until they were exhausted, had resulted in this tiny life inside her. It was incredible, miraculous! Suddenly she felt terrified.

'Are you sure the baby's all right?' she asked frantically. 'Are you *sure*?'

'We're sure.' Red smiled. 'You can talk to the doctors when they do the ward round tomorrow morning, they'll tell you the baby's fine. You can start thinking about names.' She stood up. 'I'll get you your cuppa. After that you get a good night's sleep. You can see your husband first, though. He's been waiting for hours, frantic with worry. You've got a gorgeous fella there!' She laughed. 'The best ones are always taken. Story of my bloody life.'

'My husband?' Shannon echoed. Alarm ran through her. Rob was the last person she wanted to see! What the hell could she say to him? 'Does he know about the baby?' she asked.

'Of course, sweetie! He was as shellshocked as you are. I'll get him for you now, okay?'

'No!' She raised her head. 'I don't want to see him,' she said weakly. 'We're separated, he's not the father.'

But Red had swept out of the room. Shannon heard her

cheerful voice echoing down the corridor. She lay back, exhausted and aching, trying to summon what strength she had left. Don't get in a state, she told herself. Think of the baby. Rob accepted that they were finished. He knew he couldn't be the father. She took a deep breath and willed her body to relax, her mind to stay calm.

Finbar appeared in the doorway, his eyes full of tears. He wore his black overcoat, jeans and slate blue sweater.

'Shannon!' He walked to the bed, took her hand and leaned over her, gently kissing her pale lips and forehead. 'I nearly lost you!' he whispered. His tears fell on her cheek. 'I nearly lost you! They say you're going to be fine. That you're pregnant! I couldn't believe it. They said a young girl saved your life.'

'Katherine.' She stared up at him.

'Please don't leave me now,' he begged. He stroked her hair and kissed her again. 'You're alive. Our baby's alive. We've got another chance. I love you so much! I didn't kill that guy, I swear. I didn't do it, because of you. That's the truth. I couldn't tell you what I knew, I had to protect you. But it's over now, finished. You – our love, our baby – are all that matters to me. Let me look after you. Everything's going to be all right,' he whispered. 'I love you, Shannon!'

The Trials of Nikki Hill

Christopher Darden and Dick Lochte

It's set to be the most sensational murder trial in L.A. since O.J. Simpson's!

When T.V. presenter Madeline Gray's body is found dumped in gangland Los Angeles, the police immediately have a suspect – Jamal Deschamps, a young black man arrested at the scene with Madeline's ring in his pocket.

For Nikki Hill, an ambitious African-American prosecuting attorney, it's make or break time. Having laboured away in obscurity for years, Deschamps' trial is her chance to prove herself.

Only her supposedly airtight case is springing some big-time leaks, sending Nikki and the L.A.P.D.'s homicide division scrambling to find the real killer, while an army of attorneys, spin-doctors, crooked cops and hardened gangsters starts working overtime to make the wheels of justice spin just the way they want ...

A street-smart legal thriller from Christopher Darden, renowned O.J. Simpson prosecutor, and acclaimed mystery writer Dick Lochte.

"A swift, entertaining read." *The Washington Post*

"Entertaining...convincing...Darden has delivered one heck of a closing." *People*

Blood Red Sky

Neil Gibb

One day she swore she would be in a position to fire anyone who called her girl, love, or babe.

Alex Brierley's so-called career in TV news has stalled. A serial killer is on the loose in Nottingham's red-light district – but she's still covering exploding kitchens and strange shaped marrows.

Then she gets a break. A psychiatrist is beaten to death during a break-in at a drugs rehab clinic and she's asked to cover the case. Something tells her that the story is bigger than it seems – and when her contact is suddenly killed and Alex is brutally attacked, she realises her instincts are right.

But as the serial killer turns his attention to "respectable" women, Alex has more than her career on the line ...

The Merchant's House

Kate Ellis

Archaeologist Neil Watson's dig at a merchant's house in the West Country port of Tradmouth uncovers two bodies of a woman and a child, both strangled. Meanwhile, his old university friend Detective Sergeant Wesley Peterson, the first black local police officer, is investigating the brutal murder of a young woman on a cliff path and searching for a missing toddler.

As more information is uncovered, these deaths, centuries apart, seem strangely and tragically linked by age-old motives of jealousy, sexual obsession and desperate longing.

Wes thought that Devon might be a rest cure from the fast pace of the Met, but the pressure is on if he is to prevent a further tragedy.

A thrilling crime debut from Kate Ellis.

"Fascinating" *The Bookseller*

Smoker

Greg Rucka

Atticus Kodiak is bad for your health – a professional bodyguard with a knack for attracting danger is a lethal combination. So when he is offered an assignment to babysit a pampered playboy in a plush uptown hotel he thinks it will be easy money. That is until his cool is severely unsettled by a vicious spray of submachine gun fire delivered by a hired hitman.

As the smoke clears, Atticus discovers he is the decoy in a multi-million dollar game of cat and mouse with one of the world's ten most wanted contract killers.

The two men have become united by a common obsession: to get the job done. And the stakes are high in a game where the first player who blinks – dies...

"Rucka's novel is crisply written, hard-bitten, all-action stuff"
The Times

"Twists with aplomb" *Guardian*

"A can of narrative worms so deftly deployed that the readers will bite nearly every hook" *Publishers Weekly*

Little Triggers
Martyn Waites

Stephen Larkin is back in his native Newcastle. Working as an agency journalist, he's busy blackmailing the powerful into keeping their campaign promises. But he still feels dissatisfied – which is why he jumps at the chance to track down a child abuser with friends in high places.

Cynical Larkin is automatically suspicious of people like Alan Swanson, the charismatic self-styled Minister for Youth and the man behind the 'Rebirth of the Region' project. But is his interest in the kids a chance for a photo-opportunity or something more sinister?

Larkin thinks that, as a reporter, he knows all there is to know about the evil that men do. But nothing has prepared him for this...

By the bestselling author of *Mary's Prayer*, *Little Triggers* is a tough, gutsy and brutal tale of modern city crime.

"Snappy dialogue, and the plot crackles with tension."

Daily Telegraph

Denial
Keith Ablow

"A dark and compelling debut" Jonathan Kellerman

Forensic psychiatrist Frank Clevenger is addicted. Drink, drugs, gambling, sex. They keep his personal demons at bay and hook him into the minds of the criminally insane he's paid to study. His little habits have also led to a series of spectacular misdiagnoses.

To the cops that makes Clevenger the perfect person to evaluate the mental competence of a psychotic drifter who's confessed to mutilating a young woman. But he doesn't think the vagrant did it. Clevenger has one last chance to get it right. He's living on the edge – and caught up in the hunt for a killer whose mind he can read as if it were his own ...

"Ablow writes knowledgeably, powerfully and shockingly of some very disturbed people" *Literary Review*

"*Denial* is very well written, extremely raunchy, full of stomach-turning detail and, as a portrait of addiction, exceedingly plausible" *The Evening Standard*

"... frightening, unputdownable, spellbinding, shocking, dreadful, hypnotic ..." *The Bookseller*

"a disturbing storyline which remains gripping right up to the last word" *Newcastle Evening Chronicle*

Homeport
Nora Roberts

The international bestselling author

Art historian Dr Miranda Jones arrives home after a busy lecture tour on a bitterly cold night. But her blood turns to ice when she feels the knife against her throat ... The unseen assailant steals her bags and disappears. Though deeply shaken, Miranda is distracted when she is asked to verify the authenticity of a Renaissance bronze of a Medici courtesan known as *The Dark Lady*. But the assignment nearly destroys her reputation when her judgement is called into question.

It becomes clear that no simple mugging motivated the attack on her, and that *The Dark Lady* may possess as many secrets as its beautiful namesake once did. Estranged from her family, her career in jeopardy, Miranda has no one to rely on in her quest for the truth. Except herself – and Ryan Boldari, a seductive art thief whose own agenda forces them into reluctant alliance.

Here is Nora Roberts' most thrilling bestseller yet.

"*Homeport* is vintage Roberts. The prose is taut, the story is well researched, and the bodice-ripping sex scenes are steamy."

People

The Reef
Nora Roberts

The New York Times bestseller

Tate Beaumont, a beautiful student of marine archaeology, and Matthew Lassiter, a sea-scarred young man, share a dream of finding Angelique's Curse, the jewelled amulet surrounded by legend and said to be long lost at the bottom of the Caribbean.

Forced into a reluctant partnership with Matthew and his uncle, Tate soon learns that her arrogant but attractive fellow diver holds as many secrets as the sea itself. And when the truth emerges about the mysterious death of Matthew's father eight years earlier, desire – and danger – begin to rise to the surface.

"Nora Roberts is at the top of her game." *People*

"A consistently entertaining writer" *USA Today*

"The publishing world might be hard-pressed to find an author with a more diverse style or fertile imagination than Roberts." *Publishers Weekly*